Hidden Mythics

Theos Rising

A Novel

Jennifer M. Zeiger

ZAP

Published by Jennifer M Zeiger of Zeiger Adventure Publishing (ZAP)

Printed by IngramSpark

First Edition: June 15, 2024

Edited by: Darren Thornberry

Cover Design: Justin Allen

ISBN- 978-1-7351226-6-3

jenniferzeiger.com
jennifer.m.zeiger@gmail.com

Dad

You were asking for this book as soon as you finished *Quaking Soul!*
Thanks for all the encouragement.

"Do not conform to the pattern of this world, but be transformed by the renewing of your mind…"

—Romans 12:2 (NIV)

Table of Contents

Jennifer M. Zeiger

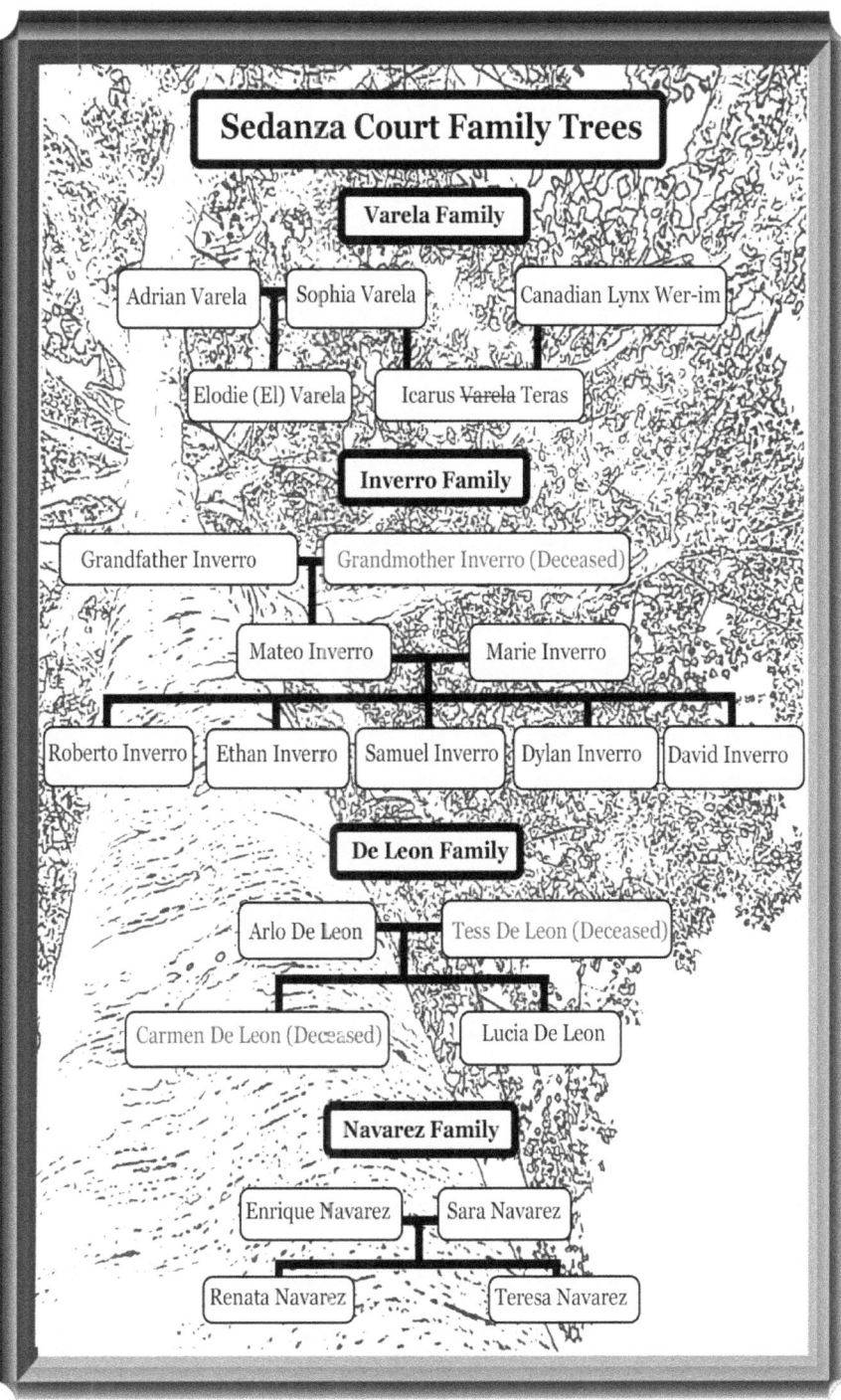

Jennifer M. Zeiger

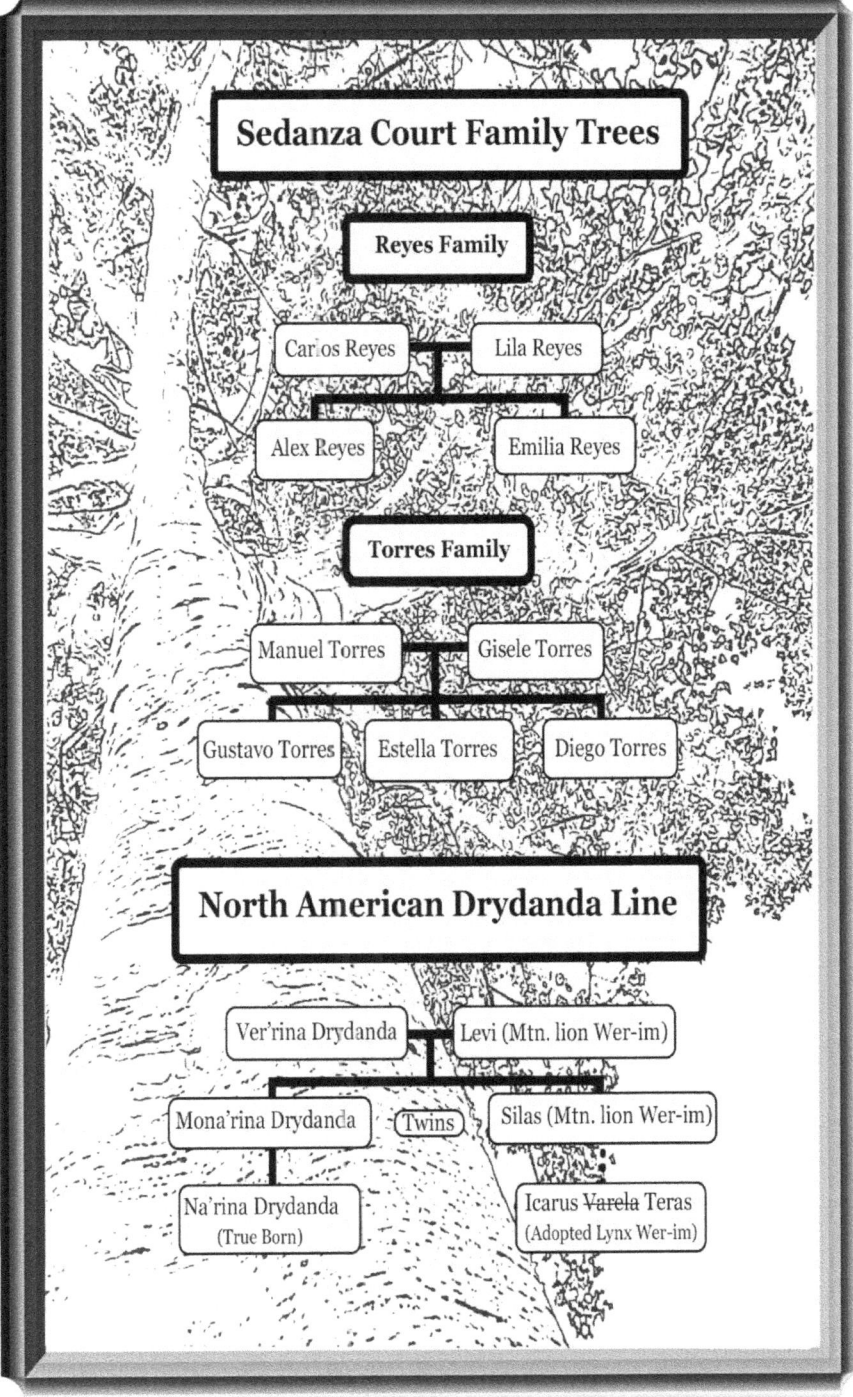

Sedanza Court Family Trees

Reyes Family

Carlos Reyes — Lila Reyes

Alex Reyes — Emilia Reyes

Torres Family

Manuel Torres — Gisele Torres

Gustavo Torres — Estella Torres — Diego Torres

North American Drydanda Line

Ver'rina Drydanda — Levi (Mtn. lion Wer-im)

Mona'rina Drydanda — Twins — Silas (Mtn. lion Wer-im)

Na'rina Drydanda
(True Born)

Icarus ~~Varela~~ Teras
(Adopted Lynx Wer-im)

Jennifer M. Zeiger

Prologue

Dear King Olbin Ak-Lea of the Appalachian Dwarves,

My name is Na'rina Drydanda and I am the Queen of the North American Dryads. You may not have heard of me. Until last spring, I enjoyed a quiet life in the Colorado mountains where I watched my grove—my Rina—grow new leaf buds while the snow melting off the mountains swelled the streams.

But our world is changing. I had never before faced a mountain nymph on the brink of eruption or been confronted by the wer-im, or were-cats, who I believed had maliciously burned our trees. And I had never faced humans who posed a true threat to the mythics' survival.

There's nothing like getting one's roots torn up by the winds of change.

Last spring, my mother was captured by a company named Intela Corp. They wanted her for what they called "scientific experimentation." She was not the only mythic taken.

To save her, I allied with the wer-im despite Rosharu the oread's caution against it. I could see no other way of saving my mother or the dryads overall.

The Wer-Kadis, Icarus Teras, and his wer-im proved my upbringing to be a mass of obscuring vines. They had indeed burned our groves but, as the truth revealed, they did so to save us from a fast-spreading disease created by the very company that kidnapped my mother. And as I dug further, I found Rosharu, who I'd befriended, was at the heart of the humans' experiments. Whorls and knots. Nothing grows in a perfectly straight line.

True friendship is as precious as the catkins that grow on my trees. Rosharu would have killed us, erupting her mountain and destroying the West Coast in the process, but the wer-im stood by my mother and me to prevent the destruction.

We all paid a terrible price. Icarus was forced to kill his mentor. I brought my nearly dead mother home to heal within her tree. After a full season, she has yet to emerge and I am beginning to wonder if the pain of losing her brother, Icarus' mentor, was too much. The mythics are growing weaker as more of our numbers disappear like the Rockies dwarves did last spring. In our desire to hide from the humans, we have become isolated and dangerously vulnerable.

I cannot ignore our dying people. If we do not strengthen ourselves, we truly will become nothing but myths. But I cling to hope. When the first aspen leaves are frozen by a late spring frost, they bud again and still have leaves in the summer.

And so I call you, King Olbin, to a summit of mythics. Will you help us protect ourselves? Together, we can survive what's ahead.

Na'xina Drydanda

The conference room was dominated by a single-slab oak table. It was a polished corpse. Na'rina didn't want to imagine the poor tree the monstrosity had come from, but her mind went there anyway while King Olbin, the King of the Appalachian dwarves, droned on.

A year ago, Na'rina would have laughed if anyone had told her she'd sit in a hotel conference room full of mythics in the middle of Charleston. Most mythics, including herself, avoided large human populations as there were too many telltale signs that marked them as "other."

But the King had insisted on the hotel and they'd desperately wanted him at the summit, so they'd catered to him. That'd been a mistake. No one, except the King, was comfortable.

Two naiads from an East Coast coalition of river nymphs sat to Na'rina's left, dipping their fingers into the cups of water they'd brought. They dripped droplets onto the conference table and ran their fingers through them, drawing designs Na'rina couldn't see. *What nearby river do they call home?* Like dryads, naiads were restricted to about a fifty mile radius from their element. One flicked her damp fingers at King Olbin, silently protesting something he said, but she didn't look up and the King ignored her and the flutter of her scarves that swathed everything but her eyes and fingertips. The scarves were the naiads' way of hiding their nonhuman features, but the disguises drew too much attention.

Na'rina's own pantsuit itched, but it at least didn't look out of place and the blouse covered her arms where aspen saplings had recently started to grow. The saplings created small, white ridges against her usual celadon green. If she ran her fingers over them, they were rough as bark instead of soft like her skin. Their roots twined between her fingers while the thin trunks sprouted up her forearms, but the roots showing below her cuff didn't stand out as she'd shifted them and her skin to white to blend in at the human hotel.

She rubbed at the aspens through her sleeves, her frustration growing as King Olbin droned on, explaining why the dwarves were safe without some mythic alliance.

Keep calm. Icarus' words played in her head. He'd spent weeks preparing her for this and she kept her face serene despite her irritation. The king reminded Na'rina of a black bear, if a black bear could be said to drink too much. Even across the table she could pick out the bloodshot veins in his eyes.

Humans were experimenting on mythics when they shouldn't even know mythics existed. Na'rina and Icarus, the wer-im leader, had dealt Intela Corp a hard blow when they'd taken out their research director the previous spring, but mythics continued to go missing and the research complexes remained active. They needed the strength found in numbers so she had to deal with the bear despite how her hands shook at his raised voice.

"What about your Rockies kin?" she interrupted. The question had already been raised, but the dwarf was adept at skirting straightforward answers.

"We've covered that!" King Olbin smacked the table and a small Asian man who Afre informed her was a phoenix jumped with a squeak. He glanced longingly at the door. Across from him, a gnome snickered.

"But you haven't answered it," Na'rina pressed. "You claim yourselves safe, but an entire line of your race has gone missing."

Afre, there to represent the fauns and not as a member of her council, touched Na'rina's knee, a subtle hint that maybe she'd pressed too far.

Olbin's face went beet red. "I don't answer to you, Drydanda! In fact, perhaps you should answer to us!"

Na'rina froze. *What's he talking about?*

The naiads wilted further into their chairs.

"Answer to you?" Na'rina pushed words past her tight throat. "What are you questioning?"

King Olbin pointed a stubby finger at her. "I'm hearing rumors that the bloodline restriction's been broken. There are laws in place to avoid a Theos mythic. We don't want more overlords, and this looks suspiciously like a reach for control over all mythics."

Na'rina's stomach rolled. *What is he talking about?* Her mother's training had not prepared her for anything more than growing and healing plants, but for six months she'd been learning from Afre, Alaya, and Icarus to avoid the naïve pitfalls she'd fallen into last spring.

Staring at King Olbin, she knew a chasm of ignorance had opened in front of her. Beside her, Afre's face had gone ashen. *He knows exactly what the King's insinuating.*

Both naiads had tilted their heads, studying her with identical frowns. They'd barely dared glance at her for the past three days but now they stared with that slightly glazed look that told Na'rina they were staring at her psychically, not physically. *Why?*

"I am unsure what you want from me," Na'rina admitted. "But I can assure you, I have no designs on controlling the mythics. There is enough to worry about with the dryads alone."

King Olbin sneered. "Then why's your council so assorted?"

Na'rina raised her chin. "As you already know, my diverse council covers vulnerabilities that were harming the dryads. A faun can travel whereas a normal dryad cannot. Alaya Oceadanda brings experience that I severely lack. I would think these things are obvious."

"Thin," King Olbin said. "Your reasoning is thin. Speaking of Alaya Oceadanda, where is she? I was led to believe she'd be here."

"The Oceadanda *did* agree to attend," Afre finally stepped in.

Na'rina thanked her stars. The faun had remained quiet for most of the summit, but King Olbin would have a harder time casting doubt on his word. "However, the demands of our people can trump any meeting like this. I suspect she was pulled away for such a demand."

"You haven't heard from her?" King Olbin pressed.

"*Na*," Afre admitted. "We will hear from her eventually."

King Olbin scoffed and slammed his hands down. "These last three days have been pointless." He shoved to his feet and stormed out, making the phoenix jump again when the door smacked the wall.

After a shocked moment, the phoenix darted out the door. The gnomes were more sedate in their departure but nonetheless didn't waste time. The naiads were slower to follow.

"The King is a bear, *sa?*" one asked softly.

Na'rina almost laughed aloud in surprise. "*Sa.*"

"Surly, angry, lashing out." The naiad dipped her finger again and dripped droplets off her long nails onto the hideous, polished table.

It was clear she was working up to a point, and so Na'rina waited for her to continue.

"True bears act this way when hungry or threatened." The naiad drew on the table again, but Na'rina still couldn't see the design. "It's unlikely the King is hungry. So perhaps he is threatened. But I am unsure whether he is more afraid of something unseen or of something directly in front of him." Finally, the naiad's amethyst eyes met hers. Then the river nymph rose with her companion, bowed, and left.

Na'rina's breath gusted out. She folded her arms on the table and laid her head on them, fighting tears. Her body craved sleep. The summit's timing was necessary, but now she needed to return to her grove to sleep for winter.

She wrinkled her nose. This close to the table, she could smell the lacquer on the oak. It reminded her of the oak twins who served on her council. Just like her, they were struggling to step into leadership thrust upon them because Intela Corp had killed their elders.

She heard Afre stand and, when she peeked, found him studying the naiad's water drawings.

"What'd she draw?"

He scratched his head, revealing a tiny horn in his curly hair. "I think it's a book title, but she used Greek letters. I'll have to look it up to be sure."

"What do you think it says?"

"Sto aima? In the Blood, maybe?"

"How do you know it's a book?"

"I think it was required reading during my training years, but that's been a long minute ago, so I'd have to check my father's library to be sure."

Na'rina nodded and rested her chin on her palm. Across the room a pegboard boasted flyers for a knitting circle, a science symposium, and a comic convention. Below them hung a sign advertising the hotel's ballroom and its famous stained-glass window but the colors blurred in her vision. She was exhausted. *We accomplished nothing.*

"Afre?" her question came out muffled against her hand. "What does a Theos mythic have to do with the wind in the trees?" She didn't even know what a Theos mythic was. *Why did Mamma not teach me this? She may as well have raised me under a rock.*

She could check the *Collective Wisdom*, a genetic history she could tap into to see previous Drydandas' experiences, but she'd come to trust Afre's knowledge more than the *Wisdom* as it could be and had been tweaked to hide things.

When Afre didn't immediately answer, she looked to where he stood by the window, his narrow shoulders hunched as he took in the bay outside.

"Afre?"

"I didn't think anyone put stock in the bloodline restrictions beyond a few random eastern groups," he said. "Common myth says Zeus, Poseidon, and Hades were Greek gods—they'd love that, I'm sure—but in reality they were mythics like the rest of us except they were born to strong, psychic parents of different races. Something about their particular mixes made them extremely powerful—Theos mythics.

Because of that power, they decided they had a *right* to rule."

"You're saying they were dictators?"

"After a fashion, yes. They split the regions between themselves and took control by force."

"How does the bloodline restriction come in?"

"During their time, the brothers instated the restrictions. Basically, they forbade a mixing of bloodlines like theirs to avoid anyone challenging their rule. It worked, and when they eventually died, there were no Theos mythics left. No one *wanted* mythics strong enough to take control by force again, so the mythics kept the restrictions. Any hint of a mythic strong enough to be another Theos was killed without question."

Na'rina slumped back in her seat, staring at Afre's curly brown hair. He'd leaned a shoulder against the window frame and still didn't turn to look at her.

"Why has no one ever mentioned this to me?"

"I don't think it's taught anymore. In fact, I think it's been centuries since it's been upheld. Think about Rosharu. She's old, and yet it never occurred to her that the oreads and oceanids refused her handfasting with Liam for any other reason than species prejudices."

Na'rina ached. The tragedy between Rosharu and her oceanid love, Liam, had set in motion everything that had happened to Na'rina in the last year. And now it made a tiny bit more sense. A twisted, terrible sense.

"Oceanids and oreads are strong enough to create a Theos mix?" she guessed.

Afre finally looked at her over his shoulder. "Hades was half oread. Poseidon half oceanid."

Na'rina shuddered, then had a thought. "Weren't they brothers?"

"All three were raised by Cronus who took them in after killing their parents. They grew up believing themselves brothers until questions started being asked. It's a messy story, but then, isn't every Greek myth?"

Na'rina moved on. "What about a Drydanda and wer-im mix?"

Afre shrugged. "That's an unknown. The Drydanda half is a definite but the wer-im are purely physical creatures. You wouldn't expect to have powerful psychic offspring. But I think some are starting to wonder."

"How does King Olbin even know? It's not like we've announced my mother's mixed heritage, and he can't see the psychic."

Afre shrugged again, looking for all the world like a lost boy. Na'rina knew he was anything but. She stared at the oak table, thinking about the summit and those who'd attended. King Olbin might as well have thrown a match into a tinder pile. Those who'd attended were local representatives from the Southwest region, and now they'd hide, afraid of getting caught between a dwarf king and a potential Zeus. It was the direct opposite of what Na'rina had hoped.

King Olbin had been the big spruce she'd needed to convince. He wasn't restricted to a location like the nymphs, and he had a decent sized population to protect. Not to mention dwarves moved among humans with a lot more ease than most mythics.

But he'd never intended to work with her. *Who poisoned his sap?*

Na'rina pushed away from the table, hating that her fingers left sticky sap-like sweat on the wood.

"Maybe I should've let Icarus come," she said. "He at least could have knocked some sense into the dwarf's hard head."

Afre chuckled. "Careful, Drydanda, or you'll be thought violent."

She strode from the conference room, her slippered steps silent on the carpeted floor. The potted lemon trees in the hall murmured greetings and she trailed her fingers along them as she passed, taking comfort in their voices. She'd been surprised to find real trees inside but loved the tiny spark of citrus they brought to her in Charleston. "I've failed, Afre. King Olbin was never interested in working with us."

Behind her, Afre's sneakers made rapid flopping noises to catch up.

"You didn't fail," he disagreed. "You got the King to attend, which is more than anyone's done in decades."

"And now everyone's more afraid of me than they are of Intela Corp!"

"Na'rina," Afre caught her elbow, "they all know the danger now. Let them thi—"

"Perdóname, Señorita." They'd stopped just before entering the hotel's cavernous entryway. The woman at the desk peeked over her tablet at them but there was nothing but curiosity on her face.

The man who'd approached was something else, however. The shimmer of his *zoi aima*, or lifeblood or energy, told Na'rina he had a tiny bit of mythic blood but was mostly human. It wasn't uncommon for humanoid mythics to mix with humans. She studied the man. His zoi aima was so diluted that even Na'rina's sensitivity couldn't tell her what kind of mythic mixed with his ancestors. When Na'rina didn't immediately respond, he said, "Buenas noches, Drydanda."

Spanish? Here?

"Common tongue, please," she requested.

"Certainly," he said with a slight accent. "I am Armando. My master has heard rumors of the—disturbance—last spring and fears something similar might be happening in South America. He begs an audience with you." His tone was courteous but bland.

"Your Master?"

"Señor Thomas Dominguez," Armando answered.

"He wants an audience now?" Afre asked.

"Yes."

South American mythics heard about the summit? Na'rina wasn't sure how that could have happened. It had been hard enough to gather North American mythics.

"We'll come," she agreed.

"You misunderstand, Señorita," Armando bowed in apology, "Master Thomas only wishes to speak with you. He is somewhat—distrustful—of fauns."

"What?" That was like saying snow wasn't cold.

"Something to do with an agreement he had with King Afren that has gone unfulfilled. I do not know the details."

Na'rina glanced at Afre. The faun had gone ash white beneath his curly hair. She touched his hand where it rested on her arm.

"Afre?"

"The fauns have been hard-pressed protecting themselves lately. We almost went extinct from, well, lots of things. I am sure this agreement can be satisfied if I can meet with Master Thomas."

Armando was already shaking his dark head. "You will have to follow up with him separately."

"But—"

Na'rina gave Afre's hand a squeeze, silencing him. He'd helped her so much; maybe this was a chance to return the favor. "I'll advocate for you," she offered.

"Excellent." Armando took Na'rina's free elbow, guiding her away toward the elevators. She was almost there when she glanced back to smile apologetically to Afre. It'd been a while since she'd seen him so shaken.

Na'rina stutter-stepped as she entered the elevator, alarmed by the panic on Afre's face. He rushed to follow her, but the doors closed behind Na'rina, cutting Afre off.

"Perhaps I should reassure the fau—" she started to say when Armando reached past her to press the button for the fifth floor.

Did he not see Afre?

"I should—" Na'rina tried again as the elevator gave that slight stomach-dropping lurch that told her it'd begun moving. *Ugh, I hate that.* She turned to insist they get off at the next floor and swallowed her words instead. Armando's face was covered by some type of mask.

"What—" Something thudded, cutting her off again, and the elevator stopped—between floors. A hiss seethed through the vents and Na'rina tasted something sweet. She met Armando's gaze through the plastic of his mask, catching a triumphant spark there.

Fight. She'd always been a pacifist, but fire sparked in her now. Surprise flashed across Armando's lifeblood as she shoved her palm against his chest, jolting zoi aima into him.

He jerked and his head smacked against the elevator wall.

Recovering, he tried to step away but there was nowhere to go.

Gathering more zoi aima to shock him again, Na'rina's vision blurred. She staggered and her legs nearly gave out. The hissing continued above and the sweet taste now coated her tongue, slowly creeping down her throat and into her chest like fingers of thick honey.

She jolted her gathered zoi aima into him again and he slammed against the wall. She could hear wheezing through his mask, but her breath was growing shallow and she couldn't gather more to keep fighting.

Na'rina staggered forward anyway and tilted into the wall. Her hand crept toward her throat and her fingers grazed the golden leaf beneath the skin of her shoulder. She couldn't draw air.

Need wind. Need breath. Fight. It's what Icarus would want her to do. She tried to step toward Armando again only to find he'd slid further along the wall until he reached the far corner from her. When she tried to follow, her legs gave out.

Tears dripped from her eyes as she gasped and her sight narrowed as though with a cloud of gnats. Na'rina clawed at her neck, struggling to breathe.

Armando's masked face appeared above. Everything in her zeroed in on his human mixed lifeblood, on his broad nose that she could barely see through the mask, on the smell of caramel-scented candles and subtle cedarwood and geranium aftershave on his skin.

"Mistake—" she breathed.

"Yes, Señorita," Armando agreed, his voice muffled.

Phantom ice spiked through Icarus' chest and disappeared.

Na'rina's hurt. He'd known when he'd made the wer-im vow to Na'rina that it'd create a connection to her. It was supposed to help him protect her, but he couldn't tell from the shaft of pain if she'd stubbed her toe or fallen off a cliff. *Can't help her right now.* He was almost 2,000 miles away, guts deep in Intela Corp's Four Corners research center where the Arizona heat baked against his skin. The place was a tomb.

Next to him, Obek clicked his ring against the revolver in his pocket. Icarus' ears twitched. He'd seen the small piece the day before while Obek cleaned it. One of Obek's own creations, the dwarven craftmanship was outstanding, the silver filagree dancing like frozen flames along the handle.

"Stop fidgeting," he said.

Obek jerked and withdrew his hand from his pocket. "Who tipped them off?" the dwarf asked.

He brushed past Icarus to try the light switch, wafting whiskey and gun powder in his wake. Against the reek of bleach, the scent was a relief. Icarus flared his nostrils, picking up chocolate and peat, maybe a bit of chicory—probably a Brownmore whiskey judging by the rich tones.

The switch on the wall clicked without effect.

"Seriously, Wer-Kadis, I think you have a leak in your people," Obek said.

Icarus said nothing. To his night-sharp eyes *something* was receiving power even if the lights weren't working. He crossed the dark room and touched the first small glow in a long row on the far wall. The monitor lit up.

Obek cursed. "Is that a prison cell?"

The monitor showed a tiny, hazy room with a single bench.

"It is." Icarus had been held in a similar room when he and Na'rina infiltrated the facility to free her mother. Walking along the wall, he switched on each monitor, revealing only empty cells. His ear twitched as steps scuffed in the hall outside. He didn't look away from the screens when the door swung open.

"Kadis, I think we have a—" Felis, his stout second in command, froze momentarily as he noticed the monitors. His yellow eyes flicked over them as he finished entering the room. "Where'd they all go?"

"We have a what?" Icarus asked.

"It looks like they left in a hurry. They tore the innards from their mainframe."

"There were people here two days ago!" Dante followed Felis in. He cast Felis a cautious glance and shifted to stay out of his line of sight. If Felis was Icarus' right-hand man, Dante was quickly becoming a close second.

Dante appeared like a straight up tabby cat. Bright orange hair, small build. Beside Felis' stalky bobcat stature, he was tiny. He'd been a stray until Na'rina had gifted him his name. He'd had a name before, of course, but by wer-im standards, it was a stray's name. She'd done it out of kindness, with no idea the ramifications of a powerful mythic recognizing him, but that didn't matter. He'd graduated from an un-positioned kit to a fully recognized wer-im with a station that befitted Na'rina's rank despite looking like a housecat. And Dante grasped that with both hands. It was causing some friction in the status quo.

"Right," Obek said, "and Intela Corp cleared out an entire complex, people and equipment, in a day? Who tipped them off?"

"Stop thinking what you're thinking," Felis snarled, his hackles rising and chop style beard bristling. "We," he motioned at the three wer-im, "were the only cats aware of this mission. Look to your own!"

Icarus gave him a raised brow and Felis subsided.

Despite Felis' overreaction, he was right. Icarus trusted his wer-im. And he had no clue how many dwarves knew about the mission. Even King Olbin, Obek's father, had reservations and had almost nixed his son's participation. Icarus remembered Obek's frustration. He had eleven brothers and yet none of them were willing to help search for their Rockies kin.

Icarus' Sedessan side salivated at the mystery behind that. Obek's mission was about as honorable as one could get, and most dwarves would jump at having such a search on their résumé. But Icarus didn't want to use the wer-im like the Sedessan Court used its information webs. On the other hand, considering the pile of nothing their search had found, perhaps he should have dug into it. Perhaps King Olbin wasn't the only one among the dwarves who disliked their interest in Intela Corp. He scowled.

Their goal had been to damage Intela Corp's files on the mythics, free their prisoners, and find information on the Rockies dwarves who had disappeared six months prior.

All three parts lay in shambles.

Felis held up a black flash drive. "Mainframe looks like rat fodder," he told Icarus. "The drive's virus is useless here." He tossed it over. "The only thing currently hooked up to power is the camera's closed feed in the cells but they're not recording."

Dante stepped up to Icarus' shoulder, staring at the screens as well. "Na'rina wanted everybody freed."

Icarus' chest tightened. Obek wasn't the only one who'd placed a lot of hope on this mission. Instinctively, he checked that other sense that gave him a feel for Na'rina's well-being. Unlike the painful spike earlier, he only got a calm sense like when she slept.

"Any indication where they took the prisoners?"

No one answered. Obek smacked the wall with an open palm.

"How am I to explain to Pa another fruitless mission? After months with nothing, he'll suspect a mole in the wer-im too."

Felis and Dante growled, then glared at each other. Obek shoved his hands in his pockets.

This was supposed to be Na'rina's ace for the summit. Icarus had hoped that while she was meeting with Obek's father, he'd be able to give her a successful mission to help convince the king to work with her.

The empty screens mocked him. He suspected a mole as well; he just wasn't convinced it was in the wer-im.

"How, Kadis? How do I convince him to let me keep searching?" Obek asked as though Icarus had answers. Despite the Rockies dwarves being their kin, King Olbin had been reluctant to keep looking for them. Every failed mission resulted in a long argument that Icarus had more than once picked Obek back up from, encouraging him that his goal was honorable.

Icarus envied the dwarves' conflict. At least Obek had a father to argue with. But that didn't mean Icarus had answers.

He finally turned, meeting the dwarf's eyes, and Obek rocked back on his heels, perhaps seeing the anger Icarus tried to keep in check. He didn't answer Obek, instead striding for the door, slamming the break bar open, and leaving those hollow screens behind.

Something whined.

Icarus froze. The door opened behind him, but Felis and Dante stopped at seeing him standing motionless. There came a faint scraping from farther within the complex.

Icarus bolted down the hall, through a cracked door, and down two flights of stairs until he skidded to a halt in a long corridor of tightly packed doors. The hall of holding cells. The haze on the monitors became clear as smoke forced its way into his nose. Another whimper drew him forward.

Unwashed body odor, salty sweat, goat hair, and burned flesh assaulted his nose a second before a small figure burst out of a doorway.

A hoof caught Icarus in the chest and pain flared through his bruised sternum. Almost immediately, the pain vanished. A benefit of his vow, he'd discovered he healed even faster from injuries. He caught the female faun before she kicked him again, pinning her arms to her sides.

She screamed, reared back to head butt him, and then fainted.

Icarus blinked his second lens over his eyes. Since his father was wer-im, that's what he resembled and he relied on that to hide his other heritage, but his mother was Sedessan and he harbored the advantages that gave him in seeing zoi aima.

The unconscious faun lit up an ugly green with brown bleeding around the edges. *Dehydrated from blood loss.*

"Almighty wonders," Obek swore as he caught up. "A faun?"

The tiny faun stared at their campfire, a half-eaten granola bar in her hand and an empty metal cup on the ground at her feet. They'd carried her from the research center and finally revived her when they reached a small campground not far off Highway 145. Besides the few other tents peeking above the sagebrush and the creek chattering on the west end of the tent sites, the place was quiet.

Still, anxiety nestled in Icarus' gut. He suspected it was due to his distance from Na'rina's grove. When he vowed to her, it'd also connected him to her Rina. Since then, the bond had matured into a connection that gave him an awareness of the grove's well-being as well as Na'rina's. He'd sworn to protect the dryad and had gotten an entire aspen grove in the bargain. At first, it'd been unsettling but now it was a golden thread that anchored him.

He did not, however, always understand what the awareness meant. The current ache was somehow *more* than the usual separation.

Is it worry? Anxiety? He didn't know.

Icarus focused again on the faun sitting across the fire from him. Dehydration tinged her lifeblood an unhealthy brown. Silas, his old mentor, would have called her a liability and left her behind. *I will not act like him.* Icarus couldn't place when Silas lost the compassionate side his dryad blood should have given him.

You're thinking too much, you kit. Cage the brain and let your instincts guide you. He buried the thought. Silas' lack of compassion would not guide him now. Besides, he might glean information about Intela Corp if he was patient.

Obek handed her a steaming mug of chamomile tea and settled on the log beside her. Side by side, they looked like a lumberjack and a child. The tea added a hint of hay to the air that Icarus focused on instead of the distinct sear of hair and flesh coming from the faun's legs. She bore burn marks the size of his hand and, even though the wounds were covered now by a pair of loose cotton pants, he could smell them.

"What's your name?" he asked.

She clutched the mug, staring at the ground.

"How can you work with him?" she whispered to Obek.

"How long have you been a captive?" Obek asked.

The faun glanced at Icarus and shook her head, clutching her tea harder.

"Some space?" Obek requested.

Icarus pushed to his feet, walking away through the scrub and juniper. He stopped beside the creek. *Maybe I should leave her behind.* Instead, he fingered the flash drive in his pocket, opening and closing it with the press of his thumb. By accident, he brushed the photo he kept there and his hand stopped. His phone buzzed. Releasing the drive, he dug the phone out from his thigh cargo pocket.

"Hello, Malon," he greeted, swallowing disquiet at a wer-im reporting to him. Someday it'd get easier.

Malon was stationed in South Carolina near the coast. He was probably a Maine Coon judging by how much he liked the water, but

Icarus had never asked. Unlike a full blooded Sedessan, he didn't really care about a wer-im's heritage beyond a friendly curiosity.

"Wer-Kadis," Malon greeted. "The *Sansabria* and *Erstwhile* moved into Charleston Harbor this evening. They're moored in the river."

The *Sansabria* and *Erstwhile* were military ships turned mobile research labs for Intela Corp. Since spring, they'd not moved much beyond wandering off the South Carolina coast. They also usually had a third ship flanking them.

"And the *Observer*?" Icarus asked.

"Currently out beyond the breakers."

"Thank you, Malon. Keep an eye on them. I want to know why they came into the harbor."

"Will do, Wer-Kadis."

Icarus hung up, staring at his phone's blank screen. After six months, he still expected sarcasm or mocking whenever someone reported to him. He was a mixed-blood outcast, after all. *Why'd you force me into this, Silas?* At first, he'd hoped Intela Corp would be handled quickly and he'd become Wer-Kadis in name only. That's how it used to be. But Intela Corp's continuing threat had shifted it into a true leadership position that the wer-im accepted. Not for the first time, he wished he could disappear into Na'rina's grove. But he couldn't hand his position to another. That's not how it worked. And besides, there was no one he trusted to step in and help Na'rina.

His stomach rumbled. Reaching into another pocket, he withdrew a stick of jerky and tore off a bite, letting the smoked teriyaki cover his tongue. His irritation at Silas, his position, even Obek and the faun, abated. Food just made it easier to be nice to people.

The soft pad of feet alerted him a moment before Felis appeared.

"What now, Kadis?" Felis asked. He squatted on his heels to fill his water bottle, his stalky frame surprisingly comfortable in the compact position. He was larger than Icarus and resembled a bobcat instead of a lynx. Long whiskers came off either side of his chin in a beard humans mistook for chops.

Icarus tore off another bite so he didn't have to answer immediately. If he'd had his way, he'd be in Charleston, helping Na'rina.

"How do you think Charleston's going?" he asked.

Felis sat back on his heels. "Better cause we're not there. Just like Obek now knows the faun's name is Aileen."

If Na'rina can learn to trust us, so can others. It was a mantra he often repeated.

"Do you know my full name?" he asked Felis.

Felis' yellow eyes twitched. He'd been caught off guard by the question.

"I'm not familiar with your surname, Kadis."

Icarus snorted, his nostrils flaring as he smelled fireball candy from across the creek. "Not my birth name. That's irrelevant. I mean the name Silas gave me."

Felis froze. Icarus had killed Silas while protecting Na'rina, and now most of the wer-im avoided saying his name like Icarus would fly into a rage if they did. He never had, nor would he. Silas made his choice and so had Icarus. His anger was not a mindless rage.

"I don't, Kadis. Didn't think it was important."

"He gave me the surname Teras. Loosely translated as 'monster.'"

After a moment, Felis shook his head. "I don't follow."

"He's wondering," came Dante's voice across the creek, "whether people will always fear us."

Felis bolted upright, a growl rumbling in his chest, and launched across the creek.

Dante surprised him…again. Felis hated when the other wer-im did that, and Dante did it a lot. Icarus suspected it was purely to goad the older wer-im. He didn't intervene despite what Silas' training urged him to do. *I won't meddle in every little thing.*

Icarus glanced toward the campsite as he finished his jerky. Through the brush, all he could see was the fire's glow. He blinked his lens down, which allowed him to see the zoi aima within creatures, and picked out Obek's and Aileen's outlines through the grass. Closer to him, a faint mist rose. Confused, he blinked again and the mist disappeared. Blinking the lens back, the mist had thickened, taking on a familiar pale green as it shifted, forming into a round, indistinct face.

Dread coiled in Icarus' chest. Many stronger nymphs could cast their zoi aima through their elements and appear ethereal at a distance, but only Drydandas would be green. Na'rina did it when she called her council to her, but it took an enormous effort from her grove and herself, meaning she had to be within her grove, which she was not.

It couldn't be Mona'rina, her mother, either, for the opposite reason because Mona'rina hadn't emerged from her grove since Mount Athos' eruption.

That left Ver'rina, Na'rina's grandmother. The face filled in until Icarus didn't need his second lens to see Ver'rina's wizened aspen bark features with her large green eyes and narrow nose.

"Ver'rina?" he asked.

Her lips moved without sound.

Icarus shook his head. "I can't hear you." *Why didn't I teach her about cell phones?* He'd started with Na'rina, but human technology made her uncomfortable and he'd assumed Ver'rina would disdain the device altogether. *Should have taught her anyway.*

Her lips kept moving.

He shook his head again and she grimaced. Concentration pinched her eyes and then a golden blob coalesced before her face. It solidified into a delicate aspen leaf hanging from a chain.

The dread within Icarus' chest hardened. "Na'rina."

With a decisive nod, Ver'rina disappeared.

"Enough!" Icarus shouted.

Felis and Dante rolled apart, spitting at each other. Blood soaked spots of their clothing. Dante's ear bled from being ripped open. Icarus refrained from touching his own ear where he bore a thick scar, a long-ago parting gift from his mother, but the wound darkened his mood further.

"I said enough." They went quiet, both looking like kits caught by their mother. "Na'rina needs us. Pack up."

The holding cell reeked of sweat, mold, and the musk of stone never allowed to dry. It wasn't the first El had ever gotten herself thrown into, but it might have been the most crowded.

Sunlight, but no breeze, trickled in through the small window of the cavern-like room. The buzzing of the invisible sensors El had stuck on her arms before the mission told her that, despite the room's rustic appearance, there was an invisible barrier over the window in addition to the bars. She rubbed her arms. The humidity clung to her skin. From her perch on a rocky ledge six feet above the cavern floor, El counted at least twenty mythics vying for space, although most of that number was the gaggle of imps scuttling beneath the other creatures' feet.

Spindly, slobbery troublemakers.

Their cackling echoed against the vaulted ceiling while three grayish-green imps spit at the eyes of a small group of gnomes. The gnomes sat back-to-back, and a wave of calm washed out from them but it evaporated under the imps' antics. Giving up on the calming, one gnome threw a rock. The imps scattered and the rock smashed against the wall, showering an ior sleeping in the corner. El snorted softly as the blocky creature, who bore the large head of all iors and appeared droopy from his nap, bowed up threateningly at everyone, unable to place who'd attacked him.

More imps ran through a group of tiny fairies and jabbed their needle-sharp claws into their delicate feet. The fairies gave high-pitched squeals of distress and danced away but their silvery blood smeared the ground from the few times they hadn't dodged fast enough. The imps dissolved into cackling fits of laughter.

Yet another imp pair tried to climb the wall around the iron-barred door, rattling the hinges and lock, and hissing and spitting at anyone else who approached.

Imps didn't usually gather in such large numbers. When they did, they fed off the group hysteria. *Either our captors have a terrible lack of knowledge about imps, or they want to keep everyone on edge.* El suspected the latter; their jailors were not stupid.

Beyond keeping an eye on the creatures, El ignored them. They would not be helpful. Having gotten thrown into the Fae embassy's holding cell on purpose, El now needed to get out—she'd gathered the information she'd come for and there were only a few in the cell capable of helping her escape.

Because of the nature of her mission, she'd come with very little tech. Other than the sensors on her arms that told her about nearby electronics, all she had was a tracking device. She was naked without a phone or comms, but her captors would have confiscated such devices anyway.

And so El considered the other mythics in the cell. People could be as useful as technology.

A gorgeous woman sat on the left side of the iron-barred door. Her jeans hugged muscular hips and calves and her red button-down blouse did nothing to hide the toning in her arms. But her curves and strength were secondary to the more telling purple buff covering her hair. The polyester cap shifted with small movements, almost like she kept lifting her ears up and down.

El wanted to stare. She'd never encountered a Daughter of Medusa before. There was good reason the imps left her alone. About a decade before, the Daughters had modified contact lenses to facilitate them interacting with other people. This one must be wearing such contacts since there were no lifelike statues in the cell but, even still, no one met her gaze.

Wonder what her range is?

Without seeing her in action or asking, there was no way to tell. El hesitated to approach the woman; she didn't relish proceeding with so little information.

The second person El considered was much harder to observe. Beyond the full-bodied Daughter, tucked into the far corner where the cell was dimmest, towered a reed-thin woman. El never would have spotted her with her dark skin and black, wispy dress blending so completely with the shadows hugging the granite. She'd picked a perfect spot where the rock jutted out, blocking the faint window light.

In the physical world, the slender woman was barely another shadow. El blinked her second lens down. It was a clear lens, naturally occurring in Sedessans, that made her eyes more shimmery to anyone watching, but it enabled El to see every creature's swirling, vibrant lifeblood, or energy. El sighed in delight. The woman smoldered with a scarlet energy like a hungry fire for that's exactly what El saw: flame beneath the woman's skin. She was a salamander or flame elemental.

As long as the other occupants left her alone, she wouldn't be a problem, but if the imps taunted her, everyone in the cell could be in danger. She might be perfect for El's purposes, however. El blinked and the woman faded to shadows.

The last member El considered didn't require her second lens to see although she had blinked her lens down, trying to decide exactly what he was. A hulking man with rough-hewn features and steely gray eyes sat against the wall below the window. The iron-barred door was really just a formality for him. El suspected it was the shock batons, batons turned cattle prods, and the sheer number of guards that kept him in the cell.

But his lifeblood rumbled within him, a thick grayish brown. Brown or russet usually indicated an earth creature—a mountain nymph, dwarf, troll, or maybe giant—but she'd never seen gray. He was obviously too big for a dwarf. From the intelligent spark in his eyes, too smart for a troll. And as far as she could tell, he hadn't spotted the salamander, which ruled out a nymph who could see the psychic world and its lifeblood.

Giant then, but what type remained a mystery. One of the door imps gave up rattling the iron and took a running leap for the window ledge above his head. It missed—claws scraping on the stone—and landed on his shoulder. The imp screeched and tried to jump away as the giant's hand flashed out. There was an audible *thwack* and the cell went silent as it smacked against the wall.

Several imps raced to him. One bared its teeth at the giant. He bared his teeth back and the imp shuddered and skittered off. Moments later, they escorted their limping companion to a spot as far away from the giant and his window as possible. *It survived then.* Imps had strangely resilient, squishy bodies. If the giant had wanted to kill the creature, however, he would have.

El narrowed her eyes, watching the giant. He smacked his palm against the floor and a deep boom, felt not heard, reverberated in the cell, a warning to some imps watching with hostile, beady eyes. They scampered away to their group where it gathered now, unfortunately, in the salamander's darkened corner.

El blinked. The salamander ignited in her vision, the scarlet sparking with electric blue flares. Three imps now crept toward her with curiosity. One darted forward and stabbed her bare foot just above the instep. She gasped and her lifeblood flared as she pressed her shoulder blades harder into the granite. Seeing it, the imps cackled.

They didn't notice the temperature spiking.

Gonna fry us all. El slipped off her rock shelf, falling the six feet and landing with a soft thud on the floor. The giant's head swiveled her way. All the creatures near her scattered, giving her as much space as the giant. She threw a look around, a cocky grin tugging at her lips.

How she hated the assumptions they made simply because she was a Sedessan, but those assumptions made her life easier in this pit. Plus, she allowed, their assumptions were justified. It *was* a Sedessan family that had captured them. But they didn't know that. She herself had just learned that.

Ah, the games we play.

El sauntered up to the three imps from behind, ignoring the wave of mythics that washed out from her path. In a way, it was humorous. She was wisp-sized. Four feet ten inches and less than a hundred pounds. The gnomes could haul her around without huffing for breath, but they all treated her like she could break them with a touch.

The imps jostled each other, cackling and pointing at the salamander, unaware of El. Quick as an adder, she snatched the right and left by their spindly arms and laid her cheek against the middle imp's rubbery cheek. It didn't matter that she couldn't hang onto the middle imp. As soon as she touched him, it was over.

El repressed a grimace as she entered their mindscapes while sweat trickled down her brow from the salamander's heat. *Sweet simmering frogs, it's hot.* She fell back on her goblin niñera's way of cursing. Thankfully, her hair tie held her long hair off her neck.

To the imps, everyone's rank sweat, mixed with garlic, mold, and the faint hint of urine, was a sweet aroma. They read so much more into the smells than El wanted to know. It was similar to how her half-brother, Icarus, perceived the world, but his mindscape was far more pleasant than the imps'.

The imps savored the hot oven scent of the salamander's blood, wondering if it would taste as good as it smelled.

El dug beyond their excitement over the blood, not bothering to be gentle, searching for something to deter them. She struck gold. A fear they shared despite being resistant to it. El grinned. *What irony.*

El painted a memory in their minds' eyes.

Fire climbed the walls and dripped from the ceiling, splattering onto their skin as more flames poured from the dark-skinned salamander's hands. Their flesh sizzled, blistering and smelling like tires melting.

The imps whimpered. Rivulets of sweat poured off them. As

suddenly as it started, El quashed the images, but it was as though the salamander knew what she'd showed the creatures because her eyes glowed amber orange and sparks fluttered around her fingertips.

Still holding their minds, El whispered, "Consider your prey with more wisdom, my pets. We don't want to end up as blackened smudges on the walls, now do we?"

El released them, straightening. They cried out, tumbling over each other to get away. The heat in the cell diminished as El met the salamander's amber-orange stare.

Perhaps she'll help me escape. El had been leaning toward asking the giant if she could get him to talk to her, but perhaps this fierce, ebony elemental would be the better choice. Even now, the woman's lips twitched in a small, grateful smile.

El winked at her.

A key rattled. Not in the cell door, but farther away, probably in the entrance at the end of the hall. Imps cried out and plastered themselves against the iron bars. Then they slumped into a disappointed pile. The shuffle and clatter of steps outside meant they weren't pulling someone out, but bringing someone in.

As the imps wandered away from the door, a twiglet crept forward from his hiding spot near the giant's hip. He tilted his leafy head in curiosity. He was less than foot tall and thin as a bedpost. If he squatted, he'd look like a tiny bush. At the door, he went motionless and then let out a keening wail as he reached a slender arm through the bars, fingers reaching in desperation toward the new prisoner. El suspected he stayed behind the bars due to fear, not because he couldn't slip through. The twiglet wailed again, piercing through the cell's chatter.

El approached him before she considered the wisdom of showing interest. As she got close, the guards beyond the door came into view escorting a female figure down the hall. One flicked his shock baton open and El's arm sensors buzzed in warning. She grabbed the twiglet by the leaves on the back of his neck and pulled him away just as the shock baton hit the bars. Electricity zapped through the iron with a dry, metallic smell.

El ignored the guard's sneer. They'd thrown a black bag over their prisoner's head. Her hands and feet, probably bare judging from their shape, were also smothered in cloth. In fact, no skin showed. *What are you?*

They pushed the woman past the door, farther down the hall toward an isolation cell. She walked with a flowing stride reminiscent of a lifetime dancer. El blinked her second lens down and her stomach dropped. The woman glowed a dancing, swirling green and blue like a solar flare.

Frog's legs! You shouldn't be here!

El glanced back at the cavern. Across the chaotic cell, the giant watched her. The twiglet, hovering near her heels, clutched his stick fingers together and stared at her through small nut-brown eyes. The woven branches that created his chin quivered. She vacated her spot at the door, and he rushed forward, keening again as he thrust his leafy head through the bars to watch the hallway. El sauntered back to her ledge and climbed up onto it to consider her options.

"Sedessan," an imp hissed at her like it was a curse.

Where am I!?

Na'rina's throat tightened with nausea. She couldn't feel her Rina. Hadn't been able to even before getting thrown into the cell. Time—a lot of time—must have passed between fainting in the elevator and waking up in a car mere minutes ago. As she tried to pull details to memory, all she got were vague sensations. Movement, the rumble of different engines, and the smell of unfamiliar, unnatural spaces. She swallowed hard, fighting the wooziness.

She'd smelled water and earth on the breeze just before an air lock's too familiar hiss cut them off. They were replaced by an isolation cell's dead air.

Cold chains held her wrists together. *Ugh!* Na'rina ripped the cloth bag off her head and cringed when the chain between her wrists scraped her face. *Not enough.* She bit at the socks covering her hands until, tearing with her teeth, they pulled free. Still not satisfied, she sat down and shucked the socks off her feet as well. Then she planted her soles against the dirt floor and sighed.

She savored the floor's grit digging into her feet. It was an earthen floor, not metal or plastic like the last two times she'd been in an isolation cell. This place was thick rock and running water although she couldn't see the water, only hear it. Moss covered the walls, its forest green zoi aima reassuring. Weak sunlight filtered down through a window above, but the sealed room blocked her ability to feed off it.

Breathe, Na'rina, Breathe. She fought the knot in her throat. *How many times does this have to happen before I learn?*

Who captured me this time? Rosharu, the mountain nymph who'd orchestrated her first capture, would be incorporeal for the next century while she healed from her mountain exploding. And Dr. Hector, who captured her the second time, was dead from a slit throat. Na'rina's uncle had seen to that after the doctor had experimented on her mother.

So, who am I dealing with now? Figuring that out might be the key to escaping. Her breath eased a fraction.

Na'rina faced the door, putting the wall against her back while she waited for whoever would come. Someone would come. They'd gone to a great deal of trouble to get her here. Swallowing down more nausea, she quested out with her zoi aima, coating the walls, searching for weaknesses in the room's buffering. The rock's dull gray and brown faded behind her lifeblood's vibrant blue and green.

When the door opened, she was tempted to harden the zoi aima, just to see if she could prevent the person from entering, but caution won out and she spooled her energy back into herself. Without strong sunlight, she couldn't restore whatever she used.

The man who entered was short and gnarled like an old pinyon pine dressed in a brown suit. His cane, a polished twist of dark oak, clicked as he stepped forward. A delighted smile bloomed below his mustache when he spotted her.

"Come, come," he gestured to someone behind him, and a group of servants bustled in, carrying a small, short table, a teapot, two cups, and two serving jars with small spoons peeking through their lids.

They arrayed the table with a white cloth in front of Na'rina. Once the teapot and mugs were set, the servants placed a blue cushion on the floor opposite her and all but one of them left. The remaining servant helped the old man forward, taking his cane and fedora as he sat. Na'rina started. The servant was Armando.

He bowed shallowly when he noticed her watching and retreated to stand beside the door, bland as always.

"You make Armando nervous, you know?"

Na'rina's eyes snapped to the man now seated across from her. *How can he tell Armando's nervous? He's as expressionless as a rock.*

"You're Master Thomas?"

The smile below the mustache grew. "Quite right. And you are Na'rina Drydanda."

Na'rina did not respond.

Master Thomas' smile sagged and then he gestured at the table.

"Tea? I assumed you would want some refreshment after your travels." He poured a dark tea into the cup in front of her and then his own, his knobby hands steady despite his age.

My travels? As if I chose to be here? And he wants me to drink tea with chains on?

She held up her wrists, raising a brow just like Icarus would have. Master Thomas stared at the roots growing along her hands. She'd shifted back to green at some point and the white was particularly stark on her skin.

"Quite right again!" he finally said. "Armando, take care of those."

Armando hesitated.

The kindly expression on Master Thomas' face vanished long enough for Armando to get the hint, bow his head, and follow orders.

Na'rina's relief as the cold metal left her skin probably showed. She tried to control it, to hide it as Icarus would have instructed, but she knew she failed when Master Thomas added, "And the ankles."

As Armando complied, Master Thomas went back to setting up the tea. He dolloped two spoonfuls of honey into each cup and then started to add cream. Na'rina's hand shot out, covering her cup before he poured.

Armando flinched.

"Animal products," Master Thomas said, ignoring the reaction as Armando retreated. "Of course, I'm sorry."

Na'rina didn't correct him. At one time, she would have easily struck up a conversation about tea and honey and how she did not particularly like milk or cream, but Icarus' low voice echoed through her thoughts. *Wait to see what they want before showing your hand.* He'd had to explain cards to her before the advice made sense, but Na'rina figured his negotiation techniques toward King Olbin would work just as well here as in the conference room.

She stirred the honey in while she waited for Master Thomas to continue.

He sipped and gave a gusty sigh. "I spent some time in a small Bavarian village in the Northwestern region of the United States and found the most delightful tea shop," he said. "Now I order it in. Did you know they make huckleberry cream tea?"

With Na'rina's first taste, she picked out the huckleberry mixed with vanilla. She wanted to fold the mug in her hands and soak in the tea's warmth and flavor. It was smooth and sweet despite being a black tea. *Don't respond, don't respond.* Na'rina held the sip on her tongue longer than necessary even as she kept her face calm, feeling the tea feed into her zoi aima like a warm spring rain. *Maybe I should imitate Armando. He's good at being expressionless.*

"Delicious, right?"

Na'rina stared at Master Thomas, fighting her natural urge to respond to his friendliness. He set his mug down with a rattle and itched at the eye of his elbow, seemingly at a loss for words. But then he spoke, "I'm sure you're wondering why I brought you here."

Finally.

"Your mother did something quite extraordinary. I'd never heard of an event like the wer-im banishment. Discounted it until recently, really…"

Na'rina stared at him.

He's human. When Armando had approached her in Charleston, she'd assumed his master was a mythic. But Master Thomas' lifeblood was an almost metallic swirl of red, brown, and blue. Unlike mythics who usually had one, maybe two colors that reliably told her their race, humans shifted through colors as easily as their moods. Like Armando, Master Thomas had some mythic in his heritage, but he was clearly mostly human. *How does he know about the banishment and the mythics?*

Realizing she'd missed what Master Thomas was saying, Na'rina refocused only to find he was still talking about the banishment.

"You believe the banishment happened?" Na'rina cut in.

"Why of course, dear. I—"

"You are human," she continued. "So how do you know about the banishment?"

For a moment, Master Thomas just smiled, inordinately thrilled about something.

Instinctively, Na'rina went utterly still, her stomach clenching.

"Did you know," he finally said, "that when Mount Athos blew last spring, we recorded a force field around the eruption? We could actually register something keeping it from being more deadly than it was, almost like a net, catching the debris."

Na'rina's alarm grew. *He knows about Mount Athos too?* She clutched her mug as its warmth seeped into her chilled fingers, fully aware that it showed her white-knuckled grip but unable to relax.

Master Thomas held up a finger. "Our psyches may be able to wrap the elements of life to fit our designs." He sounded almost like he was reciting. "The energy required for this is unknown, but a few have displayed such an ability, and if energy can be harnessed to psychic will, anything might be possible."

Na'rina blinked. *Is he crazy?*

"That does not answer my question," she said, not commenting on the recitation as she sipped her tea and finally convinced her fingers to relax.

"Ah, doesn't it? Are you familiar with simulated eugenics? No? No mind then. Our measurements from the eruption prove there are amazing, unexplained forces on this earth. Now, what do you think caused this…energy net…during the eruption?"

Maybe a mythic with mixed blood? A Theos mythic? She'd assumed she was stronger because she was *True Born*, a rare type of dryad born after the mother goes through a traumatic experience. The dryad's tree would seed in a desperate attempt to stay alive and the dryad, if she survived, would have a child just like herself, except with more concentrated abilities. Now Na'rina wasn't sure *what* made her stronger. Perhaps both things.

Na'rina's knuckles whitened around her mug again.

For Master Thomas' benefit, however, she shrugged—stiffly—and answered, "Unexplained forces. Would you mind bringing me some bread? I'm hungry after my…travels."

Master Thomas' expression became patient but his eye twitched. "Not at all, but for now, our time is done." He motioned and Armando helped him stand. "Bring the tea," he said to his servant.

Na'rina replaced her empty mug just before Armando lifted the small table. He was turning away when Master Thomas stumbled. Instantly, Armando steadied him and dumped the table. The teapot hit the floor, shattering and splashing dark liquid across the stone.

Master Thomas tisked. "Send in Marie to clean up."

Armando bowed, following his master out, and the door clanked shut, hissing as it sealed.

Na'rina let out a tight sigh. *I handled that terribly! Icarus is never going to let me out of his sight again.*

How did they connect me with the Mount Athos eruption? How do they know about my mother's involvement in the wer-im banishment? Before she could wonder longer, the door opened again and a small, round-faced woman ducked through with Armando on her heels.

"No, no, Señor." The woman shooed him. "You no look over my shoulder while I clean."

For once, Armando showed an expression—surprise, worried maybe as he glanced at Na'rina—but then he backed out and let the door close. The woman clicked her tongue. "Marie do this, Marie clean that. Marie, you missed the bathroom mirror. Oops, Marie, I spilled tea. Pheesh! Make my day harder, Armando." While she rambled, the woman got down on hands and knees to pick up the larger pottery pieces and place them in a towel.

Na'rina rolled from her crossed-legged position onto her hands and knees to help.

"No, no," Marie shooed her as well. "You no clean."

"I'll help," Na'rina said, continuing to pick up pieces.

Marie paused to actually look at her. "Bonita, what are they holding you for?"

Na'rina shrugged. "They have not told me."

"Pheesh! These men!"

They fell into silence, crawling on the floor to gather the farthest-reaching shards. Na'rina glanced at Marie's face. A knot formed in her throat. She had not wanted to ask Master Thomas where she was but—

"Where are we, Marie?" she asked.

"Island," Marie answered without looking up.

"Where?"

"Off Venezuela." Marie missed Na'rina's dismay as she grabbed a dustpan to sweep up the remaining bits.

Na'rina sat back on her heels. *I'm an ocean away from my grove!* Even if she hadn't been in an isolation cell, her insides would ache from the separation.

Marie glanced up, catching Na'rina's dismay. She paused in sweeping the shards into her pan. "You okay, Bonita?"

Na'rina couldn't answer.

Casting a cautious glance toward the door, Marie leaned closer. "These men, son peligrosos…" she paused, searching for the right word in English. "Unsafe," she finally said. "You should get out of here."

"How?" Na'rina asked.

Marie emptied the dustpan onto her towel and waved the small brush Na'rina's way. "They fear you. You are strong, no?"

Although she rarely viewed herself that way, Na'rina knew it was true. She nodded.

"Then what do you need? I will try to bring it."

Na'rina yearned for unhindered sunlight, but she doubted the servant woman could bring her the sun. She'd go for the next best thing.

"Bread," she said.

"Just bread?"

Something brushed against Na'rina and she froze, almost missing Marie's confused question.

"Just bread," she answered. The touch came again, unknown yet familiar. *It's another mythic who can reach out with their zoi aima!*

"I will try." Marie again glanced at the door. "Sí, I will try." She quickly gathered up her towel and dustpan and knocked on the door. It creaked open and she was gone.

As soon as the door closed, Na'rina quested out, bathing the room in zoi aima, seeking that touch again.

Marie's help was beyond welcome, but Na'rina doubted she would be able to get her out of the cell without Armando or Master

Thomas knowing. But if there was another nymph nearby, maybe they could help each other. The crushed leaves and damp earth flavor in the psychic touch was that of another dryad, one so steeped in the forest that she emanated a wild edge.

Na'rina extended more zoi aima, glad for the tea and honey's strengthening now as she pushed against the isolation barrier.

But as she searched, only dirt and rock greeted her. Na'rina slumped, finally allowing tears to prick her eyes. She fought a yawn, drained. *I could sleep for months.* As though her body agreed, her eyes drooped. *Na! Keep looking, Na'rina.* She wiped at her tears. Even if she was too far away to find her Rina, she had to find something.

Icarus found Afre huddled against Ver'rina's huge seed tree, sleeping uneasily in the chilly morning with his arms tucked tight into his armpits. Na'rina should have returned with the faun. But Icarus knew he'd find Afre alone. Their path had taken them through Na'rina's grove, and she'd urged him to speak with Afre, a panicked edge in her multi-hued voice as she'd explained Na'rina was missing.

They'd left Obek and Aileen behind in their rush to get here, but still Icarus wondered if he, Felis, and Dante had taken too long.

Controlling his urge to shake the faun, Icarus crouched and touched his shoulder. "Afre."

Afre jerked, bleating. Shame and dread darkened the faun's huge brown eyes as he woke.

"Wer-Kadis," he whispered. He extended his hand and Na'rina's golden leaf heirloom hung from his tufted fingers. Icarus stared at it and Afre began to tremble, making the leaf sway.

Afre had added a chain so it could be kept as a necklace, but it usually stayed beneath the skin on Na'rina's shoulder. She never removed it. Beyond being a Drydanda heirloom that could store zoi aima, it was a gift from her mother and her only sign that her mother approved of her actions during the last year.

"What happened?" Icarus finally took the necklace. He fingered the leaf until it shaped itself around the end of his pointer and middle finger.

"I messed up," Afre said.

"How?"

Afre flinched. "We were approached by a man saying he was from South America. He said something similar to the incident last spring might be happening. His employer wanted an audience with Na'rina."

"And you didn't go with?" Dante asked.

Felis smacked his shoulder. "That's the Kadis' place."

Dante bared his teeth but subsided. The smaller wer-im tended to step in where Na'rina was concerned. It irked Felis for some reason.

Icarus ignored them. *South America*. The smell of Spanish rice and beans hit him, the staple of his early years because it'd been cheap and a lone kid could beg it off the street vendors in exchange for a bit of labor. The dirt on his face in those days had easily covered his wer-im features.

Tension built in his jaw. He hadn't been to South America in years.

"The man objected to me going," Afre kept explaining, "something about an unfulfilled agreement with my father. Na'rina said she'd advocate for me. I realized within seconds that I shouldn't let her go alone but by then they were at the elevator and the doors were closing. I ran up the stairs to meet them as they stepped off."

The faun chewed on an already stubby thumbnail. "When the elevator opened, it was empty. I found that wedged into the edge of the carpet." He pointed at the leaf.

"That's it?" Dante asked.

Felis growled.

"You were thinking it too," Dante shot back.

"More rain." Ver'rina's narrow face emerged from the bark above Afre's head, the white, powdery trunk bulging to show her cheeks, lips, and nose. Her eyes were still green as emeralds, though, same as Na'rina's. For a moment, Icarus struggled to draw a full breath.

"What else?" he asked, bracing for Ver'rina's unique vernacular.

Afre moved, letting Icarus get closer to grasp Ver'rina's single hand that emerged from the bark. Her fingers scraped against his skin, holding hard enough to bruise.

"I didn't smell wind or I'd have held my mind close."

Icarus shook his head.

"She touched the leaf before you arrived, Wer-Kadis," Afre explained. "Not realizing Na'rina used it to send a message."

"Take, take." Ver'rina smacked her forehead and then grabbed his hand again.

Icarus hesitated. He hated rifling through others' minds.

"I know heart." Ver'rina poked him in the chest, hard.

He growled.

"Take," she demanded.

Resigned, he laid his free palm against Ver'rina's cheek, letting Na'rina's necklace hang from his fingers.

The mindscape he entered was early morning mist with light, almost insubstantial tendrils of thought greeting him. Then the mist burned away and Icarus found himself standing beside Ver'rina on a clear Colorado day. Most Sedessans controlled their movement through another's mindscape, but Icarus suspected that trying it with the ancient Drydanda was an abysmal idea. He'd experienced Na'rina's defenses in that regard and didn't want to know what an older Drydanda's were like.

Ver'rina grasped his hand and led him to a lake. Below its crystalline waters was the shining doors of an elevator and a hotel's unmistakable carpet instead of stones and fish.

"Take," Ver'rina said again, and pushed him in.

Tears dripped from his eyes as he gasped and his sight narrowed as though with a cloud of gnats. He clawed at his throat, his fingers grazing the leaf beneath his skin as he struggled to breathe. It rose into his palm. Hidden there, clutched tight, he conveyed everything into it.

The silver elevator wall reflected Na'rina's face back at Icarus where she lay on the floor. Her mouth hung open and wheezes pulled hard through her throat.

A masked face appeared above. Everything in him zeroed in on the human's mixed lifeblood, on his broad nose that he could barely see through the mask, on the smell of caramel-scented candles and subtle cedarwood and geranium aftershave on his skin.

As everything faded and he couldn't hold on longer, he wedged the leaf into the edge of the carpet behind the man's heel.

Icarus shoved away from Ver'rina, gasping. "What was that?"

Ver'rina closed her eyes, tears making sappy trails on the bark of her face. "I don't think memory, I live memory."

Icarus shuddered. He'd walked Na'rina's mindscape before. It was unlike anything he'd ever experienced but he'd never *become* a person in her memory. Na'rina had explained that with the Drydandas'

Collective Wisdom, she literally relived experiences when viewing it.

That's what Ver'rina had done. Shown him the Collective Wisdom.

I can smell the carpet from the elevator.

"Kadis?" Felis asked. "You about turned purple. You okay?"

Definitely not! He buried his disquiet. It would not help Na'rina.

"Call Rebecca Simms. See if she knows how to get fake ID's and passports that will pass at international airports. Dante, come here. I have a man for you to track down." Icarus paused. *South America.* He grimaced. "And a transponder I need you to fetch."

Dante looked surprised but didn't ask. Icarus appreciated that.

"Where are you going?" Felis asked.

"Visiting McCormick. I want to know if this was Intela Corp."

Ver'rina grabbed his arm. "My sprout needs help."

"That's the idea," Icarus said.

Ver'rina smacked his arm, hard, and poked his chest again. "Sprout's protector need help."

Something inside Icarus quelled. He shook his head and pretended to misunderstand Ver'rina's intent. "I've got Felis and Dante, Grandmother, I'll be fine."

The aged Drydanda tended to be…unique…but not usually unreasonable. She was even good for advice occasionally.

"Baby shoots!" she said. "This travels farther than they see."

Afre bleated behind him and Icarus registered the musk of a mountain lion a second before a huge, warm body pressed against his calves. He held still. The wer-im was Ver'rina's handfasted husband, but he'd been a lion so long Icarus wasn't sure how much wer-im remained.

"I don't understand, Grandmother. I can't take a mountain lion into a city or on an airplane."

Ver'rina glanced at Levi, frowning. "Even you not sense his stalk. He help from shadows."

Felis started to chuckle and Icarus growled. "Airplane, Grandmother. It's a metal tube the humans fly through the air. No matter how stealthy Levi is, I can't pack him into a travel bag and expect him to slip past their security search."

Levi huffed and sat on Icarus' feet. He and Ver'rina shared a long look.

They're conversing. It was Ver'rina's zoi aima that kept Levi a lion. With that contact, Levi would be able to *hear* Ver'rina just like Icarus could when Na'rina helped him shift. He again searched for the telltale zoi aima connected to Levi but even with his second lens, he couldn't spot it.

"For a season, my sun and rain," Ver'rina said to Levi, and then to Icarus, "Back up."

He pulled his feet free and joined Felis, who covered his mouth to keep from laughing aloud. Even Dante swallowed a chuckle.

Their humor vanished, however, as Levi's body became fluid. In the past, when Icarus or Silas had shifted, the change happened quickly, but Levi's form resisted, held too long as a cat. His ears slowly blurred back and forth, a lion's one moment and a wer-im's the next, until finally his body rolled upright on his hind legs, furred shoulders smoothed into tattooed, golden skin and legs elongated until a wer-im stood before them instead of a lion. Icarus knew the joint-popping, muscle-searing pain that came with changing form, but this—

Levi's entire body was tattooed. The aspen centered across his chest in stark white and knotted black. It disappeared below his loincloth and reappeared to trail down his legs, its roots running over his calves and down into his toes. The leaves spanned out in ochre, celadon, and faded yellows across his shoulders and down his arms.

Levi straightened and his eyes cleared from the agony of shifting as he adjusted his loincloth to sit more comfortably.

Age.

Wer-im were not known to live long lives but Levi's golden hair was streaked with gray and deep lines trailed from the corners of his predatory eyes. Every instinct in Icarus went on alert.

Afre tucked behind Felis, out of Levi's sight.

"This is a bad idea, Grandmother," Icarus said. *He's wearing a loincloth.* The modern-day learning curve would probably outweigh any advantage Levi gave.

"He knows the possible blizzard," Ver'rina answered. "He must watch for the snow to slide. He helps."

Usually, Icarus understood Ver'rina to some degree. This baffled him. *Disaster. This is a disaster. But he'll follow me even if I object.*

"Find him modern clothes," he told Felis.

Since Felis needed a few hours to find Levi clothes and fuel the vehicles, Icarus headed to Na'rina's seed tree and sat with his bare shoulder blades against the aspen's bark. Na'rina and her Rina were close in the way skin and body were close. If he could strengthen and encourage the grove, he could also inadvertently strengthen and encourage Na'rina.

As soon as he sat down, the giant aspen sighed, breathing in his nearness as a balm against her ache at Na'rina's absence. They shared the mountain air like sipping chilled cider together while the icy breeze brushed across Icarus' skin, speaking of the coming winter. It didn't bother him.

Since the Rina didn't immediately strike up a conversation, Icarus allowed himself to relive a memory instead. Living memory was one of the few advantages he enjoyed in being half-Sedessan.

Icarus walked beside Na'rina along the Ruby Anthracite Creek.

"She considers you family, you know," Na'rina said.

Icarus huffed. "I'm not."

"Good luck changing her mind." Na'rina nudged him with a shoulder. "Once Grandmother decides something, it's stone to her."

"Have you met many cats? We decide when someone's family, not the other way around."

Na'rina laughed, a rich, light sound that played with the burble of the creek. "Wer-Kadis."

The moment passed. "Sa, Felis," he called without looking toward the stalky wer-im.

"Your contact confirmed the flash drive's contents. She wants to talk with you but there's no cell reception here, so I told her you'd call her back."

"Coming." Icarus gave Na'rina an apologetic look. Between him being the Wer-Kadis and her the ruling Drydanda, they rarely found moments to just be. He turned to follow Felis.

Na'rina grasped his arm, her long fingers cool. "I think Grandmother's right."

He stared at her celadon-tinted fingers in the crook of his elbow. They were so pale as to almost appear white, but when the sun fully hit her skin, she glowed. He squeezed her fingers before leaving but the feel of her touch stayed with him.

Not many dared touch him. He loved that of the few who would, Na'rina topped that list.

Icarus blinked and the memory faded, making him aware of the chill in the air again.

Winter came early to the Colorado mountains. The drop in temperature signaled a change in season for the region's dryads in a natural cycle where they withdrew into their trees and rested until the spring growth and their strength returned. It was the worst time for Na'rina to be physically separated from her grove. Her body would crave sleep and the embrace of her seed tree.

Above Icarus' head, the leaves quaked, shivering their golden yellow color and dropping around his shoulders.

I need advice, Kadis, the Rina finally spoke.

Advice? Icarus' Sedessan side had always allowed him to hear the trees' psychic voices.

You know Alaya regularly meets with the oak twins, mentoring them since their elders disappeared. She missed their last meeting just before the summit. I tried to find her, but the ocean is sullen and silent.

Icarus' Sedessan side jumped into the dilemma with glee. His wer-im side sighed, exasperated.

If Alaya missed meeting with the twins, she probably missed the summit as well. Icarus scrubbed a hand down his face. King Olbin would have pounced on her absence. He'd agreed to the meeting partially because there were two Dandas involved—Na'rina and Alaya.

Frustrated, he let the Sedessan portion have its way. The grove remained silent, eternally patient as she let him think.

Alaya and the twins were part of Na'rina's unorthodox council. The diversity tied the dryads into the current world in a way they'd never been. Alaya was the most powerful of those she'd picked. An Oceadanda, Alaya had ruled in the ocean for centuries and could leave the water, unlike regular oceanids. She was uniquely capable of understanding Na'rina and her struggles.

She'd also taken the oak twins under her wing, recognizing they were adrift after Intela Corp captured their elders. Alaya took the responsibility seriously but that didn't mean she wasn't pulled away sometimes. Her duty to her own people took precedence.

He said as much to the grove.

You think she's been pulled away?

Hurricane season is in full swing to the south. She often leaves to mitigate the storms.

The Rina sighed. Through the vow, her relief manifested as an odd flush like sudden blood flow to a limb. Icarus didn't share it, but he'd shoulder that worry for them both.

I cannot feel her, Kadis, the Rina whispered. *My Na'rina and I haven't experienced this pain since we met you. And I,* she paused, sounding like an old woman catching her breath, *weaken without her.*

"I'll find her," Icarus promised. He laid his fingers against the bark behind his hips, breathing in the vibrant zoi aima within that smelled of aspen and rain, a cool kiss to his over-hot lifeblood.

"I feel the separation too," he admitted. "But our Na'rina's

53

strong, as are you."

The Rina sighed again. *She is not in the United States. I could find her—feel her—if she were.*

Icarus accepted that fact. Na'rina's grove could extend her consciousness through any root system she found, even sending it over distances to jump root systems, and by doing so, she could contact Na'rina at great distances. The grove had been growing that ability since Na'rina set up her far-flung council. Her reach covered the United States and slightly beyond now.

"What if she's in an isolation chamber like last spring?" he asked, thinking of Intela Corp.

The Rina shuddered, dropping more leaves. *I tracked her unconscious body from the hotel in Charleston. My contact ended when she rose too high off the ground, not when a door closed. I have not felt her since.*

"You can do that?"

I have been practicing. If a tree could blush, he imagined the Rina would have.

"Impressive." Judging the time was right, he pushed up from the ground to leave.

"You should not be here," said a familiar voice.

Icarus' shoulders went taut before he breathed out through his nose to relax.

He picked out Ser'ored's spiked green hair where he stood in the trees. He was an older pine dryad who, until recently, had been on Mona'rina's council. Na'rina had replaced the entire council when she took over from her mother. Other members had faded away, returning to their trees. Ser'ored had not. He hated the wer-im, but even more, he hated the loss of power. Icarus had never known a power-hungry dryad before. *Is Ser'ored's tree diseased?*

"I have the Drydanda's permission to come and go freely," he said, not mentioning his connection with the grove that now flowed so warmly in his consciousness.

Ser'ored kept his distance, his green hair looking almost black in the grove's shadow. Icarus smelled the bitter tang of pine. "I hear rumor she's not free to come and go herself."

Icarus' hackles rose. His fingers curled into fists. "She's far freer than a fifty-mile leash."

Anger pinched Ser's face. He was not a Drydanda; he was as tied to his tree as any other dryad. "She seems uniquely capable of getting captured," he said. "If she keeps it up, she'll be disposed of as a liability."

Icarus snorted, but heat built in his limbs. Right behind it, a cold layer followed that made his focus sharper than normal. Usually, the adrenaline spike was easy to handle, but it hit him hard this time and Icarus gritted his teeth, fighting it.

Breathe, Kadis. His foot rested on the Rina's roots and her multi-hued voice whispered in his head.

"Each time you attack Na'rina trying to take power," he seethed, "you look more desperate."

"Possibly," Ser'ored answered. "But if she doesn't return after the summit, if I wait until *others* start questioning where she is, then it will look natural when I start questioning her aptitude." He spun away, making an aspen branch whip off his shoulder.

Icarus stared after Ser'ored until his sharp eyes couldn't make him out anymore. Only then did he lean back against Na'rina's seed tree.

Kadis.

Sa.

How did he find out?

"I don't know," he whispered.

The Rina shuddered, and her resolve hardened in her usually soft touch on his mind.

I can't go with you, she said, *but maybe this will help.* In a rush, the tree pushed zoi aima into his back. He gasped. Na'rina shared her lifeblood with him regularly, but the grove never had. Her lifeblood was cooler even than Na'rina's tended to be, and he shivered, but it also left a familiar honeysuckle flavor on his tongue. The zoi aima traveled through his core and up to his chest, then vanished into the golden leaf he now wore around his neck.

Icarus touched the necklace, startled, and a breeze scented with aspens ran through his senses. It wasn't quite Na'rina's zoi aima, but it was still a part of her.

I'll watch Ser while you're gone, the Rina promised. Her consciousness could only focus in one place at a time, but if she wasn't searching for Na'rina, she could focus on Ser'ored. And a fifty-mile radius was a very small area for the Rina to monitor.

Icarus patted the seed tree. "And I'll find Na'rina," he promised again.

"I got nowt to say to you," the giant said.

It wasn't the warmest greeting in the world, but also not the coldest El had ever received. She'd settled beside the giant in the night-darkened cell, close enough to be heard but not so close as to be threatening.

The other occupants had settled, winding down as the light faded and some of the more dangerous mythics, including El, stirred. It was almost an ingrained thing: a predator became more threatening after dark and all that nonsense.

El almost snorted as the base vibrations from the giant's whispered greeting finally faded. She closed her eyes, taking in his accent's character and flavor. *A hearty beef stew bred from rocky, windblown mountains.* She loved how it flowed. She let it shape her tongue, asking, "Whatcha figure he's on about?" She flicked her fingers at the twiglet who stood at the door, bony fingers gripping the bars and head almost through the iron trying to see the farthest isolation cell.

"Don't know, don't care."

El leaned her head back against the stone, staring at the tiny stick creature. Its distress wrenched at her, but she couldn't show that.

An imp noticed them talking and cocked its head. It stepped toward them, but then hesitated. *Compulsion.* El had seen the

Compulsion set into its brain when she'd touched it. The imp would *want* to cause mischief and keep the other mythics from talking to each other, but it wouldn't know why. And with the giant and herself, two much stronger predators, its natural instincts were making it hesitate. Even on an imp, Compulsion was forbidden. *Things are worse than we feared.* Her mother needed to know.

El beckoned with her fingers and a wolfish grin. The imp hissed and spun away, fear winning out over the Compulsion. El returned to her conversation with the giant.

"Twiglets care for nowt but their own usually. Guess a Drydanda counts."

The giant twitched, a bare flutter in his bicep muscles, but perceptible. "Y' can't know what they bundled inta that cell."

"Aye, I can. The North American Drydanda lights up like a blue and green Christmas tree in the psychic. I seen it once before. Reckon I'll never forget it either."

He chewed on that, then asked, "Whatcha want?"

"Who says I want anythin'?"

"Y'r yatterin' at me."

El almost laughed. Definitely not dull, this one.

"This," she flicked her fingers at the crowded cell. Across the way, the imp was gathering a group and pointing at them, "ain't good, but judgin' by all of us, we might deserve a night or two stewin'. But the Drydanda? Here? Ain't right for so many reasons."

"Ain't my problem."

El laughed. It came out harsh, almost mocking. "Y' think? Y' heard of the wer-im banishment?" Most mythics had heard about the last North American Drycanda awakening entire forests to drive out the wer-im who had burned the dryads' trees. But few knew her daughter was even stronger. It was both terrifying and phenomenal. Drydandas were believed to be timid, but that one event proved them to be sleeping giants.

El relished the chance to get to know her, but that was personal, and not a part of this conversation.

"Course I heard of it. Far as I know, no one's burned no trees lately."

"Y' think this ain't as terrible? Regular dryads die if they's maybe fifty miles from their tree. She's thousands! And on this here island, there's an ocean between to boot!"

"Scared, little Sedessan?"

She gave him a sharp look. His tone didn't tell her if he meant the *little* scathingly or as a simple fact. Beside his more than seven-foot frame, she *was* tiny.

She shrugged it off. "Figure our jailers know 'bout the banishment too." El was careful not to call their captors Sedessans. As far as she knew, everyone in the cell thought they were being held by only the Fae.

Which family is behind this? The Sedanza Court was made up of six families, all of which, except for her own, could be working with the Fae. "Figure since they's captured her, they's got plans for her and I'm contrary enough to want to disrupt those plans."

The giant's brief, vicious grin flashed in the dark. "Fine. I'll help free the Drydanda." He grabbed her arm, his palm engulfing her elbow. "But don't for a tic think I ain't aware of how y' worked this

59

conversation. Y' use me to simply escape an' I'll bring the whole ceiling down on y'r head."

El stared, shocked not by his words but by his touch. No one touched a Sedessan by choice. No one.

She schooled her face as he grinned mockingly. "Just y' try me. I ain't got nothin' to worry 'bout when it comes to y'r mind games."

A shielded mind? El's curiosity raged. The Sedessans repeatedly attempted to develop technology that would shield them from another Sedessan, but so far, the surest way to block someone was a disciplined mind. It couldn't be hacked. El almost reached out mentally to test him, but better judgment reasserted itself.

He released her arm and leaned his elbows on his knees. "Tell me what y'r plannin'."

El pulled herself together, her skin tingling where he'd touched her, and glared at the imps slowly approaching. *When was the last time a stranger willingly touched me?* She couldn't recall. The imps stopped and began making faces. El smirked back at them.

Make a plan and get out of here. As she laid out her plan, she pulled her hair tie free, finding the slightly harder section in the elastic and pressing it firmly to activate the tracking device, before redoing her hair.

Na'rina sat with her eyes closed, focusing on her zoi aima as she pushed it into the island below like smoke, seeking, carefully spooling out little by little so as not to overextend herself.

With more time to investigate her cell—or should she call it a cave?—she had found a crack. It was a miniscule fissure between the wall and the floor at the back of the room. She'd missed it in her initial search probably due to wooziness.

Now she explored, searching for the dryad she'd felt earlier. So far, she'd nothing but porous rock and salty dampness. The island breathed with the tides that ebbed and flowed through every crevice. Another mythic had searched her out, but Na'rina found no trace of the creature now.

Is she avoiding me?

The faint click and creak of a lock and hinges intruded on her and Na'rina began winding her zoi aima back into her body. She fought a sudden vulnerability while also trying to conserve every drop of energy. Finally, she opened her eyes to find the servant woman, Marie, in the room. The woman gaped.

"Y-yo," she stuttered, gesturing at her face, "your eyes, son verdes!"

Na'rina blinked again. Icarus had told her that when she quested out, the green of her eyes bled into the sclera. Poor Marie must have seen this.

"What were you doing?" Marie whispered, moving forward to crouch before Na'rina.

Na'rina smiled tentatively, suddenly self-conscious. Something brushed her skin, a cool, damp touch that traveled up her back from the floor. She stiffened.

Marie reached for her hands. A second before her fingers touched Na'rina, the presence slid over Na'rina's fingers like she'd just broken out in a cold sweat, except her sweat was sticky, not wet like water. It carried the crushed leaves she'd sensed earlier and something else.

Everything in Na'rina wanted to glance down but some other sense warned her not to, and because she didn't look away, she caught the flare of displeasure on Marie's face, there and gone in a second.

What was that?

The displeasure shifted to concern. "You're fría! I can bring you a blanket, Bonita."

Na'rina shook her head, wanting desperately to look at her hands but unsure if she should draw Marie's attention to the odd zoi aima on her skin. *She's human. She can't see it.* Still, Na'rina didn't look. "I do not feel it much," she told Marie. "Now if you have sunlight, that would be another thing."

She meant it as a joke, but Marie pushed away and scrambled for a small bundle she'd brought. "Sunlight, no," she said, "but bread, sí."

She held the bundle out and flipped the edges of the cloth aside to reveal a small loaf of rough, brown bread. The heady smell of yeast hit Na'rina. Her stomach grumbled. She wrapped her hands around the bundle with a grateful smile. "Thank you."

Marie ducked her head and backed away. "I must go. You eat." She knocked on the door and it cracked open.

Na'rina cradled the bread until Marie left, torn between digging into it and setting it aside to focus on the zoi aima coating her skin. As the door clicked shut, she finally looked at her fingers. There was an aqua sheen over her skin, like the ocean she'd glimpsed before they'd forced a bag over her head. The blue shifted, streaming from her hands and over the bread. The bundle dissolved into mush, letting off a distinctly bitter odor as it did.

Na'rina gagged and dropped the soggy bread, which splatted across the floor. She spit and backed away, trying to find clean air. Still gagging, she almost missed the unfamiliar zoi aima retreating from her skin. It rushed toward the tiny fissure. Whoever it was, she knew far more about the island and its people than Na'rina did.

"Wait!" Na'rina hit her knees next to the fissure. "I need your help!" Her zoi aima streaked out to follow and this time, she didn't hold back.

The holding cell slept. Even the imps had huddled up in a pile against the wall and now a symphony of high-pitched snores emanated from the heap. El sat on her rock perch again, waiting for Amos, the giant, to make his move.

The twiglet continued to grasp the door's bars and El hoped it moved before things got exciting.

Amos rolled to his feet and stretched, his arms reaching well over El's head. Most modern giants were not the towering, aggressive, dumb creatures that myth made them out to be. The dumb part probably came from people mistaking iors for giants. The aggressive and towering parts were a matter of genetic degradation. The giants were slowly becoming shorter and had given up their aggressive nature somewhere in history. The few El had ever met were enormously strong, but gentle. Despite that, if one walked down a human street, they'd leave an impression.

Just as Amos was leaving an impression now. A couple imps and the Daughter of Medusa jerked awake at his movement. The imps collided and one smacked the other. Amos ambled toward the door but stopped to stare at them when one reached to wake their companions. It froze and its buddy smacked it again. Like guilty children, they both flopped back over and imitated snoring.

El snickered. It was satisfying to see she wasn't the only one they feared just by reputation.

Amos bent to peek through the bars of the door. The twiglet glanced up with a pitiful whine, and then climbed onto his toe and hugged his leg. El's satisfaction soured.

"Get back," came the guard's bored command.

"A privy'd be right handy 'bout now," Amos said.

The guard snorted. "Go in a corner."

As they'd been escorting people to the bathroom all day, El knew the guard was just being lazy.

Amos' hum vibrated through the floor. The Daughter of Medusa took this as a warning and vacated her spot.

"Not fond of being an exhibitionist, Mate," Amos said as he grabbed the bars.

"Back away!"

Amos' shoulders hunched just before a shudder traveled through the wall against El's back. He'd pulled on the door and a dull boom echoed in the cell. El had no idea what caused the boom—he hadn't rammed the door—but a moment later Amos groaned and the bars began to bend toward him.

Another boom pressed against El's eardrums. It had to be connected to the part of Amos' zoi aima that she couldn't place. *How irritating.* But now wasn't the time to puzzle it out.

Shouts sounded out in the hall.

The cell's occupants stirred, coming awake, while El slid off her shelf and slipped closer to Amos. She didn't want to be caught when the door gave, but she needed to be near enough to slip through once it was out of her way.

"Hurry," she whispered as the shouts grew louder. Amos gritted his teeth and his shoulders bunched again.

This time the floor rocked with the boom and even Amos appeared startled. A crack split the rock wall from the top of the door up into the ceiling. With one last heave, the door gave. Amos tumbled backward into the watching prisoners. El darted into the hall, hopping when the floor rolled under her feet. She slapped her palm to the face of the first guard she encountered.

Sleep. Resistance met her mental command but then the guard slumped and dropped his shock baton. El nabbed it and stumbled. Her head cracked against the wall.

Ugh, that'll scramble my neurons. It blurred her vision. She blinked, refocusing in time to block the next guard's descending baton. *Zap!* Sparks singed El's arms and her arm sensors buzzed. The guard snarled, leaning in and forcing their locked batons closer to El while the metal continued to sizzle. The buzz from El's sensors intensified and then quit, overloaded.

"GIANT!" El hollered.

He caught her intent and ran awkwardly the other way toward the Drydanda's isolation cell.

The guards shouted, realizing Amos' goal, but El's struggle blocked them in the narrow hall. She ducked sideways and her opponent fell onto his face. El shocked him in the back and he jerked before going limp.

Another sub-boom hollowed El's eardrums and the floor literally rolled down the hall like a mole was digging beneath it. El jumped over it and glanced back to warn Amos. *Too late.* The moving hill rammed into his heels and he fell with a shout. He'd somehow dug his fingers into the stone around the isolation door and it came with him, landing on his chest.

For a giant, the couple hundred pounds of door wasn't a big deal, but then the ceiling cracked and debris smashed over him.

"Down!"

El ducked despite not knowing who shouted. A baton swung over her head and froze, making a splintering sound as the black metal turned to stone.

The Daughter of Medusa. El wasn't sure why the woman had helped her, but she wouldn't look the gift horse in the mouth either...or look at the gift horse at all. She caught a purple streak and thanked her stars that the Daughter was focused on the guards.

With the guards struggling to get past their statued brothers, El spun for the isolation chamber. Although it lay open now, the Drydanda hadn't emerged.

"Have you seen her?" El asked as she passed Amos.

"Nowt a peep," he groaned, shoving rock off his chest.

El scrambled over the rock pile and giant into the room beyond while blinking her second lens down. Amos muttered darkly behind her.

What in the—Cracks spiraled through the walls, growing as things continued to shake. Dirt and chunks of stone rained down, but it was the chaos of zoi aima that stopped El in her tracks.

The brilliant green and blue stabbed into her already throbbing head. She stared at it anyway, trying to spot the center of that whirling mass. It spun and speared through the stone so fast it made El dizzy but someone was moving in there.

The Drydanda sat against the back wall, her eyes distant, like she was unaware of the world falling apart around her.

"Na'rina Drydanda!" El shouted and stepped closer.

The world rocked. El stumbled just as a deafening crack made her ears ring. Rock rained down and she threw up her arms to protect her head.

"DRYDANDA!"

Na'rina's emerald eyes snapped into focus. Recognition lit her face, and then the ceiling caved in. Zoi aima exploded. Usually, a creature's energy moved harmlessly with them, but this shoved El backwards against the wall like she'd been hit by a runaway horse. Her head smacked into the stone again and her vision swam as disbelief froze her synapses.

All she could see was rock where a moment before sat the most powerful mythic she'd ever known. Gone in a blaze like a dying star. Above the pile, salty ocean air rushed through the new hole.

El's brain stuttered. She couldn't picture telling her unshakable brother that his beloved was dead.

"Sedessan!" Amos' shout snapped her out of her shock. She spun to help him when the Daughter of Medusa raced past her toward the hole in the ceiling.

"No time, Sedessan," the woman shouted, "the building's coming down on our heads."

That stopped El. *I need to tell my mother what I've learned. Someone's using Compulsion.*

Amos heaved a boulder off his body. "Don't y' dare, Sedessan.

Don't y' leave me." He smacked the floor and a dull boom rocked the already unstable building.

El stumbled but caught the wall.

Shouts echoed from the guard station.

"Sedessan," yelled the Daughter of Medusa.

El spun and ran, clamoring up the pile that had buried Na'rina to reach the open air beyond even as the world continued to shudder.

I never promised him! Still, tears pricked her eyes.

Icarus walked with Levi down the street toward Richard McCormick's Denver apartment. The man was going to freak when he saw them. Icarus didn't care. Intela Corp was the most likely culprit in Na'rina's disappearance, and he needed information. His awareness of her had spiked on the drive over like claws into his chest and then gone suddenly numb. It terrified him.

He glanced at Levi. Now dressed in jeans and a buttoned flannel shirt, the large wer-im didn't draw too much attention. A few women admired his golden color, probably thinking him well tanned if a bit feral around the eyes, but his tattoos, except for the branches and leaves on his arms, were covered. The admirers looked away after a glance, however. Seeing Levi devour a plate of sushi was a bit like watching a shark attack a school of fish.

On the drive, they'd found out the hard way that Levi got motion sick. A car ride was a vast change from traveling on horseback.

"Trying to replace everything you lost?" Icarus tried to tease but there was an edge to his voice. He bit into his own sushi, hoping the food would ease his apprehension. It didn't.

Levi grinned with far too many teeth and a slim woman walking toward them clutched her purse and crossed the street to pass on the other side.

"Hide the canines while we're in public," Icarus said.

Levi tilted his head in curiosity. Icarus nabbed his empty plate and pitched it along with his own into a trash bin as they passed by it.

Levi pointed back over their shoulders. "She would have given distance because of this anyway." He trailed two fingers from his ear down across his jaw, imitating the thick scars gracing Icarus' face.

Icarus scowled.

He didn't mind the scars, despite the bottom two being thick as No. 2 pencils. Na'rina often laid her long fingers over them. *You saved my life that day*, she'd remind him. *They are beautiful to me.*

Levi stopped and Icarus stopped out of reflex. "You earned scars in the Kadivas," he said, his tone admonishing Icarus' attitude. In Levi's eyes, Icarus winning the *Kadivas*, or challenge for leadership, should be a source of pride.

Icarus rubbed at his chest, chafing at the vow's numbness again.

"Helpful among the wer-im," Icarus said, "but not while trying to blend into human society." *And they remind me of what happened with Silas.*

"Blending—" Levi chewed on the word. He pointed to the park across the street where a middle-aged man leaned against a cottonwood. His hair was died electric blue, spiked, and almost as long as Icarus'. So many piercings lined his eyebrows that Icarus couldn't tell where metal ended and eyebrow began. "Wind in the trees," Levi continued, "noticed when blowing, then forgotten."

They started walking again. Icarus rubbed at his chest and then caught himself. He had no idea what the numbness meant. They reached Richard's apartment building, a tall structure with a parking garage on the bottom three floors. Icarus led the way past the parking gates into the garage and headed for the stairs at the back corner.

Levi sniffed. "Place smells hot, oily, and like wolf pee. When did humans decide to cover the world in fake stone?" He rapped a knuckle on the stairwell wall.

Icarus snorted. The older wer-im was handling modern life remarkably well. "When was the last time you were in wer-im form?" he asked.

Levi stopped on the stairs, his expression suddenly anguished.

"I can hear Ver'rina as lion," Levi said, "even when she's in the grove and I am not."

"You can hear her psychically anywhere?"

"*Sa*. As lion, I hear her within." He tapped his chest. "As wer-im," he held up his weathered hands, "I hear silence."

"Do you—" Icarus paused. Silas had never been forthcoming with answers, saying Icarus' Sedessan side asked too many questions. *If I could do it again, I'd ask all the questions.*

Levi waited, his golden eyes intent.

"—Do you ache at the separation?" Icarus finally asked.

"My sprout explained nothing?" Levi asked.

Icarus shook his head.

Levi's lip rolled upward in a snarl. "Here," he tapped his chest, "feels like I've stood in snow too long. Painful with a dangerous dull edge. This is normal. It speaks of my Ver'rina's well-being. If it spikes, ice into my chest, my Ver'rina is physically hurting."

Icarus recalled the spike while he'd been in the Four Corners center. *I felt when Na'rina was captured.* He rocked on his heels and rubbed at the deadness in his chest again. "What about feeling numb?"

Levi tilted his head. "I do not—"

Someone opened the door below, heading up the stairs. Icarus wanted to snarl but he just gestured with his head and they started moving again. They paused briefly at the door into the building for Icarus to pass an RFID card in front of the pad. Felis' handiwork. Although Icarus stayed familiar with progressing technology, Felis loved it.

Midway down the hallway, Icarus knocked on 1059 and a heavy grunt like someone trying to stand up came from inside. A moment later, the door swung open to reveal a heavyset, balding man. His flushed face went white at seeing Icarus.

"You can't be here." He glanced both ways down the hall.

"Either let us in or chance your neighbors seeing us," Icarus said.

Richard McCormick ushered them in, glancing into the hall again before shutting and locking the door. The place was a cave. Dark walls and no lights except for a single lampstand and what filtered through drawn curtains over the only window, which happened to be the sliding glass door out onto the balcony. The apartment was a wide hallway with a few walls to delineate the kitchen and living room, and a single door that led to Richard's bedroom on the left. The TV was paused on what looked like a sci-fi movie. It always surprised Icarus that, despite being well paid as a quality control agent for Intela Corp, Richard kept his home life simple and unembellished, valuing his daughter and granddaughter far above physical things. From the binders and paperwork scattered across his coffee table, it appeared Richard had been working.

"Why'd you come here?" Richard whispered like the walls might be listening. "I always come when you ask."

"I don't have three days," Icarus answered. The usual way of contacting Richard involved slipping a pizza party flier into his mailbox in the lobby and three days later Richard would go for coffee at a café five blocks away.

"What's he doing?"

Levi stood in front of Richard's fish tank, hunched over the mesh to watch the goldfish while his large hands gripped the tank's sides.

"Fishing, I think," Icarus said. "Levi, not food."

Levi's head snapped up and his eyes shone. The laid-back feline from their walk was gone. He licked his lips. "Does he keep them for a snack?"

Richard whined an involuntary complaint. "My pets."

"Pets?"

"Richard, have your employers started research on dryads again?" Icarus pulled the conversation back to why they'd come.

"Not as far as I've seen," Richard answered while he retreated into the kitchen. He came back with a box of goldfish. "Here. It's a…it's a fish snack," he told Levi, handing him the box to draw him away from the fish tank. Then to Icarus, "They've been focusing on the naiads and some sort of holding tank lately. It's a mess, really."

"Snack?" Levi held an orange cracker in his fingers and sniffed at it. "Doesn't smell like fish."

Richard quailed. "It's food," he insisted, pulling a handkerchief from his pocket to wipe his brow.

"What happened at the Four Corners center?" Icarus pressed.

"That's umm…above my pay grade," Richard answered.

"Rumor has it the company is shifting resources to a new facility."

Levi spit, a partly chewed goldfish hitting the wall above Richard's head. Then the entire box sailed through the air at the man as Levi rushed him.

Richard squeaked, trying to back away.

Icarus' pulse spiked. Overtop the adrenaline washed a familiar veneer of ice like the crust on a frozen pond that allowed him a quick reasoning he only experienced in violent moments. It was a state Silas had never understood. A part of his Sedessan blood.

I can't outright fight Levi. We'd draw too much attention in this tiny apartment. But neither could he stand by and let Levi demolish the human.

Before Levi could hit Richard, Icarus bolted between them and rammed his shoulder low into Levi's sternum. It was like hitting an oak tree. Pain radiated through his shoulder. Air gusted from Levi a second before the huge wer-im grabbed Icarus by the throat and lifted him off the floor. For the first time, Icarus saw Silas in his father's face and his chest twinged.

What a disaster. He'd known when Levi turned wer-im from mountain lion that this would happen. *Need Ver'rina.*

Against Levi's typical wer-im rage, Ver'rina's calm was the staying force Levi had known for centuries. Icarus didn't have Ver'rina, but he did know the dryad's mannerisms and so did Levi.

Icarus laid his palms on either side of Levi's face in a gesture so familiar he longed to feel Na'rina's cool fingers against his own face. His hands trembled as he waited for the action to register.

Finally, Levi's snarl melted. Shock followed, and then shame. He dropped Icarus.

Icarus gasped.

"He tricked me," Levi whispered. "Those *snacks* are poison."

Before Icarus could answer, the *rap*, *rap*, *rap* of someone knocking at the door echoed through the apartment. Icarus raised a brow.

"Hide." Richard waved them toward the bedroom. He straightened his shirt, mopped his brow again, and grimaced at the goldfish scattered across the floor before going to answer as another *rap*, *rap*, *rap* echoed.

Icarus softly closed the bedroom door just as Richard greeted someone outside. He laid down on the floor and pressed his eye to the crack below the wood. A moment later, Levi joined him. The room was so tiny their feet hit the bed behind them.

"Martin," Richard choked, "come in."

"My god, Richard, did you throw a party for your granddaughter in here? I thought you didn't let her visit the apartment."

The voices passed by the bedroom.

Icarus closed his eyes. He knew that voice. He'd first heard it near Chattanooga when Richard and this man, Martin, had been retrieving a tracking device designed to register dryadic zoi aima. Martin slicked back his hair in a way that Na'rina said reminded her of a shell. Icarus didn't know of any shells that reeked of citrus and sugar, however.

Richard's knees and then his hands appeared as he crouched to pick up goldfish.

"What brings you out on a Saturday morning?" he asked Martin.

"Work, what else?"

"But it's Saturday."

"And yet, your coffee table looks like your desk." Black boots appeared beside Richard, crushing crackers into the carpet, and Icarus could just see the stack of papers Martin tapped Richard's shoulder with. "We never leave work, you know that."

Richard flopped over to sit on the floor and take a look while Martin leaned against the couch, crushing more crackers.

The older man groaned. "Why can't you take this one? You know I hate ships."

Sansabria and Erstwhile? Or the Observer? Icarus was unaware of any others Intela Corp owned, but that didn't mean they didn't have any.

Martin chuckled. "I've been assigned elsewhere. Grab your go-bag. I'm to drive you to DIA since your plane leaves within a few hours of mine."

Icarus gritted his teeth. He needed more information before Richard left.

Icarus elbowed Levi and they backed away from the door. The go-bag was probably in Richard's closet. It might be possible for one of them to hide in the fold of the accordion door, but it wouldn't accommodate them both. Levi squeezed his arm and disappeared into the bathroom on silent feet. Icarus tucked himself into the closet door just before Richard came in.

"I didn't think they were keeping anything on the ships lately," Richard commented over his shoulder as he reached for the black duffle sitting on the closet floor. Beads of sweat covered his upper lip. *Keep it together*, Icarus silently encouraged.

Richard glanced at Icarus. He grabbed his duffle and struggled with the zipper, holding his papers faceup against the fabric as he did.

The heading read: CRYO PROJECT – TRANSPORT OF SUBJECTS

Subjects? Dwarves? Prisoners from the Four Corners location? Icarus had no way of asking but Richard had at least given him a nugget.

"Come on, old man," Martin stood in the doorway with his arms crossed over his narrow chest. He had that lean kind of frame that hid his muscles by making them sinewy instead of bulky.

Richard huffed. "You just wait," he said. "Give it another ten years and you'll struggle to move too."

Martin scoffed and turned away.

"All right, I'm coming." Richard followed and a moment later Icarus caught the thud of the main door closing.

He peeked out to find Levi already in the bedroom with the door open. The larger wer-im stared at the living room with its mess of orange crackers.

"This Richard actually eats those things?" he asked.

"*Sa.*"

Levi appeared disturbed. "If you hadn't stopped me, he had no defense."

Icarus didn't respond as he glanced through the papers on the coffee table. None of it seemed pertinent to finding Na'rina. *Where is she?* That spike of ice haunted him. He was about to ask Levi about it again when his phone vibrated.

"Hello?" he answered.

"Faun's taken care of, Kadis," came Obek's rough voice.

"Taken care of?"

"Took her to Afre. Barely caught him. He's traveling back east to touch base with the mythics from the summit. You'd have thought I gave Aileen the world. She blubbered all over him." There was a tense edge to Obek's words as he explained.

Afre's pushing for the alliance in Na'rina's stead? He'd expressed dismay over failing her at the summit. Icarus hadn't expected the faun to jump in with both hooves, but this *was* Afre. *Good.* The faun was perfect for such negotiations, and it left Icarus able to focus on finding Na'rina. "Did Aileen know anything about Intela Corp clearing out of the Four Corners?" he asked Obek.

"*Na*, other than that they used flamethrowers to force the rougher mythics to move when they evacuated. She got caught in the scuffle and they left her for dead."

Icarus fought down an instinctual hatred for people who would use such tactics. They either viewed the mythics as rats, to be burned out, or as cattle, to be used.

"How's the Drydanda?" Obek asked. He knew about Ver'rina's call, but Icarus hadn't updated him on Na'rina's actual disappearance.

"Someone kidnapped her from the summit." The words came out dispassionately. He fought to keep them that way.

"Baldim's Beard! When will things turn for us?"

Icarus didn't answer.

"Any leads?"

"Nothing yet." Even if there were, he wasn't sure he'd share. He trusted Obek, but didn't have the authority to ask him to keep the information to himself. Icarus shifted the conversation, narrowing in on the edge in the dwarf's voice.

"How's your father?"

There came the sound of liquid pouring and a long sigh. "Pa shut down the search," Obek finally said. "He said our last mission and the summit were a disaster."

Icarus scowled. He'd suspected about the summit. "What job did he give you instead?" he asked absently. Obek was one of King Olbin's sons, true, but he was also one of his Hammers, often sent out as an extension of the king's will.

Listening, Icarus flipped through the papers on the coffee table again. Mythology research, blood tests, a biology research book. It was a scattered mess. El or his mother would love the puzzle it presented. Icarus froze. *Since when do I include Sophia in my musings?* The recent talk of South America must have stirred some things. He shook it off, not wanting to ponder what would or would not catch Sophia Varela's interest, and pocketed the blood test papers to take to Rebecca Simms.

"Shutting down our logging company in the Carolinas," Obek grumbled, explaining his current assignment. "It's one of our most productive lines, but he's shutting it down and sealing us in the caverns like we're back in Greek times, hiding from men with swords."

"It takes time to shut down a company like that," Icarus mused. "And there are Intela Corp operations in the Carolinas—" he left it hanging.

Obek grunted. "That comes suspiciously close to disobeying."

"You mentioned a friend amid the Rockies dwarves. If you let this go, can you live with that?"

Obek's heavy breathing came over the phone as the dwarf considered. Then the clink of glass against teeth and a gulp.

"Any updates on the Carolina operations recently?" Obek asked.

Icarus filled him in on the little he knew and hung up.

Levi stared at him like he was an enigma.

Icarus raised a brow.

"You feel vow here," Levi tapped his sternum, "like ice hook in guts?"

Up until the recent numbness, it described perfectly what Icarus felt when Na'rina wasn't well.

"*Sa.*"

"Yet you care about all this?" Levi indicated the papers and the phone.

"All this," Icarus answered, "is tied together."

Icarus' methodical methods had bothered Silas too, but unlike Silas, Levi accepted his explanation.

"What does numbness mean?" Icarus finally asked again.

Levi tilted his head, and then shrugged. "I do not know. My vow has never been numb."

That was not encouraging. "Come," Icarus almost snarled, "let's see if Felis and Rebecca have better intel."

El ached as she made her way to her father's study. She'd slept fitfully and the headache from her escape was now complemented by tension that throbbed down her neck. What's more, she kept seeing the giant's accusatory eyes just before she ran.

I promised him nothin'. But he'd helped her. *And now he might be dead…just like the Drydanda.* El shied away from that.

She was rubbing her temples when she reached the study. Composing herself, she peeked inside and found the room empty. El entered and leaned against the door, breathing in the smell of the books. She'd grown up on the Varela estate but that didn't mean she was unaware of its oddities.

Half Caribbean architecture and half Medieval style castle, it sprawled across the cliffs of the San Martez Island. Flower gardens grew prolifically around the dwarven-crafted, mechanical gargoyles protecting the estate. Metal storm shutters could be lowered to shelter the more sensitive areas—such as the study—during the occasional hurricane, but these went unnoticed most of the time due to the chilis drying in the sun and the massive hibiscus gracing the walls. All of it was maintained by hideous goblins who gloried in their warts and knobby knuckles.

El loved it. San Martez had character and warmth. It was the best of the Sedessan estates.

Each of the six houses in the Court claimed an island just off Venezuela. Unlike Trinidad and Tobago, the islands were small and privately owned. They'd maintained their anonymity through regular mental manipulation until about 100 years ago. Then, because of the advance of technology, they'd added an invisible surveillance dome over the entire island chain and allied with the Fae, who created an emotional resistance to the dome in exchange for the use of Riviera, the seventh, and unused, island. Humans knew the islands as a heavily fortified country called Sedanza that they had no interest in visiting.

There was a similar Court, the Asimi Court, near Egypt, but they lacked a Fae embassy like the one on Riviera.

El opened her phone to Sedanza's news sent over the nation's secured network. The top headline read, "Fae Embassy in Shambles after 5.9 Magnitude Earthquake."

Did Amos set it off? He looked just as surprised as everyone else. El's head continued to throb.

After leaving the embassy, she'd escaped to a predetermined cove where her family had a boat waiting. She couldn't say where the Daughter of Medusa had disappeared to. El huffed. *Not even near the top of my things to worry about right now.* She pushed off the door and strode for the far wall, clutching the hair tie she'd worn to Riviera with its tiny tracking device inside. It's how her family had known to send the boat to the cove.

As the thick burgundy rug covering the oak floor quieted her steps, El wished she could flop into one of the plush chairs facing the desk and take a nap. Instead, she stopped in front of the family painting on the far wall. Floor-to-ceiling bookshelves flanked it.

The room was one of the quietest in the estate simply because it was insulated by books. El loved it and hated it. Despite all the family paintings, none of them included her brother. It hinted that even her father knew the truth about Icarus. If he hadn't, he would have insisted on pictures of his late son.

Ignoring the family portrait, El ran her fingers around the heavy picture frame until she found the notches that read her fingerprints. The painting slid silently outward to reveal three shelves. The house was riddled with such hidden compartments, put in long ago by dwarves of the now extinct Cascade line. The back of the painting held the race's signature, an etching of a grand fir in the rain. *Nothing like dwarven craftmanship.*

Each shelf held seemingly normal items—bracelets, earrings, rings, tie clips—but hid antidotes, poison needles, comms devices and the like. El put the hair tie back in its spot, closed the compartment, and went to lean against the desk.

She closed her eyes and retreated to a mental room much like the study. Except it was *her* space. Her mindscape. The walls boasted several portraits, including one of a young, intense boy with dark hair and hazel eyes. El opened it in a similar way as she had the family painting. She hid everything regarding Icarus behind it. His connection to Na'rina Drydanda—their parents knew the Wer-Kadis had allied with the North American dryads but did not know his identity—the anguish El knew he'd feel over Na'rina's death, and lastly, where El had gotten the tracking device now in the hair tie. Icarus had given it to her after Intela Corp had used it on him.

Everything safely stowed, El schooled her face as someone

entered the actual study. When she blinked her eyes open, Sophia Varela, her mother, was watching her.

El had gotten her tiny size from her mother. Sophia's gray and black hair was pulled up into a bun, adding an inch or two to her height, but she was barely five feet tall. She emanated a poise that El wasn't sure she'd ever achieve. Instead of hiding her Sedessan facial markings, Sophia carefully incorporated them into her makeup. The faint lines that traced from her eyes out into her hairline looked like cat eyes to accentuate her sharp stare.

"Elodie," Sophia greeted. "Rough assignment?"

El cringed but took in the afternoon tea-and-scones accent that was uniquely Sophia. It was a voice that politely welcomed a person in, and then controlled the conversation.

Hello Mother. I'm okay. Thanks for asking. She hadn't bothered with makeup of her own that morning, and the nicks and bruises from her escape were on full display. They were minor compared to her throbbing headache and would be gone in a few hours. She envied Icarus' insanely fast healing, but at least she healed faster than a human.

"Every mission has hiccups," El answered, adopting a softer version of her mother's accent. "This one just had some—painful—hiccups."

"Indeed," Sophia tisked. "Hopefully they will heal before the upcoming ball. I've found the perfect dress for you."

El grimaced. The Sedanza Court held a yearly gathering of the families. This year it was hosted by the Inverros. In true Sedessan style, it was always held in conjunction with some human event that nicely dovetailed with the Court's love of connections, and the Inverros had planned the upcoming ball by hiding it within a science symposium held at a famous hotel in Charleston. "That's days away," she said. "I'll be right as sunshine in a few hours."

"Indeed." Sophia smiled and held her hands out, approaching.

El braced herself.

Instead of folding her into an embrace, Sophia grasped her face, her thin fingers sliding into El's loose hair.

Sophia "stepped" into El's mental study. She took in the books, her eyes skimming over Icarus' portrait, and then lighted on the paperwork on the desk. The room shifted and she stood behind the desk, reading the report's highlights.

El fought dizziness at the swift change.

"You entered the embassy under the pretense of bringing the title for one of their new boats," her mother prompted.

El climbed the steps to the Fae embassy in a dark suit. The outfit fit comfortably but the nanite mask on her face itched abominably. It was necessary, however, as her face was known at the embassy. The guard at the top stopped her with the butt of his rifle.

"Name and purpose?" he asked.

"Elizabeth Marrow. I'm from the bank." El held up a Manila envelope. "I'm supposed to see a—um—" El paused like she was checking her notes, "a Señor Dominguez."

The guard grunted and spoke into his earpiece before motioning for El to enter.

An assistant met El and led her toward Dominguez' office, her heels clicking on the stone. A janitor's closet opened just as they passed and a woman exited, revealing what looked like a wall of antique refrigerators inside.

"Odd," Sophia muttered aloud.

El agreed but didn't say anything.

Inside Dominguez' office, the old man sat behind his desk. He was not Fae but human despite being the ambassador's assistant. El blinked. His zoi aima swirled red, brown, green, and gray, then back to red.

"You have paperwork for me?" he asked.

El handed over the Manila envelope. Inside was a fake title for a speedboat the embassy had recently paid off. It wouldn't pass muster and El knew that.

"There's a note in the bank's file stating you wanted this hand-delivered," she said anyway, keeping up her ruse.

Señor Dominguez perused the papers, a fine line developing between his brows. "Give me one moment, please," he said, rising and buttoning his jacket, the gesture covering his golden, Greek-lettered tie clip. "I need to check these with our records." He grabbed his cane and stepped out.

El waited. They suspected Dominguez was the front man for an operation involving the disappearance of several notable mythics. If he was indeed involved, he'd recognize "Señorita Marrow" as an investigator for a family of elementals who had gone missing. El didn't actually know said investigator, but that wasn't important. All that mattered was that Dominguez believed she was trying to find the elementals.

Finally, the door swung open again and Señor Dominguez stood there with his hands stacked on his cane and his shoulders hunched inward.

"¿Señorita?"

"Marrow," El supplied, standing.

"Señorita Marrow. I'm afraid there's something wrong with your

paperwork." Behind him, a guard stood in the doorway.

"Wrong?" El played along, but she already knew Dominguez had taken the bait.

Sophia paused the memory, frowning at Señor Dominguez. "I always feel like I should know him."

It was an odd comment. Of course, Sophia knew him. He'd been the ambassador's assistant for years. "Beyond his association with the Fae?" El asked.

"Perhaps," Sophia answered, and dove back into El's memory without explaining.

El refrained from grinding her teeth.

The guard led her down a set of stone stairs, his grip digging into her elbow as she struggled and objected weakly. All the while, she slipped into his mindscape unawares. His zoi aima was the familiar human swirl. She dug until she came upon the last time he'd received orders. She couldn't see the person issuing the orders because he stood behind the guard, but whoever he was, he gave instructions mentally.

Sophia hissed. "A Sedessan."

"Sa."

"Who?"

"The guard did not know. But, as we suspected, they are capturing powerful mythics."

They entered a guardroom, an antechamber, below the embassy.

"Another one?" A huge man with captain insignia stood up from the table

where he was playing cards with three other men. Apprehension spiked in El. He was mostly human, but his zoï aima was tinged with a heavy dose of troll blood.

"Señor Dominguez said to have her checked," her escort said.

The captain pulled out a pair of dark sweats from a locker and pitched them at El. Then he pointed to a foldup screen in the corner. "Change."

After swiftly changing, El emerged to find a plump Fae woman sitting on the captain's desk. Her skirt, a sea green and amethyst, whirled around her ankles as she stood up and, despite her size, she floated toward El.

El's apprehension grew. Fae were a mixed bag when it came to abilities. Teleportation, telekinesis, transparency, plant and animal affinities, emotional manipulation, and sometimes what others liked to call identity finders.

El tried to back away as the woman splayed her gloved fingers wide in her face. She backed into the troll-blooded caption and the Fae woman grabbed her ears, her black satin gloves providing no skin contact. The woman dug into the edges of El's nanite mask and peeled it off. Then she hissed and flickered transparent.

"Did you touch her, Emry?" she asked El's escort.

He shoved his hands into his pockets. "Of course not."

"They're playing a dangerous game," the woman hissed. "Throw her in, but do not touch her skin."

Sophia cursed. "They saw your face!" It was only a matter of time before the Sedessans behind the embassy operation were informed and shown El's face mentally.

"That was a risk we thought necessary," El reminded her mother, keeping her voice—mostly—calm despite how tightly Sophia held her head now. "We suspected the Fae, not a Sedessan family."

"Show me the rest."

El did. Including when she stopped the imps from tormenting the salamander and found the Compulsion on their minds. Sophia's hands trembled against El's temples. It was forbidden for Sedessans to turn other people into mindless puppets. That was the one thing the mythics had risen against, almost destroying the Sedessans before both the Asimi and Sedanza Courts had promised to never use Compulsion again.

Sophia visibly calmed herself before continuing.

El blinked her second lens down...the woman glowed a dancing, swirling green and blue like a solar flare.

Sophia sighed in what El guessed was awe.

"What was that?" she suddenly asked.

"What?" El's heart spiked.

"You fear for this mythic." It was not a question. "Why?"

Boiling frogs! She'd failed to hide her reaction to seeing Na'rina.

"I know what happens to her," she said simply.

After a moment, Sophia continued through the memory, her curiosity greater than her desire to know what El meant.

El hid her relief.

The memory finally faded on El boarding the boat home. Sophia stepped back, releasing El's face, to pace the length of the study's rug.

"Someone's using Compulsion," she muttered.

El stayed quiet, leaning against the desk.

"Don't slouch, Elodie," Sophia said. "Did you see signs of stress—sweating, shaking, nervousness—on the Fae woman?"

El rolled her shoulders to straighten her posture and shook her head. "You saw her. She's well aware of what's going on. Even the imps aren't showing Compulsion stress."

Sophia scoffed, "They wouldn't. Imps aren't mentally strong enough to fight a Compelling." She paused, eyeing El with a familiar, commanding look, and El pushed off the desk, holding in a groan as her body protested. Satisfied, Sophia went back to pacing. "No one else showed signs of stress?"

"*Na*," El answered, fighting the urge to cross her arms over her chest. She was too young to remember the last time Compelling had drawn the ire of the other mythics but she knew the stories.

"You're sure?"

"I'm sure," El answered, exasperated.

Her mother spun sharply. She stopped in front of El, her dark eyes intense. "It's no light matter, Elodie. The other mythics leave us alone because we're subtle in what we do, but if someone's using Compulsion, it'll destroy us."

El was the same height as her mother, but at that moment, she felt about as tall as a pixie. She bowed her head, "Of course, Mother. I just didn't see anything besides the imps, which indicates the use isn't widespread."

Sophia eyed her and finally went back to pacing. "Compulsion's addictive. Whoever's using it *will* use it again. The desire keeps growing, keeps forcing the user to try it on stronger mythics until they run into someone they can't totally meld to their will. It *always* backfires."

Her mother spun into the bookshelves, heading for the back wall. El knew she was expected to follow.

Sophia removed the painting of a younger El sitting with Sophia on a bench in the courtyard and laid her hand on the wall's wooden paneling. It groaned as gears engaged. The panels with pictures went up into the ceiling and the others retreated down into the floor, revealing a wall-encompassing glass screen hidden behind. It lit up, showing an island group on one side and a palace with a backdrop in Egypt on the other.

"Sedanza Islands," Sophia said and the image shifted away from the Asimi Court and narrowed in on the Sedanza islands including Riviera, the seventh, at the northern edge. Sophia tapped the Reyes' island, Eglesias, at the southern edge and dozens of topics popped up beside it.

"Compulsion," Sophia ordered. The system shuffled, pulling anything in the Reyes' family that dealt with Compulsion. Sophia flipped through the results, skimming until she stepped back. "The last one to use Compulsion in the Reyes family was before we owned the islands. Check the Torres family."

El did as asked while her mother moved on to the Narvaez family. Over an hour had passed by the time they stepped back from checking each family for hints in their past of Compellers.

"The Narvaez' had an aunt who was executed for it about a hundred years ago," El said. She'd been on an assignment in Canada at the time and missed the whole debacle.

"Old Inverro was suspected of it when he was young, but it was never proven. No indication has cropped up since, so it's unlikely the rumors were true," Sophia said.

"And there's mention of a daughter in the De León family, not

Lucia, but an older sibling who tried it on Lucia when they were little. What happened to her? I don't remember Lucia having a sister."

"Hurricane, supposedly." Sophia flipped a hand dismissively. "The De León estate was devastated by a storm and the girl was never seen afterwards."

The story smacked so closely to the tale her parents told about Icarus that El bit her tongue to keep a quip from escaping. They said he got caught helping one of the staff's families prepare for a coming storm. It was plausible because even then, it was something Icarus would do. The storm hit early, however, and trapped him and the family under the wreckage of their house for two days. Icarus supposedly died before anyone could reach him.

It was true: A hurricane had trapped a family under their house, but Icarus had not been there. He'd weathered the storm on the streets of Caracas, Venezuela, in all respects a recent orphan. And El had been the one actually trapped.

Even the trapped family believed it had been Icarus, though. Her mother had seen to that. El had never figured out why Sophia didn't change *her* memories to match those of the family. At the time, El would have been too young to stop her.

As though reading her thoughts, Sophia touched her shoulder and pivoted El to face her. El flinched, caught off guard.

Her mother was not one to show concern, but she was skilled at reading body language. "You think the girl might be alive?"

"Anything's possible," El answered, choosing her words carefully. Her pulse beat in her temples, making it hard to think. "And it would not be the only time something like that's been done."

It was the closest she'd ever come to accusing Sophia of lying about Icarus. Her mother's face went blank and she turned away toward the screen again, saying, "We need to pinpoint a motive. *Why* is one of the families using Compulsion?"

El wanted to scream. *Why do you act like he never existed!? He's your son!*

"Why are they capturing other mythics?" El finally added, composing herself from long practice. "I wasn't down there long enough to figure out what they're doing with them."

"Is there a pattern?"

"A Daughter of Medusa, a salamander, a giant," El ticked them off on her fingers. She had no idea where the twiglet got to. Sophia hadn't noticed it beyond when El pulled it from the door, so El didn't add it to her list, "an ior of all things, the imps, some gnomes, me, and a Drydanda. I don't see a connection."

"The Drydanda bothers me—" Sophia tapped her chin, staring at the map.

El remained silent. The rumors regarding Na'rina centered on her odd two-tone lifeblood. It was rare and there was no way for El to keep Sophia from realizing who Na'rina was. As far as Sophia knew, El had never actually met the North American Drydanda and El wasn't going to open a discussion that might trip her up. *I still haven't, technically, met Na'rina.* El's throat ached. *And I never will.*

Sophia gave her an enigmatic look. "Two-tone zoi aima that didn't mix. That's a whole can of worms for another day."

El frowned. "Excuse me?"

Sophia waved dismissively again and El bit her tongue.

"For now, we need to focus here." She touched Riviera on the screen. The image enlarged, blurring the forests that encased most of the island, until it showed the Fae's embassy and the city with the docks on the western coast. The embassy itself sat just up the rise from the water. The other notable buildings were the library, the ambassador's mansion, the clock tower, all positioned close to the main thoroughfare running through the city center. "Go back to the embassy. So far there's no indication that the ambassador's involved with the imprisonment of mythics below his embassy. Or if he is, there's no chatter about him connecting your alias as Miss Marrow. I'm not even sure Señor Dominguez has been informed on that front. Whichever Sedessan family is imprisoning mythics is holding that close.

"Regardless, the ambassador has asked for aid from the Court…"

"What if he arrests me again?" El interrupted.

Sophia scowled at her. "Then we'll get you released through diplomatic channels and, in the process, obtain their reason for your arrest. So far, we're in the dark about their true reasons. Now respond to the ambassador's call for aid and, while there, confirm the Drydanda's death and look for any indication of which Sedessan family is pulling all the strings." Sophia paused.

When she continued, she sounded more contemplative than decisive. "If they accuse the Court of the earthquake or, stars forbid, they find out about the Compulsions, the Fae will pull their protective deterrent from Sedanza and likely declare war."

She paused again, tapping her lips with a finger. "If you have to offer another culprit, place blame at the giant's feet," she finally said. "That should keep them distracted for now."

95

El seethed. It'd do nothing if the Fae stumbled on the Compulsions. Giants couldn't Compel people. But it played to the Fae's love of cold justice. They loved executions and Sophia was right, that fascination might be enough to keep them distracted. *It'll get Amos killed.*

"The giant didn't cause the earthquake," she objected.

"Of course not," Sophia said, "but it looked like he did."

"You want me to lie?"

Sophia scoffed. "Since when do you care? *Sa*, I want you to lie. He's a perfect scapegoat."

"He might be the last of his kind."

"And?"

And I'm not interested in making giants extinct! El bit back her retort, instead saying, "And the Fae will not be fooled."

"It gives us time."

"It'll make them question our word."

"So we read someone wrong and it comes out in a trial," Sophia shrugged. "Giants are notoriously hard to read. Thick heads, you know. Now go. And Elodie," Sophia suddenly cupped El's chin between her thumb and forefinger, "our family *needs* to keep peace with the Fae. The Inverros are making waves. Your father and I are working to take advantage of it, but I need you to represent well."

Sophia's look pinned El. Getting identified during the mission had apparently compromised more than she realized.

Sophia tucked a strand of El's hair behind her ear with her free hand. "Show the Fae that the Varelas honor their agreements."

El swallowed, and nodded, feeling the imprint of her mother's fingers when she let go.

"Good. Close this up before you leave." Sophia motioned at the wall and strode from the study.

Rebecca Simms still wore high heels just like the first time Icarus met her, but now they were lined up in a neat row beside the front door and her feet were encased in puffy, pink slippers. As she welcomed Icarus and Levi into her duplex, she looked happy.

"Helps when I'm not in a tiny lab all day." She smiled, her brown eyes sparkling, when Icarus commented on it. Rebecca had worked for Intela Corp until Na'rina showed her that her test subjects were sentient. Since then, she'd worked part time in a pharmacy in a small Colorado town while also helping Na'rina and Icarus understand the technology they stole from Intela Corp. If Felis couldn't figure something out, Rebecca usually could.

The front of her home was a garden with planters on every window and hoyas hanging from the ceiling. Golden sunlight played through the leaves, creating designs on the kitchen's cream walls. Beyond, her living room was a lab with tables lining the walls and various apparatuses for distilling tinctures or whatever else the woman studied.

Icarus admired her knack for chemicals. It was something he would never understand.

Felis sat sprawled in a green recliner with his legs over one armrest. He grinned when they entered but he tracked Levi with a prey's awareness of an apex predator. Levi, for his part, bent over one of the bubbling tubes in fascination.

"Where are we at?" Icarus asked Felis.

"Got what we need to fly…with no idea where we need to go." Felis tossed a passport to Icarus.

Icarus caught it and gave it a cursory glance before dropping an envelope of cash onto Rebecca's coffee table along with the blood work reports he'd found. "To cover your expenses and to keep you busy," he told her.

Rebecca lit up and snatched the papers, ignoring the money as she added the reports to a stack on another table. Then, although Icarus knew Felis already checked with her, he asked, "You've heard nothing about Intela Corp capturing a Drydanda again?"

Rebecca shook her head, wincing apologetically. "Lots of chatter from old friends about shifting personnel around but nothing on the Zeta projects.

"Coffee anyone?" she asked, disappearing into the kitchen.

Levi followed her and Icarus picked up his quiet question regarding what food she had. It was like Levi was trying to understand the world through his stomach. Icarus hoped she didn't offer him goldfish.

"International flights are expensive," Felis said softly. "You have the resources for it?"

Icarus eyed him. Most wer-im didn't care about money. If they had wealth, it typically came from a well-placed vow far back in a family line. A sworn knight, an advisor to a king, working with a Caesar or pharaoh, that sort of thing. That was the case for Felis. He inherited a fortune that dated back to Roman times. Felis didn't offer details beyond being the youngest of seven. Icarus didn't press. He understood what it was like to lose your whole family.

And Felis' question was reasonable. Icarus had been cast out from his mother's family and he'd never known his father. Felis didn't know *all* the gritty details, but he knew Silas had found him as a destitute orphan.

"Silas had no children," Icarus answered. "Adopted son is close enough." He didn't go into detail either. It was enough for Felis to know Icarus gained Silas' fortune.

Felis accepted that with a nod.

Levi's head popped out of the kitchen. "Fish sticks? Is this better than goldfish?" Before Icarus could answer, Levi's gaze swung toward a knock on the door. "Like déjà vu," he said.

"Can you answer that?" Rebecca called.

Felis rose to do as asked. When he returned, Dante followed, clutching a stack of papers. He skirted around Felis and handed the stack over, the cinnamon of fireball candy wafting with him.

They were security camera photos. Icarus flipped through them and hissed softly. *Is that a body bag?* He nudged at the numbness in his chest, but it gave him no reassurances. The pictures showed an airport tarmac and a large private jet. A group of men were hauling luggage up the companionway. One parcel in particular looked suspiciously like a long, black bag. A familiar lean, dark-haired figure supervised the loading. The man's back was to the camera, but Icarus didn't need to see his face.

"That is the man from the elevator." Levi, who'd stepped up behind Icarus to peer over his shoulder, tapped the photo. *Ver'rina must have shared the memory with him.*

"As hard as I've tried, I can't for sure confirm she was on that plane," Dante said.

Icarus fingered the leaf now hanging from his neck. A cool mountain wind played across his skin, carrying the slight bitter fragrance of wet aspens and moldering leaves.

"Go on," he told Dante.

The orange wer-im leaned against a table and crossed his arms. "I confirmed he left on the jet," he said, pointing at the photos. "The flight plan was for Venezuela. I've tried to contact a few people down there but haven't had much success. I'd have more luck if I went there."

Venezuela. A cold sweat threatened Icarus. *Your life is forfeit. If you are ever seen here again, you are to be killed on the spot.* His mother hadn't minced words. The little boy inside him raged, wondering why she turned against him.

Focus on the here and now. The location, so close to Sedanza, is important. There were others who might want Na'rina besides Intela Corp. Icarus pictured his mother's petite, cunning face and a cold sweat broke out on his skin. It was a reaction to his mother's anger that he'd never lost.

"Maybe this isn't Intela Corp," Icarus muttered aloud, trying to process the new information without the emotional response. "We've only found evidence of them in the U.S."

"Or they are expanding," Levi said.

Icarus considered that. Na'rina was trying to build a mythic alliance in the U.S. to keep an eye on Intela Corp. If she created a strong enough net, would Intela Corp simply disappear to crop up somewhere else?

Rebecca emerged from the kitchen with mugs of coffee. Icarus accepted one and breathed in the rich, dark aroma.

The apartment was small enough; Rebecca had clearly caught their discussion. "They are moving resources around, but I haven't heard much about where. Venezuela wouldn't surprise me, though."

Icarus fingered the photos.

My contact ended when she rose too high off the ground, not when a door closed. The Rina's words fit.

It's not Sedanza. Chances are slim they'd spot me in a city as big as Caracas. Despite that, the thought of flying south was shoving a knife into old wounds. Icarus had always told himself he'd never have to see the islands again or fear a Sedessan sending a paralyzing, mental spike into his brain. *I'm no longer a helpless boy.* He'd spent years learning to defend his mind. Every time he saw El, she tested him.

Icarus tossed the photos on the coffee table. "Then to Venezuela we all go," he said aloud. "Did you get the other thing?" he asked Dante.

Dante tossed him a device similar to a sleek garage door opener. Felis snatched it out of the air. "What's this?"

"A possibility." Icarus seized it from him. Felis startled.

Icarus wasn't ready to tell him it was a transponder that would allow them entrance through the Sedanza dome. He'd sent Dante to retrieve it from a safety deposit box. Pocketing it, he opened his phone and ignored Felis' confusion. If he was going to be that close to the Court's islands, he wanted intel from his sister.

"One thing." Rebecca nudged Dante with a hip. He hissed, skipping to the side, and Felis hissed back in warning. Felis spent more time with Rebecca than anyone except Icarus.

"Sprung leaks in here," Rebecca teased.

Dante looked startled. Most humans instinctively found the wer-im disturbing, but Rebecca spent enough time around Felis to now treat them with ease. Felis grinned and flopped back into his recliner while Dante shifted out of Rebecca's way.

She gathered a few items and showed them to Icarus. "This is a sample of one of Intela Corp's recent experiments." She handed him a test tube with a greenish fluid inside. "My source couldn't say what this is other than it's got alleles often found in animals like lizards, squids or frogs but it's none of those. What they're trying to do with it—" Rebecca shrugged.

"You can hang onto that tube. I've got more of it." She held up a second tube. The liquid inside glowed with a reddish light. Felis shuddered. "This is also one of their recent endeavors. It messes with the neural transmitters in the brain, but again, I don't have a clue what their goal is with it." She handed it over to Icarus and he couldn't help but feel like she'd handed him Pandora's box disguised as Christmas lights.

El took time for a shower and braided her black hair into a tight fish tail just as Icarus taught her when she was five. She carefully applied her makeup, hiding her Sedessan facial markings instead of accentuating them as her mother had, and downed a couple painkillers for her headache. Just before leaving, she pulled on a pair of black satin gloves—ubiquitous among the Sedessans as a courtesy to other mythics.

Now El stood on the family's dock, waiting for a deckhand to bring a boat. She rubbed the thumb and forefinger of her gloves together. Icarus teased her about the impatient habit, but she figured if she had to wear them, she may as well enjoy the satin's feel.

She eyed the empty slips. It was rare for all the boats to be out, but El's father had taken one to the De León estate and the Varela staff had rushed to help those affected by the quake with the rest, which meant they had to call one back for El's use now.

An engine's thrum brought her attention to the fairway. Instead of a Varela boat with its green and purple flag, however, it boasted the yellow and blue of the Inverro fleet. A dark-haired, muscular man with an arrogant smile stood at the helm. El's stomach dropped and she instinctively reached to check that her braid was still neatly tied. Of all the people she expected, Roberto Inverro was not on the list. The last she'd known, he wasn't in South America, much less the Sedanza Islands.

He's home.

The butterflies in her stomach suddenly hardened like Medusa had caught them in her sight. She hadn't seen the eldest Inverro son in nine years. El's hand dropped from her hair like it'd burned her.

On that day years ago, they'd gone to look at a sailboat together, half-joking about sailing away on it. The next morning, news swept through the Court that the Inverros had sent their eldest son to work the networks. El had heard nothing from him since. No phone calls, no visits, not even letters. His family was even more technologically advanced than her own and there was no reason he couldn't find a way to communicate if he'd wanted. He might belong to the strongest Sedessan family and be something of royalty in the Court, but that did not excuse his silence. *You don't get special treatment from me.* El kept her face indifferent as the boat drew closer, but her chest hurt from being stuffed with too many emotions and memories.

Two smaller boys, David and Dylan, sat in the cockpit seats of Roberto's boat. It didn't hurt the Inverros' standing that they had five children. It was an anomaly considering most Sedessans struggled to conceive two or three, much less five, but in a twist of fate, Roberto's parents had conceived their two youngest recently. The boys were only twelve and fourteen, infants by mythic standards.

El knew they resented the enormous gap between them and the older three siblings. She'd seen it a number of times with Ethan and Samuel. *Roberto's been gone most of their lives. Will they treat him differently?*

"I hear," Roberto called as he drew closer, "that you could use a ride to the embassy. I relieved your deckhand from rushing his current run and told him I'd take you. Come aboard, Señorita." Faint lines

105

crinkled around his brown eyes in a smile.

That's how he comes back? Relieves my deckhand and expects me to just jump aboard? El's headache twinged, threatening to break through the painkillers already. *What would he do if I told him to shove off?* She wished she could, just to see, but she needed a boat.

El eyed him long enough to show her displeasure. Then, stepping from the dock to the boat, she passed Roberto silently to take a seat. He gave her braid a light tug and grasped her bare elbow to "steady" her. Pain ricocheted through El's head—a warning—and she slammed her mental defenses down, hearing a masculine yelp as she did. Her defense sliced through Roberto's reaching fingers, leaving a sense of him that slowly dissipated except for his teasing voice.

Just checking.

Bad form, Inverro, she snarled. *Next time I'll take more than a slice.*

"Welcome to the *Knot-i-Loose*," he chuckled aloud.

El's nerves sang as she spun around. Roberto grinned, hiding his wince, and pushed the throttle. As he did, he shucked off the glove with the hole in the palm that had given him access to her skin and slid on a new one from his pocket. El blinked, questioning if she'd seen the quick sleight of hand.

What was that?! El wanted to breathe fire. Sedessan kids often tested each other, but adults? Never. El breathed her fury out her nose and turned her spin into a flourish to take a seat. She donned a cocky expression to cover the nerves as her rage seethed. "Treating women like they're kids? Does that work for you, Roberto?" she asked, glad her voice didn't shake.

He frowned. "I treat only you that way, El. We've known each other since we were twelve."

Dylan, who was playing a game on his phone, snorted.

Roberto ignored him.

What is his angle? El stared at Roberto. He'd been Icarus' counterpart before her brother's "accident," not hers. They'd only become close years later when they'd been paired for a mission to distract a Venezuelan gang from Sedanza.

The Fae deterrent was usually enough to keep people away. When it wasn't, whichever family was currently handling the government would take care of the unwanted interest. If more force was required than the family could bring to bear, the other houses were asked to step in. On just such an occasion, the Inverros and Varelas had responded by sending Roberto and El by submersible to sneak onto the boats of a gang. They'd caught the group cleaning their rifles and dissuaded them from their course. It'd been fun and sparked what El believed was a friendship that hinted at becoming more.

At the time, she'd welcomed the possibility.

He left, never contacted me, and now acts like nothing's changed. Why? El couldn't reconcile it all in her head. She ducked into her mental library and pulled out her *Roberto* book, leafing through it for clues, but as she got to Little Italia, she found herself wanting to throw the book, so she snapped it closed. Throwing things in her mental library was not a recipe for a headache-free day.

Her phone buzzed, bringing her back to the physical world. She pulled it out and registered the number. Her heart sank; she hit the ignore button.

"It's been years," El said, tilting her face into the wind and breathing deep of the warm breeze. "You barely know me now." She might not like her present company, but she loved the ocean.

"He barely knows any of us," Dylan said, not looking up from his game.

"Hey," Roberto scowled, "I could have left you at the house. And you," he pointed at David, the younger of the two, "should be studying."

David stuck his tongue out and pointedly pushed some books farther under his leg before going back to his phone.

El chuckled and winked at David even as Roberto shot her a long-suffering look. She just smirked. From the corner of her eye, she caught David's wink back and the small grin on Dylan's face.

"In our lives, what is nine years?" Roberto asked, taking his own sideways shot at his brothers—and perhaps at El's cold reception. Both boys glared, but he continued like he didn't notice. "Besides, I do know you."

El ground her teeth. It was the Sedessan way to know as much as possible. The Inverros weren't the strongest family by might; they were that way by information. But Roberto wasn't talking about knowing facts so much as knowing her personally.

"Knowing about and actually knowing are two very different things," she said.

"I know what it's like to have brothers," he replied. Both boys were still glaring.

El's brow lifted in surprise. "What does that have to do with the price of tech in Asimi?"

"Don't you remember your brother?"

El's fingers curled into fists. *My relationship with Icarus is nothing like Roberto and his brothers.* Reason strangled her fury into submission, and she forced herself to relax. Roberto had steered their conversation here. *Why?* "I clearly remember my brother," she answered shortly.

Roberto chuckled, "Aw, yes. You have a legendary memory."

El didn't reply, but the boys were now watching her, their curiosity caught. *Go back to your phones.*

Roberto sobered, but El couldn't tell if it was an act and her chest was too tight to interrupt his next words. "I remember taking fencing lessons with him. He was a force to be reckoned with. I used to think his brain just processed faster than my brothers' and mine."

El stared at Roberto, trying to read his underlying meaning.

Does he know Icarus is mixed blood? Usually, the color of a mythic's lifeblood mimicked that of the parent they shared a gender with: father and son, mother and daughter. As far as El knew, Roberto had never seen Icarus after he'd settled from the Sedessan garnet to a violet created from the Sedessan-wer-im mix. Somehow the wer-im cobalt from his father hadn't completely taken over. *Has he seen Icarus? Does he know he's alive?* El's stomach rolled, but she kept her cockiness in place by force of will. "I miss seeing him beat the snot out of you all," she said, then looked down where she fiddled with her shirt's hem and let the smile fade, feigning grief. It wasn't hard. "I miss a lot of things about him."

After a brief silence, Roberto said, "So do I. He taught me so many things."

El had no desire to continue in that vein, so she kept her head down. The younger boys continued staring at her, something like hope on their faces. She couldn't figure why.

"I'm assuming you're responding to Ambassador Marquin's request for aid," Roberto shifted the subject. "Since I'm doing the same, perhaps we should work together."

El's head snapped up, but Roberto's expression was serious, and slightly uncertain. *Does he actually think we can work together again without an explanation?* Roberto wasn't stupid. She could see in his expression that he *knew* she was likely to tell him no. But he was asking anyway. *There's something going on here.* El wanted to flat out refuse, but a tea-and-scones voice in her head hinted she might learn something if she played along.

"Where have you been?" she asked, intentionally avoiding answering. *I ain't promisin' you a thing.*

Roberto's expression went blank. "Up north."

He may as well have said on Earth. There was a lot north of Sedanza.

"Off to a great start working together," El said, then tilted her head as she *listened* to him. She hadn't mimicked his accent earlier because she hadn't seen a reason to, but it could still tell her details about him. "You've lost some of the South American enunciation, Señor. What is that I hear? A twang?" It reminded her of the wild west with grilled steak and dried peppers, although that didn't quite fit.

His shoulders tensed—the only indication she'd hit on something. He focused intently on bringing them into the Riviera docks.

"Sounds Texan," Dylan quipped, not looking up from his game. El wondered if David, the youngest boy, ever spoke.

"No twang," Roberto said, and the tell was indeed gone. Now that he was aware of it, he wouldn't let it bleed into his speech again. "I've been running a central intel hub for one of our webs for the last several years. *My father* thought it'd give me more hands-on leadership experience."

El ignored the emphasis in his words but it was harder to ignore the intensity on his face. He wanted her to know his absence had been his father's doing. She already knew that. And it hurt for him to look at her like she should understand what he was saying without him having to say it because she *did* catch his underlying meaning. But it didn't explain why he'd abandoned her.

"Welcome back," she said coolly. "I think you'll find the Sedanza Court hasn't changed much." El rose and grabbed a dock line, wanting distance between herself and the oldest Inverro son. When the boat bumped gently against the dock, she hopped over and tied it off with a couple flicks of her wrist.

The boys joined her, helping to tie off the boat.

"Nicely done," she complimented them.

Roberto joined them. Behind him, El saw David's books hidden under a seat cushion. She could just make out the Greek title written on the top one's spine, a common Sedessan textbook.

"Mask," Roberto said. He held out two thin sheets of fabric to David. The boy groaned but accepted them and held them against his temples. Within moments, they melded to his skin and faded out the faint lines running from the corners of his eyes. It wasn't a nanite mask, but something smoother that melded almost perfectly to his skin.

Show off. The Inverros always had the best technology. *Maybe I can get some of those for Icarus.*

El turned toward Riviera, ignoring Roberto's aftershave as he came to stand beside her. *That* part of him hadn't changed.

111

The docks weren't in terrible shape from the quake, but the embassy was…gone. It had been built at the back of the city at the highest point on the island. It was still the highest point, but the hill's center had become a giant sinkhole.

El hadn't seen the complete wreckage the night before, but looking at it now, the embassy's destruction didn't make sense. To the north she could see the ambassador's mansion and the only damage it showed was a large crack in its wall. *Why did only the embassy implode?*

"Greetings, greetings!" called a voice. A thin Fae in a wet suit approached. As he drew nearer, El made out the creature's bright purple eyes and silk fine, wet hair.

Although mythology often confused the Fae for fairies, they were not. Instead, they were cousins to fairies similar to how imps and goblins were cousins except the element that separated them wasn't intelligence, but size and personality. Fairies were small, woodland-loving creatures who might play the occasional prank on a hiker.

The Fae were human-sized and far more powerful, especially in their season. Some had an affinity toward summer, others for winter, with the spring and fall their waxing and waning seasons. No matter the season, however, they were one of the few mythic races that hadn't declined with the growth of the human population. They served at the interests of their monarch, Queen Lárissa. She was supreme in the way that no ruler was anymore.

"Greetings, Elmon. Why the suit?" El greeted the Fae man, who was the head of the Riviera docks. The ambassador regularly rotated his staff to keep the Court off balance, but Elmon was one of the few who didn't change.

El and Roberto pulled gently at their dark gloves, drawing attention to them as Elmon drew closer. He tilted his chin in acknowledgment as he responded, "It's good your families sent representatives!"

Dylan frowned at the enthusiastic greeting.

Elmon led them off the dock and toward the ambassador's mansion. The boys made excuses and scampered off. El watched them go, envying their freedom. Not far away, some Fae children walked with flower baskets. One girl knelt behind a wicker chair and when she stood, the bright yellow and red flowers formed a heart surrounded by sunshine. Being tropical, Riviera drew the Fae who loved gardening and sunlight. That wasn't to say they weren't dangerous and harsh…they just embellished things with plants instead of icicles.

"What can we do for you?" Roberto asked Elmon.

"Oh! Not me." Elmon fluttered his hands toward the rubble. "I'm just checking the water for survivors since we haven't found any oceanids to help. We found a couple suspicious folks after the embassy fell, however, and have been trying to decide what to do with them."

"The embassy suffered the most damage. How did people end up in the water?" El asked.

Elmon tapped the side of his nose. "Not much gets past you. Far as I can tell, the bodies are floating out from under the island along with some detritus that got stirred up."

El swallowed disgust. *Are those other prisoners?* From where she'd left Amos, he wouldn't be one of the bodies. *Were there more holding cells below us or closer to the water?*

"Suspicious folk?" Roberto asked.

"I'll let the ambassador tell you. I wouldn't want to get anything wrong."

As Roberto knocked on the ambassador's door, El braced herself. This would be the telling moment if she were arrested again. The ambassador himself, Marquin Crostee, greeted them with noticeably less enthusiasm than Elmon had.

"Morning, Señorita Varela, Señor Inverro." Marquin's sharp accent was all kefir, bitter and thick and now laced with fatigue, but no suspicion or shout to have her apprehended. It appeared Sophia's intel on the ambassador might be correct.

Strain showed in the hollow of his porcelain-skinned cheeks and, although he was tall and thin naturally, his forest green suit hung loose on his bony frame. *He's lost weight recently.* Some of it might be because he was a summer Fae in his waning season, but not all of it.

"Good morning, Ambassador," El bowed shallowly, shifting into professional mode. There was a very thin, polite veneer expected when dealing with the Fae.

"How is your family?" Roberto asked, bowing as well and following the required Fae customs as Marquin ushered them in. The formalities were tiring but Marquin would be gravely insulted if they jumped directly into the reason for their visit.

"Marl—" the ambassador started coughing. Once the fit passed, he continued, "Excuse me. Marleen alluded to visiting soon." He didn't appear excited by the news that his wife *might* visit. It was common knowledge that she hated the islands. She preferred icicles to flowers. "How is your grandfather?" he asked Roberto.

Roberto gave a perfunctory answer about recent changes to the old man's medications that were helping his health improve as Marquin led them down the hall. On the surface, Roberto's grandfather was the head of the household, but he hadn't been seen in so long that no one believed he controlled anything anymore. Roberto's father actually led the most powerful family of the Sedanza Court.

El glanced around, keeping an eye out for Thomas Dominguez. He was the ambassador's assistant, after all. *Would he arrest me again? Right in front of Marquin?* Somehow, she doubted it. She was starting to think Dominguez was operating outside of the ambassador's interests. And she wasn't sure Dominguez would recognize her as Miss Marrow without her nanite mask on.

A spidery crack in the marble wall caught El's attention. Sunlight streaming through the windows above highlighted it, showing the entire cracked line that traveled from the doorway, down the hall, and past the massive dining room that Marquin led them into.

El answered Marquin's question regarding her own parents and sat as he gestured to the seats beside his at the table. Roberto's chair squealed on the marble.

"Earthquakes are common enough on the islands that we expect them," Marquin said dryly, gesturing back into the hallway at the crack that drew El's attention and then reaching for a slice of mango from the table.

El's stomach twisted. The table was laden with sliced fruit and warm raisin bread. It was tempting as homemade pie but neither she nor Roberto reached for the food and Marquin did not offer. The legends about the Fae's food trapping people in their land were true, and the Riviera embassy was an extension of Queen Lárissa's land according to their power. Thus, it was part of the Fae-Sedessan agreements that the Fae did not trap anyone on the island and conversely the Sedessans did not mess with the Fae's minds. With the agreements, the Fae gained neutral ground to conduct business outside of the Queen's Court and the Sedessans gained added protection for Sedanza. In the hundred years since the embassy had been established, the agreements hadn't been broken. Still, it was safer to simply forgo the food.

Marquin bit into his mango slice while he stared at them.

"Handsome pair," he said offhandedly.

El's stomach lurched and she scowled, saying, "We're not," at the same time Roberto said, "Thank you." El scowled harder and Roberto's eyes crinkled in mirth.

Marquin's eyes became predatory. "I'm glad the Varelas and Inverros are taking our recent disaster seriously," he said. "When I requested aid, I received silence. The Reyes' eventually responded, but I wasn't sure their skills lent themselves to the aid I require."

The Reyes' were rumored to be the Court's assassins. Neither Roberto nor El were going to reveal the realities behind that rumor.

"I apologize for our delayed response," El said, shaking off her irritation with Roberto. "We assumed action would be better than a verbal promise." She guessed the Reyes representative hadn't arrived yet and Marquin tilted his chin in acknowledgement.

"It is not healthy to ignore the Fae," Marquin pressed.

Roberto's fingers clenched beneath the table. El wasn't sure if it was from fear or frustration, but he was quick to respond. "We highly value the Fae-Court relationship."

Marquin's eyes flicked toward El. Despite her issues with

116

Roberto, this was not the time to be contradictory. El nodded confirmation.

A few hours of silence made him touchy? No wonder Sophia told me to keep him happy. Mutual aid was written into the agreements, but the response time wasn't set in stone. If the Court had responded within a few days, it would have fulfilled the agreements, but would have also sent a dangerous message. *He would have taken that message and shoved it in our faces.* El's stomach rolled.

"Earthquakes," Marquin said, finally moving on, "are expected. This was something else, however."

Roberto sat back, relaxing.

"How do you mean?" El asked, containing her own relief.

Marquin chewed on another mango slice, then rested his elbows on the table and steepled his fingers. "The epicenter doesn't make sense. The embassy was built in the most stable spot on the island precisely because we knew about the possibility of quakes. Plus, the caves beneath reeked of psychic energy on the elemental level."

"You suspect someone caused the quake?" Roberto asked.

Marquin's steepled fingers shook faintly and he dropped them to reach for another mango slice. *He's disturbed that it was an attack.* The Fae were not strangers to violence. El tucked Marquin's reaction away, noting it.

"We do," Marquin answered Roberto.

"What mythics would even have access to the caves below the embassy?" El asked, watching for indications that Marquin knew about the menagerie of powerful prisoners the embassy had housed. *It was a pile of tinder. How did they expect it* not *to explode?*

"We have security in place to keep people out of the caves." Marquin bit into his mango, showing a flash of teeth. "However, we've had a number of foreign visitors recently at your father's request," he motioned to Roberto with the chunk of mango in his hand. "He's been attempting...better relations...between the Court and other mythics using the Fae as his go-between since we have slightly better reputations."

Slightly better? El scoffed internally. *That's a thin margin.* Other mythics talked to the Fae but knew the dangers of making deals, which somehow always came out better on the Fae's end. That knowledge created a thin veil of security that was lacking when dealing with the Sedessans. But when mythics wanted something done without anyone else knowing, they turned to the spies of the mythic world because they specialized in intelligence, clandestine communication, and even assassinations. But there was no illusion that they were working with a "safe" party.

"We found one foreign delegate trapped in the caves and another wandering the beach," Marquin explained. "Neither should have been there."

"You have them in custody?" Roberto stood, suddenly impatient as his chair squealed against the floor again. "I'm guessing this is the aid you require, to ascertain their guilt or innocence?"

Marquin gave another predatory grin and finished the mango. "That, and I would also like you to inspect the wreckage and tell me about the zoi aima residue. My sources are...not as educated. I had hoped for Renata Narvaez because of this. I hear she is exceptional at reading lifeblood signatures."

Although the Fae were sensitive to zoi aima, they could not see it and Renata was something of a savant even among the Sedessans.

"I'm sure you're aware that the Narvaez are serving in Venezuela this decade," Roberto said. "It is not surprising they refrained from offering aid. Keeping the Venezuelan government away from the islands is important to all of us."

"Quite right," Marquin agreed grudgingly.

"The Reyes responded," El said as she rose to follow Roberto and Marquin. "What about the Torres or De Leóns?" *Give me something.* Even the smallest tidbit could clue her into who'd already been operating on Riviera and capturing mythics below the embassy.

"*Na*, they have been silent."

"The Torres family is away," Roberto said.

He's offering free information? To keep Marquin appeased or is "away" an easy way of hiding something? More than one family could be involved. Her stomach tried to tie itself in knots. The man beside her could be involved. Nine years ago, she would have emphatically said it wasn't possible. Now, she had no idea.

"So were you, technically," Marquin quipped.

"I'm sure having both the Varelas' and Inverros' assistance will suffice," Roberto pressed, apparently tired of Marquin's thinly veiled irritation.

Marquin smirked. "Of course," he agreed.

I'm in the dark about something. El kept her face professional but internally she seethed.

Venezuela, here we come. Icarus hissed a breath through his nose. He realized he was clutching the armrests of his seat, and his knuckles popped as he let go. The floor vibrated as the private jet's engines rumbled to life, reassuring him they'd be in the air leaving Denver soon. Icarus pictured the transponder he'd put in his pack before leaving. If this venture led them farther than Venezuela, he'd deal with it.

Felis and Dante bickered behind Icarus, but their voices were an afterthought as he studied Levi. He'd contemplated flying commercial but taking the older wer-im through security nixed that idea. It'd been bad enough getting him through the private security for the jet.

Why do you want him with me, Ver'rina? Try as he might, he couldn't come up with a reason that rang true for the ancient Drydanda.

The flightdeck door opened and the copilot, a short man with wispy gray hair around his crown, stepped out. He'd informed them earlier that he was filling in for the stewardess who'd called out sick. At the moment he was checking supplies. His name was Patrick. Not that it really mattered, but Icarus had always found it useful to remember names.

Levi's ears flicked backwards at the man's movement. He gulped, already fighting motion sickness with a feral grimace that showed his pointed teeth.

How did Na'rina handle her first flight? Icarus refused to believe it'd been a body bag in the picture. *Perhaps she was sedated.*

"Dryad face," he hissed to Levi when the copilot started their way. The older wer-im looked like he wanted to strangle the armrests.

Levi blinked, startled, and then the tension drained from him like water from a punctured skin.

Time for the Dramamine. Icarus leaned forward to pull a carton from the pack at his feet. Knowing how fast the wer-im metabolism worked, he'd bought three packages. Hopefully it'd be enough to get them through the flight.

He nodded to Patrick as the man passed and received a timid smile without eye contact. Neither Patrick nor the pilot, Eddy, wanted Levi or Icarus on the flight—their body language and smell said so— but they had no reason to kick their unusual passengers off the plane. Saying someone had too many facial scars to fly would probably be a company violation.

Icarus finally found the Dramamine and pulled it from his pack. A photo came out with it and fluttered toward the floor.

Levi snatched it.

Patrick recoiled, staring at Levi.

Icarus' nostrils flared. The man reeked of sudden fear.

The bickering behind him stopped and Felis asked, "There are snacks on board, right? I've a hankering for something salty."

Patrick broke away from staring. "Behind you, sir," he answered, returning to his clipboard. "The cabinets above the sink have a selection of chips and pretzels. There's also beer and sodas in the mini fridge if you'd like. I apologize that Felicia's not working today. The flu's been…"

Patrick kept rambling and Felis rolled with it, easing the man's tension with his usual charm.

Icarus listened but didn't turn around. Levi now studied the photo he'd nabbed. The dichotomy between Felis' easy chatter and Levi's intense focus was not lost on Icarus. The banishment irrevocably changed the wer-im. They were just as comfortable in the rapidly shifting human world as they were in the wilderness they traditionally called home. But Levi had missed that change, hidden away in Ver'rina's grove. Icarus suspected it was only because of Ver'rina's influence that he functioned at all in human society.

Stop reminiscing. Sometimes it was helpful, sometimes not.

Patrick headed for the flightdeck. "Wheels up for Venezuela in about ten minutes, gentlemen," he said as he passed.

Felis returned with two beers and a bowl of chips that he set on the table between Icarus and Levi. Icarus welcomed the scent of hops and salt that drove away his sudden memory of burned black beans. Venezuela always reminded him of burned beans.

"Good stuff back there," Felis said, flopping down in the chair across the aisle with his own beer and bowl.

"You picked chips over Rebecca's pastries?" Dante asked.

"How do you know about those?"

"We can all smell the sweet cinnamon from your last snack," Icarus interjected.

Dante added, "It's no secret you have a sweet tooth."

"You calling me fat?" Felis asked Dante.

Icarus' hackles rose. *Curse their bickering!* This could end up nowhere good.

Up near the flightdeck, Patrick's back was straighter than a lodgepole pine.

"Settle," Icarus ordered, too low for the man to hear.

Felis' lips snapped shut. Icarus couldn't see Dante but the smaller wer-im didn't say anything more.

"This woman," Levi broke into the awkward silence by tapping the photo. "She was Ver'rina's friend who helped us when we had our twin sprouts."

Patrick disappeared through the flightdeck door.

"*Sa*," Icarus answered, knowing Levi meant the mountain nymph, Rosharu, in the picture.

"And she's the one who betrayed you last spring."

"*Sa*."

The picture was of the Intela Corp board from around the late 1840s. Rosharu had been the rare nymph who'd learned to work within the human world, hiding in plain sight. She'd been the project manager who oversaw the human study of mythics, of all things.

The plane jerked and started taxiing.

"Swallow these." Icarus set all the Dramamine pills on the table.

Levi glanced out the window, grimaced, and popped the entire lot into his mouth. "Remind me to find some ginger later," he muttered before leaning back to stare at the picture again. "Perhaps Ver'rina was right to fear the avalanche."

Icarus' ears perked. "Avalanche?" *Is this Ver'rina's reason for sending him?*

Levi flinched and his claws appeared. When the silence lengthened, Dante peeked over Icarus' seat. Icarus couldn't tell if Levi was debating on answering or if he was fighting motion sickness. His usual tan complexion held a greenish tinge.

Levi pursed his lips.

What is he thinking? Icarus rarely wanted to use his Sedessan abilities. Resisting the temptation now, he picked up the beer Felis had served him and almost tossed it back. Then the smell hit him and he grimaced. *Too much hops.* He nabbed a chip instead and offered the beer to Dante. After a startled pause, the wer-im accepted it.

I don't truly know my family, Na'rina had once told him, talking about her mother after she'd learned the truth of the banishment.

Your grandmother's exactly who you think, Icarus had teased, *she's loony.*

Na'rina had smacked him in the stomach. *She's authentic.*

Now Icarus wondered if that were true. *What's Ver'rina hiding? What is this avalanche?*

"You think too much," Levi said.

Icarus flinched. Levi sounded just like Silas. "What avalanche?" he asked again.

Levi sighed and held up a finger for patience. Absently, the older wer-im rubbed at his arm and for a moment Icarus thought the aspen leaves there moved. "Ver'rina and I have held this close for many reasons. This does not leave us." Levi waited for them all to agree and then continued, "Ver'rina's and my handfasting was a mountainside covered in fresh fallen snow. Then we had our sprouts and a new layer was added, laying crystalline, but heavy, in the pristine woodlands."

Levi sounded like Ver'rina. Icarus adjusted his thinking.

"It was beautiful and calm, but as with any steep mountainside, it was not safe. We hoped to hide our family from outside influence to protect it. We did not succeed. Someone intruded and our world cracked. The pristine snow became a slide that tore up everything until gravity stopped it at the bottom of the mountain."

This isn't the banishment. The banishment had been caused by Intela Corp introducing a disease into the dryad population, but Levi and Ver'rina's peace had been disturbed long before that.

"The intruder was the Wer-Kadis who attempted to kidnap Mona'rina and Silas," Icarus guessed. The Wer-Kadis in the early 1800s had wanted Mona'rina and Silas for their unique abilities.

Levi tapped his nose and continued. "Two such slides happened, and then stillness."

The Wer-Kadis and then the banishment, Icarus guessed.

"Everything settled and the forest began to heal. The snow melted, trickles at a time, refreezing at night, melting again, refreezing. Then another beautiful snow fell, and the forest grew silent and soft."

"Na'rina," Dante whispered.

"But the hidden base layer was not stable. Again, none were allowed near and it was kept undisturbed—for a while. But last spring," Levi slapped his leg and everyone twitched, "cracked the snow. All it will take now is another disturbance and the rumbling will begin again, this time likely destroying everything in its path."

"Why did the events last spring only crack the snow?" Icarus asked. "Why weren't they enough to make it slide?"

Levi shrugged and tilted his head back against the seat. "Last spring brought attention to the mountainside but perhaps it was not a strong enough force."

Icarus scrubbed a hand down his face. *Intela Corp's not a strong enough force? Or its actions hadn't been?* He wanted to ask more but he could tell Levi was done. A twitch bothered his cheek. Ignoring it, he grabbed a handful of chips.

"Ver'rina sent you along because she fears this avalanche?" he asked.

Levi nodded and tried a chip. He cringed, almost spit, thought better and settled for washing it down with a sip of beer.

Why didn't Ver'rina tell me this? What came before Intela Corp that I don't know about? Levi had spoken his vow to Ver'rina along with their handfasting. She *knew* what that meant for a wer-im. *Why didn't she warn me before the summit?*

The numbness in Icarus' chest haunted him and he crunched into a chip to distract himself. They all said he thought too much, but information had always kept him a step ahead and alive.

Icarus checked his phone. El hadn't called. He attempted calling her again but no answer so he put the phone on airplane mode and pocketed it. She'd get back to him when it was safe. Not only did she need to avoid Sophia and her father, Adrian, but they suspected the Sedanza dome allowed the Inverros to listen in on calls from the islands. El was adept at bypassing that, but it usually took time. *Patience, Icarus.*

Levi handed the photo back. "Why do you keep this?"

"Can't say, exactly," Icarus admitted. "I'm missing something but haven't figured out what."

Levi sat back and hummed, closing his eyes. "The rain comes when needed."

As he'd done countless times, Icarus eyed each person in the

126

picture. Besides Rosharu, the group was all men. Five were of European decent but the last two, a bald man and a very petite man, were probably South American, judging from their features. As humans, they'd be long dead by now, but Icarus couldn't dismiss their faces.

Do I know a descendant?

Unable to place them, he finally put the photo back into his pack. He leaned back, closed his eyes, and allowed himself to relive a memory.

Na'rina's feet appeared beside him where he sat on the bank of the Ruby Anthracite Creek, her long dryadic toes curling in the rough dirt. He'd been basking in the sun, breathing in the bluebells, crocus, and occasionally the stink of bitterroot.

Whisper-light fingers pushed his hair back and traced the scar on his ear.

"Why do you hide this?" she asked.

Icarus chewed on a stalk of grass.

"Caution." He shrugged.

She lowered herself to sit beside him. "Even here?"

"Did you go to see Mona'rina?" he asked, shifting the topic.

Na'rina blew a whisp of hair out of her face and scowled. "I wandered her grove. Mama's withdrawn, and I don't want to distract her healing."

Icarus pitched his stalk of grass into the river and plucked a new one. Na'rina's reticence toward her mother was growing. He wasn't sure why. "Half-truths do not fit you, my sprite." He took her hand. Few got to see Na'rina's mischievous side, but she was the sprite who kept him on his toes. As had become habit, he tucked her hand against his stomach and held it there.

"I hide the scar to keep the habit," he admitted. "Keeps me from making mistakes."

She was silent and still for a long moment. "When you shared the memory of your mother salting your ear, she turned away afterwards, almost like she was fighting tears—" she trailed off, searching for words.

Icarus' Sedessan side raged to steer them away from the conversation. He ignored the impulse. He'd promised Na'rina that he'd hide nothing from her.

She finally just asked, "Is there no way to heal your family?"

The jet jerked, accelerating and pulling Icarus from the memory.

Na'rina's question haunted him. He'd never considered the possibility that Sophia cried at casting him out.

What other blind spots do I have? What would Na'rina see in Levi's avalanche that I don't? He ached like a limb close to frostbite.

The PA system crackled, and Patrick's voice announced, "Welcome to the air, gentlemen. It looks like we'll have a smooth flight today. Our total air time from Denver, Colorado, to Caracas, Venezuela, should take us just under seven hours. Sit back, partake of the snacks if you like, and enjoy the flight."

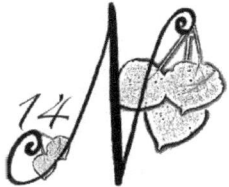

Let me go! Let me go! Somebody screeched inside Na'rina's head.

Her stomach rolled. Her body ached and her zoi aima felt…thin? She tried to stand but her legs gave out.

Let me go!

Na'rina involuntarily bolted in the pitch black and tripped, stubbing her toe on a rock. Out of control, she tried to push off the floor and run again. Terror seized her and it took a huge effort just to make her body freeze.

Let me go! screeched the other voice again.

What is going on?! Na'rina yelled back.

The voice and the struggle in her body went quiet. In the silence, Na'rina became aware of water dripping, chaotic zoi aima swirling around her, and a reek like a rotting, dead herd of deer.

Drydanda?

*What—where—*She couldn't think. Everything was wrong. Tilting her head back, she traced the zoi aima above until the streams disappeared into the rock. *Still in a cave*, she confirmed. A water drop hit her nose. *But not the one they locked me in.* There hadn't been water dripping from that ceiling, but that wasn't what caused her gut-churning nausea. No, that was caused by the swirling lifeblood above. It looked like the aurora borealis, but it wasn't anchored to anything. *Is that my zoi aima?*

It certainly isn't mine, the other voice said.

Who are you?!

Twiglet.

Did I—Na'rina swallowed hard. She shouldn't be able to meld with a walking, unrooted creature like a twiglet but her growing suspicion would explain her struggle to move. *Did I meld with you?* she finally asked. She touched her face to find a stub—like a knot on a tree—for her nose, twists of sapling branches for her cheekbones and brow ridges, and, as her search traveled upward, leaves sprouting from her head in an imitation of hair. *Oh dear!* Her limbs were branches with pliable sticks for fingers and toes. She was inside the twiglet's body.

Instinctively, Na'rina reached for the streaming zoi aima at the same time as she shoved to leave the twiglet. Fire like lightning burned into her. A scream tore through the cave and it took a moment for Na'rina to realize it was both hers and the twiglet's. They collapsed, convulsing in agony and still very much combined.

Why can't I leave him? Then, to the twiglet, she sobbed, *I'm sorry,* as the convulsions subsided.

Please don't do that again, the twiglet shuddered.

They lay motionless, staring up at the vibrant blue and green lifeblood that was dissipating like smoke. When Na'rina had reached for it, nothing happened. She couldn't pull it back to herself to form her body again.

Am I stuck? Her head swam with exhaustion. *What have I done?*

Don't know, the twiglet answered and Na'rina realized she hadn't shielded the last thought from him, *but I think we fell through the island into a cave.*

Fell through?

We're under the cell you were being held in.

Being in a different cave checked out but...*How do you know that?*

I felt us fall. We changed shape and slid through all the small spaces in the rocks. You saved us from the quake!

Not only had she melded with a twiglet and was now stuck in his body, but now they were deep under the island? Her breath stalled. *Stuck in the twiglet.* Melding with plants that were not her Rina was a temporary thing. If she stayed too long, the plant would start making unpleasant changes on her. *What will happen when it's a twiglet I'm melded with instead of a normal plant?!* She shied away from that. *First things first, we need to get out of here.* She psychically reached out, searching for the thin trickle of roots or even the moss she'd found in the cell above. Her reach wavered, alarmingly weak, and she drew the zoi aima back, cradling it close. It wasn't that she didn't have *enough* energy, it was that the body she currently inhabited couldn't take any more. Maybe if she had sunlight to gain nourishment from, she could separate from the twiglet, but there was none to be found in the cave.

No sunlight or plants within my reach. The little bit of moss she found wasn't enough. *We need a way out. May I move us?* she asked the twiglet.

Of course! I'll try to be still.

Na'rina carefully rose, feeling stunted—the twiglet only stood about a foot tall—and began trailing her hand along the wall. She stumbled on a rock and squeaked in surprise.

"She's awake!" a new, almost melodic voice spoke.

Na'rina and the twiglet froze like a startled deer.

"Look what you've done!" another voice screeched.

How many people are in here with us?

No idea.

Na'rina stayed unmoving, listening.

"She's got a physical body. That's better than us," answered the melodic voice.

Na'rina reassessed the chaotic zoi aima in an effort to spot the speakers. *If I have a body and they don't, where's their energy?*

"She's a twiglet!" the shrieked answer sounded like wind howling through dead trees.

Sounds like a banshee, Na'rina winced, and her leafy hair rustled.

"It's better than nothing," came that melodic voice again. It seemed almost familiar.

She's talking about me!

Na'rina could feel the twiglet searching the zoi aima too. The island rocked in an aftershock and sand shushed to the floor along with the dripping water.

"But now she's stuck in here!" argued the banshee.

Do you know how to get out? Na'rina asked the twiglet.

Nope. How about the same way we got in? We could change shape again!

Na'rina didn't have the heart to tell him she had no idea how to repeat the process.

"But we've made progress."

Why does she sound so familiar?

She considered asking for help and felt the twiglet's hesitation—he didn't like the banshee—but Na'rina couldn't think of another option beyond searching the dark cave while struggling to coexist with the twiglet.

"Who's there?" she finally asked.

Silence answered for so long that Na'rina began to wonder if they'd left. Then, "Na'rina, we need your help."

She *knew* that voice. Still, she couldn't place it.

"She can't be helpful in a twiglet's body," groused the banshee.

Na'rina spun and put her hands on her hips…or where her hips should be. The twiglet only had a straight twist of sprigs and no real shape.

"All right, show yourselves," she squeaked. *Ugh, I sound like a mouse.*

"Bossy for someone so young."

Two zoi aima forms coalesced into women, one made of a rich aqua and the other a vibrant leaf green.

Na'rina gaped and the twiglet screeched inside her, trying to jump up and down. Her legs twitched and she sat with a huff instead of fighting him to stay standing.

"Alaya Oceadanda," she finally placed the melodic voice.

"Na'rina Drydanda," Alaya greeted with a wry smile. Even as just zoi aima, Alaya's image held the fine details of her actual body. Long, silvery hair, delicate nose, and deep blue eyes that were pools drawn straight from the ocean. "Meet Vell'marxia, the South American Drydanda. I call her Vell for short."

Na'rina stared, then blinked, realizing she was being rude just as Vell shook her head and whirled away.

"All that effort and she's going to be useless."

Let's not tell her we mistook her for a banshee, Na'rina said to the twiglet. He heartily agreed.

Vell'marxia, like Alaya, cast her true coloring through her zoi aima. Her skin was a gorgeous mahogany and the ends of her auburn hair fluttered with the narrow, long leaves of her tree. Na'rina had never met a *Marxia*, or mahogany, dryad before. She was beautiful.

Between the two spanned a faint green and aqua zoi aima cord. *They're helping each other.*

She called me useless. The twiglet wasn't interested in Alaya and Vell casting their images from a distance. Na'rina could feel him wallowing in Vell's last words like they were mud.

"Useless?" she said aloud, cocking her head inquisitively—a twiglet gesture. She'd been called many things, but never useless.

Alaya sat down beside Na'rina. "We were trying to help you and ourselves," she admitted, "but now you're stuck and we're trapped in suspended states."

So many questions bombarded Na'rina, but one lodged in her brain above the others. "Stuck?"

Alaya's shoulders slumped. "In the quake, we collapsed the tunnel out of this cave by accident. You're in a hollow pocket with no way out."

"We got in somehow," Na'rina offered, hating the dismay in the usually indomitable oceanid.

"Do you know how?"

She'd hoped Alaya knew. Na'rina tried to remember. She'd been searching with her zoi aima, searching for the mythic who'd melted her bread—Alaya she now realized—and she'd barely been aware of her body. At least, until she'd blinked, coming back to herself and seeing Icarus' sister just before the ceiling disintegrated. *Hopefully she's okay.* In that instant, Na'rina remembered something nudging her elbow to crawl into her lap. *The twiglet.* She must have instinctively reached for the closest plant life and, although the twiglet wasn't a normal plant, he exuded the *feel* of a tree. She had no memory after that until nausea had woken her in the dark.

Seeing her crestfallen expression, Alaya said, "Water always seeps into places. There's a way out somehow."

Na'rina wanted to believe her, but Alaya's glum tone didn't match her words. In the silence, a heavy *thud*, like a boulder dropping from the ceiling, echoed in the cave.

The twiglet cocked his head. Na'rina blenched. *Do trees feel the same way when I move them?* Another *thud* sounded and the twiglet tried to jump to his feet in excitement. The impulse ran through Na'rina like an involuntary twitch.

That's probably my friend!

Your friend?

Yeah! He pulled the door off our cells, remember? The twiglet pictured himself standing on the foot of a towering giant.

Na'rina hadn't seen the person who opened her cell.

EEK! There he is again!

Na'rina fought not to screech with him. *Does your friend have a name?*

The twiglet shrugged and Na'rina's shoulders twitched. She swallowed down panic, feeling his sudden excitement flow through her like sap that wasn't her own. Would the twiglet's ability to move start pressing changes on her faster than a regular tree? She wasn't sure but his emotions seemed to naturally influence her movements.

135

He's giant, the twiglet answered.

When another *thud* echoed, an idea hit Na'rina. *What kind of giant?* she asked.

The twiglet shrugged again.

Biting back frustration, she reached out with her small store of zoi aima and found a loose rock, something bigger than the pebbles the twiglet could physically pick up. She'd learned in the last year that she could influence objects using her zoi aima, within reason, but she found now that the process tired her far more than it should. Hoisting the rock quickly in a zoi aima bubble, she dropped it three times onto the cavern floor, creating a concise *thud, thud, thud.*

Vell swung around, making the tips of the leaves in her hair brush her lower back just as they would if she were in physical form. "What are you doing?" She stared at the zoi aima bubble with the rock held inside.

Na'rina didn't answer as she waited to see if her thuds received a response. In the silence, she became uncomfortably aware of both Alaya and Vell'marxia staring at her. Then came a *thud, thud, thud,* in answer.

My friend! the twiglet screeched.

Ouch, Na'rina cringed. *That's painful.*

He cowered and she felt like she'd chastised a child. Sighing, she picked up her rock again, lifting it only high enough to make a softer thud.

"She's communicating."

"Why?" Vell sounded bitter.

"Quiet, please," Na'rina asked, barely hearing the next, softer series of vibrations over their voices. She grinned.

He's some sort of rock giant, she told the twiglet. Although rock giants appeared like flesh and blood men, they could influence stone, and this one was responding by matching her volume *and* funneling his thuds to her exact location. Na'rina scrambled to her feet and faltered as the twiglet belatedly relaxed to let her have control. Catching herself on the wall, she asked, "Where was the entrance that caved in?"

Alaya pointed.

We're not useless, she told the twiglet. A painful twinge was her only response. *Is that shame? Pain?* She couldn't say and didn't dare ask. She beat on the wall Alaya indicated with her fists. Now that the giant knew to look for her, he should be able to pinpoint her exact location without her using the rock.

Na'rina held her breath, waiting, and was lightheaded when three hollow booms soon came from the wall directly in front of her. Excitement—hers and the twiglet's—rushed through Na'rina. This time she beat the wall in what she hoped would communicate desperation. If he was indeed a rock giant like she guessed, he should be able to feel the cave she was trapped in. She hoped he'd understand her predicament and come to dig her out.

How far away is he? How long will it take for him to reach us? All she knew was that the giant's first thuds had originated from above, probably near her isolation cell. If he had to dig to reach her, it could be a while. Na'rina knew she should sit down and wait but she couldn't bring herself to move. Instead, she beat her fists against the caved-in entrance again.

"Usele…"

Crack! Sand and rock slammed into Na'rina, throwing her onto her back. She screeched and flailed, and then realized she hadn't been buried.

"Na'rina?" Alaya asked.

Na'rina spit grit from her mouth. "Fine," she answered timidly and stood back up to investigate. By touch, she found a hollow about a foot deep in the caved-in entrance. The giant wasn't coming to her, he was clearing the way.

See, he's friend, the twiglet gloated.

Indeed! Na'rina agreed. She cleared the foot-deep hollow of debris and found herself heaving for air when she finished. She flopped onto her backside, her limbs shaking. *How long did that take? Half an hour? Longer?* The prospect of digging out the entire tunnel suddenly became incredibly daunting. Na'rina beat her fists against the wall again and backed out to wait for the giant's response.

It came quickly.

This time she anticipated the explosion and stood to the side. Still, flying sand pricked at her face and arms. Na'rina scrambled back into the entrance to clear out more debris.

"Na'rina Drydanda," Alaya said, appearing beside her, "you clever, clever creature."

"How far does he have to clear?" Na'rina asked, afraid to hear the answer. "And where does this go?"

"Thirty feet maybe. It lets out into a tunnel."

"Too long!" Vell remarked. "It's going to take her forever."

"How far away is the giant?" Na'rina asked, ignoring her.

"He's stuck just outside the cell you were being held in. Last I checked, he's working on digging himself out but the area's unstable and he's injured, so he's going slowly."

"He can't get to us?"

"*Na*. And the farther you dig, the farther away you'll get from him."

Na'rina shared a look with Alaya. Rock giants could affect rock within a certain distance from their physical bodies. Hopefully the giant was a strong one or he wouldn't be able to clear the entire tunnel.

"Days!" Vell said. "It will take her days. There's no way a twiglet can dig that far without rest!"

The twiglet internally whimpered.

"You could help dig," Na'rina suggested, exasperated.

Vell's face turned livid. Na'rina froze, shocked. *She truly looks like the banshee I mistook her for*. Vell hissed and spun away, disappearing in a colorful whirl.

Alaya recoiled. They'd been connected and Vell severing that link probably stung like a branch whipping against her brain.

"On my suggestion," Alaya explained when she recovered, "she tried to pick up objects through her zoi aima like you. She can't do it. It took the two of us, building off the giant's shockwaves, to make the earthquake happen. You're different, Na'rina."

King Olbin's accusations hit Na'rina anew. *Perhaps you should answer to us*. She didn't know what to do with it and was relieved when another *crack* echoed out of the growing tunnel. Na'rina crawled back into the tunnel to keep digging. "Guess I need to keep working then."

Alaya didn't answer and when Na'rina glanced back, she was gone.

Na'rina couldn't say how long they'd been digging. Compared to her dryadic body, the twiglet's struggled to keep going and she kept having to stop for rest. Currently, she slumped against the tunnel wall, cradling her scraped-up hands while waiting for the giant. If she held still enough, the shaking didn't travel up to the leaves on her head, but she couldn't stay unmoving for long, swaying in exhaustion. She wasn't sure if the lethargy was from the twiglet's weak body or from her own struggle not to sleep. She should be curling up in her aspens right now in preparation for the first snow, not digging in a cave under an island thousands of miles away.

What would Mama think if she saw me now? Na'rina sighed, shoving the Collective Wisdom away as it tried to show her memories from Mona'rina.

What was that? the twiglet asked.

Thoughts of home.

He grew quiet, then asked, *Your mother?*

Na'rina nodded.

Is she hurt?

How did he pick up on that? Perhaps it was the memory from Mount Athos. *She's healing. Slowly,* she answered the twiglet.

He mulled that over. *How much farther do we have to go?*

Na'rina had no idea and admitted as much. The twiglet's mood went sodden.

But we've made solid progress with the giant's help, she encouraged. The twiglet hummed, still dismayed. A faint thud came from the giant above. Such telling sounds were sporadic and growing fainter as they moved away from him, but he continued to help regardless.

He is indeed friend, Na'rina said. *When we get out, we'll find him and thank him.*

The twiglet perked up, creating a small glow inside of her. The effect his moods had on her was startling.

"Na'rina."

Na'rina jumped. She'd almost dozed off. Alaya smiled sympathetically.

"I did not mean to insult Vell'marxia," Na'rina said. "Did you manage to calm her?"

Alaya swayed her head in what Na'rina took to mean "so-so." It was ironic, an oceanid trying to keep the peace between two dryads.

There came a familiar cracking and a shuddering in the wall at Na'rina's back. Once it subsided, she crawled to dig out the next section the giant had cleared.

"We need to talk," Alaya said behind her.

Na'rina cringed. Alaya was old enough that it was like her mother saying those words.

"Are you staying a twiglet to fit through a smaller tunnel or are you staying that way because you can't emerge from him?"

Panic lodged in Na'rina's throat. The memory of reaching for her zoi aima to separate from the twiglet and the agony they'd suffered made her shudder. *Why can't I separate from him?* In the hours of digging, she'd pondered it and concluded she'd done more than meld. Going incorporeal and dropping them through the island must have done something more. It somehow connected her to the twiglet's own capabilities, making them primary and leaving hers weaker. Even

141

reaching out with their zoi aima was becoming difficult. *Is this irreversible?*

Na'rina stopped digging, breathing deeply against the anxiety rolling in her stomach. *I'm stronger than this!* She pictured Icarus cupping her face as he had before the summit, confidence in his hazel eyes.

"You can do this," he said, pressing a kiss to her forehead that breathed his warmer, violet zoi aima into her along with his encouragement, feeding her like sunshine. Tears pricked Na'rina's eyes, but her panic subsided.

"Na'rina?" Alaya pressed, an edge in her voice.

Na'rina frowned. The Oceadanda walked through life as though her troubles would wash away with time. The edge wasn't irritation as far as she could tell, but she struggled to believe it might actually be fear.

"I can't separate," Na'rina finally answered. "I tried and it feels like lightning hitting my Rina."

"Is he strong enough to keep digging?" Alaya asked softly.

The question was valid. The twiglet's hands were deeply gouged from their digging and his limbs shook like flimsy saplings. Just like Na'rina, without sunlight, he couldn't heal or find sustenance. But the twiglet immediately turned the question into a statement. *I'm useless.*

Where is his melancholy coming from?

"We're still moving," Na'rina answered, pushing back against the twiglet's lethargy. She finished pushing the small rocks and sand away from the end of the tunnel and beat her fists on the wall again before backing over her heels. Alaya appeared sitting beside her when she stopped to wait.

"Vell's guessing you won't make it out," Alaya said.

"Was she snide when she guessed?" Na'rina bit her tongue, but too late. *What is it about Vell that bothers me so?*

142

"I'm not answering that."

So, sa, *she was snide.*

Alaya breathed out a gusty sigh. Na'rina agreed with the sentiment.

"I'm sorry," Alaya said, "that's got to be terrifying."

"I'm ignoring the panic," Na'rina admitted. "But the twiglet's like me: He needs sunlight, so neither of us is getting any stronger."

Alaya drew up her legs and hugged them. She appeared as drained and miserable as Na'rina felt.

"I was worried when you didn't show up at the summit." Na'rina picked up a handful of the sand that coated the floor. She let it drain through her fingers like she'd seen Icarus do once. "At first, I was relieved to see you here."

"How'd it go?"

Na'rina shrugged. "It fell apart. But that's for another day. You and Vell are as stuck as I am, aren't you? I gather you caused the earthquake to free me so I could then free you?"

Alaya tapped the back of Na'rina's hand, indicating she should hold her hand out with a cupped palm. Na'rina dropped the sand and dusted off her skin to comply. Small droplets coalesced on Alaya's nails to drip into Na'rina's cupped hand. After a short time, a small pool formed.

"Drink," Alaya instructed.

"It's not salty?"

Alaya was an oceanid, after all, not a freshwater naiad. "I can separate the two," Alaya smiled. "Drink."

Na'rina did, savoring the dampness on her tongue.

I've decided, the twiglet spoke up, *she's friend too.*

Na'rina hummed, then aloud asked, "What's going on, Alaya?"

Alaya bowed her head, her silvery hair creating a curtain across her face. "I confess," she answered. "I blamed your capture last spring on your inexperience, thinking I'd never be so stupid as to get caught in a cage."

Na'rina swallowed. She'd wondered about that, but it hurt to hear aloud, especially from Alaya.

"What happened?" she asked, holding out her hand in a silent request.

In answer, Alaya tapped her fingers to Na'rina's, leaving small aqua zoi aima pools like water fingerprints. The lifeblood slowly sank into Na'rina's skin, joining her own blue and green zoi aima.

"The Wer-Kadis warned us to be cautious of the Sedessans. I didn't heed his warning closely enough," Alaya said.

She flipped her hand and held her fingers over her opposite palm, silently indicating Na'rina should do the same. When water began dripping off Alaya's fingers, her pull on the moisture in the air reminded Na'rina of the pressure she experienced when lifting objects with her lifeblood, except this was a sensation like sucking water through a reed. When she focused on it that way, the aqua lifeblood in her fingertips responded, gathering moisture from the tunnel's air. A couple drops fell from her fingers onto her palm.

The twiglet shrieked in amazement. The sudden cry left Na'rina's throat like a muffled scream before she could contain it.

Alaya chuckled and finished filling Na'rina's small pool for her.

"We can gift abilities like this?" Na'rina asked.

"With other nymphs, absolutely. It's just not done much." Alaya shrugged. "We can gift to our elements as well. It just fades faster."

"Our elements?"

"Remember when you created a bubble of calm in the storm off the Washington coast last spring? You could have expanded it by gifting to the trees around you."

Na'rina didn't even want to consider how difficult that would be. Creating just her own tiny bubble had been tiring enough. A *crack* reverberated down the tunnel. She gulped down the water and rolled onto her hands and knees to go dig.

"I'm held now in a tank of liquid," Alaya's unsteady voice admitted behind her. "I can't wake up and they keep taking vials of my blood. Vell's held in a tank beside mine. A few days ago, we realized we can both reach out with our zoi aima despite being sedated. By helping each other, we can reach most of the island. Our bodies won't move, but our minds can't shut off either."

Na'rina stopped digging and turned to cup Alaya's transparent face. She coated her twiglet hands with warm zoi aima—which worked to Na'rina's relief—and Alaya's eyes closed, forcing out tears from the corners.

"We'll get out," Na'rina squeaked. *Gah, what a time to sound like a mouse.*

"We hoped maybe you could wake us like you did Silas on the ship."

"I'm working on it," Na'rina smiled sheepishly. "One tiny fistful at a time."

A laugh escaped Alaya. "I can feel you shaking, Drydanda, and you have about ten feet to go before reaching open tunnel."

"That's all! We've already come, what, twenty?"

"And you're stuck in a twiglet."

"Minor details. I'm sure you and Vell can help me once you're awake. I just need to get to you." Na'rina rotated to keep digging.

Another laugh came from behind her. "You've grown, Drydanda. I ne—"

A *thud* rocked the tunnel and sand cascaded out of the wall in front of Na'rina. It caught her legs and handfuls shoved their way down her throat. Another *thud* came from above, a familiar *crack* sounded directly in front of her, and two more *crack, cracks* quickly followed as sand pelted Na'rina's body.

She cowered, arms over her head, until everything settled into eerie silence. Sand pressed against her up to the waist. She coughed, spitting grit. "What was that?"

"The giant!" Alaya's image blurred as she darted away, her zoi aima streaming into the ceiling above.

El scowled. Roberto stood far too close as they surveyed the rubble blocking the tunnels below the embassy. It was distracting. She tried to ignore him as she considered that the guard station and the holding cells were under that mess, obscuring Na'rina or Amos' fate. Fae dug at the rocks but it'd be days before they finished. Even the stonified guards from the Daughter of Medusa were nowhere in sight. *Did someone crush them to hide them?* If they had, then the Sedessans involved were hiding things from the Fae. That tracked with the ambassador not knowing about Miss Marrow.

El stepped away from Roberto as she eyed the zoi aima residue coating the cave-in. It glowed a light green and aqua-like radiation off uranium. *It's a good thing Renata didn't come.* El needed to misread the residue to divert attention from Na'rina. Although the coloring didn't perfectly match hers, rumors of her two-tone lifeblood abounded and it wouldn't do to point the Fae in her direction.

"The residue's heavy," Roberto said, his eyes shining with that extra sheen that told her he was using his second lens too.

"I've never seen it linger like this." El waved a hand. She had to play close to the truth with just enough difference to keep Roberto off Na'rina's trail.

"I've seen it do this when a mythic's killed suddenly, but the coloring's strange," Roberto said.

147

Killed suddenly. El quashed the memory of Na'rina's lifeblood exploding when the ceiling came down on her head.

"Strange?" Marquin asked. His skin was pallid in the lights strung along the hallway.

Roberto reached out like he could touch the lifeblood; his fingers hovering just above. "Jewel-esque in areas," he said, "and turquoise. They don't fit together. Like maybe this is more than one mythic."

"Some elementals are jewel-esque," El offered, trying to divert Roberto. He didn't have her knack for details, but he *had* studied zoi aima coloring and would know the rumors of the North American Drydanda. "I've heard of a light, aquamarine blue for wind elementals."

"Aquamarine?" Roberto tapped his fingers on the rubble. "It's close, but this makes me think of a water mythic. Are either of your suspects an oceanid?"

Huh. That was almost too easy.

"*Na*," Marquin answered, "and none of the foreign delegates were either. Beyond fire elementals, we haven't convinced the elemental mythics to speak with us."

I can't imagine why. El's anxiety drained away as the conversation shifted. Na'rina was already dead. She didn't need to be suspected of attacking the Fae. That would drive Icarus nuts.

"There is an aquifer, though, and we've found corpses floating out from under the island since the quake." Marquin said *corpses* like it left a bitter aftertaste.

"An aquifer? Wouldn't that be sealed from the ocean?" Roberto asked Marquin.

"I'm trying to get engineers down to investigate but the quake may have split open a few of our wells."

"And the corpses aren't Fae? They're not from your staff or island residents?" El asked.

Marquin shook his head, disgust curling his lips. "We are checking on the non-Fae residents, but we don't believe any of the corpses are from the locals."

"Curious," El muttered.

"Indeed," Marquin agreed darkly, but he missed El's true meaning. The more he spoke about the dead showing up in Riviera's waters, the more convinced she was that he had no idea what had been happening beneath the embassy. She was picking up on the visceral disgust in his tone that, unless he was very shrewd, he would not know to fake.

"All right," she said. "Let's see your suspects."

Marquin led them from the ruins of the embassy and back to the city center of Riviera. Once they reached the main thoroughfare, he began greeting people as they passed. It was not unusual to see the ambassador walking as vehicles were not allowed on the island; the Fae and other mythics alike greeted him back as they righted chairs and cleaned up broken cobblestones. Marquin smiled easily with them and El noted, now that they were away from the tunnel's lights, that the ambassador's coloring looked less pallid and more naturally porcelain.

Riviera was a haven for mythics. The Fae had other havens, of course, but Riviera required less to maintain and provided neutral ground for negotiations, which led other mythics to gravitate to its shores. Plus, the Fae-Court agreements gave the Fae reasonable access to the Sedessan information network. With it, they knew who entered the dome and didn't have to expend huge amounts of energy to maintain their privacy. So, they relaxed more here than elsewhere.

Roberto stepped around a toppled street lantern, moving closer to El while they followed the ambassador. He raised a hand like he intended to touch the small of her back. Her muscles tightened. He now wore black gloves like hers, but that was beside the point. He did not touch her, however. He merely bent closer to mutter, "The zoi aima residue. You've seen it before?"

El flashed him a glare. *Why does he think I'd share such information?* He met her eyes and glanced across the street at a small restaurant, Little Italia. El refused to look, instead bending to right a toppled chair from a tavern as she fought an unexpected bout of tears. *Not here! Not now...or ever!*

"It reminds me of something, but I can't say it's the same," she admitted, regaining control.

"Reminds you of what?"

El retrieved an orange a Fae girl had dropped. She offered it back to the child. The girl giggled, a glint in her too blue eyes that wasn't altogether innocent. "Want it?" she asked.

"Amilia," Marquin scolded, "you know better."

The girl flushed and accepted the orange before scampering away.

"He knows his population by name," Roberto noted.

"It's not surprising," El said, putting a few steps between them.

"What's not surprising?" Marquin asked, catching her words.

"You know your people well," El said.

Annoyance flashed across Roberto's face.

What does he want?

Marquin bowed as he opened the front door to the island's hotel, his cheeks flushing. "I am not above flattery. Thank you, Señorita Varela."

El tilted her chin and preceded him and Roberto through the door. Once inside, Marquin took up the lead again until they approached a door at the end of a hallway. The four Fae guards standing there saluted, setting the equipment on their belts to swaying. *No shock batons.*

"We don't usually hold prisoners. Due to the nature of these two, we got creative," Marquin explained, opening the door into a round, lushly carpeted room with a mini-bar and an oval bed that came up to her shoulders and required steps to get into. Just ahead was a panoramic window with a metal sheet bowed across the glass.

El spotted four more guards around the room. *Who are they holding?* She got her answer when she stepped past the bed.

A gagged Amos sat on the floor, hands and feet tied together and a chain running from his neck to around the back of his knees. Even hunched from the chains, he dominated the room. His left foot was bandaged. El paused. *He was injured.*

Spotting her, rage blossomed in his hard, gray eyes and he strained against the chain, exasperating the large welts that were growing around his neck.

"Woah," Roberto said. "I was not aware any giants still lived in the Western Hemisphere."

"Last one that we know of," Marquin said. "His family group was displaced from Peru's Machu Picchu region by tourism. After that, they died out. He's cagey as to why. We approached him for your father and after our initial meeting he offered his services as my bodyguard. I was seriously considering it until now. Don't know what he'd hold against us to want to destroy the embassy."

El held Amos' furious gaze through Marquin's explanation. Either Marquin was laying it on thick, or he truly hadn't known about the embassy's prisoners.

No family left. Although El's family was small and broken, she couldn't imagine having none.

"One way to find out." Roberto stepped forward, pulling at his glove's fingertips to free his hands, and grasped Amos' temples. His proprietary look reminded El strongly of his father. It was new, that look. Almost instantly sweat broke out on both their brows.

Roberto's expression glazed, clearly seeing internally instead of physically. Likewise, Amos' gray eyes became hooded and a small twitch pulled at his lips. There and gone, but El caught it.

A shielded mind, she remembered. Such an ability required strict, disciplined training that few mastered. To be self-aware enough to know what to shield and self-disciplined enough to stop thinking about those things, replacing them with a barrier, was a rare thing.

Sweat trickled down Roberto's temple. *What barrier did he find in Amos' mind?* From the growing confidence on the giant's face, the Sedessan wasn't getting anywhere.

Finally, Roberto stepped back and shook his hands as though cleaning them.

"He hates the Fae," he said.

Place the blame at the giant's feet. El wasn't the only one apparently instructed to do so. *That opens some interesting possibilities.* Either Roberto's father had known about Amos, or Roberto had jumped on the first chance he got to shift blame away from Sedessan involvement. Either way, the Inverros knew there was a need to protect the Court.

"All he focused on was causing the quake. Didn't give himself an out afterwards. Didn't care," Roberto continued.

Amos sneered. "Y' think me stupid?"

Marquin considered that, tapping his chin with a finger while his eyes glazed.

It feels thin, El agreed with Amos' question. She waited for Marquin to question Roberto but as the silence lengthened, that familiar tea-and-scones voice suggested she needed to strengthen Roberto's claim. Her skin crawled. *It's not the first time I've done something distasteful. Buck up, El, we can't afford the Fae digging into this deeper.*

She stepped around Roberto while pulling her own gloves free. In Amos' current hunched position, they were almost face to face.

"El, it's not a plea—"

She grasped Amos' temples before Roberto could finish and the hotel room faded. She found herself in a box canyon with towering walls that made her feel like an ant.

Amos leaned against the stone below what might have been his father, a sharp-angled male with displeasure showing in his pursed lips. Amos crossed his arms over his powerful chest and sneered. The similarity to the carved face was striking.

"Y'all lie like snakes."

The face to his father's right was also sharp-angled, but more delicate and with a mischievous glint in her eyes. Hair formed from vines flowed around her cheeks in waves, and El wondered what color it had been in real life. "What would y' do for y'r family?" she asked.

"This got nothin' to do with family."

"When it comes to Sedessans, it's always 'bout family."

"So y'r gonna let this mountain crush me?"

El couldn't look at him. She'd done terrible things for her family before. *Why does this feel different?* Finally, she forced herself to meet his eyes, just for a second. "I'm sorry," she whispered and then retreated.

Her hands fell to her sides and El stepped away.

"Anything about what he planned here?" Marquin asked, watching Roberto suspiciously.

Words stuck in El's throat. "Nothing," she said, leaving her answer at that. "You have a second suspect?"

As soon as Marquin turned away, Roberto glared. *He expected me to back him up. Why?* She hurried out the door after the ambassador.

"It's doubtful they worked together," Marquin said. "But, *sa*, there's another." He led them farther into the hotel where rooms had been chiseled out of the hillside behind the building. This one bore its own retinue of guards as well.

Marquin paused before the door. "We took precautions," he gestured at the stone. "This one will be more difficult for you, I think." And he pushed the door open.

Heat washed out, forcing them all to take a step back or risk getting singed. The guards retrieved a hose at their feet and, when one spoke into his comms, enough water gushed out for them to bathe the room. Steam billowed, and when the guards stepped back, their skin was beet red.

"Great searing skies," Roberto swore, "what kind of mythic are you holding?"

"A fire elemental," El answered, then caught herself. "Am I right?"

Marquin nodded. "You'll forgive me for not entering. I've already come close to getting scorched."

Roberto hesitated but El entered and he reluctantly followed. The dark skinned-salamander woman huddled on the far side of what used to be a dresser. Only the frame, now smoldering charcoal, attested to what it'd once been. Soot smudged the dripping walls and a square heap of black mud spoke of what might have been the bed. Water would only ground out her fire for a short time, so El quickly knelt down, reaching out as she whispered, "Can I help you?"

The salamander's teeth chattered, her terror showing the rare mythic who had never learned to mask her feelings. Recognition lit her face. El hoped Roberto missed it but that was unlikely. The woman barely hesitated before leaning her head into El's outstretched palms. Shock shook El to the core.

She was handling a Fabergé egg; it might be as strong as jade but it might also shatter in her hands. Like many Fabergé eggs, El found a hidden treasure inside Sala: a hard, diamond center.

Figure out that mystery later. The salamander's mindscape burned. Her existence was more elemental than physical and her internal fire seethed around that diamond center. Instantly, El's headache returned with a vengeance. It was not a shielded mind, but it was more protection than most had. Nevertheless, Roberto would read her cover to cover, so El gathered what she needed and retreated to the surface.

I don't know this other Sedessan's motives, she explained, *so I'm going to hide your experiences on Riviera except for your visit to Thomas Dominguez. The rest will look like you took a few days to enjoy the heat of the beach, and then you were confused by the quake and went wandering to figure out what happened.*

It wasn't perfect but it was all El could come up with in a pinch. She desperately hoped Roberto wasn't a part of what happened below the embassy. If he was, he'd know that she hid something from him.

You can do this thing? Sala asked.

It will hurt some, but sa.

Thank you, came Sala's whisper as El retreated.

Later, Sala followed El into the Varela estate and halted, gaping at the architecture.

Roberto had cleared her almost without touching her and Marquin had accepted their claims, although El suspected he wasn't convinced about Amos. She wasn't sure why he hadn't dug more into what Roberto found in the giant's mind.

Marquin had insisted Sala be kept close until the investigation was completed, mentioning a deal between the fire elementals and the Fae that Sala needed to fulfill. She'd slumped in dismay but accepted the order until she'd realized she'd be held indefinitely at the hotel. Then she'd ignited. Taking pity on her, El had offered to have her released into her custody.

After giving her a moment to gape, El motioned for Sala to follow. Sala fluttered after her, gawking as her feet barely touched the floor like flame crawling across wood.

"I do not know what accommodations you require," El said,

leading Sala toward their guest rooms. "Do you need a nonflammable room? What are your nutrition requirements?"

"Elodie."

El cringed but schooled her face before turning to greet Sophia. Their butler, a spindly, green-skinned goblin, hustled at her mother's shoulder.

Sophia spared a glance for Sala but didn't ask about her. "I trust Ambassador Marquin is satisfied."

"We've done our part," El assured, "with the help of the Inverros."

If this surprised Sophia, she didn't show it. Instead, an alarming light came into her dark eyes. "Perfect. Dinner's at six. We have company, so dress semi-formally."

She reached over her shoulder and Gladen, the goblin, handed her the mail. El glimpsed the Inverros' crest and figured it was their invitation to the Sedanza ball. Without another word, Sophia continued past them toward the central courtyard.

Gladen didn't follow. "I will set up a room for the salamander, my lady," he said.

Sala's eyes widened. Because goblins were cousins to imps, many assumed them just as stupid. In reality, they were sharply intelligent. And they loved treasure! If you paid them in gold or silver, they made excellent servants. They also ran in territorial packs. So when you hired one, you hired about a dozen with him. Once a pack viewed an island as their territory, they guarded it jealously. Add their handy ability to change their features to appear human and they fit perfectly into the Sedessan households.

The goblins in El's case also gave her the subtle comfort of knowing she wasn't the only one who grieved Icarus' childhood "accident." Even now there were times she'd find their head cook, Marissa, holding his picture and keening.

"*Na*, Gladen," El said to the goblin. "I will see to things for her. Please let Marissa know we have another for dinner. She'll have—"

"Whatever the family is having," Sala supplied, touching her ear as she noticed the long points sticking up above Gladen's bald head.

Gladen's eyes glowed. Goblins tended to judge each other according to their knobby features. The uglier, the better.

"Set her up in the Strata room, my lady," Gladen bowed again, his eyes still gleaming, and rushed back down the hall.

Vain thing. El made a note to bring him a present the next time she was out. There couldn't be friendship between herself and the staff, but that didn't mean she couldn't spoil them.

"Did you know goblins are fire-resistant?" Sala commented, staring after Gladen.

"Come." El led her to a room that only superficially resembled the stone hotel room. Built entirely of imported cut granite, the striations in the walls made a mosaic like a winding river. On the far side, a balcony overlooked the ocean. The room's only flammable portions were the bed and the couch cushion as even the side tables were cut from stone.

"I can contain the flame," Sala said with a self-deprecating smile. "There is no need to hide the furniture."

"Is this not to your liking?" El asked as she pulled the stone wardrobe doors open. From habit, she fell into mimicking Sala's speech.

It was a caramel custard flan—more air than substance with a slight sweet aftertaste. Sala didn't notice. Most people didn't unless the change was too drastic.

Sala sat on the bed and waited for El to meet her eyes. "They let me go, which means they have a better suspect?"

El's stomach flipped. Her mother's tea-and-scones voice in her head suggested she evade the question, but Sala would find out soon enough anyway.

"The giant," she answered while scanning through the screen on the inside of the wardrobe's door. This was another dwarven-crafted piece. Everything from men's tuxes to women's dresses in every size imaginable was stored below the room. Whatever guest stayed there simply had to select the correct size and occasion and the articles that matched lifted into the wardrobe.

The temperature in the room spiked. "That makes no sense."

"You can handle the flame?" El evaded, peeking at Sala to gauge her size.

"The giant didn't cause the earthquake," Sala insisted, not even registering the question.

"What makes you so sure?" El asked, curious despite her fear at the elemental's sudden spike in heat.

Size six. Five foot nine or ten tall. El pressed the selection on the screen and the wardrobe hissed softly.

Sala fluttered her hands and sweat started to form on El's skin. *I'm not sure she can contain the flame. Am I fast enough to dive into the wardrobe before Sala turns me to ash?* The woman's zoi aima had gone from a smoldering scarlet to scarlet laced with deep cobalt sparks. The blue reminded her of the wer-im. It was a passing thought; El was far more concerned about Sala turning the Strata room into a furnace by accident.

"Don't Sedessans pride themselves on reading the races' energy?" Sala asked, looking like a cornered mouse. "Did you not realize he's a granite giant?" She gestured at the walls. "Granite's stronger than the rock of the islands. If he'd planned the quake, he wouldn't have gotten caught under it."

That's why he had a grayish tinge to his zoi aima!

"And if he caused it by accident?" El asked.

Sala scoffed. "All stone giants can feel the rock around them. The pulses he used to free the door were precise. He wouldn't have caused it 'by accident.'"

El remembered the booming during her escape. She hadn't known at the time what caused it but now it made sense.

"Roberto lied about the giant," El admitted, "and I'm unfortunately in no position to help him."

Sala froze like a startled doe and heat rolled off her in waves. El stepped back from the wardrobe, making her motions smooth and unstartling while keeping her expression cool. It was at direct odds with the sweat trailing down her spine. "Dinner's at six," she said, trying to smile. "Pick whichever outfit you'd like." Then she left, the heat prickling her back until she closed the door behind her.

Caracas' streets reeked of sewage, chickens, and that ever-present body odor found in cities with little clean drinking water, much less enough to bathe in. At least Icarus wasn't picking up burned black beans. Venezuela had been under contention about who owned it the last time Icarus visited, and it was not the same place anymore. But black beans were still a staple. As it was, the heat and stench infused Icarus with a desire to be anywhere but there. He'd been very young when he'd last seen South America, cast out and struggling to find food while hiding from the Sedanza Court. He refrained from touching his ear with its outcast mark while he followed Dante.

The smaller wer-im led the way through the streets. This was a fact finding mission…hopefully. Some of Dante's contacts claimed information about the plane from the photos. Icarus held in a growl. *I want a solid lead.*

His stomach rumbled. "I'm ready for dinner already."

Dante grunted. "What was all that avalanche stuff Levi was talking about?" He looked up the street, over at a store with music drifting out, behind them at passing people. Anywhere but at Icarus.

Icarus understood the reason behind the question, and the avoidance. Since Na'rina named Dante and thus gave him a place among the wer-im, his loyalty sat with her. If his diluted blood didn't prevent him from vowing, he would have vowed, and he acted as though he had. And that could put him at odds with Icarus because many wer-im were territorial of their Vow Protected. But Icarus was not. He respected Dante's motives.

Icarus kicked an empty can as he answered Dante, "Not sure. Levi and Ver'rina blame themselves for what happened to their twins and now Na'rina, but I haven't put together exactly why."

"Na'rina's…sheltered." Dante glanced over, probably checking to see how his words were received. Icarus raised a brow and waited. *When will they learn I'm not like Silas?* "It sounded like her mother did that to keep her from the other mythics' attention?"

"My thoughts as well," Icarus agreed.

Dante let it go at that. They walked in silence until he pointed to a storefront painted with a huge, geometric mural of a bird, possibly a duck, displayed in vibrant emeralds and browns. Graffiti tags marred the picture with thick, black lettering.

They squeezed into the alley beside the building, stepping through trash, chicken feathers, and swarms of grape-sized flies to get to the back of the store. They entered another narrow alley behind the grocery but at least it was wide enough for them to stand shoulder to shoulder. Dante sent a text and leaned against the wall.

"They'll be here shortly," he said.

"What's their connection with all this?"

"They're ground crew at the airport."

Icarus grunted. Na'rina always admired how well informed he was. This was the muddle she didn't see. The puzzle he was always piecing together.

Two figures exited the grocery and Icarus immediately understood Dante's connection. They were strays. The female had gray, salt-lined hair, not from age but from breed, and resembled a sleek, silver tabby all the way down to her sage-gray eyes.

The male was too mixed to pick out a breed. His black hair floated like a cloud and his light brown eyes snapped with enough mischief that Icarus knew he'd have to watch out for the cat's antics.

The smiles they'd worn to greet Dante melted into stony facades.

"No, amigo. We have nothing for you," the male said.

The human form of *no* startled Icarus. *They grew up in human society. It's not surprising.* After all, he'd met Dante in a computer store. Unlike other strays, however, Dante hadn't shied away. And Icarus' Sedessan side had started forming their friendship before he'd realized what he was doing. If Na'rina hadn't inadvertently named the cat, he probably would have continued to use Dante without ever offering him a place. *Bad form, Icarus.*

Dante approached them with his hands out in a friendly gesture. "Miguel. Sarah. He means no harm. The Ka—he's just scared for his Vow Protected."

Their expressions went from stony to hostile and they rocked back into wary stances. The acid tang of fear hit Icarus beneath the rotting chicken stench.

"What Wer-Kadis? He doesn't recognize us, we don't recognize him," Sarah hissed.

"Please, Sarah—" Dante began but Icarus held up his hands and the wer-im stopped talking.

"Most Wer-Kadis would take your words as a challenge," he said.

The acid tang spiked. Such a challenge, a Kadivas like he'd fought with Silas, tended to end in death. Miguel's eyes traced Icarus' facial scars and he took a half step behind Sarah. If she'd had hackles, she'd have had them raised but she too reeked of fear. *I hate that response.* "I am not," Icarus continued softly, "most Wer-Kadis."

He turned, presenting his back as he walked to the end of the alley and stepped around the corner. There he leaned against the wall within earshot. The frustration he'd hidden now made his eye twitch.

A street vendor passed with a basket of mangos over one shoulder and a bunch of bananas over the other. Icarus flagged him over, paid for a banana, and waved him away. *Does Na'rina like bananas? Has she ever had one?* He mentally prodded at the numbness in his chest, but it gave him nothing. *I'll have to see.*

His phone buzzed and he glanced at the screen.

There's rumor of trolls coming into Charleston. It was from Obek.

From the Smokies? He deleted that. Of course they were from the Smokies. Instead, he texted, *Intela Corp connection?*

Possibly. One used to roam near the Tennessee center. They gave him food for keeping people away. After a brief pause, Obek texted, *Any news on the Drydanda?*

Nothing yet.

Copy. Better luck to you than I've had.

Icarus perked his ears back to the conversation in the alley. "—have killed us," Sarah hissed.

"He's focused on finding Na'rina Drydanda," Dante answered. "He'd only kill you if you got in his way."

"What? Because he's kind of safe, you're helping him? He'll

164

throw you to the street when he's done, not even sharing his bread crust along the way," Miguel said.

"I've been working with him for years, hasn't thrown me out yet," Dante answered.

He's thrilled with scraps.

"Hasn't named you either," Sarah mocked. "Has he offered you food?"

"Gave his beer to me yesterday."

Icarus paused, then quickly finished his banana and flagged down another fruit vendor. When he returned, Dante was still speaking.

"…landed in the country about four days ago. Do you recognize it?"

Sarah scoffed. "Recognize it? I could cite the tail numbers from memory. It belongs to the Fae embassy just off the coast. They fly people in and out almost daily."

Icarus' jaw ached from his clenched teeth. *Not there. Please not there.*

El had told him about the embassy when it was established about a hundred years earlier. The Sedanza Court had granted the Fae use of the single remaining island in their property, but it continued to be the Court's land.

'From this day forward, you are a wer-im without family. You have no claim to the Varela name. Do not speak to the staff, do not stop to see Elodie, do not try to contact Adrian. You have until noon to be gone from the Sedanza Islands."

His mother's rose and lavender perfume seemed to float in the air. He'd loved that smell. Until it'd become mixed with the coppery tang of his own blood. *Why?!* He wanted to rage. Icarus buried the memory, hearing Dante asking about oddities concerning Na'rina's flight. *We haven't confirmed she was aboard.*

"Everything about the Fae is unusual," Miguel said. Then came a smack. "Ow."

"Stop being smart with him," Sarah said. "Unusual how?"

"Baggage maybe?"

"They wouldn't let us unload their bags," Miguel offered.

"And there were some rather large ones like this duffle in the picture. But they've been bringing in all sorts of odd luggage for months now. Almost makes me think they're hauling around body bags."

Dante switched tactics. "What about this man?"

"He's been on a lot of the recent flights."

"He smells weird," Miguel said.

"Weird?"

"Like his body can't figure out if it's a sweaty human or tarry goblin. He stinks of both."

"Anything else?"

"Oh, he flew in a few months ago with some really strange luggage, remember Miguel?"

"He had pods with him."

"Pods?"

"They were straight out of a science fiction movie. Big silver bullet-looking things that they loaded onto a truck. We asked about them and they said, get this, that they were portable tanning booths."

"Craziest thing," Sarah said. "I've never seen someone lie so terribly but the lady we questioned was Fae. How she justified in her brain that that was truth I have no idea."

Icarus couldn't think of a way either. The Fae didn't lie but mythology had one thing right about them: They'd mislead you all day long if they could justify how their words were technically true.

Dante thanked Miguel and Sarah and offered them something from his bag. Miguel hummed like he'd caught a whiff of grilled steak. "Where'd you find a homemade cinnamon roll?" he asked.

Seriously? Icarus almost looked but caught himself. A few moments later, Dante strolled out of the alley, letting Icarus catch up with him instead of stopping.

"You filched Felis' snack from Rebecca?" he asked as he handed over the second banana he'd gotten.

Dante accepted it after a moment and shrugged. "He ate the first one before we took off, but he put a second into his pack and I knew Miguel loved them, so I took it as a thanks." He shrugged again before peeling his banana. *Does this have something to do with why Miguel asked about food?* He suspected it did. A small jab back at the larger wer-im. Icarus followed Dante to their hotel in silence, allowing him his thoughts as he ate.

El ran a white-gloved finger over the bottom of her wine glass, glad she'd taken more painkillers before dinner. She'd tried calling Icarus back and wished that he'd answered. Hearing his voice might have steadied her for this.

The Varela dining hall echoed with the group's conversation. Sala, to El's right, cupped her soup bowl. She'd picked a gorgeous, midnight blue dress but El was more distracted by the steam she was breathing in, which made her zoi aima flare. *Does it feed or cool her fire?* The elemental glanced up and just as quickly dropped her eyes. *She'd make a terrible diplomat. She reeks of apprehension.*

El herself wore a red and white sundress and sandals, and wished she'd dressed for battle instead of dinner.

On her left sat Roberto Inverro, dressed sharply in slacks and a dark, buttoned shirt. He'd shaved again. He was one of those men who had a solid five o'clock shadow over his cleft chin if he didn't.

El ignored him and his clean profile right along with the angry flush trying to redden her face. She was *not* strangling the napkin in her lap.

Why did we invite the Inverros over? The last she'd known, her father despised Mateo, Roberto's father, after he'd stolen a lucrative connection with the Panama Canal's naiads.

And yet, here the entire Inverro family sat.

Roberto glanced at her and she pinched her lips inward, throttling her napkin despite her best efforts. Under the table, he tried to hand her a piece of paper. She flicked her fingers dismissively and the napkin flopped, heavily wrinkled, onto her legs. He tried again and she ignored him, taking a sip of wine. He huffed quietly, crumpled the paper, and slipped it into his mouth. A moment later, it disappeared with a spoonful of soup.

On Roberto's other side, his mother rapped Dylan's knuckles when he reached for another roll. Marie Inverro appeared sweet with a gentle smile and sparkling eyes in her rounded face, but she had a hidden, cruel side and El avoided her when possible. The other four Inverro boys were lined up between Marie and Mateo like ducklings: Dylan and David, then Ethan and Samuel.

Ethan caught El's eye from down the table. He sneered. Like Roberto, he had their father's cleft chin, but where Roberto had a mix of Mateo's leanness and Marie's round face, Ethan looked like all the meat had been leached off his bones. It made his sneer almost vulpine. El suppressed a shudder. He was next oldest after Roberto and had always treated her like prey he was teasing. After Icarus' "accident," she'd learned to avoid him and Samuel.

Ethan held his knife out as though he were holding a foil. It appeared normal, like he was fiddling with the utensil, but El knew the threat. She'd never won a fencing match against Ethan, and he often went beyond a mere tap to win a point.

Ting. Ethan twitched and his knife tapped the stem of his wine glass. Mateo paused while speaking. Ethan wilted under his father's censure. After a moment, Mateo went back to the conversation.

El pinched her lips inward to keep from laughing when David winked at her. He then stared studiously at his plate when Ethan glared. El couldn't tell whether David had pinched his brother or stabbed him with a fork, but she could have kissed the boy.

Roberto ignored them all. His fingers rolled against the table silently and he'd taken on a thousand-yard stare. *What's he waiting for?*

Arlo De León and his daughter, Lucia, sat on the other side of the table. Like her father, Lucia had a broad face and wide-set eyes. *Did her older sister actually use Compulsion on her? Does she remember it?* El had never connected with Lucia, but Lucia eyed everyone like she hated the air they breathed and wished she could escape it. Although, the woman *was* watching Samuel Inverro with a spark of interest. *When did that start?*

"…Marquin will be deciding his fate tomorrow night."

El's ears perked. *Does Marquin have enough evidence for a trial?* The Fae were meticulous about their hard facts and truth. Even two Sedessans' vouching for Amos' guilt was questionable. "Without a formal trial?" she asked.

Mateo swung his placid gaze toward her.

In her periphery, she caught what might be panic flash through Roberto's eyes. El wasn't sure.

"There isn't a need," Mateo answered her. "It isn't as though there will be repercussions from his nation." His accent reminded her of flour. Plain and dry.

"I'm sure—" Sophia started to speak.

"I'd think the Fae and the Sedessans would attempt to appear impartial, especially as you're reaching out to other mythics to form better alliances," El interrupted. "A questionable trial now could close every door you've knocked on." Outwardly, El ignored her mother's glare. Internally, she was pixie-sized again. She couldn't say what neurological glitch had gotten into her, but it was too late now.

"She has a point," Arlo pointed at Mateo with the same hand in which he held his wine. Then he gulped it down and held out the glass for a refill. It was hard to take an insult seriously from a man in an orange and brown sweater vest over a blue buttoned shirt and orange tie when it was easily eighty degrees outside. Arlo played fun and snuck information from people by making them laugh.

El wished she could be so skilled.

Mateo smiled, and El found herself wanting his bland flour back. "Alliances. I do believe that's what this dinner is about."

Roberto coughed and his hand twitched below the table like he had the urge to grab her hand. El flicked her fingers at him again, telling him emphatically not to touch her and irritated he'd feel familiar enough with her to even have the impulse.

El's father cleared his throat. "Indeed. We've been in discussion about tying our two families together."

El's brain froze.

Arlo rubbed his hands down the front of his vest. "Disturbing," he joked tensely. The De Leóns were not strong. An alliance between the Varelas and Inverros would weaken then further.

"We've decided," her father continued, ignoring Arlo, "that a permanent link between the Varelas and the Inverros would benefit both families. Roberto asked to court you, Elodie, and I have granted permission. Courtship will be one year and then you'll marry with the gift of a Fae blessing. We'll announce it at the upcoming ball in the U.S. in a few days."

Silence. It wasn't just in El's head. The whole room held still.

Arlo looked like he was choking on his tie and Lucia like she was calculating the chance she could score a similar courtship.

Roberto smiled at El but she detected uncertainty in the tension along his jaw. His hand twitched below the table again, but he didn't finish the motion.

Her parents had a familiar, determined set to their postures. El knew they were holding hands, sans gloves.

Mateo's placid look had returned but his wife was a canary with a mouse. El didn't spare a glance for the rest of their sons.

Her brain finally kicked into gear even as her chest suddenly constricted. *Marriage to Roberto…and blessed by the Fae.* No wonder Sophia had told her to represent well. Such a blessing would protect their marriage, and thus the families, on a whole different level. *But to Roberto?!*

A cage closed in on El. She was stuck inside with a beast she didn't know. Unexpected tears pressed behind her eyes and El pushed away from the table, walking out before they fell. She barely heard Roberto calling after her or her mother's strangled cry of exasperation.

The scraping of chairs warned her she wouldn't make a clean escape unless she moved fast. Kicking off her sandals, she rushed down the hall and ducked into the servants' corridor just outside the kitchen. Marissa glanced up from the stove in surprise as El stepped behind the kitchen door and into the large dumbwaiter that serviced the upstairs floors. She slid the waiter's doors almost completely closed, leaving a tiny crack to peek through, just as Roberto entered the kitchen.

His muscular shoulders blocked her view of Marissa for a moment as he stepped up to the metal prep table. El cringed when he addressed Marissa. "Elodie came this way."

Marissa cocked her head and continued to stir the pot on the stove, unfazed. "Elodie?" she questioned with a slight accent.

Roberto snorted. "Elodie came this way. Where did she go? ¿Dónde fue ella?"

"¿Comedor?" Marissa pointed a large-knuckled, green finger toward the dining room and El suppressed a chuckle.

Roberto's shoulders tightened and he stepped around the prep table toward Marissa, pulling off his gloves. The goblin froze, her spoon clicking against the pot as it stopped moving. Her lips pulled upward in a silent snarl.

"Our families have had amicable talks," came Adrian's voice from the doorway, "but I'd have to question your manners if you take such liberties with my household."

"His father might need to give him more lessons," Arlo chuckled. "You sure you want him as a son-in-law?"

Roberto, who'd raised a hand toward Marissa, dropped it like he'd been burned. "Of course," he said, stepping away from the cook, "I wasn't thinking. I did not expect Elodie to leave at the news."

"Piece of advice," Adrian said as Roberto joined him, "never think you know what Elodie will do."

Their voices faded down the hall. After a moment, Marissa stirred her soup and snickered. "Rana babosa." *Slimy frog.*

El almost snorted.

Even if Roberto had searched the cook's mind, he wouldn't

have gained easy access. Unlike the other Sedessan households who either restricted their goblin's access to information or regularly wiped their memories, the Varelas had gained enough trust with their pack for El to mentally train them. It wasn't perfect. A serious attack would eventually break through their defenses, but Marissa loved her cooking and if Roberto had broken through, he would have either found himself under a deluge of goblin tomato base or been forced into the memory of the last time Marissa had torn a man's head off. She was a goblin, after all.

Marrisa snickered again and came over with a frog leg in her hand. As she bit into it, she slid the dumbwaiter open, peeking inside like she used to when El was a child and liked to hide there. She grinned devilishly, crunching on her snack.

El grinned back, glad her urge to cry had subsided. She pointed upward with a hopeful lift of her brows. Marissa winked and shut the waiter. In the sudden darkness, the dumbwaiter groaned and rose. A moment later, it stopped with a dull thud. El peeked out before exiting into the empty hallway. She headed toward a window with roof access. Once there, El settled into the groove between one roofline and the next where she could see the grounds on one side and the ocean on the other. It was her usual refuge, but once settled, the reality of what had happened hit her, killing her momentary glee at escaping.

She had nothing against marriage per se and had expected it soon as most Sedessans married around her age, but somehow, she'd expected to have a say. When her parents told her to sneak into a gnome's tiny mud house, she crawled in, ignoring the dirt and enjoying the wave of calm, a natural defense mechanism, coming off the startled creatures. When they told her to get captured and find out what was hiding beneath the Fae embassy, she acted like a ditz and got herself tossed in a holding cell. When they told her to scout the Amazon for sylphs, she took bug spray and good hiking boots. None of those assignments required her prior knowledge.

Why did I think this would be different? It bothered her that even Marquin had known of the proposed courtship before her. *Na,* El corrected herself, *it bothers me that it's Roberto.* He'd abandoned what they'd had, and she didn't trust him anymore. It hurt to even look at him. She'd trusted him once. Trusted him enough to start tentatively planning a future with him and she'd seen a glimmer of possibility for a true partnership like what her parents shared. But now—

A red streak zipped out of a window, curved around, and came to a stop beside El. She blinked away the tears that were threatening again before the streak spun in a small circle and solidified into Sala. The elemental sat and drew her knees up.

"If you can go incorporeal, why didn't you escape out the door of the holding cell?" El asked.

"I'm more vulnerable." Sala hugged her legs tightly.

"You're more vulnerable as a flame?"

Sala ducked her head. "All elementals are more vulnerable as their element. Some hunters try to force us to go incorporeal because they can kill us and take our cores. They're valuable, like perfect gemstones. If they'd hit me with that hose while I was a flame, it might have killed me, extinguished my core to its diamond."

El stared at Sala, shocked. "You shouldn't tell people that."

Sala looked stricken. "You're right. I just, I—"

El's skin prickled with sudden heat.

"Sala," she said, "I have no interest in an elemental's core and it's not information I'll sell." Searching for a distraction, she asked, "How'd you find me just now?"

As the question sank in, the temperature diminished and El relaxed.

"Heat," Sala admitted proudly. "Of all the moving heat sources in the house, I figured only one had a reason to climb onto the roof."

El laughed, then covered her mouth in surprise. Sala smiled shyly, went to speak, hesitated, and snapped her mouth shut.

"What?"

Sala ducked her head again, "I've been thinking. The giant—"

"Amos," El offered and the elemental looked surprised.

"—Amos didn't cause the quake, but someone did. Our captors targeted multiple types of mythics, some quite powerful. Seems to me that equals a lot of enemies—" she left the suggestion hanging and a fresh grin spread across El's face.

"Are you enticing me to run away?"

Sala's dark eyes glinted. "I'm a lowly elemental. Surely, I wouldn't help you out of the frying pan and into the fire."

El leaned against the study's desk, waiting for Sala to retrieve her phone and a change of clothes from her room. She held a pen, ChapStick, lip balm, and comb that she'd pulled from behind the family portrait along with a sylph-made breather retrieved from under the thesaurus behind the desk. It was a bit of technology her family commissioned from the air nymphs similar to a human's emergency compressed air tank, except the breather was only three inches long and lasted forty-five minutes instead of six.

She fidgeted with the items. Conversation filtered from the dining room, but that didn't mean everyone was seated at the table, so El kept her ears primed. She heard when someone heavier than Sala approached the study.

She ducked behind a large, stuffed chair just as the door opened. Curiosity made her want to peek but she knew better—Icarus had taught her well—and so she stayed motionless.

"El, come here," her father said.

Her defiance drained away. Feeling like a chastened child, she peeked to find Adrian watching her. He could be stern and had a poker face like no one else, but right now she read his exasperation. It rankled that it was aimed at her. She rose and came around to slump into the chair.

"I got caught off guard," she whispered.

The exasperation melted into resignation. He grabbed the bottom edge of the other stuffed chair and dragged it across the heavy rug to face her. Once seated, he leaned his elbows on his knees and stared at her, thinking.

El tucked her feet up and waited, trying not to squirm.

A part of her always acknowledged that her father, with his rounded face, and Icarus, with his thin feline features, looked only glancingly alike, but his brown eyes and her brother's hazel were the only ones to ever make her feel as vulnerable and yet as safe as a child.

"I'm not surprised," he finally said. "Negotiations have been quick and we gave you no warning."

"Why?"

He shook his head. "Various reasons. You know your mother has helped build our house to its current strength. Her judgment in such things is usually unerring. I agreed because Roberto offered to take our family name."

Instead of responding offhand like she wanted to, El took a moment to consider. *So, the Inverros dull the Varela thorn in their side. They probably believe Roberto will remain loyal to them despite taking a new family but even if he doesn't, they have four other boys to strengthen their future. And we keep our family alive by adding a strong, capable member who continues the family name.*

El knew that, with only a female child, the Varelas were looking at slowly dying out. *It's a good contract.* El hated it. She now understood why Roberto had brought up Icarus and tried to point out Little Italia. He'd been trying to step right back into the friendship they'd had before. "And I don't have a choice?" she asked.

"You and Roberto were—"

"Adrian?" Sophia called from the hall.

Her father sighed. He pointed at the items El held. "Interesting mix. I'm not going to ask. Do what you need to, El, but please come talk with me before you do anything too rash."

He rose and pulled his chair back into the divots in the rug where it usually sat. "Coming," he called out the door to his wife. When he glanced back, El could have sworn he appeared regretful.

She drew in a shuddering breath once he'd left but her insides ached. *Can I do as they're asking?* She was still staring at the door, wondering, when Sala slipped in a few minutes later.

"Roberto Inverro snuck away to the bathroom and took your

phone from your room," she whispered.

El's preoccupation popped. "He what?"

"He took your phone."

Instead of anger, nostalgia and pain hit El. She and Roberto used to steal each other's phones and leave surprise pictures. In a world where their phones were their umbilical cords to the family webs, it was strangely hysterical to find a picture of someone's nostrils. *Is that why he did it or does he have other reasons now?*

Sala handed over a pair of jeans and a blue t-shirt. "I got these from the laundry. Your goblin servants jump very quickly when they know they're helping you." The statement held a suspicious edge.

"I didn't mess with their brains," El grumbled. "Horacio just likes a specific ice cream that's made in Oregon. I fly it in for him whenever I get a chance."

Sala tilted her head. "You bribe them with sweets."

"More like reward them."

"Sounds like a bribe."

The crazy part was, Sala spoke without accusation.

El huffed, tossing her sundress over the back of a leather armchair. Sophia would find it and be furious but El couldn't bring herself to care. She *should* care. She'd just insulted the Inverros—the most powerful family in the Court. The negotiations for the marriage, especially to get the Inverros to agree to give up their eldest son, probably required a lot of Sophia. But El couldn't get past the feeling that someone had just stabbed her in the chest. Amos' betrayed look haunted her. Unfortunately, it expressed perfectly how she currently felt.

Another memory hit her, that of Dylan and David's hopeful

stares on the boat paired with Roberto's uncertain but hopeful grin at the dinner table later. *There's more to this than even Sophia knows. She's working to benefit the family, but what if she's operating with too little information?*

El shrugged into a light windbreaker and pocketed the items she'd pulled out before Sala arrived. The lack of her phone would have weighed on her at any time, but right now the home screen would display half a dozen missed calls. She didn't think Roberto could get into the phone, but if Icarus called and he answered, that would be a whole different can of worms.

El smothered her unease and left out the back way with Sala, slipping through the kitchen and winking at Marissa as they passed.

Italian seasonings, spaghetti, and browned ground beef greeted Icarus' nose as he entered the hotel room. The place wasn't fancy but it had a kitchenette, small living room, and two beds. Since all of them were as likely to sleep in the forest as in a building, none cared if they slept on the floor. Icarus' stomach rumbled and he headed for the kitchenette.

Felis and Levi were eating on the couch.

"Plate's there." Felis pointed.

Icarus stared at the single plate on the counter. He peeked into the pot and confirmed his suspicions.

Turning, he caught Dante heading for the door.

"Hold up," he said, grabbing the plate. "You haven't eaten yet." He pushed it into Dante's hands. "You," he pointed at Felis, "with me."

Felis gaped, his fork halfway to his mouth. "I—"

"Now."

Felis dropped his plate onto the coffee table and scrambled out the door behind Icarus. They were deep into a section of the city that smelled of burning tires by the time Icarus spoke.

"Do you question Na'rina's rank?" he asked.

Felis spluttered. "What? Of course not. What fool would question a Drydanda's station?"

"You, apparently."

Felis stopped walking, his yellow eyes bright with startlement and anger. "Kadis, you know I respect Na'rina Drydanda."

"Your actions say she can't name a stray to our ranks. What am I to think?" Icarus snarled at a pair of kids spying on them from behind a trash bin. They froze, and he glimpsed their scrawny faces before they scampered away.

"I—" For once, Felis struggled for words. "What's his place now? My sire used to say if there's any doubt about who's mane, check who eats first."

Icarus scoffed. "You eat before me most days. Try again."

Felis rocked back on his heels. "By wer-im standards, it's whoever wins the fight, but if I fight him, Na'rina would string me up a tree."

"She would," Icarus agreed, "but she would also string you up for not preparing food for him. Stars above! *I'm* tempted to string you up for it. Why is it, Felis, that you never include him?" Icarus' hackles had risen and tension pulled at the scars on his face.

Felis shoved his hands into his pockets and hunched his shoulders in a quasi-shrug meant to make him unthreatening. Icarus suspected it was a posture learned from being the youngest of many brothers. "Because we never have?"

Icarus stared at him and Felis fidgeted.

"I'll stop that," he finally said.

Icarus fought an urge to cuff him upside the head just like Silas used to do to him. There was more to Felis' reasoning; he could feel it in the way Felis wouldn't meet his eyes.

"Fine, don't tell me the truth." Icarus turned to leave. He was a good ten paces away before Felis spoke again.

"A name doesn't change his past."

Icarus stopped and flicked an ear backward.

"He reminds me of someone."

Icarus turned back around.

Felis scuffed a toe against the ground, playing with a wrapper in the dirt. "After everyone else in the family died, my brother Attica and I joined a refugee group of mythics in the San Juan Mountains in Colorado. This was sometime in the 1850s before Silas took control of the wer-im and recruited me. We didn't want to be alone, you know, and the group needed protectors. They were mostly gnomes and fauns, a few sprites and brownies who were dislocated from the human expansion on the East Coast. Attica loved them, almost vowed to them. They eventually named us Silent Paws and Little Tail." Felis paused, his eyes glistening.

Icarus couldn't remember a time he'd seen Felis as anything but happy-go-lucky or intent on a fight. *He treats Afre like a long-lost younger brother.*

Giving his friend a moment to recover, Icarus asked, "You weren't afraid of the Drydanda? You were awfully close to her grove."

Felis shook his head. "The gnomes would becalm the trees around us, and the Drydanda never knew. For a while, this was life. It was simple, beautiful—"

Icarus waited as Felis struggled. A premonition told him he knew where this was going.

"We welcomed in a pair of strays. One in particular we

183

nicknamed Tabby. He didn't appreciate it." Felis sneered viciously. "They joined us in protecting the group but never formed that bond, you know, of fighting brothers. One night we camped in a canyon. I remember the stars that night. It was so clear."

Felis tilted his head back but the city lights obscured the stars. "The strays sold us out to a group of pelt hunters. If you remember, there was a time when trappers hunted for mythic skins. They'd warned the hunters to bring fire and lots of ammo and after they set fire to the surrounding land, it was all Attica and I could do to keep it at bay. We weren't enough to protect the group."

Icarus waited but it became clear that was all Felis intended to say. "And Attica?" he asked.

"He loved the group," Felis said.

"He died for them." It wasn't a guess. "And Dante reminds you of this Tabby."

Felis continued to stare upward like if he tried long enough, he'd spot the stars.

"Dante isn't Tabby," Icarus said. He'd worked long enough with the former stray to know that.

Felis finally met his gaze. "Neither is he a proven wer-im."

What a mess! "When we first met," Icarus said, "Silas wanted to gut you. He thought your flippant attitude was a liability. Tarn and I convinced him to give you a chance."

Felis scoffed. "He also named you monster. Not sure I'd trust his judgment."

Icarus snarled. "I trust *my* judgment. Dante's looks mean little to me. It's his actions that matter."

"There's a mole for Intela Corp somewhere."

The breath rushed out of Icarus. "What evidence do you have?"

"Nothing solid. Just…suspicion."

Is Felis correct? Icarus had no way of knowing. He'd seen nothing to indicate Dante as the mole. *But that doesn't mean I haven't missed something.* "Then it's your job to figure it out," he told Felis. The wer-im looked stricken but Icarus kept talking. "We need to know but I won't operate off of just suspicion." He turned again to walk away, saying over his shoulder, "Go find dinner."

Weariness washed over Icarus as he left. He hated the numbness in his chest. Hated doubting his friends. His stomach grumbled and he fished in a pocket for some trail mix.

He was almost back to the hotel when his phone buzzed. "¿Sí, qué pasa?" he answered in a nasally voice, not recognizing the number.

There was a pause, then, "Wer-Kadis?"

"Malon," Icarus placed the voice of the Maine Coon wer-im watching Charleston. "You have a new number."

"Lost my last one in the drink." Efficient as always, Malon went right on with the reason for his call. "The *Erstwhile* is still in the bay and the *Observer's* beyond the breakers but the *Sansabria* cruised south yesterday. I managed to place a tracker on it before it pulled out."

Cruised south…toward Sedanza.

Icarus' hackles rose again. He didn't believe in coincidences.

I'm half buried!

Earth pressed tightly to Na'rina's body from the waist down. Lightheadedness stabbed her brain as gnats swarmed the edges of her vision.

Alaya wouldn't just leave me! Her breathing rasped. *She'll be back.*

Drydanda? the twiglet, who'd been quiet for a while, whispered.

Na'rina sucked in air, choked on the residual sand in her mouth, and coughed, hacking until she could breathe again. Fighting a whimper, she pulled in another lungful through her nose and let it out on an eight count. The heavy musk of damp dirt came with it. She did it again, and again, and again, until the pungent earth was all she knew, and her pulse slowed.

Drydanda? the twiglet whispered again. *Are you alright?*

I will be, she finally answered, pulling in another breath.

Where'd you learn to calm yourself like that? the twiglet asked.

My mother, Na'rina answered, and then froze. She hadn't appreciated her mother's teaching in some time, but now she admitted, not everything she'd learned was useless.

We're kind of buried, the twiglet commented.

Panic tried to claim Na'rina again.

Breathe! Air rasped against her raw throat, expanding her chest until the surrounding earth pressed back against the expansion of her lungs. As Na'rina slowly let the air escape, she shuddered at the reduced pressure against her body as her chest contracted.

Her tongue stuck to the roof of her mouth. She could still feel Alaya's restless lifeblood in her fingertips, so she raised her hands and started pulling moisture from the air. A tingling ran through her fingers and then a couple blessed water drops appeared. She waited a few seconds and another five drops before she licked the moisture onto her tongue.

Na'rina finally answered the twiglet, *Sa, we're half-buried.*

Huh, I always wondered what it'd be like to have roots.

Roots? Unlike the twiglet, Na'rina knew exactly what it felt like to have roots. This wasn't the same, but it was close. More than half of her Rina existed underground and when Na'rina melded with her, she traveled those roots like floating in streams of water. Na'rina's panic and horror melted a fraction. The close-packed dirt wasn't exactly the same, but it did warm the twiglet's bark.

I can handle this. Na'rina gulped down the next palmful of water and felt around. The tunnel's walls were out of reach and the ceiling was too high to feel, but the debris that held her up to her armpits shifted as she searched. She flexed her knees and wiggled her toes, finding the earth not as hard packed as she'd first believed. Inch by inch she dug free, clearing her chest, waist, and legs. The sand and fist-sized rocks in her wake nearly blocked the tunnel behind her.

She was almost free when Alaya reappeared, her blue eyes huge.

"What?" Na'rina stilled, fighting a spike in her heart rate. The twiglet also froze at the oceanid's sudden appearance.

"The giant's gone. I think they recaptured him."

Na'rina swayed, dizziness hitting her. "We have ten feet?" she squeaked.

"Four-ish now," Alaya answered. "He must have realized what was happening and crushed the next big section."

That would explain all the sand that had caught Na'rina. *Four feet.* She steadied herself against the wall, her hand shaking while her legs threatened to dump her onto the floor. With the giant's help, she'd been confident of reaching the open tunnel. But now—

She slumped onto the sandy floor, and it squished like it wanted to pull her back in. "I'm tired, Alaya." She tilted her head back against the wall. "I should be preparing for winter in my Rina right now."

Alaya sat across from her.

"How do I end up in these situations?" Na'rina asked.

Alaya snorted, then said, "I have an idea for getting out, but you are going to hate it. Vell already refused to help."

"I'm pretty sure Vell hates anything to do with me," Na'rina said.

Alaya's eyes crinkled. "At least she's not Owasha."

Na'rina shuddered. Alaya's sister hated anything land-based.

"What's your idea?" she asked.

"The caved-in tunnel is mostly loose sand and grit that the giant was crushing even smaller for you. If I turn it to mud and we heal the twiglet's body, you might be able to dig through."

Inside, the twiglet hunched sullenly. He equated Alaya's mention of healing him with being weak. Na'rina's eyes felt gritty. She just wanted to sleep. *Can't, not yet.*

"Help me?" She tried to process what that would take. "You're casting your zoi aima without Vell'marxia right now. Have been for a while." Na'rina narrowed her eyes. "How far would you have to draw water from?"

Alaya ducked her head. "Does it matter? I'm not willing to die in a tank without trying to escape."

She could kill herself. Na'rina had been there once, so drained of zoi aima that she couldn't move her physical body, but determined to get out and willing to do whatever it took. "I can't ask for such a thing," she said. "There's got to be another way."

Alaya threw her hands out in frustration. "That's what Vell said but I'm not hearing any other feasible ideas!"

"I can't blame Vell for protecting her life and yours." Na'rina leaned forward earnestly. Even the small bit of zoi aima Alaya had given her to impart her water ability probably strained the oceanid. It was common to give back and forth tiny bits like offering a cup of tea, and she hadn't questioned it, but she should have. For Alaya to give enough to heal the twiglet *and* turn the tunnel to mud? Well, that'd be like taking the entire jar of honey, the tea, and the scones, and running away with them.

"Vell's not worried about her life! She's scared of—" Alaya hesitated and suspicion bloomed in Na'rina's head.

"She's scared of what?" she pressed.

Alaya pinched the bridge of her nose. "Scared of aiding a Theos mix. She spouted about you being fully grown but she's never heard of you. Asked where you've been hiding. Really, she's just scared. She knows you're stronger than she is, and it terrifies her."

"I didn't purposefully hide from the world," Na'rina said softly. For once, she commiserated with the twiglet huddling in her awareness.

"*Na,*" Alaya said. "But it's hard to explain to Vell that your grandmother hid her children to protect them and that your mother did likewise with you. It casts doubt on a subject she's already nervous about."

The words, spoken aloud, startled Na'rina. She'd begun to suspect that her lack of training was her mother's way of making her look weak, but she hadn't tied it to her protection. She clasped her hands together. Sappy sweat coated the twiglet's palms. He was making no effort to stop the changes she was making on him.

King Olbin feared me too. Is it just because of my mixed blood? Na'rina was glad Afre had explained the Theos thing or she'd be completely lost. Splaying her stumpy fingers in display, she said in exasperation, "But I'm a twiglet." Stuck in the twiglet's body, she couldn't use most of her abilities anyway.

Alaya hiccupped a sardonic laugh. "I knew Poseidon, you know. It wasn't his strength that made him such a terror. It was his assumptions paired with his strength. He lived at a time when might did equal right. That's not something I'm worried about with you." The fire in Alaya's gaze startled Na'rina and she was reminded that, although Alaya was the calmest oceanid she knew, the passion and convictions that ruled the oceanids still lived under Alaya's skin.

Na'rina swallowed and fought a cough. Once she could speak again, she voiced another objection. "You'd drain yourself so much I'd have to return you to the ocean and Vell to her tree for you both to heal," she said, "all while being a twiglet." Na'rina had no idea how she'd accomplish either of those things.

Alaya was incandescent. Not like usual with a dim glow to her skin, but dull, worn around the edges like a leaf fading on the ground. If she gave enough zoi aima for Na'rina to escape, simply waking Alaya wouldn't be enough to help her. Instead, without the ocean, it might actually kill her.

Alaya's nostrils flared. "We're four feet away from you getting out. I will not give up!"

No matter how vehemently she said it, Na'rina could see her fear. "We're going to die, aren't we?" she asked.

Inside, the twiglet cowered, becoming nothing more than a soft presence as though he'd be helping if he disappeared. He'd been doing that more and more recently. At times, she almost couldn't tell he was there.

Alaya grasped Na'rina's hand, her touch cool and damp and featherlight. If Na'rina pressed gently, her physical fingers would pass through Alaya's. Nonetheless, it was reassuring.

"Did you know," Alaya asked, "that I'm one of the strongest Oceadandas since Poseidon? No one's scared of that. They would be, if I were of mixed blood." She paused and a slight frown drew a line between her brows. "There are a lot of mythics being held above. It's not just Vell and me who need you right now."

Na'rina swallowed again, remembering the prisoners at the Four Corners research center. She'd had to leave them behind when they'd rescued her mother the spring before, but it had never settled well with her. "I *want* to help. I just don't know if I can."

"You can," Alaya said. "It doesn't matter if you're stronger. It matters how you think about it, just like it matters how you approach this situation. I know you'll help. Just take it one task at a time." She leaned forward, pinning Na'rina with an intense purpose behind her next words. "When you get out, head left. The tunnel will take you to a set of stairs. At the top, take the right-hand door, but be careful. The cavern beyond is rarely empty, and they like to have imps around. Vell's and my tanks are at the back of the chamber, last row."

"What?"

But Alaya didn't answer and Na'rina realized too late that the Oceadanda had been gathering her zoi aima while they'd been talking. In a brilliant flash, aqua lifeblood flooded through their hands, washing out of Alaya until she became translucent as a ghost. Na'rina choked, taken by surprise as the cool lifeblood flushed her with cold and began healing the scrapes and cuts on the twiglet's body.

"*Na!*" She tried to pull away, but Alaya followed her in the tiny tunnel, grasping Na'rina's face with translucent palms when Na'rina hid her hands behind her back.

"*Na,*" she objected again, but weakly, as all but Alaya's eyes disappeared and the flow of zoi aima ebbed. "I'll find you," she promised the oceanid.

Alaya's eyes pinched around the edges, but Na'rina couldn't tell if it was a smile or pain. And with that, Alaya vanished, leaving water on Na'rina's cheeks where her fingers had been.

A moment later, a trickling, hissing sound came from the tunnel ahead. Alaya's lifeblood within Na'rina responded. It washed through her and she gasped. Salt coated her tongue and a faint sheen covered her skin while her veins pounded in a rhythmic ebb and flow that was not caused by her heart. Cuts began pulling closed and bruises disappeared while the waves worked outward from her core. On an essential level, she knew the energy wasn't hers, but it swirled through her, competing for a place until she forcibly took control.

She blinked at the tears clouding her eyes.

Did she just—? the twiglet choked off.

The hissing became louder and water gushed around Na'rina's toes. Alaya was already at work softening the tunnel.

Na. Maybe. I hope not. Na'rina couldn't admit the possibility that Alaya was killing herself. The oceanid was her mentor, her friend, her ally. She stared at the aqua zoi aima in her shaking hands. It streamed around her own blue and green. *Let's not waste it.* She gathered it together and focused it on healing the worst of the twiglet's wounds. If she paused too long, the hissing, sucking sound of water pushing through sand would be too much for her.

It matters how you think… Alaya's words hit her anew.

Just focus on the next task. I'm going to get out, Na'rina told herself. *I'm going to find Alaya and Vell, and I'm going to go give the giant a hug. Just the next task. I'm going to get out, I'm going…*

She dug at the damp earth, keeping the litany rolling and ignoring her shaking limbs. After a moment, the twiglet joined in. *We're going to get out…*

20

"Eat. It's not poison," Felis said, exasperated.

"It smells—off," Dante answered.

"Are you calling my cooking bad?"

There came a huff and then, "No. It just smells off. Did you use nutmeg to season the oatmeal?"

"What've you got against nutmeg?"

"Um, nothing. Just doesn't seem right in oatmeal. Cinnamon makes sense, but nutmeg?"

A deep-chested growl answered. "Someone likes cinnamon, does he?"

"N-o-p-e." The word sounded muffled, like it was spoken through a mouthful of mush.

Icarus snickered where he lay on the floor "sleeping." The conversation was strained, but notable. Felis rarely said three or four words to Dante, much less held a whole conversation. Regardless, Felis was at least attempting to honor Icarus' desires.

Is Dante the mole? Icarus' amusement faded. Felis would figure it out. For now, Icarus had other things to worry about like the Fae embassy. He was already too close to the Sedanza Court but he'd known this might lead to the islands and he'd come prepared.

"Hey," Dante whispered.

Startled silence, then, "What?"

"I've got a problem maybe you can help with."

Felis' answer was long in coming and the tension mounted in the room. Sprawled across the couch, Levi cracked an eye open, but his breathing remained steady.

Felis' gesture with the oatmeal was an instant change, but that didn't mean he *wanted* to be friendly with the former stray.

"What kind of problem?" Felis finally asked.

Levi's eye closed again.

"This Fae embassy, it's connected with the Sedessan Court. Finding intel on them…" Dante and Felis left the room and their voices faded.

Icarus sat up and stretched. How was it that sleeping on a hotel floor made him ache when the forest didn't? He rubbed at his chest and growled in frustration.

Keep moving, Icarus. Movement, focus, was all that was keeping him sane in that moment. He stared at the two bowls Felis and Dante had left on the counter, trying to convince himself to find breakfast, but for once food didn't entice him.

Dante's intelligence pointed them to the embassy, so to the embassy they would go. A cold sweat broke out on Icarus' skin. *They'll kill me.* He was no longer a boy, but he wasn't foolish enough to believe he was invincible, either. Too many brawls with Silas had proven otherwise. All he had to do was stretch his back and feel the pull of the particularly long scar along his ribs.

Across the room, Levi started snoring again.

Icarus checked his phone but there were no notifications. He hit the speed dial for his sister. Three rings in, a male voice answered, "¿Aló?"

Icarus' breathing stuttered and the familiar ice ran through him. *I dialed El. Who's this?* A part of him wanted to fish out the answer, but a much stronger urge had him hanging up. Just as he was about to put the phone away, it buzzed with a different number.

Instantly, Levi's golden eyes popped open.

"Hello?" Icarus answered.

"Wer-Kadis?"

"Afre?"

Levi rolled off the couch and joined Icarus on the floor. Icarus put the phone on speaker although Levi could probably hear the faun without it.

"I just returned from Washington, and Grandmother Ver'rina's insistent she speak with you. Let me put you on speaker."

Icarus waited but didn't hear anything change. Finally, he asked, "Grandmother?"

"The dead bug's talking! Or is your voice on the wind?" came the startled reply.

Icarus frowned. *Bug?*

Levi grinned and tapped the phone in Icarus' hand. The device would look dead to Ver'rina.

"You wanted to tell me something?" Icarus asked.

"Granddaughter's Rina says you must know, ugly pine met with the shell man from Na'rina's memory. Pine seemed scared, insisted they follow through on their promises."

The only person Icarus knew that reminded Na'rina of a shell was Martin, Richard McCormick's counterpart in Intela Corp.

"Did she hear what promises?"

"Can I see sprout's protector?"

Icarus could tell Ver'rina wasn't talking to him, but he answered anyway.

"Sorry, Grandmother, these phones don't work that way." And even if he could video call her, it'd probably terrify her because he was fairly certain the phone wouldn't transmit the zoi aima she was so used to seeing.

"But you're talking out of a dead bug!"

"Peace, Ver'rina soul," Levi said.

Silence. Levi rubbed at the aspen tattoo across his bare chest, his golden eyes strained.

"Please tell me, Grandmother, if the Rina heard what the men promised," Icarus asked gently.

"Wings," she finally answered, her voice high pitched, scared.

"Wings?" A dryad with wings was incongruous in Icarus' head.

"Travel," Afre stepped in. "Ser'ored wants to see beyond these mountains."

Disgust raised Icarus' hackles. "Intela Corp already tried an experiment like that. They almost killed the entire dryad race!" It had been the banishment's underlying cause. Silas and Mona'rina discovered Intela Corp had injected dryads with a serum made to separate them from their trees, but instead of freeing them, it'd killed them like the plague and spread just as fast.

Silas had resorted to burning the infected trees.

Afre bleated. "I know, Wer-Kadis, but Ser'ored seems

convinced they can follow through on their promise and they're holding out on him."

"What did he give in exchange?" Icarus asked, trying not to snarl.

Afre softly bleated again. "Information. We think he notified them when Na'rina was most vulnerable."

"So Intela Corp *is* behind her disappearance somehow."

"Appears so," Afre said. Icarus could hear the clop of his hooves, indicating he was walking and had hit a patch of rock. He'd probably moved away from Ver'rina. "Wer-Kadis?" Afre sounded hesitant.

"*Sa?*"

"Do you—were you ever taught about the bloodline restrictions?"

Levi's claws appeared in what Icarus could only call a flinch.

He eyed the older wer-im, wishing people weren't always so complicated. *Bloodline restrictions?* Considering his background, his education had not exactly been traditional. It was a fair question, but it made his hackles rise again.

"I'm not familiar with it," he admitted, still watching Levi.

"Not many are anymore unless you're a radical group," Afre said conciliatorily. "It's something King Olbin hinted at during the summit." Afre explained what had happened and Icarus' muscles grew tenser as things began to piece together. "But Wer-Kadis, a naiad at the meeting hinted at a book. I didn't know its connection at the time, but I managed to find a copy. It's studies about Theos mythics. Some might connect the topic with Na'rina."

Levi looked stricken. *This is Levi's avalanche.* He and Ver'rina had unexpectedly birthed Theos-strength twins. And then the unthinkable:

Mona'rina had a True Born Daughter with abilities more concentrated than her own.

What does that make Na'rina? Dante's right. Mona'rina tried to hide her from the world.

Book? he mouthed to Levi. The older wer-im shrugged and Icarus believed the confusion on his face.

"What's the book?" Icarus asked Afre. As Afre told him the details, his cold sweat broke out again. He might have just jumped from visiting the Fae embassy to sneaking into the Varela library. *The embassy might have the book too.* He'd check there first.

He hung up with Afre and fiddled with his phone, then made another call.

"Hello?" Rebecca Simms answered.

"Rebecca. It's Icarus. Have you looked over the bloodwork stuff I left with you?"

"It's fascinating! Hold a second." Papers rustled. "Here it is. I asked a friend, since I'm not a geneticist, to look at it and he thought I was joshing with him. They're trying to isolate markers in someone's DNA that indicate certain characteristics. I think they're trying to figure out how different mythics do what they do, you know. Like Na'rina shocking Silas on the ship way back when. Actually," more papers shuffled, "I think the green test tube I gave you and the paperwork might be connected. My friend said the alleles in the solution are connected to an animal's ability to change color for camouflage."

Are they looking for abilities or weaknesses? Icarus thought of the disease that caused the banishment. *Or maybe they're looking for both.* "Can you guess what kind of mythic the bloodwork's from?" he asked.

"Erm…you might be the better one to guess that. What mythic can change its appearance?"

"Let me think on it," Icarus thanked her and hung up. He knew a number of mythics that could change their appearance, himself included. *What is going on?* The disparate pieces didn't fit together yet. They would. He knew if he dug enough, they would eventually make a whole puzzle.

Everything ached. Literally.

Absolutely everything ached.

How far have we come? the twiglet asked.

Na'rina twitched. She hadn't been able to feel him for some time.

She didn't respond. She was covered in mud, the tunnel behind them was pitch black, and she had no extra energy to answer his question. Usually reaching with her zoi aima would tell her, but she'd found she couldn't push it beyond the twiglet's bark anymore. She could, however, feel Alaya's zoi aima ebbing and flowing in her blood. It was no longer healing her, but its powerful, restless nature left a residual feel.

She scooped more muddy sand with her hands and shoved it behind her. Scoop, shove, scoop, shove, scoop—it felt almost like the tides. Scoo—her hand disappeared through the end of the tunnel. Na'rina blinked, so achingly numb that it took her a moment to realize she'd broken through.

Is that it?

A shaft of light graced her muddy hand. She pressed her other palm against the dirt and pushed, and cried out as the wall gave way and she tumbled into a hallway. Laying on her back, she wheezed.

The hallway's floor was smooth, but the walls and ceiling retained the tunnel's rough, natural texture. Utility lights hung near the ceiling. After hours—or was it days?—of being in pitch blackness, Na'rina blinked repeatedly to adjust to the dull light.

Cackling echoed down the hall and her heart spiked.

Imps, the twiglet whimpered.

Flipping over, Na'rina scrambled back into her tiny tunnel. She pushed mud and rocks into the opening to hide it just as four imps capered into sight. She hadn't fully covered the opening and she could see them through a hole at the very top of the oozing mud.

They pushed and jostled each other, careening off the walls like they'd been drinking wine all day. They probably hadn't; imps just acted that way. Passing her hiding spot, one yelped and hopped backwards, lifting his foot from a pile of mud.

His companions howled with laughter.

He ignored them, staring at the footprint he'd just made. Curious, he slid his toes through it, then took a deep sniff.

"Water? Salt? Sap?" He leaned over to taste the mud.

Na'rina shrank back and the twiglet trembled. They might be able to handle one imp. But four? She clutched her bleeding hands. It was all she could do to control their shaking.

I'm easy prey.

Na'rina didn't respond. The twiglet wasn't wrong—if the imps didn't tear her apart for the sticks in the twiglet's body, they'd haul her around like a trophy and eventually someone else would see her. But neither was she going to feed his fears.

Another imp pointed at the one tasting the mud and said, "idget?"

The taster spit and pegged his companion in the nose. The imp screeched and lunged, and a tussle ensued with all four of them rolling down the hallway until they were too far away to see. But Na'rina could hear them, and they were moving in the other direction.

Na'rina sighed, wilting. *Thank the stars imps are easily distracted.*

The twiglet continued to tremble.

Na'rina cautiously peeked out again to find the hallway empty. On shaky legs, she exited the tunnel and wandered to the left as Alaya had instructed. To Alaya, the distance wasn't that far, but for Na'rina's short legs, it was like climbing a high peak near her home. She rounded a small bend and stopped, swaying in dismay.

Stairs. They stood almost as tall as she did.

Welcome to my world, the twiglet grumbled. *No one makes things twiglet-sized.* His oozing pessimism leaked lethargy into her limbs.

Na'rina pushed off the wall before it took hold. Just like Icarus, Alaya believed in her, and she'd lose all her leaves before she let the Oceadanda down. *One stair at a time*, she said. *That's all we have to focus on.*

Na'rina groaned, hauling herself up the first step.

Step one, the twiglet counted.

By step six, her limbs were shaking so bad she tucked herself into the corner of the stair and sat, letting feeling flow through her body until the next stair didn't make her want to weep. As she recovered, she rubbed at her arms. *My saplings are gone.* In the twiglet's body, that wasn't surprising, but she still found the absence disturbing. *Will they come back when I emerge? Or will our melding kill them?* She shook her head, unwilling to consider the possibility as she focused on the next step. *I'll never discount how much work life is for a twiglet again*, she said to him, keeping her tone light.

He hunched in on himself. *Nice thought, Drydanda, but I would have quit by now.* Na'rina's shoulders twitched, trying to follow his actions. *I am a weak thing.*

Na'rina cringed. Admittedly, she'd been surprised by how much effort *everything* was for the twiglet, but that didn't mean he was weak. And if she let him wallow, the depressed lethargy would be even harder to ignore on top of her own exhaustion.

Without you, she said, *I'd be dead. Alaya and Vell wouldn't have any hope, and both North and South America would be facing life without Drydandas. Your shoulders might be small, but you've given a very valuable thing—hope.*

The twiglet froze inside like a startled doe.

After a second, he straightened and cocked his head in curiosity. In his sudden fascination, he forgot to remain relaxed, and Na'rina's head tried to tilt awkwardly as she threw her leg up over the next stair. *There's your mother if something happens to you,* the twiglet said.

Na'rina momentarily squeezed her eyes closed. *Mona'rina's ill.*

He tilted his head the other way. *But you could help her heal, right? Like Alaya helped us?*

He may as well have snapped a branch off Na'rina's aspens. He shied away from her pain, saying, *Never mind. I meant nothing by it.*

Na'rina couldn't leave him like that. As she pushed herself to attack the next stair, she said to him, *You know, when this is all over, you'll have helped not one, but two, Drydandas.*

You mean—you mean I'm a hero, like Hercules?

Or like Pegasus.

Wasn't he the son of Medusa? The twiglet shuddered and Na'rina almost slid off the next stair.

That's beside the point. According to the stories, he helped some powerful people, like Hercules. Now Na'rina questioned if the stories were even true, especially after Afre telling her about Zeus, Poseidon, and Hades, but she didn't mention that.

Or maybe I'm like Mitto.

Who?

Haven't you heard of Ara'marxia and Mitto?

The names tugged at the Collective Wisdom but Na'rina ignored it. Maybe telling her would help the twiglet.

Tell me, she encouraged.

Ten, he counted, showing he had been counting stairs during their discussion. Then he continued, *The story says that an Amazon Drydanda, Ara'marxia, was trying to mitigate massive flooding after a severe burn in the forest. All was going well until a naiad—the story doesn't name her—from the Amazon River who'd gotten displaced by the flooding thought Ara'marxia was cutting her off from returning home. She brought a flash flood against the Drydanda and stranded her on a burned section of land.*

It happened that Mitto, a twiglet, was stranded with her. Across the muddy water they could see the tall mahoganies, palms, and Ramón trees. Mitto lamented that if only he was one of those trees, then he could sink his toes deep into the ground and walk them to safety.

Ara'marxia was desperate. Some say she melded with the twiglet and wove their zoi aima into a stick. Others say she held Mitto's zoi aima in her hands and breathed it into the mahogany branch, transforming him into the tree. Either way, she transformed Mitto into a walking mahogany. He then carried her across the flood to safety.

Na'rina rolled onto the top landing, wheezing. She stared at the bulges in the ceiling. *What a strange story.* To have become a mahogany tree, Mitto would have had to let himself become nothing but zoi aima held in the Drydanda's complete control. Na'rina had never heard of such a thing, but if it helped the twiglet, she'd give it water.

Then you are indeed like Mitto, carrying me to safety.

The twiglet glowed.

Na'rina tried to calm her breathing. Thirsty, she pooled water in her hand again. Although there wasn't enough of Alaya's zoi aima to heal her now, there was plenty for the water trick. She gulped down several palmfuls until she sighed in relief. Satisfied, she turned to the next obstacle and groaned softly.

Problem? The twiglet perked up.

Doors weren't made for twiglets either, were they? The doorknob they were staring at was about three feet off the ground. Even if Na'rina stretched her arms as far above her head as she could, she'd need another foot or so to reach it.

The twiglet was silent, stumped, and then he exclaimed, *Ha! See that bulge in the wall?* The bulge he indicated was at the back of the landing about a foot off the ground. *If we stand on it, we'll be a bit closer.*

Na'rina eyed the distance between the bulge and the knob.

We'll still have to jump.

But not as far.

No pessimistic poison soured his words. Na'rina smiled. She pushed to stand and winced at the pain in her splintered fingers.

Maybe peek beneath the door first? the twiglet suggested.

Na'rina groaned softly, crouching to press an eye to the crack below the door. She blinked.

Cave spears?

Na'rina pinched her lips tight to keep from chuckling. *Stalagmites. There are probably stalactites hanging from the ceiling too.*

Are those the tanks the Oceadanda spoke of?

The twiglet referred to the long silver containers lined up between the stalagmites. They were the only things that could be Alaya's "tanks," so Na'rina just hummed. *See any movement?*

They searched, barely breathing.

Seems safe.

Na'rina agreed, although she couldn't shake the dread curdling in her stomach. She hated her reaction to fear. If she wasn't sweating sap, she was fighting not to throw up, and her reactions were almost overwhelming in the twiglet's small body. As she straightened and hauled herself up on the bulge in the wall—it was very much like crawling up the stairs—she swallowed bile. Then she carefully pivoted and stared at the knob.

Time to leap, the twiglet encouraged.

Na'rina blinked, fighting tears that she refused to let the twiglet feel. She leaped for the knob and caught it, her feet hanging free. Pain blossomed in her fingers. Na'rina whimpered, almost losing hold. She tightened her thin, knotty fingers until the knuckles threatened to pop and pushed sap to her palms to stick them to the brass. Then carefully, she rocked back and forth, turning the knob with her weight.

The lock finally came free of its frame, and she whimpered again, this time in relief. She let go, dropping to the floor to pull the door ajar just far enough to peer through. It still appeared clear, so she slipped into the room.

The twiglet whooped, forgetting to keep the sound internal.

Na'rina clamped down on the urge to cry out hard enough to make her cough. Cringing, she ducked behind a stalagmite and waited to see if anyone came to investigate. No one did.

Sorry, the twiglet apologized.

It's okay, she said, *we're almost to Alaya.*

El and Sala waited to approach Riviera until dawn, anchoring off the back side of a small island called the Hook. Once dawn grayed the horizon, El swam to Riviera to avoid checking in a Varela boat at the docks and alerting Ambassador Marquin of her visit.

Reaching the beach, El stripped out of her wet suit and changed back into the clothing she'd stored in a dry bag while crossing. They were lucky it was a calm morning. Sala wasn't a swimmer, for obvious reasons, and she'd gone incorporeal to fly above the ethereally calm water. A storm was forecast for the coming night and, as often happened, the ocean seemed to hold its breath in preparation.

Icarus would love this. Instinctively, El reached for her phone, then cursed Roberto for his theft. *What would everyone do with the engagement shenanigans if I don't show up for the ball?*

A streak of flame zipped toward her from inland and morphed into Sala. The tall, slender elemental had arrived before her, leading El to this particular beach because it was the same stretch of sand the Fae had found her wandering after the quake. It was rock-strewn and littered with tall grass, driftwood, shells, dead lobsters and jellyfish. Not a desired tourist destination.

"Where's the shack you spoke of?" El asked.

Sala said she'd found her way out of the caves through a wooden shack.

"There." Sala pointed. "I think it used to be a guard station but now it's empty. The back of it's built against the hill and there's a door that leads into the cave systems."

"Weren't the holding cells buried?" El asked. Sand and shells crunched softly underfoot as they walked.

"Maybe from the embassy side," Sala agreed, "but this is the way I got out that night. I think it's also how they found the giant."

"I should have wondered about that," El admitted ruefully.

"A Sedessan who admits fault? I didn't know that existed."

"We're not all bad."

"But there are no good stories about your people." Sala shrugged and pulled the shack's door open. They stepped into darkness that smelled of old wood and mildew. Flame flickered to life on Sala's palm, revealing a rotting floor with gaping holes that showed through to the framework and sand below. Sala pointed to a door hanging on one hinge at the back.

"How'd you end up in the holding cell?" El asked.

Sala dropped her hand and her flame snuffed out. In the darkness, El blinked her second lens into place to find Sala hunched protectively with her arms crossed over her thin frame.

El kept walking, giving Sala time as they entered the tunnel beyond the shack.

"The Salamanders have an agreement with the Fae," Sala finally said. "We provide an attachment to the queen. A single elemental who serves five years as a flame guard. In exchange, they find and protect homes for us where the humans won't destroy our habitat." Thick sorrow coated the explanation.

El didn't need to refer to her mental study to know why. "Five years away—alone—must diminish the elemental," she said. Fire elementals lived near the equator in places like Brazil and the Congo. They needed the temperature to survive or their flame would slowly die. The Fae Queen, however, was a winter being who held her court in upper Russia. "How long does it take for the representative to recover?"

"We don't." Sala grunted as she stubbed her toe on a rock. "Not fully."

What a terrible arrangement. El wouldn't put it past Queen Lárissa to have made the stipulations just to see the elementals sacrifice for what they needed. "You were being sent as the next representative?"

"I was," Sala whispered. "I was supposed to meet with Ambassador Marquin for transportation but never made it there. I don't know what that means for my people."

"Did they say why they locked you up?"

"*Na.* I was taken from the waiting room outside the ambassador's office. Thought I was being led to him. Instead, they locked me in a cell and never spoke to me."

Odd. In most hostage situations, the prisoner was told something, even if it was a lie. "The ambassador suspected you of the earthquake because you voiced dissent with being a flame guard?" Something jabbed El's fingers where she trailed them along the tunnel wall. She jerked her hand away, but whatever it was, it hadn't drawn blood. She carefully touched the wall again and kept walking.

"Not I, but there is a faction within the Salamanders who do not agree with the arrangement," Sala said. "It would not have been the first time they attempted an attack on the Fae."

They continued walking in silence.

Sala never made it to Marquin. Just as Sophia and El suspected, it all seemed to come back to Marquin's human secretary, Thomas Dominguez. Usually, visitors met with Dominguez before making it to the ambassador. *And there are a lot more visitors lately due to Mateo Inverro asking the ambassador to help negotiate stronger alliances for him.* Was Dominguez using those negotiations without Mateo's knowledge or was Mateo working with Dominguez? There were undercurrents in the Court lately regarding the Inverros' iron hold. After years of simply maintaining their position, they were now stepping out to strengthen it even more. Roberto's courtship offer was part of that. Were the happenings under the embassy part of it too?

A portion of the wall had caved in and El slowed to sidestep the rubble while she pondered.

She was fairly certain Marquin knew nothing about the embassy's prisoners. *But what about the Inverros?* They *might* be oblivious as well. El scoffed silently. *Too much coincidence,* Icarus would say. At least one Sedessan was involved, if not a whole family. *What about Roberto?* El sighed. She couldn't rule him out. With the courtship negotiations, that was troubling. *Why would anyone want to capture mythics? For what purpose?*

"Sala?"

The elemental hummed.

"How long were you detained?"

"About a fortnight, I'd guess."

"And they kept you in that cell the whole time?"

"*Na.* You did not see this when you protected me from Roberto?"

El shook her head and explained, "I glossed over your memories and did not dig." It was like looking at a jar of coins. She'd found the starting point when Sala arrived at the embassy and the end point when she'd been found wandering the beach and glossed over everything in between without seeing specific coins inside.

"I always assumed the viewing was instant," Sala said. "They held me in a tiny, isolated cell. Twice they brought me out to draw blood but that's all they did." Sala's lifeblood condensed to a dense flame around her core. "Just before you showed up, something happened. They threw everyone into the bigger cave. We only spent a day there before you and the giant made your move."

El mulled that over. She hadn't been under the embassy long enough to find out anything other than they were jailing powerful mythics. Perhaps she'd escaped too soon.

"Ho—" She cut off, hearing a scuffing ahead.

Even with her second lens, nothing lit up, but as she listened, the scuffing resolved into footsteps.

"The tunnel T's ahead," Sala whispered.

If the person passing by could see psychically, Sala's and El's zoi aima would give them away. El motioned for Sala to head back; the elemental would see the gesture even in the dark. They retreated to the caved-in portion and hid behind the rubble. El listened, peeking out occasionally. Maybe she could catch a glimpse of the other person's lifeblood.

Na'rina gaped at the cavern they'd entered. It shimmered with the same utility lights as the hallway, but here water trickled down the walls and dribbled off the stalactites like a melting candle oozing long drips. Na'rina couldn't decide if it was beautiful or disturbing. There were no roots, so although the water made the room *look* alive with motion, there wasn't anything *actually* alive. She shuddered. What she could see, or rather feel as a heavy buzzing in the air, was the electricity running to the dozens of tanks lining the floor.

Which one holds the Oceadanda? the twiglet whispered, his desire to help Alaya so strong that it pressed against her ribs. Alaya's zoi aima responded, pounding around her heart.

Na'rina shook off her amazement. *Alaya said they were at the back.* She and the twiglet had entered through a side door. The main entrance was a huge, rough, natural archway to their right with a portcullis built into the ceiling that was calcified in place.

If that was the front, then the back was to her left. Na'rina scampered to a stalagmite farther back. The effort made her gasp and her legs wobble like saplings. The pounding in her blood picked up, steadying her by driving oxygen to her legs. Na'rina wasn't sure how long the residual effect would last, but she welcomed its help.

She scanned the cavern again. She couldn't see any guards but that didn't mean there wasn't someone…she hadn't even considered cameras until that moment.

Work the problem, love, Icarus would say.

She scanned for cameras but didn't see any of the tell-tale signs she knew. No tiny red lights or bulbous glass globes, no stream of electricity to something unseen.

I can't reach or disable cameras right now even if they do exist. If there's a

214

control box or something, it's probably by the entrance, but I still don't know how to disable it without zoi aima.

She'd learned to control human electronics using her lifeblood, but she'd never learned to *use* electronics, just to enter them on an energy level. Icarus had started teaching her about cell phones recently, but she didn't figure that would help much here. *I can't disarm them even if they exist. I'll just have to avoid them if I see them.*

Na'rina scampered to the closest tank. She couldn't see through the domed top because the tank sat on a metal platform that left the bottom open for the tubes and cables snaking out beneath. Dismay filled Na'rina as she gazed up at it. She needed to see inside.

Like the stairs? the twiglet asked.

Like the stairs, she agreed.

She hauled herself on up, kicking the tank in the process. It clanged dully. Na'rina trembled, lying low across the dome while she waited to see if someone would come investigate. When no one did, she pushed to a sitting position and studied the contraption beneath her.

It's cold, the twiglet said.

It's metal. Na'rina slid along it, searching for a nameplate or something to tell her what was inside. As she neared the end, the metal flickered and turned transparent. Inside, a light flicked on, revealing the heart-shaped face of an unfamiliar oceanid with freckles flecking her otherwise white skin. She floated, suspended in fluid, her hair drifting around her shoulders.

Is she alive?

Instead of answering, Na'rina just focused on the aqua lifeblood creeping through the oceanid's face. Compared to the relentless tidal ebb and flow from Alaya's gift, this oceanid's zoi aima was water seeping from a swamp.

Na'rina carefully slid across to the next tank. She peeked inside and kept going. Each face took its place in a long list of mythics she couldn't forget, starting with the captured faun she'd seen in the Four Corners research center months before. She loathed leaving them.

At the next tank, Na'rina glanced in, saw it wasn't Alaya, and was about to move on when she did a double take. It was a dryad, which wasn't surprising. Disturbing but not surprising. What caught her was the face's familiarity.

Friend of yours? the twiglet asked.

It can't be, Na'rina answered. Anyone she knew would be dead this far from her tree. But she *knew* the dryad's face. The woman's skin was a deep chocolate brown enhanced by the greenish fluid she floated in. Small acorns hung from her lobes by the stems of oak leaves. Except for the fine wrinkles around her eyes, the dryad could have been Mia'dry, a member of Na'rina's council. *It's one of the oak twin's elders. They disappeared months ago.*

Na'rina checked the nearby tanks and found two more dryads who, by their coloring and race, were from the same forest. One was even a loblolly pine with scale-bark skin and long, needle-like hair. Loblollies were native to North America.

I can't leave them. But waking them this far from their trees would kill them. Na'rina wasn't sure what had been done to keep them alive in the first place, but she had no way to get them home.

I can't help them right now. The truth hurt in her core.

Are you alright? the twiglet whispered.

Na. She laid her hands on the tank over the loblolly's face in silent apology. *These are my people, and I can't help them. There are so many here!* She scanned the tanks, aching to do something.

Work the problem, love. She grasped Icarus' words. *Start by finding Alaya.*

Na'rina moved on, numbness creeping over her at each face she left behind.

She was almost at the cavern's far side when she found herself staring at a mahogany-skinned dryad with leaves floating around her head. It took a moment to realize it was Vell's auburn hair because, unlike in her zoi aima cast image, the leaves were browning. Sedated, Vell'marxia appeared softer. The pinching around her mouth was relaxed, leaving only faint creases in the skin at the corners of her lips.

Perhaps we should wake the Oceadanda first? the twiglet suggested.

Na'rina agreed. She'd much rather have Alaya awake before Vell. She slid to the next tank. When the lid became transparent, she gasped.

Alaya's skin was like translucent wax. Dull, aqua zoi aima crept through her body, focused around her heart. Na'rina stared at that slow ebb and flow, relief making her lightheaded. *She's alive.* Without the ocean's currents, the constant motion, Alaya couldn't rebuild the zoi aima she'd expended.

We need to get her out of here. Na'rina scanned the tank. The top was smooth, but a control panel jutted out one side. Sliding backward, Na'rina looked at it upside down and laid her hands on top.

On the *Observer*, she'd been able to open doors by "reaching" into them with her zoi aima and reading what the energy was supposed to do inside. It was similar to how she'd picked up the rocks earlier.

But she hadn't been able to extend her zoi aima for a while now. Her hands started to shake. *Why didn't I think of that!* She tried to gather and push her energy out her palms anyway. She got as far as coating her skin. When she withdrew her touch, water coated the control panel, but did nothing to the electronic itself. Tears pricked at her eyes and she sniffled.

Drydanda? the twiglet asked, alarmed.

Na'rina struggled to confess her failure. *I can't wake her. Not like she hoped.* Like the words gave it life, panic threatened to choke her again.

Reacting to her terror, the twiglet quickly suggested, *Pull the tubes out maybe?*

Several large tubes fed into the tank's sides, probably keeping whatever the fluid was fresh. Along with them were the power cables plugged into the top ends.

I've no idea what'll happen if I pull those, Na'rina admitted, but the twiglet had thrown her the branch she needed.

Oh. The twiglet sat down with a hefty sigh as he picked up what she planned to do and Na'rina sighed right along with him. At least it came out quiet.

I don't know what else to do, she said, and slid off the tank to inspect the power plug. Just as she did, a familiar cackling echoed in the cavern.

More imps. They walked between the tanks, inspecting them. Na'rina assumed they were checking all the connections, but she couldn't see much beyond their feet and the occasional flicker of a sticky note getting stuck to a tank.

They'd started on the cavern's far side, but the imps moved fast. If she was going to get Alaya out, it had to be now. Na'rina touched the power plug and electricity buzzed beneath her fingertips like millions of tiny ant feet. *I've pulled energy from a volcano and a storm before. It's all just energy.* The pep talk didn't help.

She wrapped both hands around the cable, braced herself, and "pulled" from the flowing electricity.

All at once, the lights flickered and went out, Na'rina flew backward with a scream, and the imps cried out in surprise.

Na'rina slammed into the wall and slumped to the floor, her limbs quivering in aftershocks. The lights flickered back on. She tried to quiet the twiglet's whimpering but neither of them was in complete control.

I'm sorry, she apologized. Had the imps missed her scream under their own surprised cries?

I'm a terrible Mitto! the twiglet sobbed.

Voices drifted into the cavern from the main entrance and the imps' chatter went silent.

Na'rina finally managed to roll over to crawl beneath Alaya's tank. A man entered, his voice becoming louder as he spoke to someone. *That's Master Thomas!* Cowering into a ball, she prayed he wouldn't come to the back of the cavern.

Voices farther up the tunnel grew louder.

Come on, show me who you are.

Two figures passed from left to right at the T-intersection ahead. Words trickled in their wake.

"—down here?"

"Hiding, perhaps? She worried—" and the conversation faded.

El made a snap decision and took off after them. She recognized Thomas Dominguez' lifeblood. He was the only one she knew for sure was part of the embassy operation and this was too good an opportunity to pass up.

Sala hissed in surprise, "Sedessan!"

El careened around the corner in time to catch the two figures turning right. She ran, softening her steps and flattening against the wall as she neared the corner.

A moment later, Sala joined her. Sudden heat prickled the skin on El's arm.

"What are you doing?" Sala asked.

"It's Dominguez…and a salamander."

"That can't be!"

El took in the flame running through Sala.

"Stay here," she advised. "You're too hot…they'll sense you."

"El—"

El ducked around the corner. Ahead, she found a cavern trickling with water. Utility lights lit stalagmites and reflected off the metallic domes of the refrigerators El had seen above, lying flat as round coffins.

The dark-skinned salamander with Dominguez froze like a startled animal. "—is this?"

El heard the tail end of the question.

"An experiment." Dominguez tapped a coffin with his cane. With a metallic thud and a hiss, it popped open.

El crept closer while the salamander stepped up to peek inside. Something stung El's shoulder and she winced, glancing back to find a streak of flame hovering behind her. It made Sala's energy signature tiny, but also made her vulnerable. El bit back a curse.

"I told you to stay back," she whispered. The flame poked her shoulder again. El hissed. Sala couldn't speak in her current form, but apparently, she didn't mind leaving tiny burns on El's skin.

They snuck closer, using the forest of stalagmites to follow the path up to the silver coffins where El crouched behind a long, waxy looking wall. They were just in time to see the salamander step back in horror.

"Is she dead?" the woman asked. Her lifeblood had sparked like Sala's did when threatened.

Sala hovered so close that El tilted her head away from the heat. The elemental seemed to shake.

"Just sleeping," Dominguez assured. "She wouldn't want to wake here. Believe me, Lady Ignatious, she's just fine. As is Sala."

El glanced at the tiny flame beside her.

"Sala's in *here*!" the woman took another step back and flames flickered around her fingers as she gestured at the room.

Dominguez sighed and rubbed at his mustache. "No, no, my lady. She's…"

He's stalling. El only half listened as Dominguez rambled about the earthquake and the aftermath with the Fae as she searched the cavern. Suddenly, the troll-blooded captain who had checked El into the holding cell stepped out of a doorway, raised a gun, and shot. The round barely whispered. The gun didn't have a silencer. It was something else.

Lady Ignatious gasped and slapped a hand to her neck, pulling a dart from it.

"What is this?!" She faltered and grabbed a nearby tank. The air around her wavered with heat, forcing Dominguez to step back. Two more darts whispered through the room. One hit her neck again; the other sank into the back of the hand she raised. She hissed, fury rippling in the blue flame that rose over her skin. She tried to step toward Dominguez and hit her knees instead.

Dominguez grunted and clocked her in the temple with a sharp whack of his cane. The woman collapsed.

Sala spun in a tight circle and El could imagine her panic. She was just thrilled the salamander didn't ignite the whole cavern on fire.

"You couldn't have shot her sooner?" Dominguez' question was soft but laced with frustration. "Get her situated."

The captain opened an empty coffin and gave orders to the men who entered behind him. One of them picked up the unconscious Lady Ignatious.

Sala began zipping around El's head. El patted the air, trying to get the elemental to calm down. They needed out of there before anyone noticed them. El moved to slip away. Sala streaked toward the back of Dominguez' head.

Lady Ignatious' coffin closed with a hiss and a hum and a distinctive gurgle. Sala stopped dead.

This doesn't make sense. They'd tried to tranq Lady Ignatius. Why would they now throw her in a coffin and fill it with liquid that would kill her?

The men continued to work around the coffin as Sala zipped back to her.

"Creeps me out," one of them muttered.

Dominguez paused in the doorway, glancing back. The soldier ducked and his companions cringed at his attention. "Treat her carefully," he finally said. "Abilities die with a body. We can't build the future using desiccated husks." Then he turned away, his cane clicking on the floor.

He seemed so—nonthreatening. A human serving the interests of the Fae or possibly a Sedessan house. *No one ducks away like that from a lackey.* El had seriously miscalculated somewhere. She was about to slip away when Sala zipped forward again, heading for the guards around Lady Ignatius' container. She left a wave of heat in her wake that rippled the air.

"Sala!" El hissed, but the elemental didn't pause.

Suddenly, a grayish-green imp popped up from between the rows of coffins, squealed in delight, and tried to catch Sala like she was a firefly. He got too close and howled as his clothes caught fire.

Another imp, not registering his companion's pain, jumped off a tank and batted Sala toward the floor and into a stalagmite. Instantly, he ignited into a torch.

The thump of Sala's impact was buried under his scream. The stalagmite shattered and the elemental wavered, stunned. At the commotion, the captain spun.

"Intruder!" He rushed toward the far wall. At first El thought he was going to close the main portcullis gate where she'd entered, but instead he shattered the glass on a large control box hanging on the wall and started flipping switches.

Red lights flickered to life above. El snarled. The lights highlighted piping that lined the ceiling in a massive sprinkler system.

El flipped up her hood and bolted forward, dodging silver coffins as she ran for Sala's now spinning flame. Her heat must have diminished with being stunned because imps were also converging on her. Each coffin El passed flickered. The top portions were becoming translucent at her motion.

The captain noticed her. He began shouting orders to his startled men. One jumped and raced for another control panel near the main entrance. This time El was sure they were closing the calcified portcullis. Her time was slipping away.

The heat around Sala was almost unbearable. Imps backed away, crying now in dismay. A loud hiss sounded overhead. The piping above groaned and then water rained out of the spouts.

"NO!"

But a brave—or stupid—imp had just batted at Sala, pushing her higher, and water poured onto her streak of flame. It propelled her into the nearest coffin and then washed her toward the floor.

El vaulted over the imps, heading for where the elemental vanished. They screeched and one tried to hit her. She slapped it on the forehead and it crumpled.

El's feet hit the floor and she ducked to find Sala flickering beneath the tank she'd just jumped. El cupped her hands around the flame, wincing as it burned her. *Heat's good*, she assured herself even as the pain blossomed. *Heat means she's alive.*

Sopping wet herself, she pulled the cupped flame as close as she dared, and darted for the exit.

The guard at the control panel pressed something and the heavy portcullis above shuddered, breaking the calcification encasing it, and then slammed into the floor. The debris and stalagmites below, however, crunched under its weight, and kept the portcullis from fully sealing.

El eyed the gap. *I'm small enough*. She shook water away from her face and slid for the opening. Debris scattered in her wake, and then she was past the portcullis and racing away down the hall.

Sweat and water poured down El's face, burning in her eyes, but she refused to un-cup her hands even as Sala's heat blistered her skin.

Someone shouted behind her as she hit the guard station's decrepit door with her shoulder. The wood splintered, and then she was on the beach, blinking even harder due to the rising sun.

Although the beach sported some lava rock formations, it was far too open. El scanned the dunes and beyond until she spotted a dip in the terrain. Grass grew tall in the area, making it appear almost level with the rest of the land. Running for it, El slid into the head-high stalks. She used her elbows to crawl farther into the grass, then peeked out before stepping free onto one of the lava formations.

Thank you, Icarus. She hopped from rock to rock like they used to do as kids. She dropped onto her back on the far side just as shouts echoed from the guard station and three men emerged. Two imps followed on their heels.

El seethed in vexation. Her false trail wouldn't fool the imps with their sharp sense of smell. Keeping one hand cradled around Sala, she pulled out the comb she'd brought from the study and ran her thumbnail along the tines. Small knicks caught at her nail and she counted until she found the set with three apiece. She broke them off and returned the comb to her pocket while pinching the broken tines.

With a quick peek, El found one guard beating at the grass with a baton. His two companions watched. Meanwhile, the imps ducked into the grass around his sweeps, tittering with delight.

El tossed the tines into the grass and ducked back down, waiting.

A moment later, a high-pitched sneeze ruffled the grass, followed by two more sneezes from a slightly different location. The imps popped out of the grass at a run, sneezing so violently that they flopped onto the sand behind the men, breathing heavily.

"Are they allergic?" one guard asked.

"Useless," the captain said. "Whoever it was scented the spot with cocainic. It kills their sense of smell for hours." He scanned the area, then cursed. "They're probably long gone by now."

His companions looked crestfallen. "You'll explain to Señior Dominguez, right?"

They shrank at his withering glare. "Let's go. The person must have known imps were involved, which means we *all* get to talk to Señior Dominguez."

El had to admit, the captain might have earned his rank. She'd brought the comb precisely because she knew imps were involved. Each tine contained a tiny slot full of *cocainic*, a derivative of cocaine to which imps tended to have an allergic reaction. A few tines killed an imp's smell. The whole comb would kill them in a small space. Paired with the pen she'd snagged, she could even use the tines in the pen's casing like a blow gun.

Once the men disappeared, she waited another few minutes in case they were watching from the shack, and then she relaxed, clutching Sala's small flame. The heat was dying and when El opened her fingers, the flame barely glowed above her palm, revealing a tiny diamond inside.

El blew gently like she would on an ember. It flickered. She tore off a piece of her shirt's hem and laid it below the flame, then blew again.

"Come on, Sala," she urged. "Fight!"

Nothing happened. El retreated to her mental study, desperately flipping through everything she had on flame elementals again. She found nothing on reviving them from a drenching, so she widened her search to elementals in general.

"Maybe an outside flame will help you." *Closest source of fire?* The street lanterns. It was still early enough they might be burning.

El peeked at the guard station, found it quiet, and emerged, heading toward Riviera's city center.

El breathed her relief when she reached a street with the gas lanterns and found it empty. Not many roamed at this early hour, but it'd be hard to explain her shoving her hands into a burning flame.

She gazed up at the closest one.

Seven or eight feet, she guessed, *I need a ladder, or a box, or*—

Across the street, El spotted an alley courtyard set up with metal tables and chairs for guests of a nearby café. She darted across and back, hauling a chair behind her one-handed. She settled the chair and stepped up. When she opened her fingers, she found a multifaceted diamond about the size of her pinky nail. Fire flickered inside.

"No, no, no," She pinched the diamond between thumb and forefinger—it felt like a sun-warmed rock—and held it into the lantern.

"Come on." El glanced up and down the street. Still empty. Now that the diamond was close to the flame, it became slick to the touch, but didn't reignite. "Please, Sala."

She'd finally made a friend and their first adventure together had snuffed her out. El tried to hold the diamond directly in the flame and yelped softly, singeing her fingers. The diamond clinked into the bottom of the metal lantern.

"More heat maybe," El said around the finger in her mouth. She searched around the outside base until she found the knob to turn up the flame. The lantern roared faintly like a mini blowtorch.

Something popped, and the glass dome shattered.

With another yelp, El tumbled from the chair. Fire flew from the lantern and into the alley across the street, where it settled over the flagstones in the form of a thin woman.

"Ha!" El grabbed the overturned chair and waddled back to the alley just as the flame subsided into an unconscious Sala.

"Scared the snot out of me," she scolded, kneeling beside the woman. Unsure about Sala's temperature, El grabbed a nearby broom and poked her side.

She twitched.

"Sala." El poked again and the wooden broom burst into flame.

El yelped a third time and pitched the broom onto Sala's chest.

Can't hurt, right?

"You should have left me," Sala rasped.

Surprised, El cradled her scorched fingers. "We can figure this out."

"He killed her!" Sala disagreed, sitting up and holding her head between her knees.

"Maybe not—"

The temperature spiked and El flinched, feeling like she'd been hit with a wave from the oven.

"Sala, she—"

"She's gone! Don't you get it?"

"We don't—"

"I do! He immersed her in liquid." Terror glazed her amber eyes. "He tricked her, acting all helpful, and then he killed her!"

El inched closer. "We'll figure it out," she tried again, reaching to grasp Sala's shaking hands. Touching someone to give comfort was not usually her go-to, but Sala needed something to ground her.

El barely touched Sala and the elemental recoiled, scuttling backward like a crab. "Don't you dare!"

El gaped, her hand stretched out dumbly. "I'm just—"

"What? Helping? Like you helped the giant into a death sentence? What kind of *help* do you have planned for me?"

El's anger spiked. "Do you know what would happen if I contradicted Roberto? It'd be worse than what the giant's facing!"

"You're a coward! You're no better than that man in the cavern."

El's brain stuttered and, on instinct, her face went blank. What in boiling frogs' blood was going on?

Sala snorted and fire crawled over her skin. "Friend indeed…you don't know what that even means."

Sala sparked and El flinched. Instead of torching the alley, however, the elemental whooshed, shifting to flame and vanishing over the rooftops.

El stared at her burned hand and winced. *Shouldn't have expected anything else, I guess.*

Someone shouted from the street, yelling about the shattered lantern. With a sigh, El pushed to her feet and wandered away.

Icarus stared at the glassy, aquamarine ocean. He could feel the calm before a massive storm in his bones. The bow of the *Pour Decisions*, a catamaran Dante had rented, speared through the water, rippling the smooth surface as they cruised for the Sedanza Islands.

Levi lowered himself into a cross-legged position beside him. Under his tan, his skin was waxy.

"A storm brews within you," he observed, swallowing.

Icarus didn't even know where to start but finally he withdrew two things from his pocket. The transponder he flipped on and then put away; the flash drive he held up for Levi to see. The plastic bag he'd put the drive in to protect it stuck to his fingers.

Levi frowned. "Looks like a beetle."

It was so close to Ver'rina's *dead bug* that Icarus huffed a startled laugh. "You remember how we got this?"

"A Sedessan contacted Lady Simms."

Lady Simms? Apparently, Rebecca had impressed Levi. "Specifically, Rosharu hired a Sedessan to pass it along to Na'rina. He posed as Rosharu's lawyer to do it. The lawyer part could be the Sedessan's cover for that single job, but more likely it indicates a long-term working history with Rosharu."

Levi stared at the horizon, and then he grunted. "You think the

Sedessan is rooted in Intela Corp?"

"Remember how the Rockies dwarves were tricked?"

"I do not know that story," Levi admitted.

"Prince Elbert and a group of his friends disappeared under suspicious circumstances last spring," Icarus explained. "King Bross searched for him, making a lot of noise while he did. A Sedessan showed up promising information if the dwarves would agree to a meeting outside of the Rockies—"

Levi snorted. "He fell for it."

"He did. He took a small retinue and left for the meeting. He's not been seen since."

"And now the dwarves search for their king."

"*Na.* Now their Appalachian cousins search for the entire Rockies race. We suspect the Rockies dwarves were blackmailed by the capture of their prince and king because they all disappeared a few days after King Bross."

Levi's face darkened and he rubbed a hand over the branches on his arm. "Ver'rina is right. I have been out of touch too long."

Icarus didn't disagree. Silence fell until he pocketed the flash drive again and sighed. "I don't believe in coincidences. We ran into a Sedessan lawyer with Intela Corp, the dwarves disappeared after a Sedessan contact, now we're headed to the Sedanza Islands—it's all connected somehow."

"Deep thoughts," Levi said, "but they do not explain the storm brewing within you. You are afraid of our destination."

Icarus stiffened, startled. Suddenly a wave of disinterest washed over him like he'd walked into a wall of humidity.

Felis started to power down the boat.

"Keep going," Icarus ordered.

"Why?" Dante asked. "Do we really want to see the Fae embassy?"

"Keep going," he said again. "It's the Fae's deterrent. We have to push through it."

Felis slowly powered the boat back up. He appeared sleepy at the wheel but within moments, the heaviness dissipated and Felis shook his head while buzzing his lips like a horse. "That was wild," he said. "The Fae do that?"

"For us, it makes us sleepy, disinterested," Icarus explained. "For humans, it makes them forget entirely why they're traveling toward Sedanza. It's part of the Fae agreement with the Sedessans."

"Now might be a good time," Dante said to Felis as he began pulling equipment from his backpack.

Felis powered off the boat. Icarus caught the suspicion on his friend's face while he watched Dante. *How'd I miss it?* If Dante was the mole, the Sedessans would know of Icarus' arrival at Riviera despite the use of the transponder. But until Felis provided proof, he wouldn't treat Dante any different than before.

Dante pulled out a tripod and mounted a camera on top that had more lens than body.

As the boat came to a stop, the air settled like a heavy, heated blanket over the deck, smothering them. Levi swallowed again, the sound carrying in the sudden quiet.

"Whatever you're doing," Icarus said, "be quick about it."

Dante planted the tripod on the bow near them and leaned in, manually focusing the camera. He clicked a button and stepped back. Five seconds later, it clicked a series of rapid shots. Levi grinned, starting to rise as his curiosity overrode his seasickness.

"A dead bug that clic—"

"No motion," Dante said. Levi froze in a crouched position while Dante refocused the camera.

Felis huffed, his fingers tense on the catamaran's helm. Icarus raised a brow, but Felis just shook his head.

"All right," Dante said.

Felis powered up the boat again while Dante pulled a tablet from his pack, tapping the screen. A blessed breeze began drifting across the deck.

"Dante," Icarus finally said, "explain."

Dante glanced up and the color drained from his face as he realized they were watching him. Levi, who still crouched where Dante had told him to, grinned, his sharp teeth showing.

"Um," Dante cleared his throat. "It's hard to get information about the Sedanza Islands. I mean, they shake your hand and you forget talking with them, or what you remember isn't what you actually saw. It's how they've kept humans away, they—"

"Dante," Icarus said, pointing at the tablet.

"Right." He flipped it around to show a detailed picture of an island. "Intel was hard to find and buying a strong enough scope or binoculars to see the islands from here would draw interest from the more dangerous mythics in Venezuela. Something about turf wars and snipers. Anyway, a camera doesn't draw as much interest.

"This puppy," he touched the camera, "can take pictures of the moon and show you its craters. It's not quite as good at taking pictures from a boat because of the water's motion, but I did get a bit of Riviera's layout. It also," he flipped the tablet to face him, pinched his fingers outward, and flipped it back toward Icarus, "lets us know they've experienced an earthquake or attack recently."

He'd zoomed in on what used to be a large building higher up in the coastal city.

Icarus held out his hand for the tablet. As he scrolled through the pictures, Levi leaned over his shoulder to see. Dante had gotten Riviera's entire western coastline. Icarus glanced up to confirm that he could just make out the island's hills but nothing else with his bare eyes. The pictures, on the other hand, showed Riviera in detail, all except the docks, which were blocked by the curvature of the earth.

"It was an attack," he said.

"Why do you say that?" Felis asked.

"The rubble is the embassy." He knew its location from El. "There's damage to some of the surrounding buildings but most of it's localized. Someone targeted the embassy."

"Who would do that?" Felis asked. "I don't know many who would start a war against the Fae. Plus, who would even know the embassy was there to attack?'

Icarus remembered the building in Tennessee that Na'rina had crushed using a kudzu vine. "Someone backed into a corner. Perhaps imprisoned." He zoomed in again searching for details, but the picture became grainy. "I don't see any foliage around the building but—" he shared a look with Felis.

"You once told me Na'rina wasn't the only mythic who could

crush a building. She was just the only one who'd use a vine to do it."

What are we walking into? He scanned the photo again and wished he knew who had gotten ahold of El's phone. He couldn't chance another call and without her intel, they were walking in blind.

Icarus handed Felis the tablet. He'd seen enough. Even if Na'rina hadn't caused the attack, it was too similar to disregard. It implied there were other prisoners; he couldn't walk away from that and look Na'rina in the eye when he did find her.

"She's got to be there," Felis said, shuffling through the photos before handing the tablet back to Dante. As he did, he snagged some of Dante's caramelized, cinnamon pecans and threw them in his mouth. "That building looks just like the Tennessee center when she crushed it."

Dante snarled and moved his pecans. "There's no vegetation beyond potted plants nearby for her to work with."

"Enough," Icarus interrupted, seeing the argument coming. "The Fae will know we're coming." Icarus explained briefly about the dome and the transponder. "They'll be waiting for us at the docks. Felis, I want you and Dante to greet them directly. Levi and I will sneak in afterwards." He hoped his plan would give Felis a chance to watch Dante and him and Levi the opportunity to search for Na'rina.

"Won't they react badly to our wer-im faces, Kadis?"

Most mythics would, but the Fae and the Sedessans liked to play with fire too much not to be attracted by the flames.

"Tell them you're responding to a general invitation Ambassador Marquin put out for the Inverro family. You'd like to speak with Mateo Inverro."

"Who's Mateo Inverro?" Felis asked.

"He's the head of the most powerful family in the Sedanza Court."

Felis and Dante quieted, their apprehension clear.

"He'll be civil," Icarus assured them. "Probably welcome you like princes. Treat it like the façade it is and you'll be fine. Don't let him touch you and don't leave each other alone." Then as an afterthought, "And don't eat the food. It is a Fae embassy, after all. While you're there, I want you to look for a book. There'll be a library somewhere near the embassy..." He gave them the details.

When he was done, they both wore the same nervous expression. Felis stole more pecans, but Dante didn't react. Finally, Dante turned to Felis, "So this book must be..."

Icarus tuned them out.

"The Wer-Kadis used to be a breeze we all knew was there but couldn't be bothered to throw a coat on to ward off its chill," Levi observed. "Now it's a windstorm, bending trees to its will."

"The wind can't blow forever," Icarus answered.

"Doesn't have to. It will calm, but the next time it blows, we'll find more than a coat."

How did Na'rina and I get into this mess?

"That troubles you?" Levi asked.

"I'm an outcast, half-blood feline. Since when does someone like that end up leading the wer-im?"

Levi barked a laugh. Dante and Felis glanced over, then looked away when Levi snarled at them. "The original wind was all wer-im; it garnered no respect," he said to Icarus.

Icarus took that in, surprised, and then shifted to more pressing matters. "We need disguises—any thoughts?"

Levi considered him, his eyes tracing Icarus' facial scars and then settling on the thick cartilage of his marked ear. *Don't react.*

"What did you do to earn that?" he asked softly to keep the others from hearing.

Icarus gritted his teeth. He'd said too much.

"We can touch the Drydandas' zoi aima," Levi said when Icarus didn't immediately respond, "become feline, but I won't give you secrets when I know so little."

Na'rina had changed Icarus into a lynx a couple of times by maintaining a steady stream of her zoi aima into his body. Ver'rina had kept Levi a mountain lion for centuries in the same way, although Icarus had never been able to spot the lifeblood she used to do it. This was what Levi offered: a connection to Na'rina without her present. His hackles rose. "We can touch the Drydandas' zoi aima?" he asked, seething through his teeth.

Levi tilted his head, confused. "*Sa.*"

"And you can hear Ver'rina when you're a cat?"

Understanding dawned and Levi held up his hands. "*Sa,* but this," he tapped Icarus' chest, hitting the golden leaf beneath his shirt, "was drained after the memory. No zoi aima from sprout herself. The zoi aima that fills it now is from the Rina. If you can speak to anyone as lynx, it will be the Rina. Although at this distance, it is questionable."

Icarus clenched his fists. He craved Na'rina's voice. The sudden hope swallowed by frustration left him hollow inside.

Levi's expression became thoughtful. "Perhaps not a bad thing, either."

Icarus growled.

Levi growled back. "Rina strengthens sprout, no matter where she is. A connection to her might help both."

Icarus accepted that, bowing his head. "The connection with the vow is deeper than I expected," he admitted. "Complicated."

Levi grinned. "It is beautiful as dew drops on aspen leaves and yet it is not even close to the rain or sun that *can* be. Would you want it any different?"

"*Na*," Icarus immediately answered. "I accept its growth."

Levi eyed him, absently tracing a golden leaf on his forearm. "Good," he finally said. "I am satisfied. Now…" and he tapped his ear, reminding Icarus of his earlier question regarding his scar.

Icarus sighed and ran a hand down his face. *I'm not sure I understand half of our conversations.* But this question he understood. It was easy to forget how old and experienced Levi was when he took to modern life so easily. Icarus had never run into another mythic outside of the Court who knew what his scarred ear meant.

"I'm half wer-im," he finally answered. *I fall into the same avalanche danger as Na'rina. Does Levi realize?* Icarus didn't ask, instead just saying, "That's all the offense they needed."

Levi considered that, then stated, "You want disguises not because we're wer-im but because you're Sedessan and don't want them to know it."

Icarus nodded. Levi had nailed it.

"Then perhaps," Levi continued, "it is fitting we use a wer-im disguise."

Na'rina knew that face! Even if she'd never seen Elodie before—which she had briefly—El shared Icarus' narrow nose and sharp cheekbones, the dark hair, facial lines, and the uncanny, single-minded focus.

The guards and imps chased after Icarus' sister, leaving Na'rina alone in the dripping cavern. The sprinklers kept spraying torrents of water, washing down the tanks and swirling toward large grates in the floor. The drains were not keeping up.

Tears streamed off Na'rina's stubby nose as she crawled from under Alaya's tank to follow El. Alaya's lifeblood pounded against her ears in response to the water. She tried to stand, couldn't, and crawled instead, taking the most direct route beneath the tanks and using the tubes to keep from being flushed toward a drain.

Where are we going? the twiglet asked, picturing Alaya's waxy face behind them.

We can't open Alaya's tank, Na'rina answered, *but if we can reach El, she can help us.*

The twiglet didn't say more but he didn't have to for Na'rina to feel his doubts. They'd be lucky to slip past the guards and imps who were sure to return, much less find El after reaching daylight.

One step, the twiglet finally whispered.

One step, Na'rina agreed, crawling under the portcullis that hadn't fully closed. In the tunnel beyond, puddles attested to El and the guard's path. Na'rina followed, staying close to the wall. Even crawling, she swayed, desperate for *sleep*. She longed for her Rina. She stayed upright by leaning her hip and shoulder against the stone. Grit dug into her scraped palms and added new cuts on the twiglet's knees, but he didn't complain.

A short time later, a creaking echoed from the cavern behind and Na'rina froze, peering back to find the entrance portcullis slowly rising. The booted feet of two men appeared with the wheels of a small wooden pushcart.

There was no longer the rush of running water.

They shut off the sprinklers.

A gurgling sounded from the room, attesting to the water now mixing with air as it drained.

"They'd better have a good explanation for flooding the chamber."

Thomas Dominguez! Na'rina frantically looked around. There was nothing to hide behind. She could barely crawl, much less run.

There, the twiglet directed her to a triangular shadow against the wall where one utility light and the next didn't fully overlap their spheres of light. It was darker, but not by a lot.

"I'm sure they'll spin us some excuse," the other man said.

They'll see us!

We're small, Drydanda, you'd be shocked by how many people overlook something because it's small and doesn't move. The twiglet urged her forward. She crawled, leaning heavily against the wall while sappy tears again

241

dripped off her nose. Reaching the triangular shadow, she curled into a ball of sticks and leaves.

Now hold perfectly still, the twiglet said.

An exhausted shudder tried to travel her spine.

Be strong like Mitto, the twiglet encouraged.

Na'rina tightened her muscles, halting the shudder between her shoulder blades. Only then did she peer between her knees at the approaching men. A whimper lodged in her throat. Na'rina swallowed, forcing it back down.

Master Thomas walked in front of the cart. His zoi aima flickered between brown and red. His cane clicked, echoing in the tunnel. When she'd first seen him, the cane had seemed like a fashion touch despite his gnarled appearance. Now he leaned on the rounded oak with each wobbly step.

"Have someone check the tanks for damage." He paused, then asked, "Before you dump your cargo in the well, have we heard from the divers?"

"Not yet."

Na'rina's eyes flicked to the other man who pushed the cart. *Armando.* She wasn't surprised.

Master Thomas grunted. "It probably broke in the quake. At least we don't need it much longer."

"Any word on the excavation?"

"*Na,* I can't push too hard or Marquin will balk."

"What if Marie's right and the Drydanda survived?"

Armando snorted. "That avenue's gone." As the light passed over Master Thomas' face, Na'rina started. Deep wrinkles trailed down from his eyes and disappeared into his mustache.

What happened to him?

What do you mean?

Na'rina pictured Master Thomas as she'd first seen him. The twiglet almost shrugged but caught himself. Instead, he said, *he got old…in the matter of a day or two.*

Thomas rolled up his cuff with his free left hand, revealing deep red and blue veins. He held out his arm, showing the veins to Armando.

"The serum is wearing off faster?" he asked.

Thomas hummed. "We will fix that. Later. For now, Marquin insisted I oversee the setup for the trial."

"You're almost done with all this," Armando encouraged, gesturing at Master Thomas' arm.

Thomas waved a dismissive hand. "I can handle a few more days, but I can't show up like this. The goblins in particular will notice. Where do you keep your emergency vials, Mateo?"

Mateo? Na'rina squinted but she was sure the other man was Armando.

Armando—or Mateo as Master Thomas called him—stopped the cart and Na'rina almost whimpered again. The wheels rested a mere three feet from her face. But Mateo studied the older man, his fingers tapping the cart's handle.

"You are not supposed to be the guinea pig for the experiments. What happens if you overdose?"

Thomas leaned hard on his cane, his zoi aima flashing red while his hands overlapped on the cane's handle. "Look at me! Do you think we have a choice?"

"I *am* looking at you. And we can't afford to lose you because we're rushed."

"And what would you have me do? Try it on your son? We don't have the luxury now of taking our time."

Mateo's jaw tightened and his fingers turned white on the cart handle. Then he breathed in loudly through his nose and nodded. "There's a vial on the boat, tucked under the nav station's false bottom." Mateo caught Thomas' arm when he turned away. "It's only a half dose. You might get a few hours at most."

Master Thomas grimaced but shrugged. "I'll skip the trial. The boy can handle it alone." He kept walking but Mateo was shaking his head.

"You don't think the boy's ready?" Thomas asked.

"He's distracted," Mateo answered, "but he'll do fine as long as the Varela girl doesn't pull something stupid."

Drydanda? The twiglet tugged at her attention, but she couldn't pull her eyes from Master Thomas.

He looked wrong. Not just physically older, but—*What does his zoi aima look like to you?* Na'rina asked the twiglet.

Thomas stretched, cracking his neck. "That boy better be able to handle it. We're counting on him with the Varela details."

Drydanda?

What?

Do we have enough strength to hang onto that?

Na'rina looked at the cart where the twiglet indicated. He was talking about the crossbeam holding the floor to the axel.

If he's headed outside, the twiglet said. *Maybe we can hitch a ride?*

Na'rina caught the twiglet imagining himself as a giant, walking mahogany tree. He *really* wanted to be like Mitto from his story, which might be an implausible dream, but his idea had merit. Before the two men turned back, she forced her limbs to uncurl and rolled beneath the cart.

Her body protested, spasming, and her hand almost smacked the frame. It took all she had to be still again. The metal crosspiece overhead wasn't beyond reach but Na'rina withered at the strength required to hang from it.

"He knows what's at stake," Mateo said as he grasped the cart's handles again.

Drydanda! Now!

The cart lifted.

Na'rina caught the frame before it started to move. For a moment, her heels dragged on the floor, but she hauled herself up, wrapping her arms and legs around the metal so tightly that it dug into the bark at her elbows.

The two men didn't say anything more as they moved down the tunnel again. Na'rina shuddered uncontrollably, hoping the movement was hidden by the cart's swaying.

Eventually, Thomas split from Mateo at another tunnel, going left while Mateo continued on.

Na'rina's heart fell. He wasn't headed out but farther in. Tears slid down her temples.

Mateo pushed the cart through an old wooden door. The room beyond was lit with more utility lights and Na'rina made out what appeared to be the stone circle of a well in the tiny room's center.

Mateo lifted something from the cart and grunted, throwing it down the well. She glimpsed a gnome's calloused foot before it disappeared into the floor.

The twiglet almost screamed. Na'rina swallowed the sound even as her stomach tried to revolt.

That was a body!

Mateo threw another and a splash sounded a little later. After the third body, Mateo dusted his hands on his pants and lifted the cart, hauling it from the room backwards. It rattled, now empty.

Please head outside, please head outside. Na'rina didn't know why he would though. She desperately waited for an opportunity to drop off the cart and escape.

They killed those mythics. The twiglet sobbed silently.

Mateo turned at the same intersection where he'd separated from Thomas. The cart tilted slightly and Na'rina almost lost her grip. Hauling herself tighter to the frame, she locked her hands under her arms.

Mateo grumbled and manhandled the cart past a crumbled section of wall, scraping the wheel's side as he pushed past.

A wet trickle built on Na'rina's arms where the crossbeam dug deep grooves on the inside of her elbows. Her shaking grew worse, slowly digging the metal into the bark until sap oozed freely from the wounds.

At least the sap's still flowing. She tried to stay positive but couldn't escape the memory of Mateo tossing gnomes into the well.

This step is giant-sized, the twiglet whimpered. He was trying not to affect their body, but Na'rina could feel the hiccups in his chest.

246

Ahead, a rotted wooden door appeared. It hung from a single hinge half torn off the frame. Fresh air wafted through.

Outside! He's heading outside. The twiglet's relief was palpable.

Mateo muttered at seeing it, "What in the world did those men get into?" He shoved the cart through, jostling side to side as he entered a crumbling shack.

Na'rina sobbed with longing. Sunlight filtered into the cabin from the far door.

Almost there, she stared at the light, showing the twiglet.

He whimpered aloud then, and the sound lodged in Na'rina's throat.

Mateo hit the threshold and the cart creaked, covering the small whine. Then out the door he maneuvered, at which point he stopped as the cart's wheels dug into the sand.

More sappy tears flowed from Na'rina's eyes, trailing down her temples and into the leaves over her ears. It was midday and the sun's essence filled the air with glorious, vibrant life. Thick clouds on the horizon would obscure that soon but for now, she started swaying, soaking in the slow build of zoi aima like a sunflower opening to the day's warmth. It ebbed and flowed, ebbed and flowed, washing over her earlier horror.

Drydanda?

Hmm?

Are you dancing with the waves?

Na'rina stilled, their situation rushing back to her. Not far away, ocean waves washed the sand with the incoming tide. She'd responded to their steady tempo, her zoi aima settling into their rhythm. *Oh Alaya, you're so close to the ocean, yet so far.*

The Oceadanda must not be able to absorb energy through her zoi aima like Na'rina could. She was close enough to psychically reach the ocean like she'd reached the chamber Na'rina had gotten stuck in, and yet the Oceadanda had been starving.

Mateo called out to someone, "Captain, what happened in the chamber?"

"Fire elemental, Sir," came the response.

Na'rina stared at Mateo's boot heels. He still stood far too close, but whoever he was speaking with was on the far side of the cart, out of sight if she dropped and rolled behind Mateo and into the tall grass beyond.

Mateo took a step forward. "Escaped from a tank or..."

Now or never. Na'rina tried to release the cart only to find her hands had lost all feeling. She glanced at Mateo again and then bounced to free her fingers from under her arms. Her back thumped into the sand. Groaning internally, Na'rina rolled. She moved silent on the sand, but the grass susurrated as she passed into it. Na'rina stilled and tilted her leafy head toward the cart. *I'm a small bush. I'm a small bush.*

Mateo stopped mid-sentence, glancing back. A painful tingling pulsed in Na'rina's hands.

"We think it followed Lady Ignatius," the captain answered.

"Catch it?"

"We're searching."

Mateo grunted and turned back to the captain. "Tell Master Thomas. Also, have some men wash this cart and then check the tanks."

"Of course," the captain answered, but Mateo had already

disappeared back into the crumbling hut and didn't respond.

Na'rina watched the captain's boots as he hollered commands. For the next several hours, men passed back and forth in front of her hiding spot. At one point a group of imps arrived and the twiglet cowered, but they merely wandered inside, grumbling and blowing their noses.

All the while, sunlight soaked into the twiglet's leaves. Its warmth tingled and Na'rina savored the vitality that flowed through her blood. She drank deep and all too quickly hit the limit that the twiglet's body could contain. While the twiglet hummed silently, blissfully content as his cuts and scrapes healed, Na'rina tried to hide her dismay.

She succeeded until evening rolled in and clouds obscured the sun, and then the twiglet picked up on her summoning her resolve to keep moving.

I'm sorry, Drydanda, I'm not a good Mitto.

Na'rina snorted, happy to make some sound. She hadn't seen anyone pass by in a while. *Sure you are. We're outside, free!*

The twiglet preened as Na'rina looked around. *The guards talked about the ambassador's house. I think it's that way from what they were saying.* Na'rina turned inland, silently wondering how far they had to go. *El's probably there, or somewhere nearby there. Let's go find her.*

Donning a wide sunhat, El sat on a bakery's patio and watched the alley behind the ambassador's house. The hat, along with her brown cotton pants and off-white blouse, had come from a small shop on the outskirts of Riviera central. El now blended easily into the crowd as she twirled a pen between her fingers.

It'd taken less than half an hour of gossip listening to pinpoint Amos' location to somewhere in Marquin's home. She honestly wasn't sure if she was going to free the giant or just glean information from him, but he was intelligent and highly observant, and she wanted his take on the holding cell they'd shared. As Sala had pointed out, *someone* had set off the earthquake even if it wasn't Amos.

The traffic around Marquin's home could be a problem though. The islanders usually observed a siesta after lunch, but today a mass of goblins, Fae, and sprites were coming and going in preparation for the upcoming trial. El waited, hoping things would calm some during siesta. The warm sun soaked into her skin, making her drowsy as she listened to the steel drums a Fae man was playing near the patio.

A chair scraped against the flagstones as someone sat nearby. El's eyes flew open. The new patron was a woman with large reflective sunglasses and a purple buff.

The Daughter of Medusa?

El hadn't seen her after escaping the embassy. Blinking sleep from her eyes, she eyed the hourglass-figured woman. Not a lot was known about the Daughters, but El knew their mystique was fed by gossip and assumptions. Most stories said that they'd sprung from the snakes on Medusa's severed head but beyond that, there was little agreement.

It didn't appear that the woman had spotted her. *Why is she still here?* The Daughters were often mercenaries. *Is she working a contract?* The Daughter ordered coffee, and El eventually dismissed her. If she were trying to be subtle, she wouldn't have sat down in the middle of the café where everyone nearby, the Fae, sprites, a few dwarves, and even a gnome stared at her.

El kept twirling her pen. Across the patio, a figure stooped to drop coins into the steel drum player's hat. *Manuel Torres.* Despite his glasses and droopy mustache—obviously fake—he was still clearly the head of the Torres family. As he turned to leave, his fingers brushed the player's elbow. El almost snorted. Manuel probably just stole someone's contact. Last she knew, the steel drum player was Carlos Reyes' man. *Torres is at it again.* El cocked her head. *Roberto told Marquin the Torres family was away.* In the distance, the central clock tower chimed the three-quarter hour, telling El she had fifteen minutes before siesta started.

Why would he do that? To explain their silence toward Marquin? Or was he hiding something? The Daughter's banter with the Fae server caught her ear and another thing occurred to her. *There's been no mention of statues in the rubble.* If they weren't finding statues, someone was hiding the Daughter's actions from that night, or erasing the memories of finding statues.

The Sedessan behind all this must have access to everyone excavating the embassy. She eyed the steel drum player. *Is it someone hiding like Manuel or someone in plain sight?* El wanted to close her eyes again. The family behind this was treading on very dangerous ground. *As Sophia said, they could get us all killed.*

The clock tower chimed the hour. El pocketed her pen. It was time to see Amos.

El slipped into the mansion through a small laundry room window, avoiding the garden at the back of the building because that's where the staff often hung their hammocks for siesta. *I can't believe that was a guillotine blade.* She'd spotted a group of goblins hauling the thing down the street as she'd approached. *Marquin's playing really free with the Fae's laws if he's already planning Amos' execution.*

El's feet hit the floor. She was pulling the window closed again when a voice asked, "¿Que buscas?"

Whatcha looking for?

El pivoted to find a man, only about four feet tall, standing in the doorway. He wore an Inverro uniform with a white cord over his left shoulder, indicating he was on loan to the embassy. El watched his hands, buried in a bundle of linens, but suddenly his human features melted into a goblin's rubbery skin. His face looked almost familiar but El was positive he wasn't from the Varela estate. As his human features disappeared, his teeth began to grow, but then he hesitated, and his teeth receded to their regular length.

"I mean no harm," El said, trying the common tongue. Most staff knew a smattering.

The goblin tilted his head and recognition lit his face. "El Varela."

Boiling frogs! Since when did the Inverro *staff* know her? If she could capture him, she could make him forget he ever saw her, but capturing a goblin was hard. For their spindly size, they moved fast.

"You—compras ice cream for mi cousin Horatio, *Sa?*"

El nodded, finally connecting why this goblin seemed familiar.

He pulled at one of his long ears, thinking, and then a grin spread across his face, exposing more teeth than El cared to count. "If ice cream were aparecer—ah—were to—"

"Appear?"

"*Sa,* to appear in mi cuarto, maybe I no remember this—" he nodded toward El.

El returned the goblin's grin. As far as bribes went, this she could deal with. "What flavor do you like?"

Not only would Horaz conveniently forget seeing her, he led her to where Amos was being held and unlocked the door into the storage room. Goblins apparently loved ice cream. At El's insistence, Horaz relocked the door behind her and walked away, whistling softly as he went.

El found the pull string for the light. A single bulb flooded the windowless room, which held exactly one piece of furniture—a thick, metal chair that had recently been bolted to the floor, judging by the metal shards around the feet.

Amos sat shackled to the chair and the floor with enough chains to hold several giants. The floor, interestingly, was covered in a thick sheet of metal to separate him from any stone.

He looked—tired. El studied his rough-hewn face, noticing the red around his gray eyes and the sag to his shoulders. The fierce anger she'd encountered before had dimmed to a wary mistrust.

"Now what?" he asked.

Now that she stood before him, El hesitated. *Where do I start?*

She walked around his chair, finding small scrapes on his fingers, blood smeared around his wrists, and minute scratches on one of the bolts holding an O-ring on the chair through which his chain ran.

His fingers curled slightly, appearing relaxed. El tapped the back of his hand.

Amos grunted, and curled his fingers tighter, refusing to give up whatever metal shard he was using to work at the screw. Despite all his efforts, he hadn't made much progress. El continued around the chair to stand before him again. Tired he might be, but not weak. He'd mangled the chair, pulling at its legs and bowing them outward before he'd moved on to the bolt. He wasn't giving up. *I wish we hadn't gotten off on the wrong foot.* He'd trusted her. It was unlikely to happen again. She thought of Sala's accusation and swallowed hard.

"What'd they want? The folks as captured you?" El asked.

Amos snorted. "Don't rightly know."

"Why'd they lock you up?"

"Wasn't told."

"They take blood?"

Amos twitched like she'd poked him with a needle. "What's it to you?"

El didn't answer. "Anything else?"

Amos' expression turned dull as he looked away.

El changed topics. "Y' didn't start the quake?"

A snort was his response.

"See any Sedessans besides me?"

"Like I'd know. Y'r the only one ta show y'r face."

El didn't want to ask her next question but Sophia's orders and Icarus' heart demanded she at least try. "Do y' know what they'll find when they clear out the Drydanda's cell?"

Amos' intelligent, gray eyes swung back toward her. "Y'r still on that?"

El waited, but he just seemed amused. For once, she was at a loss about what tactic to use. *I can't tell Icarus without confirming Na'rina's death.*

Amos' amusement was unsettling. Usually, she knew more about the person she was dealing with, or she gained more in quick order. That wouldn't work here. Icarus would chide her. He'd always warned her to rely less on her abilities. *They'll fail you one day, El,* he said, *or by using them, they'll become the very thing that ruins your success.*

As she met Amos' hard gaze, she realized this might be that day. El looked down at her feet. "Last spring, the Drydanda found out that humans are experimenting on mythics. We're a growing field of study for them. She was uniting the North American mythics to protect them. No more dodgy alliances," she thought again of Sala, "no more finding out that an entire dwarven race is missing, no more fauns ending up on the black market as a curiosity. With her death, any chances of an alliance vanish. She had fauns, dwarves, oceanids, wer-im, naiads, dryads, and others willing to negotiate. With her dead—" El couldn't finish. With her dead, Icarus himself would make war on the humans.

Amos sat back. "Knew y'r accent wasn't real."

El threw up her hands, turning away. She'd just vomited information and he was laughing at her!

"Still don't explain why y' care."

El spun back. "Humans! Experimenting on mythics. What more do I have to say?"

Amos shook his head and his long hair fell across his face. With another shake, he said, "Sedessans trapse amongst humans like they belong there. Y've no reason to worry about such things. Why. Do. Y'. Care?"

El stared at him. *Why does he have to be so stubborn?* She'd just spewed more information than a Sedessan ever gave, and he wanted *more?* Her mother would be horrified.

She spun away. "I'm done." She'd meant to ask more, a lot more, but apparently the giant didn't understand the give and take she was offering...or he understood it too well.

El pulled the pen from her pocket and uncapped it. She started pulling out the innards to get to the thin picks inside. In the silence, the tiny scraping and clicking of El's tools sounded loud in the door's lock.

"She ain't dead," Amos said, his words dropping like stones into the quiet.

El glanced over her shoulder. She barely kept her sudden hope from her expression. "How do you know?"

Amos shook his head. "That's all y' get until y' get me outta here."

El snorted. "Not enough. I'd be risking too much if you're lying." She went back to the lock.

"I's not the one who's a liar here."

El sighed and her forehead thunked against the door. It wasn't like she *enjoyed* lying. But neither did she like leaving the giant to Marquin's justice. The ambassador wouldn't have brought in a guillotine blade unless he intended to use it. The lock clicked. El withdrew her tools, slid them back into her pen, and allowed another tool to slide free as she turned back toward Amos. She was halfway around his chair when voices sounded through the door.

She cursed, sliding the long, thin carbide rod she'd pulled out into Amos' hand instead of using it to cut him free.

"Get y'r shackles loose," she said, "an' be ready." Then she slipped out the door. She'd barely made it around the corner when a group of guards entered the hallway, heading for Amos' door.

Icarus could smell the Fae before they finished docking, but then, as a lynx, he could also hear the scuttle of bare feet on the wooden dock and the rustle of birds landing on the masts of nearby sailboats. He sighed. The sun was finally setting and its heat no longer baked the deck.

Na'rina's golden leaf itched beneath the skin of his shoulder, but it brought a cool wind through his fur and reminded him of the faint scent of warmed aspen he'd get just before she'd sit down beside him. He almost expected her to appear and lean into his side.

Instead, it was Levi in leonine form who sat beside him in the cockpit. Just like Icarus' golden aspen leaf, Levi carried a fuzzy golden catkin that contained some of Ver'rina's zoi aima. He'd shown Icarus how to breathe in the lifeblood to initiate the shift. For Levi, it flowed smooth as silk. For Icarus it'd been torture. He ached in every joint and muscle now. But he finally understood why he'd never seen a link between Ver'rina and Levi.

Apparently changing back and forth would drain Icarus' leaf quickly, but he could stay a lynx almost indefinitely. He had no desire to shift again without Na'rina guiding it. But now that he was a lynx, he treasured the part of her that held him there. His vow sat numb in his chest but around that hole there was now a soft coolness—the connection to her Rina had grown stronger—buffering it. Icarus couldn't hear the Rina, but that did not surprise him with the distance between them.

Levi brushed his shoulder, shifting his attention to Felis and Dante. They finished tying off the boat and wandered down the dock, making its boards squeak. Icarus and Levi stayed hunched between the seats in the boat, waiting.

The Fae weren't likely to inspect the vessel until Felis and Dante were gone, giving Icarus and Levi time to slip off the boat unseen.

"Disturbing," Felis grumbled, talking about Levi and Icarus' shift. "The Drydanda's not even here."

Icarus huffed and Levi nudged him again, putting more weight behind it to encourage Icarus to stay quiet. It had the opposite effect, forcing Icarus' breath from his chest in a gust. Levi didn't mean anything aggressive by it, but he was huge.

After his Kadivas fight against Silas where he'd shifted, Icarus had searched for lore on the wer-im shift because he'd been shocked by Silas' size. From the little he'd been able to find, it wasn't uncommon for the wer-im's feline form to be bigger than a normal cat. Icarus himself was closer to eighty pounds whereas a regular lynx was twenty to forty. But even then, a regular mountain lion would outweigh Icarus by at least seventy pounds. And Levi was just as big compared to his normal counterpart as Icarus—more like a small gorilla than a feline.

Levi eased away, giving Icarus breathing space.

"I'm not a diplomat," Felis continued to grouse. "How the Kadis expects me to not mess things up with the Fae, I've no idea."

"Quiet," Dante whispered.

Then, to someone else, he said, "Greetings."

"Wer-im! Here! Welcome to Riviera," said a distinctly happy Fae. "I'm afraid it's a bad time to visit the embassy."

"Why?" Felis asked.

Icarus cringed. Beside him, Levi snorted a soft laugh.

"My apologies! I am Elmon, the dock master here…Master?"

"Felis Callas—and this is Dante."

He introduced him. Icarus, hiding on the boat, warmed with pride.

"We're not here to visit the embassy, per se," Dante stepped in. "We're responding to an invitation from Mateo Inverro."

The air became tense as a lute string and Icarus' hackles rose.

"That is, of course, different," Elmon said. "There is a private event tonight that Señor Mateo will be attending. I can take you to a hotel to wait for him, but it will be late."

"That's fine," Felis grumbled. Icarus cringed again. He should have given Dante the lead.

"This way please."

As their steps faded down the dock, Dante asked, "In the meantime, would it be possible to see the library? I hea—" They moved beyond even Icarus' sensitive ears.

He and Levi waited, listening. When the silence continued, Icarus peeked his head up. Dew from the cooling air had collected on his thick coat and he shook it off. He'd inherited the dense fur from his father, a Canadian lynx. Already he'd begun to shed in the heat and his skin itched.

He ignored it and stretched, grimacing as his back popped. The discomfort from shifting had never lasted this long with Na'rina's help.

Beside him, Levi whined through his nose, fast asleep.

Icarus pawed his shoulder and a large, golden eye popped open. Levi huffed, coming awake from his brief nap. He rose, stretched, and followed Icarus to the starboard rail, away from the dock. They both stared at the water with distaste before slipping over the side.

The water instantly cooled Icarus and, for once, he didn't mind being wet. They swam for the shore just as voices sounded from the dock.

"Master Elmon's wringing his hands on this one," a voice said. "Two wer-im showing up on the same night as the trial."

Fae, Icarus scoffed, *they do love their trials.*

"They had a transponder," another voice said. The *Pour Decisions* swayed as someone stepped aboard. "Although it does seem opportune."

"They'll smell us, you know?"

"What?"

"They're cats. They'll smell we've been aboard their boat."

"Master Elmon gave me a spray to kill our scent."

They wouldn't find anything other than the fur Icarus had shed. Icarus and Levi continued toward the boat launch while the Fae were distracted.

The "event" Elmon mentioned is a trial. That supported Icarus' theory that someone attacked the embassy. *Is it Na'rina's trial?* His chest tightened. They reached shore and shook, spraying water across the ramp's crushed rock.

With the embassy in shambles, a trial would be held at the next largest building. Icarus recalled Dante's photos, locating a manor that had to be the ambassador's house. His memory wasn't quite like El's, but he retained the knack for hanging onto details.

He led the way into the city with Levi padding behind. As the sun set, they slipped between the growing shadows while the fragrance of hibiscus, jasmine, and orchids surrounded them. It'd be overwhelming except for the breeze that carried the heavier musk of approaching rain.

Rose and lavender perfume.

Icarus froze mid-step and sniffed, fielding out the flowers and rain for the perfume again. His gut clenched when he found it.

Sophia.

After years of not seeing her, the memory of that fateful day when she'd cast him out smacked him in the face.

He walked into the dining room for breakfast and Sophia smiled in greeting. The smile melted, replaced by a look of betrayal.

"Rus, you look purple!" El exclaimed.

"Follow me." Sophia rose from the table and Icarus' twelve-year-old self hesitated, suddenly afraid.

Icarus stumbled. Levi had pushed him with his forehead, breaking him from the memory. He ducked into an alley, sliding behind a stack of woven baskets that reeked of fish just as Sophia Varela turned the corner from the docks and headed their way with her phone to her ear.

She'd always worn a high-waisted dress and a tight bun hairstyle that enhanced her height. Now she wore heels, dress slacks, and a maroon blouse. The bun, messy instead of neat, still sat high on her head.

Just like any mythic that mingled with the human world, she'd adapted to the current styles, but other than the clothes, Sophia hadn't changed.

"Any luck?" Sophia asked whoever she'd called. She sighed. "I'll see if I can salvage this." She paused, listening. "Don't start with me. We've been over this. I'm almost to the…" and her voice faded as she turned toward the ambassador's house.

Icarus stared after her.

Levi nudged him.

I should've known I'd see her.

Levi nudged him again but this time he leaned his forehead into Icarus' shoulder until he had to take a step or be pushed over. A deep rumble vibrated from Levi's chest. A purr so low it shuddered in Icarus' ribs. His eyes burned with tears he couldn't shed as a lynx. Icarus leaned back, adding his own purr until he could breathe again and the tears passed.

Sophia will be at the ambassador's. And possibly El, Adrian, Na'rina's abductor, and hopefully Na'rina.

The familiar, icy calm slid over Icarus. He let it settle and continued on to the ambassador's house again.

Marquin had changed his enormous dining room into a quasi-court room, complete with podium at the far end for the judge (presumably Marquin), the defendant's chair, and, as she'd seen before, a guillotine with its blade gleaming in the chandeliers' light.

El narrowed her eyes. She did *not* want to witness Amos' head getting cut off although she wasn't sure how to free him now without anyone connecting his escape to her. But she needed him alive. Hopefully he'd made use of the carbide blade because whatever she did now, it'd be a hasty plan.

El kept her head lowered with her sunhat in place as the room filled. She'd altered her outfit to include sandals, a chestnut-colored wig, and a shawl that concealed her skinny frame. The room was mostly occupied with Fae but there were a few goblin servants, some Sedessans, and a couple brave dwarves. Nothing would truly conceal her from the other Sedessans if they used their second lens, but she hoped they wouldn't need to see the psychic during the trail.

El's spot at the back of the room offered easy egress. Try as she might, though, she couldn't see a way to help Amos without being noticed. She'd brought a smoke bomb in her collection of items from the study, but if she used it, hiding in the back wouldn't keep the Sedessans from recognizing her.

Roberto strode in with David and their mother. He stutter-stepped upon seeing the guillotine and his brother trod on his heels. El snickered and ducked her head. Roberto's expression had almost immediately gone blank, but for the briefest moment there was surprise. Roberto's mother peeled off to speak to someone on the far side of the room and El lost sight of her.

El kept her head down as Roberto and his younger brother filed into the seats in front of her. David pulled at the collar of his tailored grey suit, only belatedly remembering to unbutton his coat to sit after Roberto did it. Titanium cufflinks flashed on Roberto's wrists.

He dressed to the nines to testify. He always had known how to cut a clean figure.

El wondered how long her parents had searched for her, knowing the Fae would want a second witness. *I can't testify.* She'd never openly acted against her mother, but this was the first time she was sure Sophia was operating with too little information. *Na'rina might be alive but to find out for sure, I have to free Amos.* Apprehension ached in her stomach. She spotted her mother's telltale bun passing through the crowd and not far behind, her father's dark hair. She wished she'd gotten a chance to speak more with him. *Is Amos' death part of their plans?* Her parents rarely set someone up like this. *How does it hurt them if he escapes?*

Roberto's brother tugged on his sleeve and Roberto handed him a mint without looking, giving El another glimpse of his cuff links. She made out the Greek "rho" and "iota" that stood for Roberto Inverro. She also noticed the phone-shaped bulge in his pocket. While he was leaned forward, deep in conversation with a Fae man, David had that bored, dull look the young reserved for adult business.

El fumbled her pen. It pinged against the back leg of Roberto's chair. Leaning forward, she reclaimed it—and pinched the phone from his pocket with two fingers. It slid into her sleeve before she was upright again. When David glanced back, her head was down while she wrote in a small notebook. The bored expression never left his eyes.

The room's double doors opened and a round Fae man stepped through. He pounded the floor with a wooden staff. "Marquin Crostee, Ambassador of Queen Lárissa of the Fae."

The room quieted as Marquin entered. A long, scarlet justice robe floated around his narrow legs as he took center stage, susurrating in the quiet.

"Welcome," he said. "Everyone please take your seats."

The atmosphere in the room shifted, taking on that somber tone of official proceedings. El couldn't think of another race that garnered such instant respect and caution from all the mythics. Over the years, the Fae had become more subtle in their use of power but that did not mean they were not as formidable as in the days of myth. On Riviera, Marquin embodied everything the Fae valued. He'd gained his position partly due to being swift and decisive when he needed to be. Plus, he was the heart, or focus, of the emotional deterrent around Sedanza, which meant he was incredibly strong in his abilities.

"Please bring him in," Marquin instructed his guards. They ducked away, smoothly combining their bows with their leaving. "As most of you know, our embassy was attacked recently. We have good cause to believe it's the fault of this mythic."

They could hear his steps before they could see Amos. Then the guards returned and Amos ducked in behind, his head tilting to the side to avoid hitting the doorframe. He towered over the guards but there was none of the self-conscious hunching that many tall people adopted in an effort not to stand out or appear threatening.

His ankle was no longer bandaged. It must not have been a bad injury. He looked exhausted but that did not diminish his stature as he met the eyes of everyone present. El savored the uncomfortable shifting of chairs and ducked her head again as those gray eyes traveled the room.

"Take your seat, Amos Granum," Marquin said.

It looked like he might refuse—his height granted him a certain gravity—but the moment passed, and Amos took the heavy chair set beside the guillotine without acknowledging the device.

"I had offered Amos Granum employment and, as far as I knew, he had left to consider." As he spoke, Marquin paced the front of the room restlessly. He paused and pinched the bridge of his nose. "Then he was found in the rubble below the embassy. We suspected he might be involved, so we requested aid from our allies to confirm our suspicions."

At this, Roberto stood and nodded to the ambassador. When Marquin motioned for him to speak, he overlapped his hands on the seatback in front of him. "Thank you, Ambassador. It is our honor to help." El repressed a shudder. He sounded like his father, Mateo. "I've read the giant and found a deep hatred for the Fae. A bitterness born from the collapse of the Areopagus treaty that he believes led to the decimation of his family…"

El checked her mental study and couldn't see how the treaty connected. Roberto was stretching. *Why doesn't Marquin see it?*

"In his rage, he did not care about the consequences and allowed himself to be buried—"

A laugh rumbled through the floor and Roberto paused, irritation in his eyes.

"You will contain yourself, giant, or I will hang you upside down where you can't touch the ground." El had never seen Marquin levitate an object, much less a giant, but she wouldn't be surprised by the ability. She filed the knowledge away as Amos grinned.

"Y' believe in justice, *na?*"

Again, Marquin pinched his nose. "All here are familiar with Fae justice."

"Hard facts, *na?*"

El leaned forward.

"Of course."

"Why'd I wait?"

"What?" Roberto asked.

His cuff links caught her eye again. *Where have I seen that lettering before?* Something about the Greek initials tugged at El. Watching the trial, she retreated into her mental study again, trying to place the familiarity.

Marquin stared at Amos and he took that as permission to say more.

"I ain't coolheaded enough to plan an escape but I waited a week to attack? Not to mention, that farce of a treaty's been dead for decades."

"Preparation?" someone guessed. The Fae loved riddles and Amos had drawn them in.

In answer, Amos drummed his heel once against the marble. Vibrations shuddered through the floor, growing stronger until the whole building rattled. Fae and guests alike jumped to their feet but even standing, the tremble made everyone's legs like jelly. The glass in the chandeliers tinkled violently and then all at once shattered into tiny flying shards.

Marquin caught them with a wave of his hand and plastered the sparkling shrapnel against the back wall.

Yep, levitation, or rather, telekinesis. El confirmed as she was forcibly pulled from her mental study to stand and clutch her chair. The wall beneath the glass shards began showing stress cracks, and El's eyes widened. Just as she feared those cracks would grow bigger, the vibrations subsided like someone was sucking them up into a vacuum.

"Contain yourself!" Marquin pointed at Amos, but the giant's face was pinched in concentration and the vibrations fully stopped.

"No preparations needed," Amos addressed the crowd, a bit breathless, as they resettled chairs. "Consider," he continued, "Marquin believed me gone. Y' monitor all traffic on and off the island with your transponder thin—"

"You dare question the ambassador's honesty?" Roberto bellowed. He'd remained standing and leaned forward on the chairback with his hands still stacked.

The posture clicked in El's head. *Thomas Dominguez.* The resemblance was so uncanny El experienced a disconnect in her head. How in the world did they share postures?

"I'm questioning th'r allies!"

"Marquin has long proven faithful to this alliance—"

"The ambassador believed I'd left, why?"

"We'd have no reason to compromise—"

"Cause someone lied to 'im or messed with 'is brain."

"—Our relationship simply to have a giant killed."

A line formed between Marquin's brows and a sheen appeared on his skin as he looked between Amos and Roberto.

"It is an oddity," he muttered into the sudden hush. Marquin cupped his chin in a show of thought, but his fingers shook ever so slightly. "But I cannot ignore that we found you in the epicenter of the quake."

El stared at the ambassador's hands. Shaking and sweats were not normal for him. *Compelling stress?* She wanted to shy away from the possibility. Compelling imps was one thing but Compelling the Fae ambassador—Sophia's fear of the mythics destroying the Court would be a very real possibility. The Fae wouldn't even need help doing it. *Any Sedessan who thinks they can successfully Compel a Fae would have to be insane.* The Fae were too strong-minded for it to hold.

Did someone actually lay a Compelling on Marquin? Roberto's not strong enough for that. After their brief mental spat on the boat, El knew that for sure. He was arrogant and lacked subtlety. But as El watched Marquin regain control, her doubt disappeared. He tried to hide his shaking and sweating but couldn't control it. And Marquin's shaking hands when they'd met with him earlier made more sense if it was Compulsion stress rather than a reaction to the embassy's quake.

Roberto's connected to Thomas Dominguez somehow and Dominguez is knee-deep in whatever was going on under the embassy. The Compeller has to be someone in the Inverros' house.

"We had a witness from the Varelas corroborate Señor Inverro's account," Marquin was saying, "but she was pulled away unexpectedly so we've asked her mother, Señora Sophia Varela, to stand in."

El twitched. Sophia wouldn't bandy words like El had. She'd fully commit to backing Roberto's testimony. *And there'll be no separating our houses in the Fae's minds after that. If the Inverros burn for Compelling, so will we.*

But her father had asked her to come talk with him before doing anything drastic. *I don't have time now.* Her brain scampered. Helping Amos escape would destroy the alliance with the Inverros, but tying themselves to a Compeller in the Court was worse.

She hadn't figured out a way to help Amos without implicating herself. *So be it.* As Icarus used to tell her, *Others hate us, that's on them. How we actually act, that's on us.* She'd deal with the consequences later.

Her mother walked toward Amos.

El met the giant's eyes.

Her hand slid into her pocket as she gave Amos a single nod. Marquin had obstructed the giant's mouth with an air block, evidenced by the slight, forced parting of his lips and the tension around his jawline, but his eyes crinkled in a smile just before he hung his head in what appeared to be defeat. At the same time, he lifted his heels and bunched his shoulders just like when he'd torn their cell door free.

Here goes. Committed, El stood, throwing the jar of lip balm hard against the wall.

Icarus and Levi hid below an open window on the northern side of the ambassador's house. A massive garden surrounded them, hiding them while they took in the sounds and smells from inside.

Icarus mostly caught the Fae's multi-hued fragrance, the rubbery skin of goblins, and the even dirtier stink of imps. As he filtered through those, another scent hit him. He shook his head, trying to clear his senses. Catching it again, his hackles rose.

Caramel-scented wax. It lacked the cedarwood aftershave from Na'rina's kidnapping memory, but the caramel paraffin was definitely there.

Levi bared his teeth, letting Icarus know he'd caught it too, and nodded up toward the open window. They'd remained low due to the aftershock that had rippled through the ground a moment before. Now, Icarus stood on his hind legs, peeking through.

A guillotine? Overkill much? But then, these were the Fae. Icarus

271

frowned. *Roberto?* Despite his son's presence, Mateo did not appear to be in attendance. Nor was there anyone fitting the kidnapper's appearance. Icarus spotted the mythic on trial. *Mateo's event is a giant's execution?*

Icarus dropped back to the dirt. A localized quake could have been caused by a giant, but that didn't fit with most giants' behavior.

With the heady mixture of mythics, it was impossible to pinpoint the one wafting caramel wax. He needed something more to confirm the kidnapper was present.

A thud and angry yell came from inside followed by the crack of a gunshot. Then two more shots in quick succession. People screamed and chairs screeched. Icarus hopped back up to look but immediately dropped back down, coughing and sneezing. *Smoke bomb!* Holding his breath, he hopped up again. A Fae man stood on a chair and shouted but the crowd's babble drowned him out. The giant and guillotine were gone, leaving behind a jagged hole in the far wall. *Way to go, giant!* Finally, the Fae man caught someone's attention. A moment later, a group of guards hustled through the hole after the escaped prisoner. Seeing them exit, the crowd rushed to follow.

Icarus pushed off the window and trotted through the garden, hoping to get a look at everyone as they left. Levi followed.

They barely made it to the corner, however, when a sound made them freeze. Icarus' ears twitched, picking out muffled chaos inside the house, the patter of running feet, and the quiet conversation of two people.

At his side, Levi nudged him. It was supposed to be gentle, but adrenaline coursed through them both and Icarus stumbled sideways.

"You're sure it wasn't her?" a woman asked.

"I'll give my next assignment to Dylan if it was."

Icarus slinked behind a rain barrel and Levi jumped onto a nearby roof just as Roberto Inverro and his mother entered the alley behind the ambassador's mansion. Icarus' ears twitched as they approached.

"Find Elodie anyway. We can't have her running loose right now," the woman ordered.

"What do you want me to do?" Roberto asked mockingly. "We blindsided her. She's unlikely to want to see me."

Icarus tilted his head. He'd never heard Roberto take that tone with his parents. A whiff of paraffin hit him as they passed and Icarus' lips pulled back from his canines in a silent hiss.

"Woo her," the woman scolded. "We need the Varelas and she's the key. Make it happen."

Icarus didn't catch the response. Fury coursed through him. Every fiber in him wanted to find Na'rina's kidnapper but as he moved back into the alley, he caught the distinct cinnamon and cumin that was his sister. There was a coppery tang to it. *She's bleeding.* He needed to find her before Roberto did. He thought of that whiff of paraffin. *One thing might lead to the other.*

Levi dropped from the rooftop beside Icarus, his golden eyes glowing with excitement. Icarus huffed and took off after his sister.

Na'rina crawled over a fallen oak. Distances had never been a problem before but now traversing even a few miles was going to take days.

I've never been this far from home, the twiglet mused. His good spirits had grown after spending time in the sun.

Na'rina tripped and caught herself on a palm tree.

Aw, aren't you sweet.

Na'rina jerked her hand away. She couldn't hear the trees at a distance like usual. And the first one she'd touched couldn't tell she was a Drydanda. *Please don't let these changes be permanent.* The trees did, however, gift energy in greeting like normal, which maintained her zoi aima but also added to the unfamiliar sensations running through her. Usually, such gifts were so diluted against Na'rina's overflowing energy that any effects were unnoticeable.

A heavy coconut flavor from the palm's greeting coated her tongue. Na'rina shook it off, missing her grove's light honeysuckle essence, and asked the twiglet, *Are you from this island?*

I'm from Venezuela.

Na'rina leaned against a pine.

Where're your roots, kid? the pine asked.

Na'rina pushed away without answering but gleaned reassurance in the familiar sharp taste left on her tongue.

How'd you end up here? she asked the twiglet.

He became shy, mentally ducking away to make himself smaller.

Are you trying to hide? Although he diminished in her mind, he didn't disappear and Na'rina almost chuckled as it reminded her of playing hide and seek, but then she caught something else. *Shame? Fear?*

What happened? She nudged him. He slumped, making her trip again over nothing as her body tried to follow.

Twiglets grow up in stands, you know? We usually have five or six of us together.

The Collective Wisdom kicked in to show her past twiglet stands that other Drydandas had known. She let it show her a little and then hummed her understanding.

We don't move around much so usually people just assume we're part of the foliage. One day some gnomes wandered into our field and settled down for a snack of mushrooms and potatoes. They were grumbling away, giving each other raspberries with their lips, when there came a repeated thumping sound and they all slumped over.

These people showed up and stuck one with a long needle. They withdrew some blood, placed it on a strip of paper and waited, staring until the paper turned dark red, which made them crazy excited. They bundled all the gnomes into burlap sacks and were leaving when one of the men looked back and caught me watching.

The twiglet stopped talking but his trembling shook Na'rina.

The man...the man dropped his sack and said, "Can't have witnesses."
He came at us with a machete and I screamed, waking my stand. None of them had seen what happened, but then I woke them up and they saw him and he saw them...

Na'rina shushed him. *You don't have to continue.*

...He mowed through them and was coming at me when a lady stopped him

and told him to bag me like the gnomes. Said, "Maybe it's useful." I'm not useful; I'm not good. They're gone cause I'm dumb and—

Enough. Na'rina startled herself with her tone. She sounded like Icarus. *Enough,* she softened as she sat down on the sandy, leaf-covered ground. The twiglet's sobs hiccupped in her chest. She wrapped her short, stubby arms tightly around his stomach and leaned into the one-person embrace, letting the sobs explode from inside.

The faint ebb and flow in her zoi aima, that strange synchrony with the ocean, picked up the rocking and grew, washing through them in cleansing waves until the surf pounded behind her ears. The forest would do something similar for a dryad's grief, offering solace in its embrace. She and the twiglet leaned into the rolling comfort until his sobs faded into occasional gasps. Once they subsided enough that they wouldn't hinder her, Na'rina pushed to her feet and kept moving, letting the twiglet calm himself until he said, *Sorry.*

You have nothing to be sorry about.

He was quiet for a long time as Na'rina stumbled through the quickly darkening trees. She'd started up a hill and the terrain slanted to the side, testing her footing.

*This El lady—*he hesitated. *She can help Alaya?* Again, his desire bled into the question. It was connected to his grief, like if he failed Alaya, he'd fail his family again.

She can help us, Na'rina said. She didn't actually know El but she believed Icarus' stories about his sister. If there was anything she could do, she'd help.

Na'rina steadied herself against a magnolia's long, reaching branch.

Thud, thud, thud.

The Nolia stirred, muttering, *What rattles my leaves?*

Na'rina had the same question. The steady thudding grew.

Something big is coming, the twiglet said.

Before Na'rina could respond, a man flew past, his huge strides in time with the sound.

My friend! The twiglet squealed and an eek escaped Na'rina.

The giant?

Another softer sound stilled her. Heavy, rasping breathing and running feet. A moment later, El stumbled past, clutching a hand against her side.

Na'rina didn't have Icarus' powerful sense of smell, but she didn't need it. Something red was leaking through El's fingers.

El!

Na'rina stepped away from the magnolia, hope rising like a wave in her chest. Something smacked her shoulder and she spun, hitting the ground.

"Ah!" yelled the Fae who'd run into her. He wore a guard uniform. "Dang imp!" And he kept going, chasing El and the giant.

Na'rina shoved off the ground only to be grabbed by a second guard who snatched her leafy hair. She kicked and the leaves tore free. The twiglet screamed.

"Come back here, you imp!" the guard snatched at her again. Na'rina ducked and ran into the thick, intertwining branches of the magnolia. As the guard thrashed into the tree's branches, she ran out the other side, wincing at the pain she'd just caused the poor Nolia.

She dove into a long hollow log and froze, hoping the growing darkness would hide her. The guard broke free of the tree, cursing at the "useless little imp."

A metallic snap!

Stay still, stay still, stay still.

Something stabbed through the rotting log and *zapped* as it hit her shoulder.

Na'rina screamed. The guard stabbed again, hitting her leg but also fully busting open the log. It cracked apart, exposing all the ants and beetles living inside.

"Ew!" The guard jumped back.

We're not useless or an imp! Fighting to move, Na'rina found a familiar, painful weakness shaking through her limbs. She gave up on running and rolled instead, letting the natural slant of the land carry her. The guard hollered. She picked up speed, holding her legs and arms tightly and not caring if she hit trees or rocks along the way.

Suddenly, the ground disappeared and she sailed out over a small cliff. Air whistled past her ears, and then she hit a mimosa's canopy and tumbled through to the ground.

She shuddered in the dead leaves under the tree. Her passage had created a tiny hole in the branches above and she watched as the guard peeked over the cliff.

"Aw, forget it!" he cursed again and left.

Tears flowed. Na'rina ached, bleeding from dozens of scrapes and cuts. They began to heal sluggishly but she fought exhaustion with the pain. It wasn't a lack of zoi aima so much as mental fatigue. She wasn't sure how they'd get back up the cliff they'd just sailed off, so she simply laid there, staring at the branches and the darkening sky while a cacophony of bugs started talking around them. Typically, Na'rina would thank her stars for being alive, but those lights were dimmed by clouds and looked so so far away. What would usually be a reflexive thought felt hollow now. If the gods were just stronger mythics, and the stars distant balls of light without a care, what was she thanking when she thanked her stars?

Strange reflections at such a time as this.

El— Na'rina struggled.

And my friend, the twiglet helped.

Either one could help us, Na'rina finally got the words together.

Sa, the twiglet agreed.

Just another minute, Na'rina said, *we'll follow them in just another minute.* But the twiglet's despair mirrored her own. Gazing at the hazy night sky, she reached as though stretching for her Rina, hoping *something* would give her the strength to keep going.

So close. We're so close.

El's heart beat so hard she couldn't draw breath and her side screamed with each step as warm blood leaked against her fingers.

Stupid, trigger-happy guard! She couldn't remember the last time someone actually got *shot* on the Sedanza Islands.

Ahead, Amos' heavy strides thudded, but no matter how she pushed, she wasn't gaining on him. If anything, she was quickly losing ground. She blinked her second lens down, trying to see him in the dusk, but that didn't help. They'd made it out of the city center and into the forest, but Marquin's guards were close behind, probably using his silencing gag as a beacon.

The gag would break with distance or time. As far as El knew, Marquin had to consciously fuel it. But El had no idea if they could get far enough away or if Marquin would give up. El's ankle twisted. She stumbled and tumbled down a small hill with barely a cry because she couldn't draw enough air.

She finally found the bottom of the hill and was pretty sure she couldn't have hit more trees and rocks if she'd tried. Her side screamed and her fingers were soaked in blood. The Fae would smell it. That shot terror down her spine. *It's quiet.* There was no thud from Amos' feet, no night bugs chattering, not even the sounds of their pursuers.

Where's Amos?

A guard shouted, shattering the momentary calm. El groaned, rolling over to find somewhere to hide. Pain radiated through her; she whimpered instead.

"Hold still."

She almost yelped as Amos dropped to his knees beside her.

"Where'd y' come from?" she asked through gritted teeth.

He rolled a shoulder and repeated, "Hold still," as he engulfed her in a hug.

Shocked, El felt tiny against his chest as he hunched over farther. Granite cracked, sprouting from his shoulders and growing down his back and up his arms. Then it stretched out to form walls between his limbs and body. All light dimmed until a dome of rock encased them.

"It's an island. They can't have gotten far," someone said.

"Unless he had more than one accomplice."

Footsteps approached.

"I smell fresh blood."

"But the trail ends here. What'd they do, vanish into thin air?"

As her eyes adjusted, El picked out tiny pricks of light attesting to air holes Amos left along the ground. One dimmed and Amos huffed softly as the guard leaned against his rocky back.

"The air block's gone. Try to feel him out."

El wanted to curse. Some Fae were gifted with the ability to *feel* what creatures were nearby. It wasn't precise, more like that prickling you get when you feel someone watching, but it'd be enough to tell the guard a direction.

El laid her hand over the granite behind the guard's heel. Amos obligingly crushed a tiny section to dust and El slid her hand up the guard's pant leg to touch his calf above his sock.

He jerked until she touched skin and "convinced" him a gecko had wandered up his leg and his twitch had dislodged it. Thankfully, he didn't realize a gecko wouldn't be moving as the day cooled.

El typically wasn't the bludgeoning sort when she coaxed a mind. She hated the feeling of someone's mind gone limp. Instead, she nudged. A tiny suggestion here, a thought there, and she was gone. Such subtle maneuvering was more reliable anyway.

The Fae quested out, searching for them. El marveled at his connection to the world. It wasn't beautifully complex like a Drydanda's, but he sensed all nearby warmer-blooded creatures. He'd miss a dryad or oceanid altogether, but the warmth he sensed would identify the size and temperature of most everything else.

Amos, interestingly, only vaguely showed as an overly warm rock. El ran with the sensation, gently pressing on the likelihood that the rock had been bathed in sunlight most of the day. The guard dismissed the rock and moved on. El carefully pulled her hand away.

"Nothing," he finally said.

"Too clever by half," his companion grumbled. "He can't be faster than us. Where's he hiding?" The guards wandered away, their voices fading.

Around El, Amos' arms remained tense.

"Y' okay?" she whispered.

"Takes a mite to break," he admitted. His forehead pressed against hers and she felt the sweat on his brow.

El snapped her mouth shut. Except for Icarus, no one hugged her, and she found herself a tiny bit glad it'd take him a minute longer.

And staying motionless helped the screaming in her side.

Just as he began to relax, there came a faint huffing sound. El tilted her head and gasped as a large feline nose pressed close to a hole at the bottom of Amos' dome.

The rock in front of Icarus exploded as though shattered with a hammer. It cascaded off massive shoulders. Icarus sprang away with a yowl and barely avoided the huge fist that swung past his nose. He glimpsed El curled up around her stomach where she lay in the giant's protective shell. Adrenaline spiked through Icarus and then the familiar icy reasoning took over.

This is El's ally. He didn't want to harm him. *I have to slow him down.* Icarus launched off a tree to slide between the giant's legs as he took a step forward. Spinning, he braced for when Levi smashed into the mythic's chest. More than 300 pounds hitting all at once was enough to knock even a giant backwards. His heels smacked into Icarus' side.

Icarus' breath huffed from him as the massive creature fell on top of him. Vibrations shuddered the ground, then rolled back toward the giant like he was sucking them into himself. What should have been a loud thud came out as a soft whoosh.

Levi had ridden the giant to the ground and now lunged for his throat. Huge hands batted him back, but it was clear Levi knew what he was doing. He rolled and came right back.

El whimpered, her lips forming a protest as she inched toward the pair while clutching her stomach. Blood scented the air, stronger as she moved.

Icarus' heart thundered. *Levi's past his reasoning!* He dug his claws into the ground to pull himself free of the giant's legs and swatted Levi's hindquarters just as he bunched to lunge again. Levi twitched, swatted at Icarus sideways, and spun back toward the giant.

Icarus knew that single-mindedness. He did *not* want to go head-to-head with Levi while a bunch of Fae were close by. But he couldn't employ his other abilities as a lynx.

He pulled in a deep breath and held it. His heart slowed and the adrenaline abated until he could focus on the zoi aima coming from Na'rina's leaf. Regretfully, he pushed it away. It dissipated like mist in morning light and the change seared through him so fast he yowled before he could stop himself. His muscles and joints flared in one excruciating moment.

Then the change was done. El and the giant gaped at him but Levi lunged for the giant's throat again.

Icarus smacked a hand against him mid-air.

Relax! he ordered psychically.

Levi went limp but he was mid-jump. He slammed into the giant's face and kept rolling until he lay on his side, panting from what Icarus guessed was shock.

Bitter guilt coated Icarus' tongue. He loathed using his Sedessan abilities. It wasn't Compelling precisely. A victim wasn't aware of what had happened when a Sedessan Compelled, but it came far too close. Icarus gagged and spun away, suddenly understanding why some things made Na'rina ill.

The giant spit, spluttering at the lion fur in his mouth as Levi stood and shook himself.

El chuckled and groaned, hugging her middle. "Rus, you do know how to make an entrance."

"Y' know 'm?" the giant sputtered.

Icarus ignored him, rushing to El's side. "Let me see."

She lay back and removed her hands, her brown eyes twinkling despite her pain. The wound had bled profusely from her running, not from how deep it was. "It only grazed you," he assured her. He stripped off his shirt and pressed it to her side. "Hold this tight. With how much noise we just made, we need to get moving." He helped El to sit up, then pulled her to her feet. When he turned, he found the giant staring at them in confusion. "Let's go," he said, leading them farther into the forest and away from the sounds of the Fae searchers.

Pinched between their bodies, his phone vibrated. He grumbled but fished it out.

"Hello?"

"Kadis," Afre bleated, "they've done it!"

"Done what?" Icarus fought a wave of exhaustion. His joints hurt. *Afre doesn't call often. It's important.*

"Followed through on their deal with Ser'ored."

Icarus stopped walking and El stumbled. He grimaced apologetically at her. Then to Afre he said, "Explain."

"I returned from Tennessee to find Ver'rina panicking. The shell man came back and afterward Ser'ored left. And now I'm staring at a very diseased pine tree, Kadis. I think he killed his tree."

The familiar ice washed through Icarus. "Has the Rina touched it?"

"I—the Rina—"

"Did she come into contact with the pine, Afre?" Icarus' patience was long gone.

"*Na*, Kadis. She didn't."

Icarus's hands trembled. "Destroy the pine," he ordered.

"Destroy? As in cut it down?"

"It could infect the Rinas, Faun. Cut it down and burn it." They couldn't do much about Ser'ored right then, but they needed to protect the rest of the forest. Ser'ored might even die from whatever he'd done before he infected someone else. Icarus knew that shouldn't give him hope, but it did.

After a pause, Afre answered, "I'll figure it out, Kadis."

El may as well have passed through a rock tumbler. Bruises were starting to appear on her arms, her ankle throbbed, and her side pulsed in tandem with it, pounding like a bass drum.

Icarus gingerly peeled her shirt away to see her injury. "It needs bandaging."

They'd found a small alcove to hide in long enough to patch El up. Heavy rock walls surrounded them, which would provide warning if anyone approached. El tilted her head against a palm tree and let out a sigh as she watched the wind whip at the fronds above. A storm was rolling in. They were farther up the coast from where she and Sala had landed, so at least they were more sheltered. *Where is Sala?*

El hissed as Icarus flushed water over her wound. She wished briefly for his ridiculous healing but then bit her lip. *He was treated like a pariah because of his heritage. I have no business bemoaning my lot.*

A deep line showed between his brows and El reached to touch it, then hesitated, her fingers inches from his skin. That phone call had alarmed him.

Icarus teasingly nipped at her hand to get it out of his way as he started tying a long strip of fabric ripped from the bottom of his shirt around her middle. El snatched her hand back but knew there was no reproach to his action. Icarus had never shied away from her.

Does it hurt to shift? Where do his clothes go while he's a lynx?

El bit her cheek. She was rambling. She didn't fully recognize Icarus anymore. It wasn't that the young boy she'd known was gone from his sharp cheekbones and hazel eyes. She'd long ago adjusted to that. It wasn't even that he sported new scars since she'd last seen him. He'd told her about the Kadivas with his brutal mentor.

Why are you here? They'll kill you!

She reached for his hand. A light touch and she could ask him.

With a tug, he finished her bandage and moved away. Over Icarus' shoulder, she caught Amos' gaze. Guilt, confusion, distrust, fascination. Such a glut of emotions.

Icarus settled back on his heels with preternatural grace. His companion padded out of the forest, slipped around Amos, and sat down against Icarus's hip.

El stared and the huge golden eyes stared back. She was under no illusions as to how Icarus had stopped the massive feline's attack. And yet he sat down touching her brother. Even let Icarus rest a hand on his shoulder.

Envy burned in El. *Stop it, stop it, stop it! He's worked hard for such trust.* But she couldn't help thinking of Sala, who'd backed away without El ever violating her trust. *Why's it hurt so much?* She'd experienced rejection before. Perhaps it was that Sala had actually given her a chance at first.

"Levi says the Fae have given up the search for now," Icarus said. "We'll need to find shelter soon."

El closed her eyes, drinking in her brother's unique dark chocolate-and-whiskey voice.

"He's a wer-im?" she asked. For all she knew, Icarus could draw normal animals to him, but the puma's size made that unlikely.

"*Sa,*" Icarus said.

"He's massive."

The puma raised his head and huffed, then rubbed the side of his head against Icarus' knee. Icarus caught himself with a hand as the gesture threatened to knock him over. El could swear the puma was laughing as he laid his head back down.

"Who're you?" Amos asked, staring at Icarus.

El shot him a look.

"What? History's writ all over y'r faces."

Icarus' jaw tensed. It was bad enough he was on Sedanza; they didn't need to make it worse by telling people who he was. But El found she *wanted* to earn Amos' trust. It was a very un-Sedessan desire. Before she could figure out what to say, however, Icarus asked, "Where's a good place to shelter before this rolls in?" He indicated the heavy clouds above.

Amos' eyes shuttered. "I'll find me own place." He stood, wincing probably from the chain lacerations where they'd dug into him.

"*Na*," El blurted, flushing at her lack of tact. But there was a cavern full of captured mythics to free, a Sedessan Compelling Ambassador Marquin to capture, and a missing Drydanda they needed to find. They didn't have a lot of allies they could trust and, despite everything, she trusted Amos. As both Amos and Icarus looked at her in surprise, she tried to settle into her negotiation façade and found it uncomfortable. She pressed on anyway. "First, you owe me some information," she said, "and second, we've got a whole cavern of people to help."

"Cavern of people?" Icarus asked.

El didn't answer. She held Amos' stare until he relaxed back into his seated position and then she flushed in what suspiciously might be a blush. *It's relief,* she told herself.

"Guess y'r right," Amos finally said. "Y' did finally follow through."

Intrigued, Icarus leaned forward with his elbows balanced on his knees while the giant paused, chewing on his words.

"Y' know I have a connection to rock," Amos said. "There was the large cavern where we met, the Drydanda's small cavern—"

Na'rina's here! Finally, some confirmation. Icarus held up a hand. "Back up. Give me context."

El explained quickly about the holding cells below the embassy and the earthquake, finishing with, "Amos claims to know what happened to the Drydanda."

Another holding cell. Levi rubbed his head, hard, against his hip and Icarus unconsciously rested a hand on his furry shoulder to steady himself. "Go on," he told Amos.

"There was the Drydanda's small room," Amos picked up his story, "and three other chambers. One huge cavern to the south of ours, and two below."

"The huge cavern," El interjected. "It's full of sedated mythics."

"I can't confirm that," Amos said.

"I can. I saw it earlier today. Now, the two chambers below us?"

Icarus let El guide the conversation.

"One was porous and full of water. An aquifer, I guess."

"And the other?"

"It was tiny. I would'a missed it, but when the quake hit, the water in the aquafer pushed up into the tiny chamber and seemed to, er, shake the walls."

"Was there a water mythic in the aquafer?"

Amos rolled a shoulder. "'Spect so. I only feel rock, not people, but water flowed upwards during that quake, so I'd bet so."

"How does the Drydanda fit?" Icarus asked, unable to hold his silence longer.

"I think she fell into the tiny chamber."

"While it was filled with water?"

"You think?" El sat up straighter, then gasped and grasped her side.

Amos patted the air to calm them, and then scratched behind his ear in consternation. "The water drained," he assured Icarus. "The tiny chamber sits directly below the Drydanda's. Since I was buried in rock and iron door not ten feet from her," he shot El a glare, but it lacked any heat, "I saw her poof—gone—when the ceiling caved. But after everything settled, I feel this *tap, tap, tapping* from the tiny chamber below."

"You don't know for sure that it was her?" Icarus asked. He *wanted* to believe it was her, but neither did he want to pursue an empty lead.

Amos held up a finger, unease playing across his face. "There's not many who would trust enough to communicate like that. Guards with their batons, imps running amok, yet whoever it was purposefully responded to me." He patted his chest, then leaned forward as the gusty wind blew his hair about his face. "Sounds an awful lot like something a dryad would do, though, *na?*"

Levi growled softly as Icarus sat back on his heels again.

He's leaving something out, Levi said, *pushing* the thought at Icarus, trusting his Sedessan side to hear. *Were there pants or roots?*

"Levi thinks you're leaving something out," Icarus said aloud. "Were there roots near the Drydanda's cave?"

"Some above it."

"They go deeper than her cave?"

"*Na.* Nothin' deeper."

Icarus rubbed a hand down his face.

"What is it?" El asked.

"She needs some sort of body. Like a cell tower; she can send out signals, but it has to have a place to originate. The only time she fully disappears is into a plant. If there's no plant, and her body disappeared, then she had to have melded into something. How did she answer Amos' tapping?"

Neither El nor Amos offered an answer and Icarus growled. El twitched and he realized he was showing his canines.

Amos rolled a shoulder awkwardly.

"Y' su—" Amos cut off as something thumped into the forest behind them. A keening pierced the air, high and pained, and El winced.

Both Icarus' and Levi's heads came up, but it was Amos who shoved to his feet, shock and concern on his face. He took off running through the trees toward the sound.

"Rus?" El asked Icarus.

He didn't answer as Amos returned. Everything within him zeroed in on the torn, weeping twiglet cradled in the giant's hands.

Na'rina clung to Amos' wrist. It wasn't quite the hug she'd hoped to give him, but in her torn and broken state, it was the best she could do.

"Is that—" a woman started to ask but Na'rina couldn't hear the rest of the question over her sobs and the shaking of her leafy hair. The twiglet's relief intensified her emotions.

She'd reached the giant! That's all she'd been able to focus on after she'd convinced herself to get up and stumble after them. Then she'd fallen down another cliff as she'd tried to climb down toward the beach.

"How'd it survive the quake?" the woman asked.

"This," the giant proudly lifted Na'rina, clinging hard, toward the woman, "is how your Drydanda survived."

He knows? Na'rina peeked over her shoulder, sniffling.

That's El.

Motion drew her eye farther and Na'rina's heart stuttered.

Icarus!

She screeched before she even realized the sound was building in her throat. Hopping out of the giant's hands, she barely caught his shirt long enough to climb down his pants to the ground. Once there, she scampered to Icarus, who gracelessly flopped off his heels to sit.

Na'rina scrambled into his lap.

Those beloved hazel eyes blurred. *My tears or his?* She couldn't say. Raising trembling hands, she grasped his face and whispered, *Hello, my love.*

A heavy sigh escaped Icarus' lips, rustling her leaves.

A twiglet? I didn't know that was possible.

Neither did I, she hesitated but then admitted, *but now I'm stuck.*

Behind her, El exclaimed, "Heavens above, she looks like a star stuffed inside a log."

Not very tactful, is she?

Icarus chuckled. *Caught her by surprise.*

A raindrop splattered onto Icarus' forehead, then his nose. Na'rina flinched when another hit her shoulder. The energy surge she'd experienced at seeing Icarus faded and her hands trembled.

She dropped her arms and thumped her head against Icarus' sternum instead, shuddering with exhaustion. He pushed something into her hands. Sappy tears trailed down Na'rina's nose. *Will I ever stop crying?* But these were joyful as her Rina's zoi aima whispered into her from the golden leaf. *Should I attempt to separate from the twiglet again?* Na, I *can't draw enough zoi aima and until I figure out why, it won't work.*

"We need shelter," Amos rumbled as the rain fell harder.

Icarus fished his phone from his pocket.

Alaya, the twiglet urged. *Say something about Alaya.*

"Alaya's stuck in a tank," she muttered, fighting a yawn. *When did I last sleep?* She wasn't sure, but it might have been when Armando— *Mateo,* she reminded herself. *Armando is Mateo*—drugged her.

No one answered but Icarus stiffened briefly. A second later, he made a call and Felis' playful voice answered.

"Kadis, you must be back in regular shape! Please tell me you've found the Drydanda and Dante and I don't have to actually meet this Inverro guy."

"Not quite," Icarus said, his breath rustling the leaves on Na'rina's head. "What's a better location to hide seven mythics, the library or the hotel you're at?"

"Seven? Huh. That'd be tight here at the hotel. But there's a study room at the library we might be able to slip into."

"Good. Did you find the book?"

"*Na*, this place is a labyrinth."

"Keep looking. We'll meet you there. Oh, and bring me a shirt."

That was the last thing Na'rina heard as she drifted to sleep.

Na'rina woke as they entered the Fae library. She knew, without opening her eyes, that Icarus was carrying her from the spice of his zoi aima and the warmth against her skin.

"Never liked this place," El muttered.

Na'rina popped an eye open.

Their steps whispered across a marble floor, past massive white columns and floor-to-ceiling shelves. A part of Na'rina intrinsically knew those shelves were covered in books, paper made from the corpses of thousands of trees. The faint vanilla aroma of decomposing paper filled the air like mountain flowers on a soft night.

Would they mind such a burial? To grant knowledge long after they'd passed? Her sleepy mind started to ponder it but stopped when Amos asked, "Don't Sedessans love information? Y'r surrounded by the stuff here."

El snorted. "Sure. Except if you walk down that row and turn around to come back, I can guarantee you won't find yourself back out in this main hallway. It's a labyrinth. I'm not even sure how he's leading us right now."

At her envious tone, Felis shot her a grin with too many teeth.

"Plus," El continued, "do you hear our steps?"

Na'rina certainly didn't, but she had just figured everyone walked as lightly as the wer-im. Now that she thought about it, though, that didn't make any sense.

El stomped a foot. She winced and clutched at her side. "Hear anything?" she asked. None of them had. El threw her hands up in a "see" gesture and kept walking. "I'm not sure if it's Fae magic or construction, but something about this place ain't right."

"The poor Fae try but it's hard to trick a wer-im's senses," Felis joked.

Icarus scoffed. "He's following his nose."

Na'rina understood a moment later when Felis led them into an alcove in the library's marble back wall. There was no door, but the marble took them around a curved hallway and opened into a room with a heavy mahogany table laden with bread, fruit, sliced deli meat and goat cheese.

Na'rina stared at the polished table, reminded of the oak monstrosity from the summit, but then Icarus was lowering her to stand on the mahogany and the aroma of yeast hit her.

"Fae food?" El asked, her suspicion clear.

"Brownie bakery," Felis answered. "Oddest place ever. Sign said, 'You're on the honor system. Pay for what you take or we'll come rearrange your house. Pay for more than you take and you might find an extra loaf of bread on your counter.'"

Definitely brownies. Sure of that, Na'rina searched the table for the bread she smelled. "Bread?" she rasped.

"And honey." Icarus set the jar in front of her along with an herb-covered white loaf.

Na'rina grasped the rim of the jar, half wanting to climb into it. *Is that a twiglet desire?* The twiglet didn't answer but at the back of the room, she caught Dante's knowing chuckle and shared a silent laugh with him before she pulled a chunk of bread off the loaf and dipped it.

Satisfied, Icarus accepted a new shirt from Felis and then loaded a plate.

El filled a bowl with pineapple chunks and sat across from them. It was a simple move, comfortable, but something about Icarus and El at the same table rang true like a catkin budding on a snow-laden branch.

Na'rina took another bite and flopped across the table with a blissful sigh, her hands resting on her distended stomach. A splash of red caught her eye and she gazed longingly at the bowl of strawberries, but then she slumped back into her contented bliss. She didn't want to make the poor twiglet sick by overeating.

"You're welcome to eat," Icarus told Amos while tossing a chunk of meat to Levi, who'd curled up against his feet.

The giant stood in the doorway. "Not sure I should stay."

"Come, Amos," El said. "There's a cavern full of mythics that needs us."

"Accordin' to you, but you lie. And it almost got me head cut off."

Icarus shot El a look and she blushed. *Is that shame?* Na'rina didn't get to ponder it as Felis spoke up.

"Kadis, you sure about the mindwalker?" Felis jabbed a thumb toward El.

Fire lit Icarus' eyes and Felis backtracked. "I'm just saying—"

Inside, the twiglet whimpered.

Na'rina's bliss evaporated. *This can't be happening. It's like the summit all over again.*

"Stop it!" Na'rina pushed to her feet. Blood rushed to her head and she wobbled. Once her dizziness passed, she realized everyone was staring. The twiglet cowered, and Na'rina's shoulders tried to hunch inward. *Now I've done it.* But she refused to back down. "Look at us! We're being experimented on and dying! There's a cavern full of sedated mythics, yet we can't even agree to help each other.

"I don't know you," Na'rina pinned El with a look and the petite woman's eyes glittered back. It wasn't threatening; if anything, El was enjoying this. Na'rina pressed on, "but I know him," she pointed at Icarus, "and he trusts you." She spun toward Amos and took a couple steps across the table. "I don't know you either, but you saved my life without asking for a thing. You don't trust El. Fine. I saw the cavern too. If you don't trust her, at least accept a second witness that there are mythics who need your help.

"And you," she whirled back toward Icarus and stalked over to him. Words failed her. She cupped his face instead and just stared, begging.

"All right," he said, "I'll throw my cards on the table if everyone else will."

Levi, of all people, protested from the floor. Icarus dropped a hand onto his head. "She needs to know," he said. "I'll not hold your secret."

Levi bared his teeth. Icarus bared his right back.

"Why's he protesting?" Na'rina asked, disturbed.

"Has to do with an avalanche," Icarus said. "I'll explain."

Levi huffed and padded from the room.

Amos harrumphed, watching him go, and then stood to his full height. "One question, Drydanda, and I'll agree."

Na'rina turned, uneasy, especially after her own grandfather voiced an objection. She swayed again and caught herself on the honey. Her exhaustion, an almost physical call to return to her grove, was starting to ache within her.

"How many members in the twiglet's stand?"

Grief washed through Na'rina like he'd ripped a branch from her. *Na*, not her, from the twiglet. Memory flickered across their connection…the twiglet with his stand, the tiny creature huddling against the giant, then curling against the base of a white tree. Just as quickly, the images vanished.

He's friend, the twiglet whispered. *He cares.* Na'rina's shoulders slumped. In that moment she understood why the twiglet trusted the giant so completely. They'd both lost everyone they loved.

Amos recognized the grief. He pulled out a chair and sat.

"What was that?" Felis muttered.

"Making sure Na'rina didn't kill the twiglet," Icarus growled.

Na'rina pointed a warning finger and he subsided.

"Introductions first," she insisted, sitting against the honey jar.

"I'm Na'rina Drydanda and a twiglet, at the moment."

Amos, Felis, and Dante spoke next, taking the introductions in stride. When it came to El, however, she hesitated and shot a glance at Icarus. Only because she knew him did Na'rina sense Icarus' apprehension.

I hate secrets. But Icarus had agreed to lay his cards out and so she just waited.

"Thinking up a lie?" Amos asked El. He'd leaned back his chair against the wall but still his legs easily reached the floor. It was good the chair was marble, or it might have collapsed under him.

El glared. "Not all truths are mine to give."

"This one's mine, though," Icarus cut in. "I'm Icarus Teras, the Wer-Kadis of the wer-im, Na'rina's Vow Protector, and El's outcast half-brother."

Adrenaline spiked through El at Icarus' bold words.

Felis huffed a laugh. "I knew you weren't all cat, but sheesh."

Na'rina just handed Icarus a chunk of pineapple and then shifted to lean against his arm.

Can I drop my mask here? Bracing herself, El said, "I'm Elodie Varela of the Sedanza Court. And as Icarus just said, I'm his sister."

Amos tapped his finger on the table. "Always about family, eh?" There was a gleam, not forgiveness exactly, but maybe understanding, in his eyes. Something inside El melted.

"All right," Dante said, breaking the moment like El hadn't just made herself vulnerable, "now what?" he asked Na'rina.

The Drydanda stood up and grabbed another pineapple chunk. Seemingly on a whim, she dipped it in the honey and tasted it. Her lips puckered. She shook her head, hard, as a shudder went through her body. "Ugh! Bad idea," she said. Once she'd gathered herself, she continued, "Let's combine what we know. I'll start…"

El's brain went into overdrive as they shared.

Bloodline restrictions. Both King Olbin and Drydanda Vell'marxia fear Na'rina because of it. Does that connect with what Sophia did to Icarus?

Alaya Oceadanda is being held captive. North American dryads are captives too. They can't be freed here. They'd die away from their trees, but the

Oceadanda needs help now.

Na'rina and the twiglet need help too. Time is crucial there, but how do we separate them? Na'rina estimates they have…what? Maybe a day or two left before changes start to become permanent. That terrifies her. El glanced at Icarus. *Scares him too.*

Thomas Dominguez and Mateo Inverro are working together. I knew they were connected! That gave El both relief—she'd been right to throw the trial—and anxiety. *Who's leading whom between Thomas and Mateo? Mateo is one of the leaders of the Court, probably the most powerful person individually in Sedanza, but Na'rina's story makes him sound subservient to Thomas. Dumping bodies. That's menial for Mateo.*

"Wait, let me get this straight," Felis interrupted Na'rina, who'd been explaining her recent experiences. El paused her contemplation to listen, "The guy who kidnapped you introduced himself as Armando, but he's really Mateo Inverro, who happens to be a big cheese in the Court?"

Na'rina nodded.

"And he's somehow working with the human guy who's the aid to the Fae ambassador here on the island?"

She nodded again.

"Eesh. Talk about confusing."

"It's not unusual for Sedessans to use aliases," El said.

"Can't you just be you?"

"Not often."

Felis grimaced. El shared a look with Icarus. He understood the reality of her world. When the silence lengthened, Na'rina picked up her story again.

El, only half listening, swung back to Dominguez. *There's something not right about that man. Asking for injections from Mateo? What for? What does he want?*

A disturbing possibility occurred to El. She mentally pulled up pictures of Dominguez, Mateo, and Roberto. Even went so far as to remember Dominguez leaning on his cane and Roberto leaning on the chair with his hands stacked. A pang ran through her at connecting the two, but she ignored it. If Roberto was involved, she wanted to know. *Uncanny resemblance.* She added Sedessan facial lines to Dominguez and aged him. *Too uncanny. But Na'rina and I have seen his human zoi aima. He's worked as Marquin's aid for years. A lot of Sedessans have seen his lifeblood. Maybe…oh, maybe that's why he wants the injections. Is that even possible?* She distinctly remembered Roberto giving Marquin a perfunctory answer about his grandfather's medications helping him when he'd asked after the man. *That'd be just like Roberto to answer that way.* Another thought chased that. *The eldest Inverro was suspected of Compelling in his youth.* She needed to confirm her sudden suspicions.

"…priority is to free Alaya. She'll know how to help Na'rina and the twiglet," Icarus was saying.

El glanced around the table, noting that everyone deferred to her brother naturally. *Does he even realize?* It was somewhat odd for El to see him as the Wer-Kadis. To her he was just—Icarus.

As he spoke, Icarus dipped a pineapple chunk into the honey and tried it. His shudder wasn't as pronounced as Na'rina's, but he set the pineapple aside on a napkin.

"We need to meet with Ambassador Marquin as well," El added.

Na'rina cocked her head, but it was Icarus who asked, "Why?"

El hesitated. She'd told them about the last few days, but she hadn't gone into depth about a few things, including the Compelling. It was the worst thing to accuse a Sedessan of. "I suspect," she finally said, "that someone Compelled him."

El held in her cringe as the two wer-im, Felis and Dante, looked at her in alarm. Icarus leaned back, clearly absorbing the idea.

"That'd explain the farce of a trial earlier," Amos said.

"Exactly. Fae are many things, but lax on truth isn't one of them."

They started to discuss details to free Alaya *and* get the ambassador to meet with them.

El retreated inward again to process the unlikely coincidence of Intela Corp's ship, the *Sansabria*, floating off Riviera's coastline—without anyone apparently noticing it entering the dome—and the Inverros wanting injections of something. *The injections are probably an Intela Corp creation. Are the Inverros buying from Intela Corp? Are they giving Intela Corp mythics to study? Is that why they've captured so many?* El grimaced in disgust. The idea that a mythic would hand other mythics over to humans for study was disturbing.

The heavy pounding of rain and the deep boom of thunder caught El off guard. The room had grown quiet.

"Dante and Felis, get the Fae's attention and insist on a meeting with the ambassador instead of Mateo," Icarus finally said. "Convince him to meet with us back here later tonight."

"How?" Felis asked. "He's not likely to come alone with the likes of us."

"Play to his pride," El suggested. "He's a powerful telekinetic. Hint at your surprise that he'd have anything to fear from you."

Dante snickered. "Not the first time that's worked."

"Copy that," Felis said, sounding unconvinced.

"One other thing," Icarus stopped them before they disappeared. "I'll need your backpack, Dante." The wer-im picked it up off the floor and tossed it across the table. Apparently, it was almost empty.

"All right," Icarus said after they'd left. "Let's go figure out how to get Alaya out of that tank."

Na'rina watched water drip down Icarus' neck as she clung to the top edge of the backpack she rode inside. The pack's sodden material squished under her toes. It'd protected her from the howling wind but not the torrential rain.

They followed El into the tunnel she'd escaped from earlier and Amos brought up the rear, his steps leaving huge puddles on the floor. Somewhere farther behind them Levi padded along, but Na'rina only caught flashes of his golden eyes.

She'd never seen him outside of Ver'rina's grove. Until last spring, she'd never even met him. Icarus had given a recap of their avalanche discussion, and it left a deep disquiet in her. *So many secrets.* And Levi hadn't wanted to share this one. *Can I blame Mamma for hiding me when Ver'rina and Levi set such a precedent?* A longing settled in her heart like a lode stone. She missed her grove and her mother. Behind them, she glimpsed golden eyes again. Watching for another flash, she spotted something else.

"Icarus," she whispered. "We're not the only ones leaving puddles."

"We're not the only ones using the storm for cover," he whispered back, unsurprised.

Na'rina shivered. She curled her fingers against Icarus' skin, letting his warmth seep into her fingers while the utility lights lining the walls guided their way. She spotted the small triangle of shadow she'd hidden in only hours earlier. *We're not alone this time.*

Drydanda, the twiglet said, *I don't want to be alone.*

She froze. Had he heard her? *Na.* She caught snatches of his thoughts. Images of digging in his roots among her trees. Of smelling the aspen sap and connecting it with a new home. He missed his stand and he was scared of being left alone again.

You won't be alone, she promised.

"I hear imps ahead," Icarus whispered.

El paused and pulled something from her pocket. She snapped tines off the comb and a faint smell reached Na'rina's nose.

"Cocainic?" Icarus asked.

El winked and continued forward.

She's so confident.

"Cold, cold, cold," an imp complained somewhere ahead. There came a shriek and a scuffle that ended with cackling.

A few moments later, the cavern entrance appeared, freshly swept of rubble. El crept forward to peek inside and immediately stepped back like she'd been hit.

"Eh?" Amos grabbed her shoulder to steady her.

"Drydanda, were there eleven rows of tanks when you left the cavern today?"

Na'rina swallowed and tried to remember but she hadn't counted. She'd only been looking for Alaya's tank. "I don't know," she admitted, "but the rows ran all the way from the back wall up to three rows past the side door."

El slumped against the tunnel and dirt crumbled onto her shoulders.

Amos peeked into the cavern. "That ain't good," he rumbled. "There're only five rows now."

"Is the back one still there?" Na'rina squeaked. *I left Alaya!*

"It's there," Amos said. Na'rina buried her face against Icarus' neck in relief. "But those imps are preparin' things to be moved."

"We're losing our chance to free everyone," El said

"Maybe not," Icarus said. "I think I know where they're moving them, but we'll need Alaya free now to take advantage of it."

El pushed off the wall. "See anyone but the imps?"

Icarus blinked and peered into the cavern for a long moment. Amos checked too.

Does the giant see energy like us? the twiglet asked.

I don't think so, Na'rina answered, *but he might pick up on the vibration of footsteps.*

Oh, the twiglet sat back. *That's cool. I want to tell him that's cool.*

You'll get your chance.

"Nothin'," Amos muttered.

Icarus nodded.

El accepted that and stepped into the cavern, humming.

Na'rina leaned close to Icarus' ear. "Where do you think they're taking everyone?"

"The *Sansabria.*"

Na'rina shuddered at the mention of the ship.

In the cavern, four imps popped their heads up among the tanks. They zeroed in on El as she sauntered between stalagmites; then one shrieked and vaulted over a tank toward her. She spun and brought what looked like a pen to her mouth. With a puff, she sent something sailing into the imp's face. He shrieked again and dropped like a swatted fly. In quick succession, El pivoted and hit the other three imps in the same way. Na'rina stared, stunned, and then Amos chuckled, breaking the moment.

She learn that from you? Na'rina asked Icarus.

His hazel eyes glittered at her as he stepped into the cavern to join his sister.

"The control panels are that way." El pointed to the right and unconsciously checked her side with her fingertips.

"Alaya's that way." Na'rina pointed toward the back wall.

"See if there's a manual," Icarus told his sister and then strode in the direction Na'rina indicated.

Manual? Na'rina asked.

A binder with instructions.

Ugh. Humans and their ways of keeping information.

Amos whistled softly, drawing their attention to the far-right wall and a row of larger tanks strapped together. "Think they tried to construct a tank big enough for me?"

"They took your blood," Icarus said over his shoulder. "I suspect if there was something they found useful, they'd have figured out a way to make you fit."

"Maybe it's a blessing y' convinced me to act," Amos said to El.

El paused in searching the control area. "As you said, I about got your head chopped off. Not too sure about that blessing."

Amos huffed. "'bout and did are two different things."

El went back to searching without responding. If Na'rina didn't know better, she'd think the woman didn't have a response.

"Found the manual," El called a moment later, her low voice carrying across the cavern to where the other three stood now in the back. "Disconnecting anything without the proper procedure will kill whoever's inside."

"Which one?" Icarus asked Na'rina.

Na'rina pointed. As they neared, the lid turned translucent.

"Almighty wonders," Icarus breathed, "she's paler than you were after Tennessee."

"Good thing she's close to the ocean, then," Na'rina said as Amos stepped up beside them. El joined them with a huge, blue three-ring binder in her hands.

"This thing's ridiculous," she flipped through the pages. "Na'rina, crawl below the tank and disconnect the power cord. Icarus, hit that button before she does."

Icarus shrugged out of the pack and let Na'rina climb out to do as directed.

"You're sure?" Na'rina asked. She'd considered removing the cable before but had been scared it would kill Alaya.

"It'll switch to battery power, and we'll be able to move it," El assured. Then she puzzled, "Huh."

"What?" Icarus asked.

"Take a look at the panel above her head."

"It's a light."

"It's a UV light. Meant to keep dryads and certain other mythics alive."

"Does that mean what I think it means?" Na'rina asked, squeaking as she tugged on the power cable. It resisted.

Icarus' face appeared under the tank's bottom edge as he answered, "Mimics sunlight."

We were that close to a source of sunlight? She pulled harder and the cable came free, depositing her with a thump onto the floor. *What about Vell'marxia?* The other Drydanda's leafy hair was browning. "Must not work well," Na'rina said.

"Or it works too well," El said. "Looks like they struggle to keep the lights at a perfect level."

"Ah." That tracked. Na'rina had seen plenty of plants brown if they were being cooked by the sun. "Whatever happened to the fire elemental you were with?" she asked, thinking about someone being cooked…or who could do the cooking.

When Na'rina peeked out from under the tank, she found El staring at the control panel on the side.

"She spooked and ran."

Oh. Na'rina ducked back under the tank.

Amos watched El, reading more into her answer than she'd like. *Ignore 'im.* Aloud, she said, "We'll have to move the whole tank. There's supposed to be an external, electronic key to open it but since we don't have that, we'll let the battery keep her alive until we reach the ocean and then we'll crack it open." She pushed a couple buttons and the tank hummed. "We can disconnect the other tubes now."

Icarus grabbed her arm. She froze.

A second later, footsteps echoed in the tunnel. *What happened to that giant puma guarding our backs?* They all ducked below the line of tanks. El wanted to curse. Even if no one spotted them, they'd notice the unconscious imps on the floor.

Suddenly, a young voice called, "Elodie? Elodie Varela?"

Icarus hissed but El shook her head. She couldn't imagine why Dylan Inverro, of all people, would be looking for her. *Maybe the puma didn't deem him a threat.*

"I know you're here." Dylan's steps drew closer.

Will he leave if we stay silent?

El peered around the tank. Dylan was nudging an unconscious imp with the toe of his tennis shoe. He shrugged, making the ratty blue pack on his shoulders flop against his back, and stepped around the limp creature. Alone, he appeared to be just a human boy with his jeans and gray t-shirt. There was no hint of his facial markings.

She stood up and Dylan flinched.

"Hello, Elodie," he said, timidly. Besides his brother, David, Dylan was the youngest Sedessan in the Sedanza Court. He rarely dealt with adult Court members alone. El stepped forward, and her brother hissed. She side-kicked him in the shin and walked away from Alaya's tank. *Cool-headed around everybody…except Sedessans,* she grumbled.

"Dylan," El greeted the boy. "I'm Elodie to my mother. Call me El." She stopped at the front row of tanks and leaned back on the nearest one, folding her arms and schooling her face into a cool expression. The move made her side twinge, and she bit her tongue to keep from wincing. "What's up?"

He scanned the cavern, looking unnerved.

Is it an act?

He glanced at his phone, took a second to shut it off, and shoved it into his pocket.

"We keep track of our brothers' whereabouts. You know, cause they're a pain and we like to avoid them," he said.

El cocked her head and raised a brow.

Dylan laughed and hunched his shoulders. "David saw you take Berto's phone."

"You tracked me here." *Duly noted. Get rid of the phone.* She hadn't had a chance to decide what to do with it after finding out it wasn't hers.

He nodded.

"Why?" El searched the entrance behind him. *Is he a distraction?*

"I'm alone," he said.

"Forgive me for not taking your word for it."

He actually grinned at that. "That's why we like you," he said. "You never talk down to us." He ducked his head, flushing. He shuffled his feet and silence fell as he glanced around the cavern again.

Not an act.

"Dylan," El pressed. "I don't mean to rush you, but neither you nor I want to be caught here. Why'd you track me down?"

"Right." He dropped his pack and knelt to pull it open. El tensed but Dylan only hauled out a book. He set it on the floor and stepped back, reshouldering the bag.

"David wanted me to give you this."

El couldn't read the cover, but she recognized the thick spine and inlaid title despite that.

"Dylan," she stalled him before he pivoted to leave. "Forgive me, but you're well aware of how distrusting we Sedessans are. Why would David want me to have his textbook?"

He glanced at the cavern entrance again and swallowed. "It's scary in our house. All because of that," he said, jabbing a finger at the book like it was a snake. "That's why they're doing this," he indicated the cavern. "And maybe if you know what's going on, David and I will be okay. Maybe you can keep Berto from getting sucked into the crazy too far too!"

He spun and ran. El stared after him until she couldn't hear the pattering of his feet anymore.

Icarus walked past her and picked up the book. "That's not a coincidence," he muttered.

"What's not?" El finally looked away from where Dylan ran. He'd seemed terrified. *How long has he been hiding that terror?* Was the hostility more than the sibling rivalry she'd assumed?

Icarus tilted the book toward her. "It's the book about bloodline restrictions that I've been searching for."

"*Na*, mate," Amos said from behind El, "that's a bunch of drivel 'bout making gods. It's nuttier than a squirrel's cheeks."

"El, is 'Berto' Roberto Inverro?" Icarus asked.

El wandered back to the Oceadanda's tank. She did not want to talk about Roberto right now.

Icarus put the book in his pack as he pressed, "Why did Dylan think you could help Roberto?"

And there it was. She'd left out the engagement stuff while sharing about the last few days.

Na'rina had climbed on top of the tank, and she tilted her head in curiosity, perhaps catching El's discomfort. *Too perceptive.*

El entered the last code for moving the tank while Amos pulled a dolly off the cavern wall.

"El?" Icarus asked again, joining her at the tank.

"If you'd never been cast out and they told you to marry Lucia De León, would you have done it?"

Na'rina swayed and then stilled, her emerald eyes huge. The wilder mythics called it handfasting, but Na'rina clearly knew what "marry" meant.

Icarus hissed. "Roberto asked you to marry him."

"*Na.* Sophia and Adrian announced our year of courtship and then marriage over dinner the other night. No Elodie agreement needed. Not to worry, though, I threw all that to the wind when I helped Amos escape."

The silence was palpable. El's head throbbed and she rubbed a thumb over her brow ridge to relieve the pressure.

"You might not have thrown it." Icarus pivoted her away from the tank by her shoulders. "Roberto was denying it was you right after the escape."

Roberto covered for me?

"What happens if y' refuse?"

"You have a choice." Icarus said to El.

"I'll hamstring the family if I don't agree."

"Do you still trust him?"

Nine years ago, she would have answered with a solid affirmative. *Now,* El pulled away and Icarus let her go, *I can't answer that. He's at least somewhat involved in all of this.* She pulled the last few hoses from Alaya's tank with a little too much force.

Icarus helped Amos tilt the tank onto the dolly and lifted Na'rina to a better position on top in the awkward silence. As the giant maneuvered out of the row, the wheels squeaked. "Wha—" Icarus started and then froze. He slapped a hand onto Amos' shoulder. "Someone's coming." He pointed to the far side of the room's control panel where the larger, empty tanks stood up on end. Just beyond them peeked the frame of another doorway.

"I hate this cavern," El said. "Amos, get Alaya and Na'rina out of here."

"I ain't got a clue how to open this thing," Amos protested.

"Didn't you hear earlier? Once you dump it in the ocean, rip the lid off and make sure the oceanid's submerged. She'll do the rest. Icarus and I will provide a distraction. We'll meet back in the library. Now go!"

Amos hesitated.

Is that worry? El shoved his shoulder—didn't really budge him—and took off for the suspicious doorway. Icarus already stood beside it with his back against the wall, waiting for the first person to step through.

Where is that puma?

Na'rina clung to the tank as it bounced and rattled into the tunnel. She wanted to stay. Wanted to help. But there was nothing she could do.

Levi appeared, leading them back down the tunnel.

We could bite people like the cat, the twiglet offered.

Na'rina hiccupped a laugh.

"Enjoying y'r ride?" Amos asked, puffing.

"Twiglet offered to bite people."

The giant grinned. "Always have liked twiglets. They's got a sense of right."

Na'rina shared his grin, then yelped as he stopped suddenly.

"Dang rocks." Amos set the dolly upright and turned to address the rubble.

Levi disappeared into the darkness, scouting ahead.

While she waited, Na'rina hauled herself into a more secure position near the dolly's handles. There came a familiar, deep booming and the rock crumbled.

"Better." Amos grabbed the dolly and continued.

"I haven't—haven't really thanked you for saving me," Na'rina said while they bumped toward the guard shack's dilapidated door. As they drew nearer, she could hear the storm howling outside even over the squealing of the wheels.

Amos shrugged. "Would'a done it for anyone."

"But you did it for me and I'm grateful."

Amos pivoted the dolly and pulled it through the doorway backwards, ducking to avoid smacking his head.

"What the—"

Na'rina screamed as Amos toppled backwards over Levi, who'd stopped on the far side of the door, confronted by guards with long, metal sticks. The dolly banged into the floor, and the tank gave an alarming gurgle.

The shack's rotted floor popped and Amos sank into the splintered wood. Guards darted forward, thrusting their batons against Levi and Amos. Two sharp zaps sang out, followed by an angry yowl. The odor of burnt fur filled the air.

Amos bellowed, reaching to pull himself from the floor.

"Shock him again!" a man shouted.

Levi pounced, hitting the man in the stomach. His baton flew from his hand. They slammed into the shack's thin wall and, just like the floor, it crumbled. Levi and the guard disappeared into the rain beyond.

The other man jabbed Amos' side and the giant convulsed.

My friend!

Na'rina scampered off the tank and across the floor, getting pelted by the rain pouring in through the hole in the wall. Something crunched and she glanced back. Amos had rolled sideways, trying to extricate himself from the floor before he got zapped again.

She looked away just before the guard jabbed him in the back. Amos bellowed and Na'rina choked on a sob.

Move faster! She fought the wind to wrap her small fingers around the fallen baton's handle. She got under it and heaved, but it was like lifting a fallen tree by only one end.

She turned and dragged the baton backwards. The tip scraped against the wood, but with the storm's howling, the guard didn't hear. Once she was close enough, Na'rina pivoted and pushed the tip of the baton toward the guard's boot. Then she hesitated. *The boots will insulate him from the shock.*

Amos saw her problem and kicked, catching the side of the guard's knee. It cracked. The man screamed and landed on his backside directly on the baton.

Good enough. Na'rina pushed the button on the handle and jumped back when the baton bucked from her hands. The man screamed again and slumped onto the floor, still convulsing.

Na'rina fought an urge to throw up.

He would've killed my friend. The twiglet did not share her remorse.

Amos pulled himself from the floor with a groan.

"The tank's gurgling." Na'rina scampered back to Alaya's tank. She hoped Levi was alright but knew she couldn't help him even if she did spot him in the storm.

She found a cracked and leaking tubing connection on the bottom of the tank. Na'rina shoved her hands against it and saltwater coated her hands. Her lifeblood responded with the faint tidal whooshing. "I can't stop it!"

"Here." Amos nabbed the guard's jacket and held it against the crack. Na'rina took it so he could go back to moving the tank. She pressed hard, thought she missed a crack, then realized the faint lines were some sort of etching, and shifted the jacket back. No matter how she pressed, though, the fabric didn't fully stop the leak.

"Hang tight." Amos lifted the dolly.

Na'rina curled around the bars of the frame. It left her under the tank but maybe that was better anyway as Amos hauled them out the door into the storm's full strength. The giant lurched against the wind and trudged toward the pounding surf.

Its angry rhythm throbbed in Na'rina's blood. *How long will Alaya's zoi aima affect me?* She'd assumed it'd fade quickly—Alaya's gift was long gone—but she continued to feel the effects.

"Almost there!" Amos bellowed.

Na'rina tightened her grip.

Amos turned the dolly and tilted it, rolling the tank into the surf. Na'rina jumped free only to land in the water too. Waves surged over her. The pounding in her lifeblood spiked, and then Amos pulled her out by her leafy hair. She spluttered as he tucked her into the neck of his shirt. She expected to feel the warmth of his skin like she would Icarus, but Amos was just as cold as she was. She bunched his shirt in her shaking fists to hang on.

"Rip the lid off, eh?" Amos grabbed the tank, his fingers sinking into the metal, and heaved. The tank groaned and split apart like a melon. Rolling it over, he dumped Alaya into the waves. "She'll do the rest?" Amos stepped back, teetering as the wind buffeted him.

The waves tossed Alaya's body. Na'rina whimpered. If this had been her Rina, it would have pulled her in immediately to start healing her, but Alaya was getting smashed like a bleached piece of driftwood in the water.

Levi appeared on the shore. He shook, splaying water from his fur, but it didn't help as the rain continued to drench them.

Suddenly, Alaya sank, disappearing so fast that Na'rina gasped and had the urge to grab for the Oceadanda.

"Huh," Amos said. "Now what?"

"Alaya?!" Na'rina yelled. The wind swallowed her voice whole. She remembered pulling energy from the storm in Washington and creating a calm bubble around herself. It'd been a horrifying experience but she'd been able to do it. Now she chafed at the inability.

We're useless, the twiglet moaned.

Na'rina swiped rain from her eyes as she scanned the water. *We just need to wait.* Alaya knew they needed her. If she was capable, she'd at least show herself and reassure them.

"Not sure how long we can stay here!" Amos warned.

"Just a little longer!"

The wind gusted and sand pelted them from the side. Much more of this and they wouldn't be able to see Alaya even if she did surface.

Amos hunched his shoulders and a vibration traveled through him, followed by a cracking. Na'rina held tighter, instinctively looking down. He'd encased his feet in rock to anchor himself.

Levi leaned against his legs, lending support or needing the anchor, Na'rina wasn't sure. Amos curved his shoulders against the wind to take the brunt of it on his back and give her a tiny, sheltered spot in the protection of his body.

Na'rina kept her focus on the waves. *Come on, Alaya.*

A silver-haired woman appeared and Na'rina cried out, pointing.

But her hand fell as she made out the woman's face.

"My, my, Drydanda, how you've grown," Owasha, Alaya's sister, mocked.

"Will she survive?" Na'rina asked in a regular tone, knowing Owasha would hear her. The fury in the storm made more sense now. Owasha loved inciting storms into hurricanes.

The oceanid dropped her mocking smile. "It's too early to tell."

Na'rina wanted to bury her face in Amos' shirt and cry but showing Owasha such an emotion would be disastrous.

"Why are you here, Owasha?" she asked. Unless Owasha had known where Alaya was being held, she had no reason to be in the area.

Furious wind whirled Owasha's hair around her head. She glowered at Na'rina, only sparing Amos and Levi a quick glance.

"Are you mocking me?"

Na'rina stuttered. She'd only been trying to understand the oceanid, not insult her.

Owasha snickered. "How oblivious you are, Drydanda!" She lifted her arms like she could grab the storm in her fists. "Can't you feel it? This is a child throwing a fit with a new toy. With Alaya incapacitated, someone has to mitigate the monstrous mess they're leaving."

"You're not feeding the storm?"

"As much as I'd like to torment the mindwalkers, the joy of it isn't worth the effort to drag a storm over the Sedanza Islands."

Na'rina's stomach revolted but she fought not to lose it down Amos' front. The storm wasn't natural. *Did Dominguez synthesize Alaya's abilities?*

"Did Alaya send you?" she asked, fighting her nausea.

322

"Alaya says she owes you a life debt. I do not agree with her."

Amos rumbled something ill-tempered under his breath. Na'rina leaned into him a little harder, trying to caution patience.

Finally, Owasha explained, "But I promised to pass along a message." The mocking smile returned and Na'rina's heart sank. "You have maybe a day before you're irreparably changed by the melding with the twiglet. Alaya suspects grief or fear made him dig in and hide. Now he's so twined into your psyche that you can't naturally tell where he ends and you begin. Unfortunately, or fortunately, Alaya in her present condition cannot help you.

"Two things you need, Drydanda. Someone to disentangle him from your mind, and sunlight. Oceans of sunlight. The twiglet's body cannot hold enough zoi ama for what you need. If you attempt to separate without enough sunlight readily available, it will kill one or both of you." Owasha held her arms up in the storm. "Good luck with finding that." She turned to leave.

Na'rina's mind raced. Inside, the twiglet cowered, guilt wafting from him in waves, and then he disappeared altogether.

Now wasn't the time to search him out.

"Owasha," Na'rina called, stalling her. Icarus had mentioned the *Sansabria.* If they let the ship slip away, they'd lose their chance of freeing the imprisoned mythics. Although Owasha hated her, Na'rina couldn't let their one hope of getting to the ship swim away. "There's a ship nearby like the one they used to experiment on oceanids last spring. Can you help us get to it?"

Owasha hissed and the storm seethed as she spun back. "Why would I help you?"

"These are the same people who took Alaya. What if we can rescue all the captives from them?" In Na'rina's limited experience with Owasha, the only one she cared about was her sister. She hoped that'd weigh heavily enough to convince the oceanid.

Owasha's nostrils flared. "You cannot even get out of the twiglet, Drydanda. I will not leave Alaya longer to help you on a fool's quest." She shoved her hand at them and the world became solid water in their faces.

Na'rina sucked in a breath but not fast enough as the wave smashed against Amos. He hunched into it and came out spitting when the wave subsided back into the surf. Na'rina coughed at the saltwater filling her throat and stomach. She gagged, unable to keep from throwing up.

"Sorry," she squeaked.

Amos chuckled. "We're in a torrential shower. What's a little more water?"

Na'rina peeked down Amos' shoulder to check on Levi just as he shook. She ducked back and then looked to find him miserably staring up at her.

"Let's go." Na'rina glanced at the now empty, tossing ocean.

I've failed again. She shielded the thought from the twiglet.

"Nasty creature," Amos muttered, stomping to break off his granite shoes. "But perhaps more helpful than she intended."

Nasty creature, the twiglet agreed, but Na'rina cocked her head, considering Amos' words. As he headed back to the library, she huddled against his chest and pondered Alaya's message.

Icarus counted footsteps, the familiar ice washing out into his fingertips while he waited. *Four people, five, six…*he glanced to his left where his sister had disappeared behind the control panel. He could hear her rummaging and muttering and then her head popped back up. She'd found a shock baton. She snapped it open and raced to duck behind a row of tanks.

Seven, eight, nine…At least ten against us two. Icarus didn't care for the odds.

The door beside him opened and a tall, heavy-shouldered man stepped through. Icarus extended his claws, glad Na'rina left with the giant because what happened now would turn her stomach. The man wore the insignia of the Inverro guards. Icarus grabbed him by the neck and pulled, throwing him out of the way and slicing his throat at the same time.

Shock held the group for a moment. Icarus got ahold of the next man in line. Suddenly, the two at the far back of the group spun and ran.

Icarus doubted it was from fear. They worked for a Sedessan household. The punishment for cowardice was typically death. He and El had to be gone before those two returned with backup.

The third man blocked Icarus' swipe with his arm. Icarus' claws raked across something metal, setting his teeth on edge. The man grinned and rammed him.

Icarus stumbled backward, shifted it into a roll to avoid a swing, and blinked. The man lit up with human zoi aima except a thick brown overlaid the swirl of colors. *Troll blood. Don't let him get ahold of you.*

Behind Icarus, something zapped and a man grunted. Two men had slipped past him into the cavern, and El had surprised the first when he'd tried to circle Icarus. Now she faced off with the second.

The rest of the group flooded out the door as Icarus circled with the troll-blooded man, and Icarus snarled.

A wrench caught his eye. He snatched it, feinted toward the troll-blooded man, who flinched, and flung the wrench across the room. It smacked El's opponent in the shoulder and she lunged forward, zapping him in the chest and ducking as a shot cracked through the cavern. El cringed, instinctively clutching her side.

Icarus' ears rang hollow and then high pitched while the shot sparked off a tank and ricocheted back toward the group of men. One of them cursed.

"Don't shoot!" someone shouted. "They'll kill us if we damage the tanks."

Too late. There was a large dent in the tank's lid and its control panel had gone dark.

Icarus' opponent shouted and charged. Icarus jumped backward, startled at his speed as a metal shield shook out from the man's arm. It expanded to cover his torso, locking into a solid sheet. Icarus saw the etchings on the rim and then it smashed into his chest. The man leaned in hard, pinning him to the wall.

A couple of ribs cracked, flaring pain through his body. The backpack with the textbook gave him a tiny bit more room but also pressed sharp corners into Icarus' back. Belatedly, his ribs popped, trying to heal. *I'm not healing as fast.* Na'rina in the twiglet must affect that connection too. Try as he might, Icarus couldn't get his arms around the man's shield, and he didn't have leverage to push back.

Another rib cracked and Icarus howled.

He scrambled for options. *Nothing to throw or stab with. My claws don't work against the metal shield. What else can I use?* His mind stuttered, craving air. *The empty tanks.* Taking a chance, he quit pushing back with his left hand to swing out to his side. His fingers brushed the tail end of webbing that strapped the empty tanks together.

This is going to hurt. Icarus wrapped his hand in the webbing and hauled on it, howling in defiance so suddenly that the troll-blooded man flinched. It was enough. Icarus strained. His shoulder socket burned, stretching, but the tanks rocked. Forward and then backward. When they rocked forward again, he yanked harder.

He began to black out as the shield pressed harder into his chest.

The tanks rocked again. *Now!* Icarus hauled one last time. His shoulder popped and the tanks toppled. The pressure on his chest disappeared, replaced instantly by pain in his shoulder and weight from the tanks as they buried him. His head cracked against the floor, and he lost time for a moment.

His shoulder popping back into place woke him. A second longer and his ribs popped too. It was fire and then blessed relief. He pushed against the tank pinning him to the ground and lifted it enough to slide free.

Not more than two feet away, the edge of the shield peeked from under another tank. Icarus pressed a shoulder into the thing to roll it away. The troll-blooded man lay pinned and unconscious under a third tank, but his arm was exposed, showing the straps holding the shield and a tiny button in the middle of his palm. Curious, Icarus pressed it and the shield retracted against the man's forearm.

A vicious smirk pulled at Icarus' lips. He detached the device and tucked it into his pack. Usually, he'd also finish the man off but fighting echoed in the chamber and he was more worried about El.

He climbed out of the mess of tanks instead.

El fenced with a guard using her shock baton. Both batons zapped at each contact but neither one could get around the other. A dark stain was seeping through El's shirt, and she was clearly tiring.

Icarus circled behind the man. His sister parried a swing and broke away, dodging around a tank to put space between her and her opponent. The man followed, so focused on El that he missed Icarus pouncing from behind. Icarus rode him to the ground, finished him, and jumped after El.

"I got five to your three," El teased.

Icarus grunted. "Last one was a team effort. Besides, you can have the troll next time."

El just laughed. They were leaving a mess behind that would put the Inverros on guard, but Icarus couldn't help the thrill that washed through him as they ran.

Na'rina's shivering wouldn't stop. It wasn't from the rain that had soaked her but from leftover nerves. She huddled against Levi, trying to absorb comfort from his solid presence. Somehow, he was already dry. The twiglet's bark was heavy with moisture and, not for the first time, Na'rina missed her own body.

Levi had unerringly led them back to their study room and

they'd found that no one else had returned to the library yet. Na'rina craved the strawberries she'd seen earlier but she hadn't convinced herself to climb onto the table yet. Her shivering might make her fall and she'd already put the twiglet through too much.

She searched for him but didn't find him in her thoughts. Ever since Owasha's message, he'd vanished, leaving residual fear and guilt in his wake.

Amos lowered himself to sit against the wall beside them. He handed over the cork from a wine bottle. It'd been hollowed out and filled with water for her to use as a cup.

"Thank you," she whispered, surprised.

He hummed and the sound rumbled in the floor. It reminded her of Rosharu.

"Figure they're alive?" Amos asked.

Na'rina started. "Why would you ask that?"

"Cause those guards 'r no joke and it's been a while."

Na'rina's insides rolled. She carefully set the cork cup down and crawled onto Amos' knee to look him in the eye. One thing about being a twiglet—people didn't think twice about her getting into their personal space. Amos just gave her a bemused expression. It pulled his brows up and reminded Na'rina of the heavy ridges in a spruce's bark.

"They'll come back alive."

"Life ain't always that pretty, Drydanda."

Definitely ain't, the twiglet agreed, then vanished again.

So, he's not unaware of what's happening, Na'rina noted, *just hiding.*

Beside them, Levi lifted his head, his rounded ears twitching, and then padded away on silent paws.

Na'rina tilted her head, trying to think of something that might ease the loneliness in Amos. It was not a loneliness she knew. Even so far from her grove, a hidden assurance like a deeply buried seed let her know the Rina was there. The closest she'd come, she supposed, was when she'd been held in an isolation chamber, but even then, a part of her had known her Rina lived.

"You goin' to trust 'em to help you if they do return?" Amos asked before she could put together the right words.

"Of course," Na'rina answered, perplexed. "Why wouldn't I?"

"Sounds like you'll be needin' one of 'em to sort through y'r head." He gently touched her forehead for emphasis.

"I trust them both," Na'rina said simply. She didn't mention that she and Icarus communicated mentally all the time. It was a connection she treasured and continued to foster. *Hopefully we can figure out Alaya's information. If I can't emerge from the twiglet, growing with Icarus might be...impossible.* She refused to look at her arms where her aspen saplings were missing.

Amos rolled his fingers, pinky to pointer, on his pant leg. "This group—confuses me."

Na'rina smiled. "Not what you expected?"

His eyes turned distant. "Not at all."

Soft conversation whispered in from the main library. Na'rina patted Amos' knee and slid off.

"Who's the Sedessan loyal to?" Amos asked. "Her parents or her brother?"

Na'rina stilled. El's parents had insisted she help Roberto blame Amos for the quake. She'd gone against that, but nevertheless, El was clearly torn and it was only natural that Amos would question it. Na'rina couldn't answer his question. She didn't know what El would do if her parents again told her to do something contrary to what Icarus asked. But Icarus insisted El had never betrayed him and Na'rina trusted that.

How did Na'rina put into words the assurance she felt due to past experience Amos didn't have? Before she could answer, El and Icarus walked through the archway with Levi shadowing Icarus' heel.

"...didn't wake while you were carrying him," El was saying.

Behind them came Felis and Dante, carrying an unconscious Fae.

Felis snorted, "He's not like you, Sedessan. I'm not worried."

"You should've been," El said. "Fae have long memories for disrespect."

The wer-im dumped the Fae on the floor and Na'rina approached, swaying in surprise at the gag and cord binding his wrists and ankles.

"What did you do?" she breathed.

El smoothed her clean shirt, a gift from the orange-haired wer-im, down her hips while she eyed Marquin. The shirt was baggy, but it hid her fresh bandage.

The wer-im were supposed to entice the ambassador to come to the library, not truss him up and haul him back like a sack of potatoes. She wasn't sure she believed their story about finding him in his study already unconscious and bound. *Did he start questioning the Compulsion? Was he tied up to get him out of the way?* If that was the case, they had to work fast. Such treatment meant the culprit wasn't worried about staying in the Fae's good graces anymore. El sat across from Ambassador Marquin at the table waiting for his grogginess to pass.

They'd ungagged him and released his feet but left his wrists bound until they knew he wouldn't lash out. El wasn't sure how strong his telekinesis was but most with the ability needed motion to use it.

"Ambassador, can you hear me?" she asked.

He blinked and swayed.

Icarus, who stood behind him, caught his shoulder to keep him upright. El sat across the table from the ambassador. If he was suffering from Compulsion stress, she wanted him to know she hadn't caused it. Icarus, also being Sedessan, didn't play into it. What the ambassador didn't know wouldn't hurt him in this case. It was just the three of them in the room. The Fae didn't need to know their numbers.

"Ambassador?"

"Señorita Varela," Marquin slurred, his kefir accent particularly bitter. "You will pay for this."

El shifted into negotiations, hoping the façade hid her sudden nervousness. "My associate found you like this," she said. "I will have him unbind you as a sign of good faith."

Marquin's pupils constricted and his eyes flew around the room until they landed on Icarus at his shoulder. "I don't know you."

"*Na*, I am the Wer-Kadis."

"Stop touching me."

Icarus lifted his hand and Marquin tilted, barely catching himself before he toppled out of the chair.

He *didn't return the introduction.* El wasn't sure if that was from anger or disorientation, but it didn't bode well either way.

"Kadis, please undo his hands," El said. She might regret it momentarily, but she had to gain some goodwill.

Icarus didn't question it. Before he'd become the Kadis, he might have, but now he was honoring this as her conversation to lead. Both warmth and uncertainty blossomed inside El. She'd always been the background player, never the spearhead.

Marquin massaged his wrists. El leaned forward, offering him water, but he stared at it impassively. Finally, she set the cup on the table.

"How are…"

"Forgo the pleasantries," Marquin interrupted her. He was a good ambassador in part because he could adjust as the situation necessitated.

El shifted gears, hoping it didn't portend an unsuccessful outcome for this meeting. "At the trial earlier," she said, "you appeared ill, shaking, sweating, uncertain, not your normal composed self. I think it had to do with how you started with a guillotine regardless of the facts. No Fae in his right mind would ignore the truth. Perhaps you weren't in your right mind. Perhaps—" El hesitated. Just saying the words could sink the Court. The Fae could crush the Sedessans if they wanted. Bracing herself, El pushed forward, "—perhaps you're suffering from Compulsion stress."

The silence dragged. Marquin's fingers had stopped massaging his wrist and instead had closed around it. They began to tremble. Behind him, Icarus stepped closer, cautious.

"It would be devious of you to say such a thing to shift suspicion," Marquin said.

El couldn't deny that. She held up her hands, fingers splayed. "It would also be detrimental, if I or my family Compelled you, to offer help in breaking the hold. If you agree to let us help, my associate and I will not touch you. I'll ask questions and see if we can help fill in the holes you're experiencing in your memory."

"Your family," Marquin swallowed and licked his lips. "Your engagement. Who do you align with?"

El paused. *I should have expected that question.* It was dangerous to admit she was acting alone but also inadvisable to connect herself or her parents to the Inverros when she suspected them of Compulsion.

El's mouth went dry. She knew what her brother would advise and it made her nauseous. But it was the safest bet. She reached for the water pitcher, pouring herself a glass as she admitted, "I am acting alone but I am sure, if I were to consult my parents, that they would fully support my actions."

Marquin leaned his elbows on the table and interlaced his thin fingers, smiling a predatory grin that dissolved into a grimace as he said, "Ask your questions." His body instantly reacted. Sweat broke out on his brow, beaded, and ran, dripping off his chin.

El retreated to her mental library briefly. Her search confirmed her suspicions regarding his physical reaction. He subconsciously knew something was wrong and had just consciously decided to fight. The more they dug, the harder this was going to get for him.

"Here," she pushed the water closer to him. "You're going to need it."

Marquin sneered but he snatched the glass as soon as her hand left it.

Good.

He chugged the water and El leaned back, giving him more space.

"Where were you the first time someone Compelled you?" she asked, hoping to jolt his memory with the sudden question.

Marquin dropped the glass and Icarus caught it before it could shatter on the floor. Her brother refilled it and went to set it on the table again, then thought better of it and transferred the water to a plastic bottle before giving it back to Marquin.

Marquin trembled, starting to wheeze. More sweat poured off his brow. "The ba—the bay on the northern side of Riviera," he said.

El had never seen someone fight a Compulsion. The ambassador looked almost skeletal. *This is why they hate us.* She hated it herself. A person's decisions should be their own.

"Why were you there?" she pressed. The northern bay was an unusual spot to visit. It wasn't deep enough to serve as a dock for the island and, like the beach outside the shack, it was littered with rocks and shells.

The ambassador's teeth ground against each other.

"Why were you there?" El asked again.

"Marleen!"

El straightened. She'd leaned forward, fascinated despite herself. She could see the dawning surprise in Marquin's eyes. *He didn't know his wife came to visit.* He always said she *might* come but it was well known she hated the warmer climates.

"Did someone lure you to the bay or was she actually there?"

Marquin turned green. He gulped more water, almost splashing liquid against his face as the plastic bottle squished in his fingers. "She was there."

"Who else was there?"

"I—I don't—" he shook his head and groaned, "I don't know."

"What happened?"

"—grabbed…from behind."

"El, he might need a moment."

El had been so intent, she'd forgotten about her brother. He tilted his chin at the water pitcher. It was only half full now, but the water was plastered sideways against the glass. Apparently, Marquin didn't need hand gestures to use his telekinesis. A moment later, the water sloshed back into the bottom of the pitcher.

"Continue," Marquin rasped.

"What happened when you were grabbed?"

The ambassador's eyes glazed but then he shook his head once, hard. "It becomes a blur."

El wasn't sure what to do with that. Now that they'd breached that part of his memory, he should be able to recall anything exchanged between Marleen and whoever grabbed him.

"What urge did you suddenly have?" Icarus asked.

Marquin spun and almost toppled from his chair. *He forgot about Icarus.* "I showed them the elephant room."

El frowned, leaning in and drawing Marquin's attention back to her. "The what?"

"It's a cave under the embassy. The stalagmites and stalactites on the back wall create the shape of an elephant. I somehow—somehow thought Marleen would love it." He frowned, confused.

El pictured the cavern with the tanks and mentally removed the equipment, envisioning the unobscured back wall. *It's the same room.* The Sedessan that Compelled him had wanted access to that cavern. Another thought struck her, but she wasn't sure if she should pursue that line of questioning.

Marquin reached for the water again but hesitated as his fingers shook uncontrollably.

El pushed the bottle toward him. "You need it."

The ambassador vacillated, but finally grabbed it and drank, spilling some down his front where it disappeared into the sweat stain appearing on his silk shirt. Icarus refilled the bottle again for him.

"What does Marleen look like?" she asked, deciding to touch on her suspicion briefly.

"Beautiful." This was laced with sadness and suddenly Marquin not only appeared emaciated but old. El didn't know his age but Fae usually wore their years well. This was the old of disappointment, not of long life.

"Go on."

Marquin eyed her, perhaps hesitant to implicate his wife even more, but then his shoulders sagged. "Eyes of deep violet in a heart-shaped face. She's graceful, floats as she walks."

El hesitated. She wanted to ask if Marleen was plump, but that'd be insulting, so she took a different tack. "Can she turn transparent?"

The ambassador's eyes dilated. "I dislike how Sedessans always know far more than they should!" he snarled.

El took that as a yes. She bowed, acknowledging his distaste, and resumed her previous line of questioning. "What's wrong with showing her the elephant room?"

Marquin twitched. Clearly this struck closer to the Compulsion. Finally, he blurted, "She hates caves."

"Have you been back to the elephant room?"

Marquin opened his mouth, grimaced, and then simply shook his head, wiping his brow with his cuff.

"Why not?"

"Dominguez' domain," he moaned, holding his head in his palm.

"Thomas Dominguez? The human?" El *knew* he was connected. Now to figure out if Dominguez was who she feared.

A hysterical laugh and then a sob answered her. If her studies were right, Marquin's head must be pounding.

"I don't know," Marquin whispered. "He's my human assistant!

But he's wrong. All wrong!"

"Is he Sedessan?" El's own head throbbed.

Marquin rocked and then stopped by slapping his hands onto the table.

"Is he Sedessan?"

His jaw clenched and the water pitcher slid a foot down the table with a screech.

"Ambassador?" El pressed.

Marquin's fingers curled into fists. "He's Thomas Inverro!"

Glass shattered outward. El ducked but not fast enough as splinters tore across her cheek. Glass struck the marble wall, leaving splats of water and shimmering slivers that stuck there as though frozen.

"I'll have the entire Court for this!" Marquin rose, hands planted on the table.

"Ambassador Mar—"

"Don't play me for a fool, Sedessan!" Invisible fingers grabbed El by the neck. Her windpipe shut off for a terrifying moment—and then the hold disappeared as Icarus grabbed the Fae by the throat and shoved him against the wall.

"Enough!" he roared.

Marquin trembled, terror replacing his rage. Then his eyes rolled upward and he passed out. In the sudden silence, the shattered glass plinked against the floor.

Icarus gently lowered Marquin.

We did this to him. El pushed away from the table and strode out, gently touching her sore neck. Blood trickled down her cheek and her throat spasmed. She didn't care. *We're monsters.* Wind howled, but it only echoed her turmoil. *Marquin's a good man. Harsh, but good, and now he's a wreck.* Lightning cracked and she jumped, startled to find the after image burned across her sight.

A hand grabbed her shoulder just before she walked out into the storm. She expected Icarus but spun to find Amos instead. Her surprise must have shown because he cracked a grin and pulled her back into the dry library.

"Ain't safe fer fish out there, much less one little Sedessan," he teased.

Something in El broke and she flung her arms around him, burying her face in his sternum. He stiffened, then relaxed and held her. He smelled of wet granite and moss. And he was solid against the insanity pounding in El's head.

"Come now." He pushed El back to see her face. "Y've got me shirt bloody."

She just let her forehead thunk against his chest, exhausted. "No wonder the world hates us," she muttered.

"What happened to the ambassador wasn't y'r doin'." Amos sat down against the wall and pulled El down to sit across from him. He tore a chunk off his shirt and dabbed at her face.

"Y' still got cuts bleedin' here."

El touched her cheek and winced. Amos moved on to her forehead. She hadn't even realized she was bleeding there too, but now it added to her headache.

"I always thought the Varela household was different, you know," she said. "*Sa*, we're Sedessans, but that doesn't mean we hurt people."

Amos briefly stopped attending to her wounds. "What's changed?"

"I'm expected to marry an Inverro and I don't know if I can trust him not to do that." She flung a hand back toward the study room.

Amos harrumphed. "Y'r parents ain't dumb. Surely, they considered that."

El pulled the rag from his fingers and held it to her forehead, refusing to meet his eyes. *Is he right?*

"Hey now." Amos' finger was firm under her chin. "Where's the spunk? Y'r never without that shield."

El tried to give him a cocky smile.

"Eesh. Looks like y'r havin' a stroke."

A surprised chuckle hiccupped from El and her lips relaxed.

"Better," he said.

El dropped her head again as she fiddled with the rag. "Maybe my parents don't know me as well as I hoped," she admitted. "Maybe they think I can infiltrate the Inverros, but I can't. I can't *act* like what they're doing is okay."

Amos clasped her hands. She'd tried to find gloves for her meeting with Marquin but hadn't found any. Her fingers were tiny in Amos' hands. Splayed out, the tips would only reach his first knuckle. As it was, his callused hands engulfed hers and he began running his thumb across the edge of her thumbnail. *How can he be so gentle?*

It was a simple gesture, holding her hands, but El stared at his blunt fingers with their short, dirt-crusted nails, and didn't want to let go. He'd never shied away from her, even after she'd left him buried in rocks.

"Me sister used to say there's a big difference between doin' what's expected and doin' what's right. Seems to me y've got to figure out what's what."

"What's right? Or what's right for whom?"

Amos stopped running his thumb across her nail, and she glanced up. His frown made her look away again.

"There's a right right," he said. "Might not be easy, might hurt, but that's what separates the fish as follow the stream and the fish as fight the current. Always easier to follow the stream, but it's often flowing the wrong way."

"El." Icarus had come from the library with Na'rina on his shoulder. In each fist she held a large strawberry. There were bites out of each one and red staining the twiglet's lips.

Icarus eyed El clinging to Amos' hands but didn't comment. Instead, he leaned against a bookshelf and folded his arms. "This Thomas Inverro. Is he who I think he is?"

El nodded. Roberto's grandfather, Thomas Inverro, was the one behind the Compellings and the operation in the elephant cavern.

Was Roberto left out of all that while he was gone? Or has he been complicit in his grandfather's Compelling for years? A tension headache started climbing its way up El's neck.

Icarus fished a photo from his pocket and handed it to her. She was glad for the distraction until he tapped the bottom corner. "Na'rina called this person Marie when I showed this to her. She insisted that despite the getup, the person's female. Is it Marie Inverro?"

Na'rina paused in biting a strawberry to see El's reaction.

El tilted the photo toward a wall sconce. Although Icarus was asking about a specific person, she scanned the whole photo and found the text across the bottom.

Intela Corp Board 1848. She'd seen the photo before, back when he originally found it in the spring. At the time she'd been surprised the group lacked the CEO but apparently the man feared photographs and it became tradition for him to never be pictured. But that wasn't what Icarus was asking about. The person he'd indicated was a small Latino man. El mentally removed the hat and altered the clothing to something modern and her tension headache climbed higher. Na'rina was right. The person was Roberto's mother. El said so and Icarus' cheek started to twitch. *Roberto grew up with Intela Corp.* El couldn't believe he knew nothing about it.

"All this time I thought humans were experimenting on mythics," Icarus said. "Turns out they're just pawns. Got another question for you." Instead of asking a question, though, Icarus stepped back and shook his arm. As he did, Na'rina put the last of a strawberry into her mouth and grabbed his shirt. El understood why a second later when a familiar metal shield snapped into place in front of him.

Amos whistled. "Fancy that."

"Took that off the captain?" El asked, rising to look.

She traced a finger along the shield's paper-thin plates. She'd seen the thing about crush Icarus, so she knew its strength despite the apparently delicate construction. The thinness allowed the plates to layer into a thick bracer on his forearm, overlapping for storage and snapping into place along grooves on each metal edge. El's fingers settled into etchings on the top and Icarus shifted to allow her to see them better.

"That's the Inverros' arms," El said.

Icarus nodded. "But this," he rolled the shield sideways, "isn't. Do you recognize them?"

El tilted the shield even closer to the light. She'd mistaken the new etchings as tiny nicks but they were faint lines like silk in the metal. She traced them and huffed, surprised. Similar ones graced the inside of her dresser, except instead of the grand fir and rain signature of the Cascade dwarves, these belonged to the Rockies.

"This is the mountain crest and sun of the Rockies dwarves," she said.

Icarus flashed his long canines. "I think the Inverros are the ones who kidnapped the dwarves. Na'rina found a similar etching on the underside of Alaya's tank."

"Remarkable craftsmanship," Amos commented, studying the shield as well.

"Precisely," Icarus said. "The technology the Inverros have been coming out with in the last year requires skill they don't have in their human or goblin workers. They needed the dwarves. But I think the dwarves are working under duress and they're leaving breadcrumbs on their work." He snapped the shield closed. "It all comes back to the Inverros."

He headed back into the library, saying over his shoulder, "First things first. We need to plan. We've got Na'rina and the twiglet to separate, prisoners to rescue, and a ship to steal."

Icarus ended his call with Richard McCormick. He'd suspected the prisoners were being taken to the *Sansabria* because Malon's tracker placed the ship just east of Riviera. Now he had his confirmation, and he even had an ace, in a way, as Richard happened to be on board.

Now he turned back to continue his argument with El. Frustration hardened his expression. They'd solved one portion of the Na'rina-twiglet problem. Alaya said they needed lots of sunlight and after seeing the manual on the stasis tanks, both El and Icarus were positive the tank's UV lights would suffice.

That left three obstacles:

How to get to the *Sansabria* and the empty tanks.

How to open a tank without damaging it since they lacked the electronic key. (Richard hadn't known.)

And who was best suited to go into the tank with Na'rina once they had it open. It wasn't that Icarus didn't trust El, as Amos so pointedly suggested, it was that Icarus knew Na'rina better and El had never wandered Na'rina's mindscape.

"I'm more likely to find the twiglet," he insisted. Na'rina's mind acted like her grove. It'd be easy to spot the difference the twiglet made.

"You hate messing inside people's heads." El wasn't backing down. He'd usually be proud of that. "This isn't just a walk-through!"

"I'm not clumsy."

"You'll take longer and time's not a luxury."

Icarus' cheek twitched just under his lowest scar as he stood across the table from El. She wasn't wrong. He lacked El's mental practice. But when he pictured El stepping into Na'rina's mind, the potential disasters were numerous.

A heavy shudder traveled through the table and Icarus and El glared at Amos. "Y'r Drydanda's trying to say somethin'," he said.

Na'rina stood on the table beside Amos' hand. Icarus twitched. *She moved.* He hadn't noticed. *Bad form.*

"Who helps me won't matter unless we can get to the ship," Na'rina said. "Since Owasha laughed in our faces, how are we getting out there in this storm?"

Icarus stowed his irritation and sat down. Looking to Dante, he asked, "You're sure using the boats isn't an option?"

Dante had the most experience besides El on a boat. At the moment, his face was lit pale blue from his tablet's screen. "Oh, it's an option," he answered, studying radar of the storm. "But it's a terrible idea. Depending on when we leave, we'll be near the hurricane's eye."

"Could we use that?" Felis asked.

Dante shook his head. "It's not calm on water like it is on land and if we get caught by the eyewall the winds could be upwards of 150 miles per hour. This storm's moving fast."

Icarus scrubbed a hand down his face. They were so close. Na'rina wandered over and slumped against his arm. She always appeared delicate but as a twiglet she was diminished. It was like the fierce light inside her had nothing to keep it alive.

Icarus rubbed at his chest, still feeling numb from the vow despite Na'rina sitting beside him. *What if she gets stuck this way?*

"How did the Inverros do it?" Na'rina muttered. "How'd they move everyone to the ship?"

Across the table, El's nostrils flared and Icarus caught her faint huff. It was a tell she'd had even as a child.

"El?"

Her face went blank. Icarus raised a brow.

"Submersibles," she finally admitted. "The Inverros have a small fleet of subs. They're going under the storm."

There was more. It was written all over El's face.

"And?"

She pulled a phone from her pocket and held it up. "I might be able to convince Roberto to let us use his."

"Would he have an electronic key as well?" Icarus asked

El grimaced. "He might." That clearly bothered her. She stared at the phone in her hand.

"Think he'll betray us to 'is family?"

"I don't know. He's been out of the family loop for years, but I have no idea how involved he's been with the Compelling stuff."

"Do we have another choice?" Dante asked.

"*Na*," Icarus said softly. Time was slipping away, but he shared El's doubts and couldn't force her to make that call. Not with how much she might have to give to convince Roberto to help.

El grimaced again and dialed, setting the phone on the table for all to hear. After two rings, there came a faintly accented, "Hello, Elodie."

Roberto had agreed far too readily over the phone and every nerve in El suspected an ambush as they approached the black pod on the sandy beach. He'd just set a place and time to meet and hung up, but now, as El approached the open hatch of the submersible, Roberto watched with an almost hungry look. His eyes reminded her a bit too much of his brother's vulpine smile.

As agreed, only Levi walked at her heels. The sub was something from a sci-fi movie with the back opening upward on hydraulic pistons to allow entry. El could see the backs of the passenger seats and beyond that, the front windshield and the pilot's seat.

Icarus and the others hid in the trees, waiting for her signal.

"It's good to see you," Roberto shouted over the wind, holding out her phone when she got nearer. She'd guessed his passcode on the first try and reverse called him to get ahold of him. He spotted the puma and unconsciously took a half step back. "You keep odd company anymore."

El ducked under the partial shelter of the raised hatch and snatched her phone. She stalled by tucking her hands into her armpits to warm them, scowling at the water dripping from her jacket in rivulets as she did. "I've always kept odd company. Where's your family, Roberto?"

"You think I'd bring them to a rendezvous with you?"

"They're searching for me. Why wouldn't you notify them that you'd found me?"

He smirked nervously. "I don't share everything with mi madre, you know."

El ground her teeth. He was being evasive. Not surprising but she still wasn't sure what his angle was.

While they spoke, she eyed the submersible and Levi inched forward, getting a good sniff at the air. His ears flicked and then he circled behind Roberto.

Roberto tentatively reached a hand to touch Levi's back as he passed and received a snarl in warning. He wisely sidestepped away.

"Forgive me if I'm not totally trusting," El said.

"I hid your imprisonment, you know?"

The only imprisonment he could be talking about was when she'd gotten thrown into the embassy cells and the Fae woman— Marleen Crostee, the ambassador's wife—had identified her. *He hid that too?*

According to Icarus, Roberto had denied she was the one to help Amos escape as well. El followed the reasoning. *Marleen reported to Roberto…which means—* "You *knew* about the Compelling and the experiments and—"

"I didn't know about the Compelling!"

El snapped her mouth shut. *But you knew about the experiments!* It wouldn't help to shout that though.

"I didn't know. Not until I returned home."

"That hardly makes experimenting on people okay!"

His eyes went flat and El hissed through her nose. As much as his involvement disgusted her, this wasn't helping. "I'm well aware nothing comes for free. What is this going to cost, Roberto?"

His frustration appeared real as he shoved his hands into his pockets and stared at his toes. "You don't believe I'd just help you?"

"Even when we were younger, we didn't give freely."

Irritation flashed across his face, quickly replaced by sadness.

Who is this man? He was involved in Dominguez' experiments and yet is helping me? How does that work in his head?

Roberto sighed and pulled a small, black velvet box from his pocket. He held it out on his palm. "At least consider it."

El pushed her hands harder into her armpits. "I can't be a part of what your family is doing."

His hand dropped. "The Varelas are too strong. My parents want them destroyed. They were going to use the storm. Haul it directly over San Martez and—poof—no more Varela family. I convinced them to let me try another way. That maybe I could slowly pull you under the Inverro umbrella instead. They don't realize—" He stopped, looking away as he pocketed the ring.

Dylan's panic played through El's head. She grimaced. "What was your plan? Marry me and later have the boys come visit? They'd just conveniently never go home?"

Roberto's head swung up, a hungry hope back in his eyes. El could see him clutching the ring box in his pocket. *I'm his ticket out.*

"I'll consider it," she agreed.

He held out the ring again. "Take it while you do…please."

Please? Roberto was not one to beg.

"I will consider it," she repeated. He took the hint and slipped the ring back into his pocket.

El nodded and turned to wave at the trees. Moments later, the group emerged and Roberto mutter, "Sweet summer, you keep odd company." But he stepped aside to let everyone pass into the submersible, including Amos who gave him a level look. Icarus was the last to enter and El held her breath. There was a chance Roberto wouldn't recognize him.

Roberto frowned and reached for Icarus' elbow. Faster than El could process, Icarus grabbed Roberto's shirt and pinned him against the wall.

"Don't touch anyone," Icarus hissed.

The color drained from Roberto's face. He wheezed softly but held still.

"We'll be leaving Levi on the sub," Icarus continued, his canines showing as he pressed hard against Roberto's chest. He didn't say it was mostly because of Levi's motion sickness. The implication hinted they didn't trust Roberto, who'd agreed to take them off the ship later.

"He'll be good company," Roberto tried to tease.

Icarus sneered and let go. El savored Roberto's distress until his terror faded to confusion as he watched Icarus find his seat. "You look—"

Icarus glanced back with a raised brow.

Roberto cursed softly. "Fantasma de los muertos."

Ghost of the dead.

"If you mean your good intentions," El said, "you'll leave him that way."

She waited for his shock to fade and then held out Roberto's phone that she'd stolen. He shook his head and closed the hatch.

"Keep it for now," he said. "It's the key you'll need to open a tank. Just be aware I'll report it lost to my parents soon."

How long will he play both sides? El slipped the phone back into her pocket, wondering if she should have taken a picture of the rat's tail she'd found sticking out of a hole in the library wall. Roberto would've laughed uproariously when he found it...at least, he would have when they were younger.

The *Sansabria* swayed and heeled with the storm and Na'rina's blood responded to the seething ocean. Infiltrating the ship felt like déjà vu from their experience freeing Silas except, this time, they weren't on calm water.

Na'rina's heart raced and the twiglet's shivering fluttered the leaves on her head. She wasn't sure, however, if they were nervous for the same reasons. Besides a snide comment or two, he hadn't spoken to her since the beach. All she sensed from him now was fear and grief so thick it tasted like a bitter mushroom.

"We won't be here long," Icarus said over his shoulder.

He was too perceptive. She touched his shoulder, calming the tremble against his warmth.

"Hopefully that's true," Na'rina whispered. She searched for the twiglet but couldn't find him. He was like a vine twining into her psyche, becoming an indistinguishable part of it.

Icarus asked, "Has the extended melding started changing you?"

Na'rina was caught off guard that he'd been thinking so closely to the same thing she was. "Some," she admitted, thinking about how twitchy she was. "How permanent they are remains to be seen."

El paused ahead, waiting at the hatch labeled "Cargo." Amos hunched beside her, too tall for the ship's hallway. Most people unconsciously gave the Sedessan space, but Amos seemed unaware of that as he stood almost shoulder to shoulder—or rather elbow to shoulder—with El.

Na'rina wished Felis and Dante were with them. Their teasing might distract her from the ship's dead rattle, but Icarus had sent them on their own mission to take over the bridge and Na'rina couldn't fault his reasoning. The easiest way to free the captives was to steal the ship. It was an ambitious venture, but Na'rina trusted that the two wer-im knew what they were doing. Plus, they had Richard McCormick to help them access the bridge.

"Ready?" El asked as they joined her. Except for a flush across her cheeks, she looked calm as she wrapped her small hands around the hatch to spin it open. Na'rina wished she could be so composed.

The hatch squealed as El pulled on it. After a quick check to make sure it was empty, they slipped through into the cavernous room beyond. Faint red lights housed in metal cages circled the ceiling. Their reddish glow gilded dozens of rows of gray tanks. Na'rina could hear the dull hum of their electricity.

"Richard's intel was good," Icarus whispered. "No one's here."

"Empty tanks are this way." El pointed.

As they threaded through the tanks, one of the unconscious occupants caught Na'rina's eye. *It's one of the Four Corners prisoners!* She gave the storage bay another scan. There were more tanks than what the Riviera cavern could hold. *Is this all of Intela Corp's prisoners?* The possibility filled Na'rina with heady hope.

El spun suddenly and pointed at Na'rina. "If we survive this," she said, "you owe me a vacation in the Colorado mountains."

Na'rina barked a laugh and slapped a hand over her mouth as the high-pitched sound ricocheted. "That's *all* you want?"

"That's it," El said. "I want somewhere where I can eat bread and honey," she grinned, "and soak in the sun without anyone expecting me to crawl into a gnome's dirt-caked home."

Na'rina wasn't even sure what gnomes had to do with it, but she grinned back. "Agreed."

El winked and turned away, heading for the empty tanks.

Warmth spread through Na'rina, reminding her of the comradery she sometimes shared with Afre. The warmth faded, though, as they stopped before the empty tanks. They were strapped to the wall with ratcheted webbing.

"We'll open the end one." El strode for it and began freeing the rachets. Amos helped.

Na'rina stared at the dull, gray metal. It was like the ship, hollow and lifeless. *And I'm about to crawl inside and close myself in.* She shuddered and clutched at the backpack as the memory of Lady Ignatius came to her. She hadn't been able to see what was happening, but she'd heard the gurgle as the tank had filled with fluid. Na'rina swallowed bile.

Don't throw up on Icarus' shoulder.

"Let's move it away from the wall," Icarus said, grabbing a corner to help.

"Is that the fill station?" Na'rina asked, pointing to a hose hanging from a hook. Everyone followed where she pointed. The ship heaved, catching El and Icarus off guard.

"Looks like," Amos answered, holding steady while the other two found their balance.

Na'rina pinched her lips together. Perhaps it was best not to distract them while moving the tank. They set the thing on one of the platforms meant to hold it off the floor and El slid beneath to screw in the hose. Roberto's phone lit up as Icarus pulled it from his pocket. When he passed it over the keypad, the tank hissed open.

"Icarus," Na'rina swallowed, "it's like a tiny isolation chamber."

He swung the pack off his back and picked her up. Hating that she couldn't wrap her arms around him, Na'rina reached for his face. He gently tilted his forehead against hers. She laid her fingers against his warm skin to trace his scars.

"It'll be brief, love," he promised.

She breathed in his spicy smell and savored the violet zoi aima that brushed against her fingers. By the time Icarus lifted his head, El had already climbed up to sit on the tank's edge with her feet inside. When Na'rina found out that Roberto's parents were on the *Sansabria*, she'd asked El to accompany her into the tank instead of Icarus, ending the siblings' argument. There was no way she was going to leave him vulnerable.

"Trust me, Drydanda?" El held her hands out. Her tone was teasing, but Na'rina cocked her head as she picked up on an undertone. *She's nervous.*

"Of course." Na'rina reached out her arms and smiled.

The twiglet was hardy but El felt like she was holding a newborn child. *You're not going to break her.* Na'rina grasped her forearms and El turned her around to hold her against her chest. Laying back, El flushed with relief that her side didn't even twinge. She was healing.

"Here." Icarus set the sylph-made breather between El's teeth. She met his eyes as she slid into the tank and laid back. "I'll be right here when you all come out." His intensity sent a shock through El. She knew that look. He'd worn it when fencing with the Inverro brothers. It spoke of focus and violence, of a commitment to do anything to reach his goal.

He looked away to dab a cloth with the sedative for Na'rina. Richard McCormick had instructed him that each tank contained a bottle tucked into a compartment below the control panel for just this purpose.

El swallowed and held her breath to keep from inhaling it.

Amos leaned his hands on the tank's edge, meeting her eyes upside down.

"Always 'bout family, eh Sedessan?" he asked, tucking a strand of her hair behind her ear. El flushed and grinned around the breather, still holding her breath as Icarus leaned toward Na'rina.

"See you soon." Icarus held Na'rina's hands until she went limp.

El exhaled.

She wanted to repeat her promise to take care of her but couldn't speak around the breather. Instead, she held her brother's gaze, trying to don confidence like armor to reassure him. She hadn't seen such emotion in his eyes since their mother salted his ear.

He closed the tank, engulfing them in darkness. The tank hissed and gurgled. El pulled in a deep breath through the breather and dropped the confidence for forced calm. Armor didn't work in water; she needed something lighter, like a buoy. It bolstered her against the terror roiling inside her like a miniature storm.

Focus on Na'rina.

El reached out and met a mind of crisp air and mountain starlight. Faint traces of cloying grief, like heavy mist, hovered in the twilight.

Go away, the twiglet hissed, there for a moment, and then gone.

Icarus' claws screeched against the tank's lid. He couldn't prevent Na'rina's terror over being closed inside. He spun away and scanned the wall for the power cord they'd need. Richard said all the tanks initiated their sequence off their batteries, but once they were running, the tank needed to be plugged in.

Amos held out the coil of cable. "Nabbed it along with the hose."

Icarus nodded in thanks. He accepted one end and pulled it toward the tank while Amos headed for the bulkhead to plug in the other end. Amos had just reached the outlet when the hatch squealed.

Icarus ducked, cursing that they hadn't shifted the tank into line with the others yet. It'd be obvious to even a casual observer that it wasn't stored like the rest. Begrudging the oversight, he crawled below it and plugged the cord in.

Then he searched for Amos. The giant was too big to fit beneath the tanks, but neither was he near the outlet now. He spotted Amos' pants between two empty tanks strapped along the wall.

The hatch squealed again and thudded closed. A moment later, footsteps clicked on the metal floor. At least one of the people who entered was wearing heels. That eliminated anyone in his group.

"Why didn't he report it?" asked a woman.

"And admit he lost the electronic key we trusted him with?"

"Pheesh. That boy."

Icarus slid from under Na'rina and El's tank and crawled below the nearest row.

"It's moving."

He froze, waited for the two people to move closer, and peeked out. *Mateo and Marie.*

He hadn't seen them in years. Like his mother, Marie was a small but forceful woman. But it was Mateo who captured his attention. He blinked and Mateo lit up with a Sedessan's seething garnet zoi aima. Blinking again, Icarus found himself staring at the apparently human man who had kidnapped Na'rina, but now he boasted the facial markings of all Sedessans.

When Na'rina saw his zoi aima, though, it'd been human.

Thomas isn't the only one playing human. Miguel's comment, "He smells weird…like his body can't figure out if it's a sweaty human or tarry goblin," connected with the bloodwork Rebecca had checked out for him. *They synthesized the goblin's ability to appear human and somehow advanced it to affect the zoi aima too. They can disguise both physical and psychic.* He tracked that further. The vial Rebecca gave him probably contained an injection of the drug. *Such a drug explains why the Sedessans never realized Dominguez wasn't human.*

Disturbing.

Mateo and Marie turned down Icarus' row. A cell phone's glow lit Marie's face and Mateo's eyes scanned the floor.

Icarus slid Roberto's phone from his pocket. He wiped it with the end of his shirt—he wouldn't put it past them to fingerprint it—and set it on the floor before rolling out the far side of the row.

"What was that?" Marie's head swung up.

Icarus hadn't made any noise. *What caught Marie's attention? Amos?* It didn't matter, for now she stared at Na'rina and El's tank with a frown.

"Either the captain's men got careless," she muttered, "or we have a problem."

They can't inspect the tank. Need a distraction. Icarus needed something that couldn't be easily checked out and then forgotten. Needed something to draw them out of the room. The only thing he could think of was himself. They'd know Amos on sight and, although he was strong, he wasn't fast enough to get past the Sedessans without having to actually confront them. Until Na'rina and El were out of that tank, Icarus wasn't chancing a confrontation in the cargo bay.

Amos peeked out and then ducked back again. In a stroke of luck, Marie was staring at the misplaced tank and didn't notice.

I have to move before he does. What if they recognize me? Marie and Mateo wouldn't hesitate to kill him. *Roberto didn't recognize me at first.* If any Sedessan was going to outside of his family, it would have been Roberto. *So, keep the encounter brief and wer-im.*

Icarus sprang from between the tanks and landed on the one in front of Marie with a roar. On instinct, Marie rocked back a step and reached a hand toward him. He smacked the phone from her and vaulted over her, landing two rows away and racing for the hatch.

Her phone cracked against a tank, but Icarus barely caught the sound under Marie's scream.

"Seal the room!" Mateo bellowed.

But it was too late. Icarus had the door open and slammed shut before either of them moved. He raced down the hall, sometimes vaulting off the wall as the ship rolled, and kept a sharp ear behind him.

Finally, he caught the squeak of the cargo door and Mateo and Marie's arguing voices.

Good, they hadn't stayed to inspect the tank. He'd have to double back to help Amos but first, he had to lose the Inverros. Careening around the corner, Icarus sprang for the ladder to head topside at the same moment a man closed the hatch above. Icarus glimpsed the troll-blooded captain's face before the metal door slammed into his head.

Pain shot down his spine and his hands went numb. He dropped to the floor where his legs gave out and his vision narrowed.

"It *is* a wer-im," someone said.

His vision sparked as he reached for the ladder. Growling, he hauled himself to a standing position just in time to turn into the reaching hands of Mateo and Marie.

El gaped at Na'rina's mindscape.

When entering a mind, a Sedessan usually conducted business in a place familiar to the person. For El, it was her mental study. For Icarus, it was a shallow cave with a campfire highlighting the walls. When El tested him and escaped his cave, she found a swampy forest at night with vines, insects, and predators lurking. It gave her the creeps, which was kind of the purpose.

But Na'rina's mind was something else altogether. Instead of a contained mental room or cave, El stood on an open ridgeline looking down into a valley. For miles, the hillside glowed golden with fall aspen leaves topped by a brilliant robin's egg blue sky.

When El used her second lens, she saw creatures' lifeblood. This was different. Zoi aima flowed and flickered through every plant, animal, person, and even the ground under her feet. The wind gusted and small puffs of glittering crystals floated past El's nose.

Focus, El! But the complexity of the world on this scale was stunning. She just wanted to stare. *Focus. We don't have time for me to play tourist.*

El forced herself to critically survey the forest below. It not only swayed with golden light, but the green zoi aima running through it sparkled like a massive river flowing down the valley.

It's so open. Why hasn't Icarus built up Na'rina's mental defenses? Her brother wouldn't overlook something so vital, but here she stood in a mindscape so open she could see for miles. *Not the time to worry about that!* Somewhere in that flowing, green river was the twiglet. El closed her eyes, feeling the mind around her. Usually, she could sense what she wanted and move like mist to reach it. This time, she became immersed in the dry mountain wind brushing her skin and the aroma of warmed aspens and pines. The smooth, seamless whole of it surrounded her, denying her Na'rina's individual memories.

She felt a presence beside her and looked over. Na'rina—the woman and not the twiglet—swayed in the chill breeze. She was unreal. A thin sprite with sparkling, emerald eyes and a haunting beauty that reflected the aspen forest below.

"He's in there somewhere," she said, "terrified."

El breathed in Na'rina's accent, feeling like she'd found a patch of sweet, wild raspberries. She scanned the valley below. "Any idea where?"

Na'rina shook her head, her brown hair swaying. "I cannot distinguish him from my Rina." Na'rina held out her hand, a silent offer to guide El.

El ignored it. It wasn't that she didn't appreciate Na'rina's offer, but this was what El did. She'd wandered more minds than she had places. And a new perspective might help them locate the twiglet.

"We'll start there," she pointed to a creek trickling down the hillside into the forest. For a moment, El was taken in by the swirling white and blue zoi aima that mixed with the water. She caught herself and cleared her throat. "Water should be attractive to the twiglet."

Na'rina shrugged and gestured for El to lead. She didn't appear hurt, just confused. Briefly, El was at loose ends. There was no resistance to her here and it seemed—wrong. Even Sala's mind had burned, fighting back out of instinct. Remembering Sala's fear, El had a sudden insight regarding the elemental. She had almost no experience away from home. When she'd watched Lady Ignatius get tricked, that reality may have dawned. Perhaps her spooking didn't have anything to do with El herself.

Feeling a bit better, El shifted them to where the stream entered the trees. Na'rina stumbled and grasped the nearest aspen, and El pitied her the disorientation. "Let's follow the stream," she said.

El stepped and the world shuddered like a giant rousing itself beneath the ground and she was the ant on its back.

"Wait!"

The warning came too late. The ground shifted. Thick roots curled around El's ankles and, with a jerk, pulled her into a grave of heavy dirt and darkness. El's stomach dropped. Panicked, she smacked her hand against the tank, suddenly becoming aware of her body again. She gasped against the breather. *It's not real! It's not real!* But grit packed tight to her body, clogging her nostrils with every breath.

Amos' face appeared above, his brows drawn in a thick frown. He reached for the control panel and El shook her head hard. She wasn't ready for him to open the tank.

Just as suddenly, someone grabbed her hair and pulled, and then she was back in Na'rina's mind. Blessed air hit her face. When Na'rina let go, El hit her knees, gasping and spitting.

Na'rina knelt in front of her, holding her shoulders.

"I'm sorry!" She brushed dirt from El's face. "The Rina didn't recognize you and I didn't warn her fast enough."

"What was that?!" El had seen many defenses over the years but she'd never experienced anything so real. She could still feel earth pressing against her ribs.

Na'rina ducked her head, a blush staining her cheeks a deeper green. "I'm sorry. My mind acts like my Rina when threatened. I thought since I was with you, she wouldn't attack, but—" Na'rina shrugged, chagrined.

El shuddered. If Na'rina hadn't hauled her back up, she wouldn't have been able to dig her way out. Not many outside the Sedessan world realized it, but what happened in the mind could happen to the physical body. She would've suffocated on nothing but Na'rina's mindscape.

Rus, you could've warned me! She wouldn't have listened though. She was stronger than him in their mental capabilities and her pride would've made her shrug off his warning. But now El knew why Icarus hadn't messed with Na'rina's mindscape. El shuddered and spit again.

"I'm sorry," Na'rina said again, appearing at a loss.

"You don't even have to *think* about triggering that defense?"

Na'rina shook her head. She was so innocent, so contrite, that El struggled to hold a temper despite her recent terror.

"That's both marvelous and disturbing."

Na'rina smiled tentatively and El was struck by how beautifully open she was. *No wonder Icarus loves her. She's the exact opposite of a Sedessan.*

"Is there a way," she asked, replanning her approach, "to touch on recent memories and not trigger—that?" She pointed at the disturbed earth. Na'rina's recent memories might have a trail leading to the twiglet, but El did not want to end up sucked underground again.

"If I lead you, we can move freely." Na'rina again offered her hand.

No hesitation, no fear. El's heart clenched and she inhaled hard on the breather. She trembled, more aware of the liquid covering her than the mindscape she wandered. Steadying herself, she finally took the Drydanda's slender fingers.

"We want newer memories," El said.

Na'rina nodded and closed her eyes. The forest shifted, dozens of white trunks flying past, memories flashing by with them, and then the world stopped.

El's head spun. She grabbed a tree, battling the dizziness.

Hello, Icarus' sister.

El pushed off the aspen so fast she stumbled.

Na'rina chuckled. "My Rina can sense you."

"Wait, what?" She was in Na'rina's mind. Anything that happened here, other than Na'rina and El herself moving around, should be from the past.

Na'rina touched the necklace around her neck. "Icarus brought my leaf that my Rina filled with her zoi aima. Sometimes, briefly, we can feel each other because of it."

Seriously? This might be the strangest mindscape El'd ever explored. An idea struck her. "She can talk with you now?"

"Some."

"Can she sense the twiglet too?" The Rina was intrinsically connected to Na'rina but still her own entity. She might be able to

367

pinpoint the difference the twiglet made in Na'rina's mind.

Na'rina closed her eyes and the forest shifted again.

El swallowed hard. "I don't see the twiglet," she said.

Na'rina sighed. "The connection with my Rina is brief. She pushed us in the right direction before it faded again."

"Will she be back soon?"

Na'rina shrugged, then pointed. "She directed us that way."

They walked and the grove grew smaller. Not in expansiveness, but in the newness of trees. The aspens went from towering giants to tiny, stick-thin saplings.

"After Intela Corp chopped down this section of my mother's grove, her trees should have pressed up new suckers to fill it back in," Na'rina said over her shoulder as she led the way. "They didn't. My Rina waited initially, leaving the area open, but it stood out like a sore on the groves so she began expanding."

El missed a step. Na'rina may have been talking about the physical Rina, but the representation here meant something else entirely. "You're telling me this is all new memory from after you met Icarus?"

Na'rina brushed a new trunk with her fingers. "This was when Icarus first felt my grove when he made his vow. I didn't know at the time what he'd done."

El caught herself marveling and hurried to follow before she got left behind. The saplings started to thin and blackened, cut stumps poked through the new growth. Icarus had told El about Intela Corp weakening the Mother Drydanda by cutting down her trees.

"This," El touched a stump and her fingers burned. "This is just like the real grove?"

Na'rina didn't pause. "Just like it," she said.

El stared at the white saplings growing in stark contrast to the blackened, dead stumps. She gulped. Not only was Na'rina's mind expanding as she learned, but her Rina expanded with her and was trying to heal the attack against her mother. It spoke of a deep defiance within the young Drydanda and the phenomenal connection between Na'rina and her grove. *How vast is her ability to grow? When does it stop?* As far as El knew, an aspen grove never stopped expanding. *Is Na'rina the same?*

They reached a spot where the desecrated trunks disappeared and a more mature section of forest began. The hairs on El's arms stood on end. She knew, again from Icarus, that this was no longer Na'rina's grove but her mother's. There was an otherness to it that reminded her of a ghost watching from the creaking branches.

"This isn't your grove," El noted, confused as to their direction.

"The Rina pointed this way. I see no reason not to search here."

El shivered. "Your mother can't communicate with you mentally at a distance, can she?"

To El's relief, Na'rina chuckled. "*Na,* thankfully, or my younger years would have been—uncomfortable. What you feel is what the actual grove feels like. My grandmother tells me that otherness means my mother is alive within her Rina. The stronger the sense, the more aware she is."

What a strange existence.

Ahead, Na'rina stopped and tilted her head again. She pinched a leaf between her thumb and forefinger. "The memories here are in an unusual place," she said, and took them into a memory.

...That's probably my friend!

Your friend?

Yeah! He pulled the door off our cells, remember? And the twiglet pictured himself standing on the foot of a towering giant...

"We're headed in the right direction," El said.

Na'rina hummed, her confusion written in the crease between her brows. She walked a little farther and laid her hand on a knot in another aspen.

...She could kill herself.

Did she just—? the twiglet choked off.

Na. Maybe. I hope not. Na'rina couldn't admit the possibility... She stared at the aqua zoi aima in her shaking hands. It streamed around her own blue and green. *Let's not waste it.*

Na'rina moved again to touch another tree.

...when this is all over, you'll have helped not one, but two, Drydandas.

You mean—you mean I'm a hero like Hercules?

Or like Pegasus.

Or maybe I'm like Mitto.

...I'm sorry, the twiglet sobbed. *I'm no Mitto...*

El sensed fear. That cloying fear that he might lose what he loved. She didn't mention it as Na'rina wandered farther and picked another memory.

…One step, the twiglet finally whispered.

One step, Na'rina agreed, crawling under the portcullis…

…There, the twiglet directed her gaze to the bit of shadow against the wall…*You're small, Drydanda, you'd be shocked by how many people overlook something because it's small and doesn't move…*

…Drydanda?

What?

Do we have enough strength to hang onto that? If he's headed outside, maybe we can hitch a ride…

The fear subsided, then returned in waves of agony with the next memory.

…I screamed, waking my stand. None of them had seen what happened, but I woke them up and they saw him and he saw them.

…He mowed through them…I'm not useful, I'm not good…

El yanked them from the memory, gasping. She thrust her hair out of her face, her hands shaking. "Where would the twiglet go to help someone?" she asked.

"Help someone? It's just us here."

El shook her head. "You showed him that helping you buffers his grief. He's scared of losing you, or becoming what he sees as useless again. Where would he go that he feels like he can help?"

"I—I don't—" Na'rina went silent. She gazed up at the old-growth aspens in sudden understanding. "But he can't actually help her here," she whispered.

El snapped her fingers to draw Na'rina's eyes back down. "Help who?"

"My mother. We're in her grove. There's no reason these memories would be here and not in the saplings unless he left them like footprints. But he can't actually help Mona'rina here."

"Doesn't matter. It feels real and, deep down, he knows it's a safe place. Melding must have bypassed your defenses and let him wander freely."

Without warning, the grove shifted. El groaned, fighting dizziness again as she found herself facing a large, split-trunked aspen. At its base sprouted a bright green cluster of shiny leaves that stirred when Na'rina brushed her fingers over them.

The twiglet lifted his head. His arms were wrapped tight around his knees and sappy tears stuck to his cheeks.

"You weren't helping her," he accused Na'rina.

Na'rina's breath stalled. The accusation was a shield, she knew, but it hurt. She *had* been avoiding her mother when she could be helping her heal. A part of her ached for the twiglet's grief, but another, larger part flushed in angry frustration. They couldn't help *anyone* if he wouldn't let go. He'd grown shoots out his back and pressed them deep into the trunk of Mona'rina's seed tree, explaining why she'd been unable to distinguish him from this part of the grove.

El gently pushed Na'rina away and crouched beside the twiglet. She traced the shoots with her fingers. The twiglet shrank and would have spun away, refusing her touch, if he wasn't attached to the aspen.

"I'm not useless!" he shouted.

"Of course not," El agreed, "but you've got yourself entangled here." She continued to run her fingers down the twiglet's back. "It's hard to help people when you can't control your own body."

The twiglet whimpered. "The Drydanda knows better than me."

Na'rina almost scoffed. *He's angry that I want to separate from him but insists I know better?* Icarus' voice seemed to speak to her. *He's scared, love. If you're controlling him, he avoids blame if something goes wrong.*

Wind fluttered the leaves above, and the twiglet shot scared eyes upward. Na'rina slowly backed away. She was projecting her emotions. It wasn't helping.

As though El heard Icarus' remembered words, she took a different tack. "You know, my brother loved to tease me. He'd string yarn through my clothes hanging in the closet and then lie in wait to watch me try and pull a shirt out. How about you? Your brothers like to play tricks?"

Na'rina could just picture a small Icarus meticulously stringing yarn through his sister's clothing.

The twiglet wiped at his tears and shook his head hard enough to lose a couple leaves from his hair. "They were good brothers."

El scoffed. "Even good brothers enjoy a little teasing now and then. Or was it you who instigated the jokes?"

The twiglet scowled. "I'd never! It was Mio who tripped us all up, not me!"

El grinned and the twiglet scowled harder, realizing his mistake. He hunched over his knees, admitting, "We can grow our toes long and twine them into things. Mio would wrap his toes around my feet while I was sleeping and then shout for us to run. I'd wake and try to take off and fall on my face because he'd tied my feet together."

A thick shoot came free in El's hand, slowly retwining itself into the twiglet's back.

Na'rina swayed as a needle-prick shot through her and then was gone. A subtle warmth suffused her limbs as though dawn had just broken on her aspen's bark. *It's working!*

She craved that warmth and almost reached for it but then stopped. That might distract El and the twiglet because the grove would reach with her. But that warmth called to her! It was the sun baking against her Rina's bark. She involuntarily took a small step forward. The twiglet whimpered and pressed his back tighter against the aspen.

Na'rina stilled again. She'd never had another creature look at her with such terror. She wanted to comfort him. *Let El handle this.* She swayed, feeling as though she should be able to help. She was good with plants after all.

But this isn't a plant, Na'rina.

It doesn't matter if you're stronger…it matters how you approach the current situation, Alaya's voice filtered through her mind.

Sometimes the required approach meant doing nothing at all. Na'rina swayed and forced herself to retreat a step, then another, as El continued to speak softly to the twiglet.

A second shoot came free and warmth suffused her as mist evaporating off bark in the morning sun. She almost swooned. *Don't step forward.* She twisted her fingers together and shuffled another step backward instead.

A third shoot let go, the sun rising, warming sap and filling the air with juniper and aspen leaves perfume. Na'rina jerked sideways, stepping behind another aspen before she ruined El's work. Her forehead thumped against the aspen she'd stepped behind.

The UV lights are working. She quested outward, testing with her zoi aima. She pushed at the twiglet's familiar barky skin, and her lifeblood misted beyond his body like a tendril of smoke.

A sharp flavor, like the buzz of electricity when lightning strikes nearby, coated her tongue. Her reach wavered but she pushed harder, stretching, savoring the vulnerability she always experienced when extended like this. It was an exquisite agony, the sharp bite of wind that brings life-giving rain. Sensations came with it. The vibration of an enormous engine, damp granite, that sharp electrical flavor, and a warm, spicy scent so faint she almost missed it. She swallowed back tears. That scent had become a part of *home* to her.

Icarus.

She reached for him, but he was farther away than expected and she faltered.

Wait, Na'rina, El's almost done. She stopped pushing outward and waited.

Two unfamiliar minds rushed in to overwhelm Icarus.

He threw up the mental world he and El had created. A heavy duff of leaves and sandy dirt formed under his feet. Humidity grew sticky and hot against his skin, and everything darkened into the heavy night only found in thick woods. Ancient oaks, black walnuts, and slender pines towered behind him, and a damp cave formed before him, covered in moss and dripping vines. This was a world he and Silas had lived in for years and he knew it all the way down to the fragrance of the crushed poison ivy leaves growing around the cave's entrance.

I'm not ready for this. He'd never be ready for this.

Mateo and Marie seeped like oil across the cave's floor. Icarus waited for them at the cave's entrance. At his feet lay a dead fire. Usually, he'd have it lit and throwing shadows, but his mental world was far more disorienting in the dark and he wanted the advantage as the cave itself wouldn't last long with two arrayed against him.

Use that.

He and El had fought time and again in this space, testing his limits. He barely held his own against El; he had little hope against two much older Sedessans. What he did have was a small element of surprise. If he could knock them out, he could escape their mental cage and return to the physical world where he'd hold the advantage.

Their mental fingers explored the mossy walls, testing them. Finally, they materialized as dark silhouettes. To Icarus' sensitive eyes, the darkness meant little. He could see Mateo's dull eyes and smell his cedarwood aftershave.

Marie flicked her fingers toward the walls and tisked. "Hardly a secure location."

Mateo tapped his ear. "Did you see the scarring?"

Icarus' cheek twitched. He'd hoped they'd miss the ear among the rest of his scars but of course they hadn't.

"Nooo," Marie gasped. "You don't think he's *their* hijo?"

The mocking tone sank claws into him. Marie was as vicious as always. But it was Mateo he had to watch out for. The two always worked in tandem. Marie as the distraction, Mateo as the spear.

This is my nightmare. Icarus shook his head. *Na'rina's safe. That's all that matters.* The vow was still numb in his chest though. *She needs more time.*

"He's not their son," Mateo huffed in derision. "He's no one's son. He's an outcast who tried to come back."

"Which means we can ki—"

"Enough," Icarus interrupted them. He stepped back and raised his hands in a "come get me" gesture. Mateo sneered and Icarus clapped his hands together, hard, setting off a shudder in the earth.

The cave crumbled, burying the two under heavy boulders. A surprised "oomph" mixed with the thud of rock. Maybe he'd knocked one of them out already! Icarus spun and vanished into the thick foliage. If he'd been El, he would have added a barrage of snide thoughts just in case they were conscious, but he wasn't El.

A moment later, water gushed from the rocks and reformed into Marie and Mateo. Marie was laughing delightedly. They stretched out their hands and water misted into long, searching fingers.

Icarus seethed fustration. He'd hoped they wouldn't spread out so quickly. A full-blooded Sedessan's mind could be deployed through another's psyche like a spiderweb, collecting details from multiple places just by the vibrations in the atmosphere.

That was his problem now. Those fingers of water were the threads of their web, growing and beginning to touch the leaves, ground, and air. They were just waiting for him to create the smallest vibration. He held unmoving against a cypress with his feet in the thick mire at the swamp's edge while he tried to think.

Make other vibrations, Dummy. It's what El would say. But simply distracting Marie and Mateo wouldn't help him in the long haul. He didn't have the ability to keep up multiple disturbances for long. *Then use them as a lure.*

Icarus formed realistic replicas of Levi, Felis, and Dante. A dull throbbing kicked up in his head. *This won't last long.* He sent the replicas racing in opposite directions away from him.

Marie and Mateo shot thick spears of water after each running figure. Mateo after Levi and Felis, Marie after Dante. She stepped forward as she focused on his running back, drawing nearer to Icarus. He stayed against the cypress' peeling bark. A fantom itch appeared between his shoulder blades as he watched her water spear draw within inches of Dante's back.

A second before Marie's spear reached the smaller wer-im, Mateo's slashed into the fake Levi and Felis. They exploded into sticky

378

webbing that clung to Mateo's mental reach. He gasped and hit his knees, fighting the strands. The more he fought, the more they clung. If Icarus could hold him long enough, he'd pass out.

Marie swore, stopping her spear just shy of piercing Dante. A small shift in her weight was all the warning Icarus got. She spun, stabbing an obsidian knife at his chest.

In the physical world, he'd take her out easily, but not here. That knife could do more than just puncture a hole in him. Icarus ducked and dove, submerging himself in the swamp's sludgy water. A real, sharp pain shot through his back. He hadn't been fast enough. Marie had stabbed him in his right shoulder and left the dagger in as he disappeared into the swamp.

His grip on Mateo slipped and disappeared. The dagger was Marie's construct, creating a link between Icarus and her. Around him, his carefully wrought world fuzzed. Icarus forcibly pulled the trees and swamp back into their protective layer. Warm blood seeped down his actual shoulder while the blasted knife started pulling on him mentally, trying to draw memories.

"What an abject failure you are," Marie's voice spoke as though she were directly beside him. He recoiled. "You barely hold your defenses after only a few minutes. What must your father think? Oh, that's right, he doesn't care." She chuckled and kept digging. "Who was it who cast you out? Adrian? Sophia? Hmm. Somehow, I doubt Adrian had the nerve. Unless…Unless he didn't know you were a bastard and the surprise pushed him over the edge. But that doesn't seem quite right. It must have been Sophia. Your own mother marked you to die."

The words were a punch to the chest. Icarus sank into the

swamp until his feet settled into the grime at the bottom.

He contorted to wrap his fingers around the knife's hilt. Even as he grasped it, her words heaved at the memory of his mother slicing open and salting his ear.

"Follow me," Sophia Varela rose from the table and his twelve-year-old self hesitated, suddenly afraid. Sophia strode back to him and caught him by the back of his neck.

"I sense something delicious," Marie taunted.

It didn't help that he'd just seen Sophia in the streets of Riviera. He could picture her in stark clarity, making it all the harder to ignore the memory trying to break through. He pulled the dagger free and muffled a scream through his teeth. Bubbles blurped toward the swamp's surface despite this being his own world. It was hard not to exactly mimic the physical world.

Blood soaked through his shirt. Something about the mental injuries made them harder for his body to heal. Until he was in control again, the wound would continue to seep. Instinctively, he wanted to hang onto the dagger but he knew better.

"Was it your mother who cut your ear? Did she have the nerve to do it herself or did she order a goblin to do it?" Marie pressed. "Sophia always has been a hands-on kind—"

Icarus pitched the dagger and her voice disappeared. The pulling on his memories disappeared.

Where's Mateo? He'd lost track of the man. *Idiot. Marie's a distraction.*

He fought the urge to surface for air despite not needing to in his mindscape. Staying under felt wrong, but it kept him from breaking the swamp's murky surface and revealing his location. He inched away from Marie by creeping across the bottom like an alligator.

The image struck him, and he resisted a grin.

Faint movement drew his attention and Icarus paused. Turtles. Mateo or Marie—he wasn't sure which one—was flooding the swamp's surface with turtles. They were just like the water spears—extensions of consciousness that would reveal Icarus' location.

Concentrating hard again, Icarus crafted two large alligators and sent them swimming for the surface with barely a ripple. His head throbbed. Once they were close enough, they struck, chomping down on swaths of turtles before diving again.

Behind him, Mateo grunted and something hit the water. *Mateo's turtles.* Taking advantage of Mateo's distraction, Icarus swam into the knobby roots of a cypress stand and surfaced. Not far away, Mateo slumped on his knees, bleeding from multiple puncture wounds like the alligator's teeth had bit into his arms. Seconds later, Marie hit her knees beside him and wrapped her arms around him. It wasn't a comforting gesture but a way to strengthen Mateo. Marie had initiated physical contact with not only Icarus, but now Mateo as well. Mateo's wounds began to close, and Icarus' mental world stretched and then snapped back into place.

Icarus muffled a grunt. His world frayed like worn fabric.

Now or never, Rus. He shot the alligators forward. Marie and Mateo were growing, pushing at his world, stretching it thin until holes started letting in pinpricks of memory. He smelled warm blood and snorted, trying to clear his nose as the blood trickled out of his nostrils.

Marie finally spotted him.

Mateo tried to haul her away from the approaching alligators, but Marie dug her fingers into his arms while pushing hard against the boundaries of Icarus' world.

The alligators shot from the water, their jaws wide to chomp down on the pair. Marie pressed harder and the gators turned translucent. Icarus gritted his teeth, remembering how *real* Na'rina's world felt. He wanted—*needed*—that now. Pain pierced his skull and the gators exploded, his carefully crafted world shattering into tiny shards of agony. With a delighted crow, Marie elbowed her way into his memories and Mateo appeared behind him, caging him in heavy bars.

Icarus screamed and Na'rina's patience shattered.

"I'm sorry!" She ripped away from the twiglet, her zoi aima streaming through metal walls and empty space to reach Icarus. The twiglet shrieked, but then Na'rina emerged fully from him and his pain vanished from her, replaced by the cold against her bare feet, the sharp smell of damp steel, and the nausea climbing her throat as the ship pitched.

I'm me again!

She'd emerged next to Icarus and two Sedessans. She caught the glow of a fourth person's lifeblood in the hallway but then her psychic awareness became overwhelmed by the ship's hollow rumble. She trembled. Na'rina shook her head, trying to bring the world into a cohesive whole, and then she gagged as a musky sweat filled her nose. She ducked just as the fourth person she'd sensed grabbed for her. She stumbled on her gangly legs. Using the motion, she hit her knees and rolled past Icarus, putting him and the Sedessans between herself and whoever she'd startled. When she looked back, she whimpered.

The troll-blooded captain?

She remembered him from the beach outside the tunnels. His musky sweat in the confined space made her gag.

"Where'd you come from?" he rumbled. He eyed the gap she'd

rolled through, hesitating. He couldn't pass without touching the Sedessans.

Na'rina did a double take at the Sedessans. *Armon—Na, Mateo and Marie.* After seeing Icarus' photo, she knew Marie was Sedessan, that she was Roberto's mother, but seeing her slammed that reality home. *I almost trusted her. How naïve!* Na'rina swayed, caught off guard by her pessimism.

The two Sedessans were holding Icarus in white-knuckled grips.

The captain shouldered past the trio.

Na'rina yelped and pushed to her feet just as he grabbed for her again. A fresh wave of dizziness washed through her, making her stumble. The captain caught her arm and forced her face-first against the wall. Her head smacked the metal. The gray wall swam in her vision.

A familiar buzz tickled the hands she'd raised to blunt her impact. *I can feel it!* Na'rina breathed it in, glorying in the electricity's bitter, beetle-like taste. Her body tingled with its energy. Focusing it on the pressure of the captain against her back, energy shot from her skin with a sharp *zap.*

The man jolted into the opposite wall. Na'rina spun, intending to jostle Icarus and break the Sedessans' contact, but she froze. Blood soaked Icarus' shirt.

Why's he not healing?

Her hesitation cost her. The captain was moving. In two steps he'd be within touching distance again. She couldn't get to the ladder or the hatch above so Na'rina spun, darting toward the hatch behind her. Her bare feet slapped against the floor, carrying her in long strides. It was *good* to be back in her own body!

"Get back here!"

Right. And let you catch me? But she was now running away from Icarus too and she couldn't get his bleeding back out of her head. *He needs me. How do I get rid of the brute?* She reached the hatch and ducked through just as the door swung with the roll of the ship. Someone hadn't secured it. Na'rina squeaked as it banged closed and then open, almost catching her.

It gave her an idea. She stopped and spun, pushing her zoi aima back the way she'd come.

The captain wasn't that far behind.

The ship pitched and Na'rina almost fell, catching herself on the wall. The brute appeared in the hatchway. Na'rina curled her reaching zoi aima around the door and found he'd taken a second to secure it.

"There's nowhere to run to, little nymph."

Na'rina snarled. It was a very Icarus response and it suited her just fine. She flipped the securing pin open again with her zoi aima and yanked on the door. It shrieked and smacked the man from behind. He gave an *oomph* before his head slammed into the opposite wall. Even as elation surged through Na'rina, he pulled his hands toward his shoulders to push back from the wall.

How did that not knock him out!? Icarus' bleeding haunted her. She did *not* have time for this! Grabbing whatever came to hand, she swung a paint bucket at him and caught him upside his head. The bucket exploded, spraying gray paint across them both. He came back at her, furious. It should have terrified Na'rina. Instead, her fury tinged her vision scarlet. *Icarus needs me.*

All this talk about her being a Theos mix and she couldn't deal with a stupid troll? *Am I just a weak dryad?* The brute lunged and caught her arm as she tried to dodge. His grip crushed the bones in her wrist. She tried to pull away, but she was a tiny seed caught in a storm. Satisfied he'd subdued her, his grip loosened. Her wrist immediately *popped* as it reset.

His mouth fell open in shock.

Enough of this! Na'rina smacked her free hand against the conduit buzzing in the wall. The brute released her, trying to back away. Na'rina bared her teeth, again seeing scarlet. It even flickered up the branches on her arms. Before he got too far, she slapped her newly healed hand against his chest.

Electricity slammed into him and again he hit the wall, denting in the metal with a loud *crunch*. He slumped to the floor like a boneless doll.

For a moment, Na'rina just stared at him. *I did that.* A shudder traveled her spine as her fury faded. *Deal with it later.* She stepped past the brute to return to the hallway where Icarus faced the Sedessans. She couldn't risk touching Marie or Mateo. Icarus had already shown he'd protect her at any cost when he'd killed Silas. If the Sedessans could see that memory, they'd know she was his weak point. It'd be like adding wind to a forest fire. She didn't necessarily have to touch anyone, however, for Icarus to hear or feel her. Na'rina entered the hallway and then paused. *Best hide while I do this.* She grabbed the large conduits that lined the ceiling and swung up to hide on top of them.

Warmth blossomed in Icarus' chest, dissolving the numbness

that had plagued him. *Na'rina's free!* He carefully kept the knowledge buried as Marie watched his memories.

"Get some sleep." Silas waved Icarus away. They'd been discussing the disappearance of the Rockies dwarves again but nothing new would come to light tonight.

Icarus slammed his shoulder against Mateo's cage again, startling both Marie and Mateo. He was a bird in a tiny cage but that didn't mean he couldn't resist. Snagging Mateo's collar, he hauled him against the far side of the bars. Panic suffused Mateo's face and then electricity ran through the cage and Icarus' muscles froze. Mateo stepped out of his grip. Icarus snarled, enjoying the worry Mateo couldn't quite hide.

"Might step back farther, dear," Marie suggested. "Felines have an uncanny ability to slip their shoulders through tight spaces."

Mateo took another two steps back. The cage was his. Icarus could feel the man's unwavering nature in the bars, the rounded ceiling that looked like it could be hung from a hook, and the thick metal floor beneath his feet. If he recalled right, Mateo kept a pet macaw. He'd fashioned the cage after something familiar.

The rest of the mental world was Marie's. The small woman sat on a chocolate microfiber couch in a home theatre. Across from her was a whitewashed wall displaying images from the projector at her elbow. With her feet propped up on a coffee table, she tossed popcorn into her mouth as she watched Icarus' life like a movie.

Icarus climbed into a sprawling oak and settled into the juncture where two thick branches sprouted from the massive trunk. As he dozed off, he could see Silas' reflective green eyes watching the night below.

Someone screamed and Icarus rolled out of the tree, landing amid Silas and two men he didn't know. They weren't the only unfamiliar people in the forest. Men moved through the trees, targeting other wer-im who awoke at Silas' cry.

Something zipped past Icarus' ear and someone grunted. Silas. *His mentor hit his knees, a small red dart jutting from between his neck and shoulder. His eyes rolled upward, and he slumped forward.*

"Na!" More men surged forward and Icarus had to dart away to avoid getting shot. Each time he tried to reach Silas, he was pushed back, and he finally registered that the wer-im were being decimated.

"Retreat!" he shouted.

Icarus grated his claws against the gold bars. Marie scowled, pausing her movie.

"Would you rather experience them again instead of watch?" she asked, eating another handful of popcorn. "I did that for Rosharu, you know." Icarus knew she could force him back into the memory and make him relive it over and over again. *Would that stall her?* He needed to give El and Na'rina time to get off the ship. The second part of Marie's taunting hit him. *She drove Rosharu mad.*

He'd find other ways to stall her. Icarus remained quiet and Marie shrugged.

Another memory started:

Silas gripped Na'rina's arms, ready to kill her. Icarus lunged, tearing his mentor away from her. It ripped Silas' claws out of her skin, sending pricks like needles into Icarus' chest. He rolled with Silas, trying yet again to speak to him, to reach into his mind.

Silas spun on him instead, attacking in blind rage.

Icarus couldn't reach him…

"Silas!" Icarus roared. Surely some part of his mentor heard.

Na'rina ducked and Silas' jump went long. Icarus followed…Silas' vicious snarl showed none of the wer-im Icarus knew. He's beyond my reach. *Bucking him off, Icarus spun and locked onto Silas' head. He didn't even notice the tears running down his face as he twisted. The pop felt far too loud in his ears.*

Marie laughed. "Let me get this straight. You abandoned him to be captured and then, after freeing him, you killed him. No wonder your parents cast you out. You've no family loyalty."

Her words were a punch to the chest. Silas had been Icarus' father in every way except biologically. Icarus had lived in Silas' shadow and been content to stay there, but the events of the last year had pushed Silas too far.

Perhaps he saw it coming. Perhaps he chose me to be Wer-Kadis before he could destroy the wer-im. Icarus couldn't shake the possibility. That sort of planning was exactly like Silas. *He trusted me to be Wer-Kadis.*

While he struggled to accept the possibility, Marie turned back to her projector and kept scrolling for more *entertaining* memories.

Icarus' forehead thumped against the bars. He glanced back at Mateo. Impassive as always, Mateo stood with his hands clasped behind his back. He didn't have to stay so close to maintain Icarus' cage, but for whatever reason he wasn't joining Marie on her made up couch.

He's humoring her. Now that they had control, they could simply kill him, but Marie was enjoying herself and so Mateo waited. When she was done, he'd squash Icarus' cage until it was a tiny ball of nothing with Icarus left inside…and without a mind to speak of in the physical world.

Icarus probed at the cage again and a mental slap hit his knuckles. Icarus hissed.

"Stop interrupting my show," Marie ordered.

He stared at the back of her head, fury making him see red. Seconds later, the familiar ice rushed through his limbs, bringing the eerie calm. The longer he held Marie's interest, the longer El and Na'rina had. He paused. His sense of Na'rina had become a hot fist in his chest that almost mimicked his own fury.

What is she doing?

It didn't matter. He just had to buy her time.

He refocused on Marie. *Irritate her or leave her alone?*

Marie paused her scrolling and chortled as, in the memory, Silas hit him upside the head.

"Where's your head, dumb kit? These knots should be second nature by now."

"Terrible wer-im apparently too," Marie commented.

She didn't know Silas. If he'd been really irritated, it would've been more than a slap to the head. Icarus almost smirked.

Irritate her. The woman liked to talk. It might stall her longer if she had to correct him in between scrolling.

"If you—" Icarus cut off with a howl. Joint-popping pain washed through him like a wildfire and then vanished, leaving behind a cool wind that rose the hair on his arms.

Marie rolled off her couch in a crouch and Mateo took a nervous step backward.

Icarus held onto the bars, shaking.

When nothing else happened, Marie tossed her popcorn bowl at him. "*Pheesh!* Trying to take years off my life? I'll take years off your own!"

He barely heard her. He *knew* that touch.

Na'rina's hands shook against the conduits beneath her. *What just happened?*

She'd reached for Icarus with her zoi aima just like she'd always done, but instead of shifting him into a lynx, and thereby breaking the Sedessans' hold on him, he'd screamed. Pain washed through him. *I just added to his agony. Me…I hurt him. I—,* Na'rina stopped. *I can do this.*

She braced herself and tentatively quested out again, avoiding the sharper, more pungent smell of Marie and Mateo to settle around Icarus. Her cooler lifeblood often soothed his pain. She swallowed, wetting her dry throat.

Why didn't he shift?

She knew the heart rate that usually triggered the shift as well as she knew her own heartbeat, and yet he'd screamed and stayed in his wer-im form. *Why?*

Marie's lifeblood suddenly turned sour a second before Icarus threw back his head and howled again. The scream echoed against the metal walls.

What do I do? Na'rina held in a sob. *I could shock them like I did the brute, but that might hit Icarus too.* The possibility made her nauseous. *Maybe I can speak to him.* Na'rina didn't totally understand why—perhaps it was the combination of his Sedessan abilities and her own psychic nature—but Icarus could hear her when she streamed zoi aima into him. She couldn't hear back, but did that matter?

Na'rina closed her eyes to block out the agony rippling in his lifeblood. Below her, Icarus gagged. Tears dripped off her nose onto the metal between her hands. As she misted zoi aima into him, she called, *Icarus, I see you.*

Marie's fingers squeezed Icarus' throat. Handcuffs had appeared on his wrists and the cage shrank so he couldn't back away from her.

"Stop your noise," she snarled, "or I'll make you relive every scar on your worthless body." Her nails punctured his neck and warm blood trickled down into the hollow of his throat.

Icarus, I see you. A cool breeze brushed his mind.

"What was that?" Marie slammed his face into the bars. "Your eyes dilated. What was that?"

I see the blood running down your back and the crescents, like nails, on your neck. The breeze brushed across the wounds as Na'rina spoke. They sluggishly began to close despite the Sedessans' hold stunting his healing.

In her anger, Marie didn't notice. She slammed him again and Icarus groaned. His head throbbed but he seized on the faint, beautiful whisper in his ear.

"Pain," he croaked.

"I know what pain looks like!" Marie shouted, "and what excitement looks like. What caught your interest?"

Na'rina was free and Marie couldn't hear her. *She can see me...which means she's close.* His heart thudded with both hope and fear.

I can't touch you, her whisper breathed around him, *I don't know if that would do more harm than good. I tried to shift you but that didn't work either. I can only figure you're more Sedessan right now than wer-im, like when Mama's skin started looking like bark when Silas changed into a lion. More dryad and more wer-im to balance things. You're out of balance, but I don't know how to fix it.*

Na'rina was rambling. She tended to do that when scared. He clung to her voice, fighting to stay aware.

Marie jeered and loosened her grip as he started to pass out. She tapped a finger against his cheek. "As much as I love toying with you," she said, "we have work to finish and you're keeping us from it."

She flicked her fingers, letting go of him. "Have your fun, mi amor," she said to Mateo as she backed away.

Mateo's dull expression melted into fierce joy. He raised a hand to clench his fingers and the bars against Icarus' back shuddered and pressed tight to his shoulder blades. *I need to move fast.*

I don't know how to fix things, Na'rina continued. *But I know you're strong enough to win.*

Her words echoed as the cage buckled inward, pressing downward on his head. Before him, Marie's face blurred. She was speaking. "—a failure. You can't—"

The floor heaved upward, buckling his knees.

You're everything a wer-im should be. He pulled on Na'rina's confidence.

"—you failed your family. Failed—"

Fierce, loyal, intelligent. It's exactly what he needed to hear. He screamed, pressing hard against the mental cage. It shuddered.

"—worthless imp of a—"

You're the Wer-Kadis that your people need, Na'rina sobbed. *You're my Icarus.*

"Worthless—"

You can do anything.

Na'rina's zoi aima built within him like the pressure behind a dam. It overshadowed the agony in his legs as the cage shrank farther. The cage convulsed again and something snapped.

Fight, Icarus! Lifeblood sparked along his nerves, no longer cool but sharp as lightning.

"—u're no one."

"*Naaa!*" Energy exploded, bursting from his core in a wave of violet, green, and blue, all lined in a scarlet he'd only ever seen when someone threatened Na'rina's grove. A concussive *boom* hollowed out his ears, followed immediately by a high-pitched ringing, and then pain.

His mind finally registered that his legs had broken and he collapsed.

Na'rina had gripped the conduits so hard she dented in the pipes. Blood dripped from her nose but the shock from the psychic blast locked her fingers in place. It'd been lightning striking her body. She was surprised that her skin wasn't singed black.

Below her, Icarus convulsed, his legs twisted in odd directions.

Move, Na'rina. She rolled off the conduit and landed beside him. A screech pierced through the hall just before uniformed men rushed through the far hatch.

Spasms rocked Icarus and his hand smacked her leg.

Is he healing?

Something twitched to the right and Na'rina jumped, noticing Marie for the first time. She lay in a heap with blood coming from her ears and nose. She groaned and twitched again but her eyes didn't open.

Mateo sat up on the far side of Icarus, grasping his head.

Icarus whimpered and his left foot smacked the wall. A sharp *pop* sounded as his leg straightened just below the knee. Nausea rolled through Na'rina.

He needs time.

But they didn't have time. The group of men were almost to them. Na'rina swiped at the tears coursing off her chin and stood over Icarus. His psychic shout had drained her zoi aima but not depleted it.

I only need a bubble. She gathered in everything she had left and pushed outward in a small circle, hardening the outside edge just as Mateo pushed to his feet.

Na'rina snarled at him.

He stepped backward, panicked, and then noticed the men coming up behind him. The panic disappeared beneath a placid curiosity, and he grabbed at her.

His hand hit Na'rina's invisible wall.

Na'rina swayed as the impact rippled her extended zoi aima.

Mateo stepped back, startled. He blinked and his Sedessan lens added a sheen to his eyes. In awe, he tentatively ran a hand along the green and blue barrier between them. His fingertips flattened not more than five inches from Na'rina's face.

Icarus whimpered again and latched onto her ankle as he bowed inward. She'd never seen him in such agony, not even when Silas shredded his face during the Kadivas.

Mateo shook his head, drawing her attention again. "He kept saying you were the key. Now I know why." He knocked his knuckles on her shield and it rippled again.

Na'rina desperately hoped he assumed her hold was fluid instead of realizing how fragile it was.

He stepped back into the men who'd stopped behind him. "Bombard her."

Daft! Gritting her teeth and closing her eyes, Na'rina braced for impact.

"Capture the nymph. Kill—"

Something thudded and tremors vibrated up through her bare feet. Mateo glanced backward in irritation. The men around him faltered as a metallic clang filled the hall. Someone bellowed and the group's discipline disintegrated. The men closest to Na'rina were rammed against her shield by something from behind.

It flexed inward. She couldn't hold it against their combined weight. Collapsing over Icarus, she held her weight on her knees and elbows and shrank the shield down to just their bodies. Her muscles ached like she was holding a physical shield against the onslaught. Tears blurred her vision and dripped onto Icarus' chest.

Something stirred on her opposite side. The brute scooped Marie into his arms and then vanished through the hatch. Na'rina lost sight of him when Mateo and another man stumbled over her shield, landing on their backs on the far side.

Seeing them fall, the others stepped on the shield to get over her. Na'rina had no idea what they were running from but their weight kept pounding on her like a rockslide until they were past and escaping through the hatch. The last man swung the door closed and spun the wheel, locking it.

Na'rina's body trembled, threatening to dump her on Icarus' healing body.

Pop.

It sounded loud in the sudden silence.

"Was that his leg?"

Na'rina finally pushed away from Icarus to lay on her back beside him. She stared up at his sister who stood with the twiglet on her shoulder. Amos loomed behind them, swinging his arms like he was stretching after a good workout.

Icarus moaned.

"They shattered his legs," Na'rina said. She laced her fingers with his. After a brief moment, he returned the pressure. El stared at their hands until Icarus started chuckling.

It wasn't totally humorous.

"Care to share?" El asked.

"I picked their brains," Icarus croaked.

"Your humor's not up to par, Rus."

"It'll recover. Any word from Felis or Dante?"

El's jaw worked, but then she held up her phone and read, "'Bridge is ours. Hope freeing the nymph is as easy.'" Then she asked

Icarus. "Now what did you pick from the Inverros' brains?"

He shook his head. "Let's get out of here and then I'll share details."

"Fine." El huffed and offered Na'rina a hand up. "We'll talk later."

Icarus had asked to come to San Martez, but his hackles still rose as their headlights swept across the marble entry pillars and he glimpsed the lofty gargoyles' eyes. They looked miserable but then again, they'd looked miserable when he was a kid, rain or shine, so it wasn't the rain that soured their moods.

The estate was flooded past the front door and Icarus almost hydroplaned coming to a stop. Both Na'rina and the twiglet squeaked.

"Rus, what are we doing here?" El asked again.

He knew she hated being left in the dark, but he'd needed time to think. "I'll explain once we're inside." He shifted the car into park and reached for the door, but Na'rina caught his hand.

Are you alright?

He just smiled at her. He wanted to do more. To hold her now that she was Na'rina again—to simply breathe in her aspen fragrance—but they were short on time.

"Inside," he said again, and opened the car door. Water covered his feet as he pushed through the monstrous front doors of the estate. Icarus spotted the entryway rug rolled up and leaning on the second-floor landing. The staff knew what to do when a hurricane hit.

Na'rina's slender fingers slid into his hand. On her other side, Levi padded along, his golden eyes glittering in the faint house lights.

How is he holding up under his separation from Ver'rina? Icarus continued to feel the ache of being away from Na'rina's grove but with her beside him it was a small wound.

Icarus paused, water lapping against his ankles, as his fingers encountered the tiny divots in the banister where he'd tried to climb it when he was four. *No one buffed them out or stained over them.* After reliving a number of his memories, the place felt hollow and cold like a tomb for his childhood.

He sighed. He had not wanted to come here but if all went well, he'd be in and out with Sophia and Adrian none the wiser. He started up the stairs again. Suddenly the poignant aroma of Marissa's cooking—the goblin loved her Mexican spices and frog legs—struck him, and the tomb feeling disappeared.

Icarus led everyone to the study and El peeked inside for him before opening the doors for everyone. Then she pushed them closed and leaned against them. "Now, what are we doing here?"

"Do you know the name of Intela Corp's CEO?" Icarus asked as he leaned against the desk. Irritation flashed across El's face. Icarus just waited. He'd had more freedom in Mateo's cage than the man had realized and what he'd found answered a lot of questions.

Na'rina joined him, hopping up to sit on the desk. Her feet were bare, but she still wore a cream pantsuit. *From the summit.* If it bothered her that it was in rags now, she didn't show it.

Amos shrugged. He considered sitting on the floor but settled for leaning against the end of a bookshelf. Perhaps he didn't want to disturb the twiglet sleeping in his cargo pocket. Icarus could just see the leafy hair sticking out and hear a high-pitched snore.

El huffed. "Dom Endo, or something like that," she answered with a flip of her hand. "He's super reclusive."

"For a reason. He looks exactly like Thomas Dominguez."

Na'rina froze like a startled deer. He didn't blame her.

"Dom Endo, Thomas Dominguez, Thomas Inverro. How many names does this guy have?" Amos asked.

"He's been using Intela Corp to study mythic abilities, making them into injectable serums," Icarus explained. "The goblins' ability to appear human, enhanced to alter not only their physical appearance but their zoi aima signatures as well, the salamanders' control of fire, the giants' strength. One plus: He can only inject one or two at a time as they interact with each other in unpleasant ways. But he's planning to use Intela Corp's tech symposium to Compel some of the smartest minds this century. He *needs* something from them."

"What, all at once?" El asked. "That doesn't make any sense. Compelling takes focus. It's incredibly tiring."

"I don't know how he plans to do it. I just know Mateo believes he has a way. On top of that, he created this hurricane and is hauling it up the coast, perhaps to trap everyone at the symposium long enough to accomplish what he hopes."

Na'rina shuddered, coming out of her shock. "Owasha was right," she muttered. "The storm's not natural."

El pushed off the door and paced the length of the rug. "He's headed to Charleston then," she said.

Icarus raised a brow.

"It's not just Intela Corp's symposium, it's the Court's ball this year."

"How do we stop 'im?" Amos asked, watching El like he wanted to halt her pacing. Wouldn't work. El never sat still for long unless she was on mission.

"You want the jet," El guessed, pointing at Icarus. "But I can't just ask Gladen to fly us there. He'll never go for it without approval."

"I didn't think he would," Icarus said. This was what he'd been mulling over the whole ride to the estate. How to get to the symposium in the first place. He knew the goblins ultimately reported to their parents, not El. "What if you tell Sophia and Adrian about Dominguez?"

El shook her head. "They'll insist on going with and I doubt we can hide you."

"Not if we give them the ship." Icarus had anticipated El's objection.

"What do you mean?"

"Oh, that could work!" Na'rina's eyes lit up but then she touched Icarus' shoulder, a line appearing between her brows. "But will your parents take care of everyone?"

He couldn't help a grin. "It's in their best interest to."

"What are you suggesting?" El asked again, exasperation leaking through.

Icarus took pity on her. "Give Sophia and Adrian the ship with all its hostages. Vell'marxia's still in her tank. They'd gain one of Intela Corp's ships *and* a grudging introduction to the South American Drydanda."

He could see El's mind stutter. A connection with Vell'marxia would be a big win, but the Drydanda wasn't the only hostage their parents would love an opening to. In one move, this could massively expand their influence and vault the Varelas to the top of the Court.

El grinned. "That could work. Go hide." She pointed to the room's far back corner. "There's a nook built into the window back there. It stays dark unless you switch on the reading light. Take the puma with you."

Icarus headed for it with Levi at his heels. Amos grunted as he moved to follow.

"I'll explain about Amos," Na'rina offered. "We'll have to explain about the cells under the embassy anyway and the Compulsion stuff for this to make sense to your parents."

Na'rina standing face to face with his parents—

Icarus' hackles rose again, but he curbed the reaction. He trusted Na'rina as a Drydanda probably more than she did. He just trusted Sophia to also use any weaknesses to wrest control.

"We'll make it work," El said and reached for the pull cord to call for Gladen. Before her fingers could grasp it, the study doors flew open and Sophia stormed in with Adrian at her heels.

"Elodie Varela, you have no—" Sophia cut off as she spotted him.

Icarus' heart rate spiked. He was twelve years old again, about to be cast out by his mother. His ears twitched with remembered agony and his claws dug into his palms. Na'rina moved so quickly, hopping off the desk and reaching his side, that Sophia flinched belatedly. Cool fingers gripped his arm hard enough to press muscle against bone and the discomfort pulled him from his shock. Icarus hardened his expression.

We survived Mateo and Marie. We'll survive this. Na'rina encouraged, shifting to face his parents with him as she settled her hand on his arm.

Sophia's spine went rigid, her own face becoming a cool mask.

Icarus stretched his claws. He'd always wondered how this confrontation would play out. He wasn't surprised to find Sophia showed no remorse. Adrian made a choking sound—and then he was moving, coming straight for Icarus.

Icarus rocked backward. In his peripheral, he glimpsed golden eyes between the shelves.

Sophia let out a startled protest.

Adrian halted before Icarus like he'd hit a wall. He scanned Icarus' face, his ears, his facial markings, the tips of his canines pressing against his bottom lip. Icarus couldn't figure out if he was cataloging or trying to fit the wer-im with the boy he'd known.

Icarus struggled to reconcile that Adrian, the man he both loved and resented, was looking *up* at him. When he'd been twelve, Adrian had towered over him.

"My son," Adrian choked, and threw his arms around Icarus.

Icarus' breath huffed out of him. Cool zoi aima misted into him from Na'rina's fingers that rested on his arm. Icarus didn't need it. Not like he'd expected. Adrian just held on and suddenly it wasn't the lack of air in Icarus' lungs that made his chest hurt. He returned Adrian's embrace, engulfing the smaller man, and Na'rina moved away.

Back in the shelves, Levi's eyes glittered and disappeared.

The room seemed frozen. Years of rejection crowded into Icarus' mind. *Adrian suffered too? Why?*

"This is a disaster," Sophia said, massaging her temples. "If anyone sees you, they'll kill you."

"They already tried," Na'rina said at the same time El muttered, "And whose fault is that?"

"They failed," Icarus said, stepping away from Adrian.

Adrian grabbed his arm. "We had our reasons," he said. "They were stupid reasons born of our inexperience and cowardice—"

"Adrian!"

"—but by the time we understood that, we'd already buried you and it was *safer* for you to hate us all."

"Safer! You cast him out to starve on the streets of Caracas!"

Sophia scoffed. "You took him food."

That brought El up short. Even at eight, she'd been very careful when contacting him. *They tracked her.* If they knew about El's trips to see him even then, it stood to reason they'd known all along.

Icarus chuckled. It held an incredulous edge, but it was a better response than fury.

El and Sophia swung their heads toward him. They looked startlingly alike in that moment.

"They've always known, El," he said. "I should've guessed. They've always known you kept contact with me."

"That—I—but—" El couldn't put words together. It was a good thing she couldn't see Amos' grin.

They didn't have the luxury of hashing out their past right now, but Icarus couldn't help but ask, "What reasons?" as he remembered Na'rina's long ago question about healing his family.

Adrian hesitated, finally taking in the whole room. His earnestness receded into caution. "That is a conversation better left for a private meeting."

Icarus snorted. There was nothing Adrian or Sophia could say that would be any more damaging than what the group already knew. Icarus shook his head and said, "*Na*, You don't get to bury this for another time."

"We can bury it forever," Sophia said.

"Darl—" Adrian started.

"You could," Icarus interrupted, "but then I walk and she walks with me. And you lose your one chance this century to turn the tables on the Inverro family."

Taking the hint, Na'rina stepped up to his side again and slid her fingers into the crook of his elbow. She swayed, mimicking her trees so perfectly it looked like a slight breeze swirled around her, fluttering the tatters of her shirt. She watched his parents with the same indifference as her aspens would.

He could kiss her for that.

He could also swear the gears were spinning in Sophia's brain. Who was Na'rina that she was such a bargaining chip? How did it help the Varelas? Sudden understanding appeared in Sophia's eyes. And the dawning pride and calculations in her made him very wary.

"You're the Wer-Kadis," Sophia said, smugly.

They knew. El boiled inside. *For years I defied them, and I was doing exactly what they wanted!* She was only slightly mollified that they'd never connected Icarus with the Wer-Kadis or the Drydanda she'd reported on from North America. *I managed to keep something from them.*

Adrian had invited them to sit but El couldn't stand being still. She paced beside the desk while Adrian tried to find words. Sophia sat curled into one of the plush chairs. She looked like she was putting together the puzzle of people before her, making them fit whether they were the right shapes or not.

El spun on her heel, ignoring Sophia's stare. *I don't want to know what shape she thinks I fit.*

Icarus waited in the chair he'd hauled from the reading nook with Na'rina sitting on the floor beside his legs. *How is he so calm?!*

Across the room, Amos had lowered himself to the floor like Na'rina and now leaned against the end of a bookcase, watching but also separating himself from the conversation. Where Levi was, El didn't know. Even her second lens didn't reveal his zoi aima signature back in the bookshelves.

"Fertility wasn't as understood in the early 1800s," Adrian suddenly said and El swung around. *He sounds—uncertain? Apologetic?*

Icarus raised a brow, disturbingly relaxed.

El forced herself to stop pacing and leaned against the desk instead, crossing her arms over her chest.

"As you know," Adrian tried again, "a large portion of a family's strength comes from its long-term goals." He swallowed and reached for the pull cord near his seat, giving it two sharp tugs. A call for drinks. Then he leaned forward, elbows on knees, and kept going. "We tried for fifty years to conceive. We were seen by every doctor, mythic or human, we could think of—"

"Nothing worked," Sophia interrupted, her tea-and-scones accent bitter as lemon.

Adrian took the hint and didn't go into details as he continued, "Even in those days, the Inverros were strong. Mateo and Marie had conceived Roberto and Ethan, firmly setting their future in the Court. The only way for us to counterbalance them was to have a child, and our years were running short."

"How y' mean?" Amos asked. Sophia scowled but Amos ignored her as he continued, "A few years difference in ages don't mean much in y'r lives. Even another fifty wouldn't a made a huge dent in the grand scheme."

"A Sedessan doesn't usually conceive after three hundred," Sophia spat. "I was running out of time."

"And y' had to keep power?"

"If they hadn't conceived, their decline would have been slow, but certain," Icarus answered coolly. "They'd be cut out of meetings involving planning for the next generation. Down the road, they'd lose a lucrative association because of it. Contacts would slowly shift alliances, seeing the Varelas as a short-term family. Other contacts would simply disappear. The Inverros and Varelas have been jockeying back and forth for power for centuries. Without offspring, the Varelas had a huge target painted on them, prime for the Inverros to not just weaken them, but kill them."

"Just so," Adrian whispered, looking disturbed at Icarus' dispassionate assessment. "I was raised to take over the Varelas. Sophia was raised by the lowest family in the Asimi Court. She knew better than anyone how dangerous our position was. Her parents were killed in a freak carriage accident. My father had just passed, and we were losing ground, still uncomfortable in our positions. We were young, and with neither of our families alive, we made a desperate decision. An emissary from the Canadian wer-im came to the islands saying he wanted to establish an alliance. With the Wer-Kadis of the time, it made sense. We found out later the Wer-Kadis didn't even know this 'emissary's' name but—"

"That's neither here nor there," Sophia interrupted. "We sought to steal the alliance with him from under the Inverros and solve our childlessness problem at the same time. So, I seduced him."

Sophia's bluntness settled like an oppressive, sticky layer of humidity. El couldn't help her incredulous stare. They'd *both* planned it? She'd assumed Sophia had a weak moment that produced Icarus, but then, nothing Sophia did was from lack of self-control. *I should have known better.*

"Does he know I exist?" Icarus finally asked.

El's heart ached. All these years he must have wondered why his biological father never sought him out.

Sophia waved a hand over her shoulder like she was tossing salt.

"He was gone before we knew I was pregnant."

"And you never tried to tell him?" El asked.

"Why should we have?"

"You—"

"Leave it," Icarus interrupted. "As much as I'd like to know, we're short on time and I'd rather hear the reasons for casting me out."

El literally bit her tongue to keep from venting her anger. *How is Icarus so calm? This is insane!*

The study doors opened and Gladen backed into the room with a pitcher of iced tea and three glasses on a tray.

He stopped short at the group he found.

"Serve them first," Adrian gestured to Icarus and Na'rina, who was drawing designs in the heavy rug with her finger. El couldn't tell what the designs were but they left her with the impression of vines.

Gladen's huge eyes bugged. The spindly goblin strode across the room, thumped his tray onto the table, grabbed Icarus' face in his knobby hands, and stood nose to nose with him.

"Gladen!" Sophia protested

She went silent as Icarus raised his finger.

Gladen took in Icarus' scent with a long sniff. Then he thunked him in the forehead and grinned, his long fangs showing. Icarus grinned back, pulling up his lips to reveal his own sharp teeth.

"Bueno," Gladen declared, spun on his heel, and left. It was only after he exited that El registered Na'rina's fingers had hovered over Gladen's long, bare toes for the exchange. *What would she have done if Gladen turned violent?*

Sophia huffed, clearly perturbed.

Icarus offered Na'rina a glass of iced tea and took one himself. He motioned for Amos to take the last glass, but the giant rolled a shoulder in refusal. Since her parents weren't moving for it, El claimed it. She loved Marissa's tea.

"Please continue," Icarus said once she'd returned to lean against the desk.

"We obviously didn't need to do as we did," Sophia flicked her nails at El, "but we didn't regret you either. We've known a few half-bloods who kept their garnet zoi aima despite their mixed parentage. So, we hoped. We might have even kept you, despite your settling to violet, except for the rumors that began to circulate about a year before you settled."

Sophia stopped there, gesturing for Adrian to explain the rest.

"Most myths about us are from Greece or that region, and they pertain to the mythics who live, or lived, there," he said. "The Medusa myths…" El straightened, thinking of the Daughter she'd seen, and then gulped her tea to hide the tell. Adrian continued, "…the Hercules myths, the myths about the Greek gods. In the western hemisphere, most of those barely touched our lives. Did Zeus live? Sure. None of the Western Hemisphere mythics ever met him.

"We didn't think much of the bloodline restrictions…" Na'rina went utterly still. El was sure Sophia noticed. "…until we heard about a group that was killing mixed-blood mythics in the name of enforcing the restrictions. These weren't just back-alley killings either. They reached into the Fae court, into the giants despite them being so secluded, even into our own Court. If you remember Lucia's older sister, we believe she was a bloodline killing.

"Thomas Inverro claimed he'd established contact with this group. He threatened us, saying if he could prove his suspicions about Icarus being a half-blood, he'd have him killed. Of course, it wasn't that blunt, but that was the gist."

Adrian shot Sophia a glance.

Is that bitterness? Pain? Resignation? El couldn't even name half of what showed in Adrian's eyes. She was tempted to say something snide to break the terrible silence. Instead, she finished her tea.

Adrian sighed and continued, "About a month before you settled, two men hired us for a contract to deliver a message to a cyclops. We wondered why they hadn't gone to the Inverros, but we were too desperate to look too far into our luck. We'd hashed out the contract and Gladen was taking them out when they ran into the two of you in the entry hall—"

"I remember them." El hadn't meant to interrupt, but in light of the conversation, the odd encounter made a lot more sense. Sophia gestured for her to go on. El almost refused—this was Sophia's explanation, not hers—but Icarus tilted his head in curiosity and El didn't want to refuse him. "Do you remember those Egyptian men who smelled so strongly of myrrh and cinnamon?"

Icarus' curiosity vanished as his nostrils flared. "They debated what a girl like you would go for in the market if you were up for sale," Icarus answered, disgust pulling his lips upward and revealing his teeth.

El pictured him shifting from a lynx earlier and she stopped herself right there. "You charged one of them," she said.

"You caught my hands," Icarus pointed to Sophia. "I suspect my claws gave you scars."

Sophia held up her hands, showing faint white dots on her palms. "I didn't act fast enough. They may as well have been licking their lips when they left. I almost had Gladen follow them and eat them. I *should* have had Gladen follow them and eat them." Vitriol dripped from her words. "The evening before you settled, the Court met in a meeting Inverro insisted on. At it, he pushed for us to unilaterally support the bloodline restrictions. He argued that it offered us a powerful ally we couldn't ignore. None of the other families had reason to object, so everyone agreed.

"Then you settled and every Court member had a reason to turn you in because it'd weaken our house. When you walked in for breakfast with violet zoi aima, I knew you'd be safer if they all believed you were dead. If they forgot about you long enough for you to mature, if you could disappear and grow up as a wer-im who could tear out their throats by the time they found you, you'd have a chance.

"And I also knew, because you're too much like me, that unless you believed we didn't want you, you'd find a way to come back and protect us. Our one reassurance was how easily people underestimate Elodie. I watched for Elodie to seek you out, and I made sure no one ever suspected our eight year-old-daughter knew you were alive."

El shoved off the desk, furious. "So you sliced open his ear and left him to fend for himself?! You didn't think to send him away for training or to contact the Fae to shelter him? They would have! For a far smaller price, they would have!"

Anger flared across Sophia's face but El was prepared to confront it.

"It wouldn't have worked." The soft words dropped like cool

water on their seething anger. Na'rina repeated. "It wouldn't have worked. The Oceanids and Oreads refused a handfasting of their children for fear of a Theos mix long before Icarus was born. The fear was already there." She ticked off the example on a finger. If it'd been anyone else, El would have unleashed her fury on them, but Na'rina's earnest words sucked the ire right out of her.

"My grandmother tried to hide her twins because of their mixed blood but the Wer-Kadis at the time found them and tried to use them," Na'rina continued, ticking off another finger. "The South American Drydanda would rather kill me—and dozens of others, I might add—than have anything to do with my mixed blood." Another finger went up. "And now the Appalachian Dwarven King would rather hide than negotiate with me, implying I'm trying to take control like Zeus. Someone's been slowly building this fear.

"The Fae, or any other race strong enough to protect Icarus, would have gladly taken him in under the pretense of protecting him, and then used him or traded him to form an alliance with this group. He had to disappear.

"Although—" a small line formed between Na'rina's brows and her head tilted in a curious fashion. She pointed at Sophia. "You knew about the old Wer-Kadis' greed for power. It stands to reason you also knew about his play for stealing my mother and uncle. If we follow that vine, that means you knew about their power and that's something you would keep tabs on."

Sophia gave Na'rina a pleased smirk. It sent adrenaline through El. Her mother only showed that smile when she was viewing a very good prospect like a cat spotting a bowl of cream.

"Meaning?" El prompted when Na'rina didn't continue.

Icarus had tilted his head back and closed his eyes. Dark circles smudged the skin under his eyes and El couldn't help but glance at his legs. The legs that only hours before had been shattered. *That's just the physical trauma. How much of Mateo and Marie's attack lingers?* He scrubbed both hands over his face and said, his words muffled, "Meaning Silas didn't find me by accident."

Marissa burst through the study doors and everyone jumped, even Icarus. The goblin carried a tray of burritos, of all things, and scurried across the floor, almost dumping the entire tray into Icarus' lap.

Na'rina rolled to her knees to keep from getting stepped on as Icarus shot to his feet, a snarl frozen on his lips. Marissa thrust the tray into his hands, the metal clicking against his extended claws, and reached out a curious finger to tap one of his canines. Her own teeth elongated with her smile. Then she set the tray aside and grabbed his hands, holding up his claws in utter fascination.

El couldn't look away. She'd never seen his claws fully extended. They were as long as his fingers and thick enough to rival Marissa's, which she now held out in comparison. Marissa's glee pushed the skin in her cheeks up into folds, showing her dimples. Her pointed ears quivered and huge tears pooled in her eyes.

"Niñera," Icarus greeted her and Marissa cried out. Surprise, joy, maybe even anger all mixed together. Her tears wandered the folds in her skin as she let him go and grabbed a burrito that she thrust into his hands.

"Comes. ¡Eres demasiado delgado!" she ordered, and just like Gladen, she spun on a heel and left.

Amos laughed, the sound rolling through the room and shuddering the marble.

"What was that?" Na'rina asked.

El snickered. "She thinks he's too skinny."

Even Sophia's lips quirked in amusement. Then she said, "Let's get down to why you've actually come."

The storm meant they were stuck on San Martez for the night and would arrive in Charleston the day of the symposium. Icarus chewed on one of Marissa's burritos, savoring the spices that burned in his sinuses while staring out the window. Against the storm, the dark, water-streaked glass reflected his haggard face.

This had been his bedroom. The window latch was still broken from the time he'd had an argument with Sophia and forced it open to escape onto the roof. He also knew that, right at the edge of the roofline, the forest rose in thick foliage although he couldn't see it through the rain. It was all dreamlike to him.

Na'rina came up beside him and slid her arms around his waist. Sophia had apparently found her some light cotton pants and a shirt as her tattered suit was gone. "My mother tried to hide me; yours tried to make you disappear," she said. "Are your roots still strong?"

She had perhaps spent too much time around Ver'rina. She was starting to sound like her. Icarus finished his burrito and turned into her embrace, breathing in her fragrance of aspen and mountain air. "Shaken," he answered, "but firm."

"Will you forgive them, now that you know their reasons?"

"Will you forgive your mother?"

Na'rina answered with a long sigh. "I think I already

have…mostly. Although I don't agree with her choices."

Icarus' phone buzzed. He fished it from his pocket to find a brief, terse message from Obek. *Pa called me home. Warn your wer-im to avoid the dwarves. He blames you for my disobedience.*

"Poor Obek," Na'rina said, reading the message with him. She paused, then asked, "Are we something to be feared?"

Icarus didn't reply at first. He'd been feared most of his life for one reason or another, but that wasn't what Na'rina was asking. She was asking if such fear was justified.

"Perhaps," he finally said. "But what truly matters is what we do. We will not react as your mother or my parents did. We will do better than that." It was a promise to himself as much as her.

Na'rina looked startled but before he could ask about it, someone knocked.

"Come in."

Amos peeked through the door. "Seen the twiglet anywhere?"

"*Na*," Na'rina answered. "Is he alright?"

"'E wanted to check out the courtyard despite the rain but now I can't find 'im." Amos shrugged and ducked back out.

"I should go look for him." Na'rina tried to pull away but Icarus held on. "I hurt him, Icarus. I need to speak with him anyway."

"In a moment." Finding her in the twiglet had relieved Icarus' worry about her being dead, but it wasn't until now that he'd had a chance to hold her and let the fear wash away. She smelled of home and felt like spring in his arms. Leaning his temple against hers, he breathed deep and savored the brush of her hands sliding back around his waist.

Sophia gloated that he was strong enough now to protect

himself. She'd even insinuated that his meeting Na'rina was a byproduct of her sending Silas his way. Icarus didn't accept that. Sophia couldn't take credit for the relationships that anchored him. She didn't understand what Na'rina was to him.

"You survived coming back to Sedanza," Na'rina said.

"Only because you helped me."

She stiffened, pushing back to see his face. "What do you mean?"

"Mateo and Marie are far stronger than me in the mindscape." The admittance tasted bitter.

"Of course they're stronger!" Na'rina spun away, throwing her hands up as her gemlike eyes flashed. "That's their world! But you walk two worlds…and that is where you're stronger. You are uniquely wer-im *and* Sedessan. Don't separate the two."

Icarus caught her hand and pulled her back, noticing the branches on her arms had budded with catkins. "What's this mean?" He traced one of them.

Na'rina pulled away again, hiding her arms behind her back. Then she shuddered and relaxed. "Ugh. Twiglet habits." She folded her arms across her stomach instead. "Just means growth."

Icarus raised a brow.

"On the ship," she said, "when I emerged and couldn't get to you, I started to see red. It traced these," she held her arms out, "like lightning running through my grove. Is that the wer-im in me?"

Icarus had rarely experienced what she spoke of—his Sedessan side was terrified of losing control—but he knew the rage. Silas had wanted him to give into it. "*Sa,*" he answered, pulling her back into a hug. She let him. Her willingness surprised him. The vow did not give him permission to treat her as more, but she never resisted and it settled something in him. He *wanted* more, but he also knew that for a dryad—especially a Drydanda—that choice was hers. *It is enough.* Aloud, he said, "That is the wer-im in you."

"It was…useful," Na'rina said, laying her cheek against his chest. "It seemed—"

Another knock interrupted her. Icarus seethed frustration through his teeth and called, "Enter."

Levi, in wer-im form, opened the door. He paused at seeing Na'rina in Icarus' arms, but then ignored it. "I would like a word with my sprout."

Na'rina's fingers tightened in Icarus' shirt. He laid his temple against hers and asked, *You good?*

Sa, her fingers relaxed, *I've just never spoken to him before.*

I won't be far.

She gave him a squeeze and stepped back. Icarus took the hint and left, intending to find El. He'd had a thought regarding the synthesized abilities Rebecca had given him and now was as good a time as any to speak with her about it.

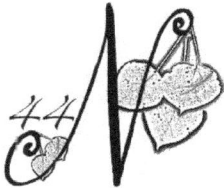

Levi's golden hair, flecked with gray, was pulled back at the nape of his neck by a leather strap. He wore jeans and a brown t-shirt and walked barefoot just like Na'rina. In his face, she recognized her mother's brows and even more the nose and chin Silas had inherited.

He joined her at the window, leaning on the frame and folding his arms as he studied her in turn. He was huge. Another trait that Silas inherited but she and her mother had not. Na'rina's eyes dropped and caught on his forearms.

"You know what they mean?"

Na'rina touched the aspens growing on her arms. She'd been relieved the sprouts were unharmed after her time in the twiglet. "I know."

"And yet you choose it? Even knowing the avalanche it'll bring?"

Na'rina's head came up, her eyes flashing.

His tone softened. "I must ask," he said. "There are those who would tell you no."

"It is not their place."

He chuckled. "They would still try."

"I will not live by fear."

He studied her a moment longer. "Good," he said and pushed off the window frame to leave.

"That's it?" Na'rina asked. "You sought me out for that?"

He stopped with his hand on the doorknob. "You do not know me, but I was there when you were born. I watched you play with the fauns and swim with the naiads in the mountain streams. I've seen you grow from a tiny sapling into a slender, resilient grove, weathering storms that topple larger trees. I wanted to know if you were still that resilient aspen or if recent events had hollowed your core." He finally looked back at her. "I have answered that question, and I am satisfied." He opened the door to leave.

"You would have kept me in the dark about the possible avalanche," Na'rina stalled him.

"We thought it safer."

"Safer? For me to bumble around like an idiot?"

"*Na*. Sometimes leaving the snow alone keeps it from sliding and the danger passes. But now you know and—" he nodded, "I am satisfied." Then he left.

Na'rina swayed and caught the window frame. *Both my grandparents are loony.* But not insane. Levi's repeated *I am satisfied* dropped like rain onto her heart.

She'd handled things to his satisfaction. *But not totally to mine. I need to find the twiglet.* She left Icarus' room, heading down the hall toward the courtyard in the center of the estate. Sophia had given her a room painted in greens and purples, perhaps thinking it was semi-foresty, but it'd been the scent of wet palms and magnolias that had caught Na'rina's attention earlier because, if anything, she'd sleep among the trees. Even Icarus looked uncomfortable in his old room, and she suspected she'd find him in the branches later too.

422

Na'rina stepped through the archway into the courtyard, tilting her head up into the pouring rain. Instantly she was drenched but it was a relief to be outside again. And here in the courtyard, the house protected her somewhat from the heavy winds.

She quested out with her zoi aima, searching for the familiar essence of the twiglet. She'd tried speaking with him on the sub ride to San Martez but he'd hidden in Amos' pocket. She now encountered stone benches, gravel walkways, palms and magnolias, hibiscus and orchids, but no twiglet. She was about to leave when a green zoi aima moving opposite the silvery gusts of wind caught her eye. The small grouping of leaves nestled amid the jasmine vines growing up a pillar to the second-floor veranda.

Na'rina spooled her lifeblood back and meandered farther into the yard. "Leafy toes, curly nose, run and hide your berry," she called out in the familiar game she'd seen in the twiglet's memory. "Now I look, now I find, now I search my query." She purposefully walked past the twiglet's spot, then spun back.

He'd moved. "You're not my brothers, Drydanda." His small voice barely carried over the wind.

Na'rina grasped a magnolia branch beside the veranda and hauled herself into the tree. She climbed, gaining the second-story balcony. She left wet footprints on the sheltered stone as she searched around the jasmine-covered pillar.

"*Na*," she agreed, "I am not your brothers." She jumped to the next pillar in two bounds and ducked to check the far side. Several hibiscus blossoms lay on the marble, broken off recently. Na'rina tucked one behind her ear and jumped off the side of the veranda to land in the courtyard. "But that does not mean I don't care."

A palm not far away boasted a new cluster of leaves against its base. Na'rina checked inside the azalea beside her. When she glanced back, the cluster was gone.

"We don't hurt those we care about."

Na'rina almost missed the words over the wind. "Sometimes we don't have perfect choices," she answered, "and we do the best we can." She checked the palm and wandered past it toward the center of the courtyard.

"I wasn't good enough."

Na'rina paused. *Good enough?* She checked the azalea beside her and moved onto a magnolia, stepping into its wandering branches to reach the trunk. "It's not a question of good enough. It's a question of timing," she laid her hand on the trunk to peek around the far side. The twiglet sat at the Nolia's base, huddled in its deep roots. He tilted his head up at her. "The timing was perfect for you to keep us alive during the earthquake. It was then perfect for me to help Icarus when he needed me. There will be a time when you're able to help again because you can and you're there at the right time. It's just a matter of willingness, which you have in oceanfuls."

The twiglet sniffled and wiped his nose across the back of his arm. "But I'm a terrible Mitto."

Na'rina sat cross-legged in the roots, facing him. "Mitto carried the Drydanda across a river. He didn't carry her the rest of her life." She pulled the hibiscus from her hair and offered it to him. "Like him, you saved me. I'm sorry I hurt you."

Instead of accepting the flower, he crawled into her lap and hugged her. He was tiny in her arms, but Na'rina knew his strength. Letting go, he grabbed the red hibiscus blossom and scampered away with it through the rain, shouting, "Giant! Giant! I got a flower!"

"You did good, my sprite."

Na'rina bolted to her feet, then caught herself on a branch as she spotted Icarus. Even after months of him being around, he snuck up on her more often than not. Rain had plastered his dark hair around his face, and she pushed it behind his ears as he caught her around the waist. His eyes glittered, warning her as he leaned in to kiss her. He did not do so often. She wasn't totally sure why, but now she encouraged him. Warm zoi aima drifted through her senses, both teasing and stirring.

I will not live by fear. Na'rina stroked the scars on his face, the aspens on her arms growing, and savored the moment.

El stared at the red and green vials Icarus had just given her. *Synthesized mythic abilities.* She pocketed the red one as Icarus had no idea what it contained. The green one containing the goblin's illusion ability, however, could be useful. *Except it was made by capturing mythics.* That bothered her and Icarus. *But do we have a choice if it helps us?* El stared at it, considering.

She jerked out of her reverie at the sound of footsteps and pocketed the green vial too. She'd retreated to the kitchen for some of the burritos Marrisa dumped in Icarus' lap, and now the last bite of her second serving sat on a plate in front of her. She ate it. *What now?* She fought the urge to simply cross her arms on the metal prep table and fall asleep.

"Elodie?"

Boiling frogs! I've had enough for one day.

Her mother walked through the door with Roberto behind her. El blinked. Not to use her second lens but to process that Roberto was standing in her kitchen already. She'd texted him on the new number he'd given her, knowing they needed to settle some things before the symposium, but hadn't expected him to walk into the kitchen ten minutes later.

"You have a visitor," her mother said. "We'll be ready in ten," she told Roberto and left, for once not telling El how to handle the situation. Perhaps heading out to the *Sansabria* was occupying her mind.

Roberto joined her at the prep table. "May I?" he gestured at the last burrito. El waved permission.

"You didn't leave after dropping us off," she said. It was the only explanation for how fast he'd responded.

He tilted his head back, ecstasy on his face as he took his first bite. He was handsome. Dark hair glistening in the single light over the stove, cheek bones high and lips full. Well-trimmed. He'd matured into his physique. *Should I marry him?* The silence lengthened and suddenly the kitchen was too small and intimate for El's liking.

Roberto hummed, breaking the moment. "Our goblins don't cook like Marrisa."

"Won't your family be looking for you?" El stood up, carrying the now empty tray to the sink.

"It's odd," he answered, following her and finding a glass of water. El moved to the prep table to wipe it down. "It's easier to evade them within the dome than it is outside of it. I destroyed the trackers on the sub already and I conveniently don't have my phone. At least, I don't have the phone they know about."

"They'll notice the trackers went dead."

"True, but they're notoriously sensitive and who's to say the weather didn't mess with the signal?" He sat across from her again and his light tone shifted. "El, I—"

She turned away to rinse the rag. She needed his help at the symposium, but it hurt to have a conversation like they used to. He was apparently, finally, not being evasive, and she wasn't sure she was ready for that. She hung the rag over the edge of the sink but didn't turn back.

"Please sit, El."

She'd checked her phone after he'd returned it. There'd been a single new picture, taken from the deck of a sailboat with the sunrise streaming over the ocean, painting it vibrantly orange. It was so striking El could almost smell the morning breeze. *He's offering the escape we always joked about.*

She finally sat across from him. "What do you actually want, Roberto?"

He bit into the burrito and stared at her while he chewed. *Stalling.* El resisted the urge to touch his hand to glimpse what was going on behind his eyes.

"Do you remember when we climbed on the roof and spied on my brothers through a window?" he asked.

El snorted. "We burned our soles," she recalled. They'd lain on their stomachs to listen, exposing their bare feet.

He leaned toward her and El could smell the cumin on his breath as he said, "I want that. I want the partner in crime who's not afraid to hang off a roof with me."

The memory stabbed at El. They'd stayed there for well over an hour, listening to his brothers planning their next mission. A mission Roberto should have received but Mateo had given it to Ethan and Samuel instead.

It'd been a test. Mateo had wanted Roberto to prove that he would not allow his brothers to take contracts from him. That was the first time Roberto and El had stolen a contract from his brothers. That night was also the first time Roberto took her to Little Italia to celebrate.

"I'm not sure I can trust a partner who disappears for nine years," she admitted.

He jerked back like she'd slapped him. "Disappeared? El, I wrote to you. Dozens of times. You never responded."

Wrote to me?

"Electronic communication would have been intercepted by one of our parents, so I wrote like I was a contact."

El couldn't breathe. She pushed away from the table and started pacing. Retreating to her mental study, she scanned postcards, letters, cards, anything that could have been from Roberto. Almost immediately, a headache began pounding at her temples. "I never—" she couldn't say it. She had no idea where his communications could have gone. *Is he lying?*

"El?"

She glanced at him. He held out a hand. "I don't have a lot of time. Despite the trackers, I do need to get back to my family."

Trap or honesty? She wasn't sure. Grabbing his hand, she asked, *Did you sic your parents on Icarus on the ship?*

What?! That'd be a terrible idea. I want you to marry me, not hate me.

El let go and spun away to pace again.

He smacked the table behind her. "El, I'm serious."

"So am I! I don't know you anymore. I don't know if you're working for your family or honestly trying to escape them."

"Escape, El. I want that sailboat! You have no idea about my family."

"I know who your grandfather is."

Roberto deflated onto his stool. He downed the last of his water, thumping the glass back on the table before saying, "I don't know what he ultimately wants but I do know I want no part of it. We used flamethrowers on fauns, El. It was terrible."

El didn't know what he was talking about, but she sat down and snagged the last bite of his burrito, chewing on it angrily. "Dylan said it was scary in your house."

"He's not wrong. You got lucky, you know, when you came to the embassy. Grandfather had started experimenting beyond the goblin-human serum. It messed with his Sedessan lens, and he couldn't see your zoi aima. If he had, you'd probably be dead."

The burrito stuck in El's throat. She grabbed Roberto's empty glass and refilled it, chugging the water before returning to the table. "That's why I texted you," she admitted. "We know about the symposium. Know he's hauling this hurricane toward Charleston and that he's going to Compel some key people there. I can't let him, Roberto. I don't know exactly what we'll be walking into, but I can't let him turn people into puppets. Will you help us?" She thought better of her word choice. "Will you help me?"

She clutched the empty glass, watching his face. If he publicly opposed his family, he'd end up houseless, just as dead to the Sedanza Court as Icarus. She wanted his answer before she answered his marriage proposal. Did he oppose his family enough that he'd act against them without Varela protection?

He wrapped his hands around hers on the glass. *I will. I'll help you.*

El "listened" hard to his answer. Honesty was incredibly hard to fake mentally. She caught conviction, anger maybe, and grief on the level of clouds without rain. It was heavy.

Good, she accepted his answer and tried to pull away. He didn't let her.

"I imagined asking you to marry me differently."

"Family hijacking," El agreed, trying for teasing.

"Understatement." He extracted the empty glass from between her hands and interlaced their fingers. El stared, wishing the contact didn't fill her with pain. She wanted to recapture what they'd had, but bittersweet knowledge told her that wasn't possible. "So let me make up for it." The ring box appeared from his pocket. He snapped it open one-handed to reveal a deep red ruby in a silver band. "Will you marry me, Elodie Varela?"

"I—" she swallowed, searching for an answer. "I—"

He squeezed her hand and slid the ring over her finger. "You don't have to answer now. Tomorrow at the symposium, it might come in handy if my family believes you've accepted. As for your actual answer, that can be between us later." Kissing her knuckles, he let go and left.

El's head thunked onto the table. *I might just sleep here tonight.* She was too exhausted to move.

Someone entered the kitchen but El didn't look up. The stool across from her groaned. The person tapped her new ring and El's head shot up in surprise.

"Nice rock," Amos commented.

El's head thunked back to the table. "Roberto thinks it'll help with his family." Her breath fanned across the metal below her.

"Might," Amos agreed. "Could use all the help we can get."

El looked up again. "You'll be there, right?"

431

"What's wrong, little Sedessan? Scared?" When she didn't answer, his grin faded. "Y'r butler and I've been practicing. We'll be there."

El couldn't help the relief that brought her.

Soft conversation filtered through the jet to Icarus who leaned against the conference room doorway watching the other passengers. When the Varelas bought a jet, they bought a jet, complete with sleeping rooms, conference room, and full bar.

Na'rina sat in a captain's chair with her face fully in the sun. A book sat open on her lap but she was soaking in the rays like a starving orphan and the book was forgotten. In the psychic, she glowed like a mini starburst. *She needs it.* While in the twiglet, she'd been seriously restricted. The UV lights on the ship had worked to feed her, but it'd been unnatural and she'd drained herself, again, helping Icarus. Only now, after the storm had moved north and they were flying in daylight, did she have a chance to fully restore herself. Her celadon skin gave off a faint radiance. He could stare at her all day.

He didn't. Especially with the Fae at the back of the plane. One of the ambassador's guards snickered at Marissa for trying to bring them a charcuterie board. Icarus wished he could throw the man off the plane.

They'd shown up that morning asking for the use of the jet to get to Charleston. Marquin claimed his own transportation had been damaged. Being Fae, that was technically true somehow, but the damage might just be a scratch to the paint for all Icarus knew. *They're going after Dominguez.* How they had found out he'd be in Charleston, Icarus didn't know, but that was the only reason Marquin would leave Riviera when he resembled a warmed-over fish. He was suffering from the Compelling.

Marquin refused to meet Icarus' eye. He was avoiding interacting with either Na'rina or himself. Propriety would demand the usual Fae pleasantries if he did; they were the North American Drydanda and the Wer-Kadis after all, and the waters were murky as to how much deference he'd owe them. Too little or too much would send the wrong message. Judging by his almost green complexion, the ambassador didn't want to figure out such details right now.

Icarus finally looked away from the man. Between Na'rina and the Fae, Levi lay sprawled with his legs draped over the armrest of a couch. He'd downed a package of Dramamine just before the flight and now Icarus could hear his soft snore over the engine's hum. The nub of a gingerroot that he'd chewed while waiting for the medication to knock him out rested in his fingers.

The plane jolted and Na'rina squeaked, grabbing her armrests while the book hit the floor. They were flying wide of the storm to reach Charleston before it hit the States, but it still made for an eventful flight.

A Fae snickered but Na'rina just went back to absorbing the sunlight and left the book where it'd landed. Dante, sitting across from her, snarled softly at the Fae and retrieved the book.

This is a tinderbox if we're not careful.

"Kadis?" Felis asked from behind him. Icarus turned. Felis wanted a private word. He and Dante had arrived on San Martez that morning, having passed control of the *Sansabria* to Adrian and Sophia the night before.

The stalky wer-im peeked through the door and then tossed a stack of papers onto the table.

"What's this?" Icarus asked.

Felis itched at his beard. "Truth."

"That doesn't sit well with you?"

"That shows me I need to get over myself."

Curious, Icarus perused the papers. "Where'd you get these?"

"Off the *Sansabria*."

"Dante's not our mole."

"Not even close," Felis said.

Icarus' relief was palpable. "Good," he said. "We're going to need to trust each other for what's coming next."

Felis hummed and scratched at his beard again.

"What else?" Icarus asked.

"Speaking of trust, I—we're working with Roberto Inverro?"

Icarus folded his arms and waited. Felis clearly had more to say.

"We're working with Roberto," he finally continued, "but his dad's the one who kidnapped Na'rina. On top of that, his grandfather's the Sedessan CEO of Intela Corp who's planning to Compel someone at this ball?"

"About sums it up."

"That's a lot of messed up. We're trusting Roberto why?"

"Not much choice otherwise," he admitted.

Na'rina opened her eyes. She was satisfied. She couldn't remember the last time she'd gloried in the sun to the full. It was marred only by her discomfort from being disconnected from her Rina.

She absently observed Amos and Marissa chatting in the galley. She'd watched in fascination as the cook shifted to appear human before boarding. Her zoi aima had contracted in on itself until it was almost solid. It was different from when Icarus shifted into a lynx. He physically changed. The goblin did not and if Na'rina stared really hard, her skin blurred, struggling to keep the illusion of pale pink instead of rough green. Na'rina stopped trying to see through the illusion when Marissa noticed and bared her teeth, but the question remained: If Thomas Inverro made himself look human by using a serum from the goblins, was it an illusion she could see through?

"Want this?" Dante offered her the book she'd dropped. She accepted it back. "The Fae say you squeak like a mouse."

Na'rina snorted. Of course, the wer-im could hear the Fae's conversation farther back. "If the only residual effect of my melding with the twiglet is a tendency to squeak, I'll take it." She would not show them her unease over flying but she was hyperaware that she sat in a luxurious but hollow metal tube that was flying over a chasm of empty air.

"Have you seen this?" Dante asked. He offered her a colorful flyer.

Na'rina stared at the picture of a ballroom. The back wall housed a stage, but it was the oak tree standing in the lefthand corner that the flyer advertised. The wall had been built around its massive trunk but the branches that would usually extend low on the base had been shorn off, leaving large nobs instead. Those branches had then been added to the oak's canopy above, extending its already expansive reach to span the entire slanted ballroom ceiling. There were no natural leaves. Instead, the humans had designed stained-glass leaves that shone deep green on the left and changing like seasons to reddish-yellow on the right, transforming the ceiling into a green and gold skylight between the branches.

They called it a marvel of Charleston. Na'rina knew the oak itself was dead. She didn't want to know how the humans sealed the poor Dry to make him structurally sound for their building.

"They fashioned it after the famous Angel Oak that grows just outside of Charleston. Wasn't sure if you saw it when you were at the summit," Dante said.

Na'rina swallowed. "The hotel's big. We didn't enter the ballroom while we were there." She fingered the flyer, trying to decide if the stained-glass grave was beautiful or just morbid. "Thank you. It would have startled me."

Dante patted her knee and leaned back again, closing his eyes to nap.

Na'rina slid the flyer into the back of the book and tucked her legs up beside her. Wanting a distraction, she slanted her body toward the window to see better and opened the book again. Na'rina was not a good reader, especially of Greek, but her mother *had* taught her. And for once, she reached out to the Collective Wisdom to help her when she struggled. The intro again held her, just as it had the first time she'd read it.

Our psyches may be able to wrap the elements of life to fit our designs. The energy required for this is unknown, but a few have displayed such an ability, and if energy can be harnessed to psychic will, anything might be possible.

Thomas Dominguez had quoted directly from the book over tea.

Na'rina jumped when Icarus flopped into the seat beside her with a handful of summer sausage. He set the food aside, however, to pull her hand away from her leg. She'd been absently running her fingertips over her burn scar, the one she'd gained from stopping Rosharu's volcano last spring, where it showed below her dress' hem. El had scrounged the pale blouse and green maxi skirt for her that morning.

Icarus traced the thick ridges of her scar with a feather-light fingertip. "Enjoying Dylan's textbook?"

She wasn't really. This was the book the naiad had pointed her to after King Olbin's accusations, but she wasn't far enough into it yet to understand why. It was odd, containing genetics, biology, and chemistry, right alongside history, mythic bloodlines, and more.

She shrugged. "I'm not sure this is Dylan's textbook."

"El saw him with it," Icarus assured.

"I'm sure she saw him with a copy of it," Na'rina said, "but I don't think it was *this* copy. I think he stole this from his grandfather."

El's head popped up overtop her seat back. "What?"

Na'rina held up the book and tapped the margin. Acute interest lit El's face. She sat on the couch across from them on the opposite wall and held out a hand for the book. Na'rina gladly passed it over.

While she thumbed through the pages, Amos settled beside her with a huge bowl of cereal and a glass of orange juice.

Na'rina's mouth watered at the sight of the juice, but she ignored it as she waited for El. The woman flipped a page every couple of seconds. *Is she actually reading or just scanning the handwriting in the margins?*

That's what had clued Na'rina in that the book wasn't the boy's. Someone had filled the margins with notes…and they weren't study notes for school.

After several minutes, Icarus finally asked, "El?" When she didn't respond, he repeated with a little volume, "El?"

She looked up and blinked. "She's right. This is Thomas' handwriting." She tapped the current page.

"Y' know his handwriting?" Amos asked.

"I've seen it before."

Icarus held out a hand and El reluctantly passed the book over. He didn't skim through it as fast as El, but Na'rina could see his eyes shifting over the words and she laughed at herself for envying him and his sister.

"Why did the boy give it to y'?" Amos asked around a mouthful of cereal.

El folded her legs beneath her and rubbed her fingers together. When Amos lifted the juice to drink, she absently nabbed it from his fingers and took a long drink before handing it back.

"I wanted that sip," Amos groused.

"There's more in the galley." El pointed and moved on. "Why would he ally himself with whoever's killing half-bloods when he's studying the effects of mixed abilities?" she asked.

"Keepin' tabs?" Amos guessed.

"That would track," Icarus said. "Maybe he wants to outdo them." He tapped the book. "His notes speculate on what mixes produce what. It's never been understood why some, like a sylph and a fire drake, produced Zeus. Or an oread and a salamander produced Hades, yet if you mix an oread with a sylph, you don't get an equally powerful mythic."

Icarus leaned forward, lowering his voice to keep the Fae from overhearing. "The common thought is at least one of the parents has to be psychically oriented. But as far as we know, no Theos mixes have ever come from a Sedessan, but that may be due to the Sedessans' secrecy, not from a lack of it happening. Sophia and Adrian had every reason to believe the wer-im would augment the Sedessan in me to produce a Theos mix, yet it didn't. On the other hand, a Drydanda and a wer-im apparently does.

"Dominguez questions why. He's trying to artificially create powerful mixes with his serums. That's why he wanted you so badly." He pointed at Na'rina. "He's never had an actual Theos mix to study."

"Simulated eugenics," Na'rina remembered. Both Icarus and El looked startled. Na'rina ignored that and asked, "Did he succeed at mixing abilities into a Theos serum? Can he suddenly become like Zeus or Hades?"

Icarus flipped through the book again, checking notes. El's eyes glazed. Amos made a face at the small woman, and she swatted his arm without losing focus. Na'rina wondered which one, Icarus or El, would find the answer faster.

"Kind of," El finally said. "He enhanced Alaya's abilities by mixing them with a sylph's. That's how he's hauling the storm up the coast, but there are limits. Apparently, it's really painful in the lungs—a drawback Alaya or a true Theos wouldn't have.

"He also melded salamander abilities with a sylph's to make it hotter but according to the book, he's probably not immune to the fire like a salamander would be. And he can't mix that with the oceanid's serum because they counteract each other—"

"Hotter?" Felis interrupted as he joined them in the chair beside Dante. "Seriously? He'd make buildings melt if he uses that one."

That gave everyone pause.

"Maybe that's the point," said a voice behind them.

Na'rina squeaked.

The Fae guard who'd spoken bowed, but she could swear he was laughing at her. When he finished his bow, however, his face was notably blank.

Amos may have caught the look, though, because he eyed the Fae like he wanted to attack him with his spoon.

"The point?" El asked.

"Perhaps he wants to announce mythics to the world," the guard answered. "If he wants the humans to fear us, controlling hurricanes and melting buildings would do that beautifully."

Na'rina shuddered. "How do we counteract him?"

The Fae held up his hands in a weighing gesture. "That depends on which serum he's relying on, which we won't know until we get there."

Amos dropped his spoon into his empty bowl with a loud clatter. "Kill 'm. Far as I seen, no mythic rains down fire or water when he's dead."

The guard smirked. "Lovely thought but highly unlikely to succeed." He turned to El. "Señorita Varela, the ambassador would like a word?"

El's bright, engaged eyes went flat but she followed the guard. As they reached the back of the plane, there was a shift in the air and Na'rina's ears popped. She looked at Icarus questioningly.

"Powerful telekinesis. Marquin created a bubble of hardened air to keep us from hearing them."

"Don't mean I can't see 'im," Amos said, "and she ain't thrilled."

"Not at all," Felis agreed. "Can't hear them but I certainly smell her frustration."

"Frustration? Seriously?" Dante asked.

"Sure. Can't you? It's almost like a rancid grape."

"Don't know about that, but she's about ta throttle me orange juice," Amos interrupted.

Na'rina hadn't even noticed when El took the juice again, but Amos was right. El's fingers gripped the glass so hard she hoped it didn't shatter in the woman's hands.

"Whatcha' think 'e wants?"

Icarus shook his head. "Politics…or a contract. Probably both." He thumped the book shut.

The twiglet scampered down the aisle. He'd been snoozing on another seat, and now he held out a bowl full of dandelion fluff toward Amos, silently asking the giant to add milk. Amos huffed and picked the creature up.

"I never should've shown you that, kid," Amos stood, hunching to avoid the ceiling, and wandered away with the twiglet in his hands.

Na'rina stared after, delighted at the twiglet's interaction. *He's not hiding.*

Marissa appeared from the galley, plopping a charcuterie board

442

on the table in front of Na'rina and Icarus.

"Gracias, Niñera," Icarus thanked her.

The goblin's cheeks darkened in pleasure.

Na'rina wasn't familiar with goblins as they avoided dryads' homes, preferring instead to live underground or on the plains. The Collective Wisdom flashed a memory of a goblin digging beneath a dryad's tree and the dryad collapsing the entire cave system in a fifty-mile radius. That explained why they stayed clear of her and her mother's groves.

The Wisdom had hit so quickly that Na'rina's smile of thanks became a bit frozen when Marissa glanced her way. The goblin responded with her own wooden smile that didn't reach her eyes.

Before Na'rina could fix her mistake, Marissa was shuffling away. *Gah, why are the simple things the logs I trip over?* Marissa clearly loved Icarus like one of her pack. Besides El, she was top on the list of people Na'rina wanted to know from his young life.

Icarus raised a brow, catching the exchange and Na'rina's consternation. Na'rina just shook her head. He let it go. Taking her hand and threading their fingers together, his thumb began tracing the roots on her skin.

Do you think we can succeed? she asked.

When Icarus didn't answer, she looked up to find him watching her. She both loved and shied away from the searching gaze he gave her now. He deciphered an inordinate amount of what was going through her head simply by paying close attention. But this time she wanted him to know her fear. It wasn't just the airplane's hollow vibration that threatened to make her sick.

I believe we have a shot, he finally answered.

The mental communication reminded her of her Rina. A pang twinged through her chest. *How long has it been since I felt my Rina? A couple days? A week?* She wasn't sure.

Icarus continued, *But only if we work together like we did at Mount Athos. There are more players this time, which could be good—or could mean something goes sideways and we don't even see it coming.*

Na'rina gripped his hand between her own, appreciating his honesty. *I'm scared,* she admitted. *At Mount Athos, I acted without experience, just hoping I could do what I needed to. This time I know more, and it terrifies me. I'm not sure I can do it.*

It's not the pain you fear but the ability?

Na'rina caught his wry edge. *Even before getting stuck in the twiglet, I've always felt about the size of one.*

It gives you an edge.

Na'rina frowned.

He explained, *People see me, they're automatically on guard. People see you and they're fascinated, but they never expect what lies inside. You can do this, Na'rina.*

His confidence flowed through her like a balm for her jittery nerves. Shifting the conversation again, she said, *People, like Mateo and Marie, underestimate you too.*

He tensed but she only held tighter and massaged the heel of his hand until the muscles relaxed again. At the same time, she misted zoi aima into their contact like sprinkling water on a hot rock to cool its surface. His lifeblood curled into the touch and sent a whiff of spice through Na'rina's senses.

If you say so, he finally replied.

She ached at the uncertainty in that single statement. *You made Marie bleed from her ears, you know.* She wouldn't usually bring that up, but she shared the memory with him now because he'd probably missed Marie's state while his legs were healing. *They're not invulnerable.*

Icarus huffed but she could tell he wasn't convinced. *Brace yourself,* he said, squeezing her hand a moment before El slumped into her seat. She reminded Na'rina of a prowling feline with its hackles ruffled.

"Everything alright?" Icarus asked, offering his sister a slice of cheese off the charcuterie board.

"Fine," she said, nabbing the cheese and chewing.

Clearly not fine, Icarus muttered before letting Na'rina's hand go.

"So, I've been thinking," El's expression shifted from frustrated to serious, "it might be good if we can communicate during the symposium. I brought these." She pulled from her pocket several tiny cone-shaped devices.

"Comms," Icarus said, picking one up. He showed Na'rina how he held it and then slid the thing into his ear. It all but disappeared.

"They work like this," El said, also slipping one into her ear. "There's a main channel where we'll all be able to hear each other." She held up her hand and tapped her thumb and pinky against each other. "That opens the channel. We have enough of us that it could get confusing, so we'll use it sparingly. The other three fingers can be individually programmed for specific people. I'll be with Roberto, so I won't program him. I'll have Na'rina as my ring finger, Amos as my middle, and Icarus as my pointer."

445

Na'rina tentatively picked one up and inserted it into her ear. She could hear a slight buzz from the energy in the device.

"Hello," El said and her voice echoed oddly.

Na'rina jerked.

"We'll practice with it," Icarus encouraged.

"I'll program everyone here in a moment," El's eyes took on a mischievous light as she addressed Felis across the aisle. "Before I do, though, I hear you like gadgets."

"Mayybeee." Felis fidgeted.

"Then I've got a thing or two to show you. Come on." She left her seat and headed forward.

Felis shot Icarus a worried look.

"She doesn't bite." Icarus waved him off.

"This place gives me the shivers," Na'rina said from the hotel room window.

El gave the wainscoting and crown molding another glance. As hotels went, it was a gorgeous room. The King's Cathedral had been built as an actual cathedral on Charleston Bay in the 1800s. At some point, it was turned into a historic hotel with rooms added on either side of the original building.

The hotel didn't hold much interest for El. Instead, she stared at the velvet dress draped over the back of an upholstered chair from where she sat on the bed. Roberto, who'd flown to Charleston with his family, and Icarus would be by within the hour to collect them for the ball-symposium downstairs. She should be donning that dress and mentally preparing for the evening ahead.

"It's ethereally calm," Na'rina craned to see the sky through the window.

"That'll change," El said. Before they'd landed, radar had shown the dense, fast-moving hurricane they'd skirted around in the jet had missed the Georgia-Florida coast, turned back out to sea and curved inward again at speed. It'd soon slam into South Carolina instead.

Na'rina joined El on the bed. She stared at the satin dress draped beside El's velvet one and shuddered. "Seems weak armor for this evening," she noted.

The name Dom Endo was on the program as the guest speaker, so they knew Dominguez would be in the ballroom. But what he planned, where his family was, whatever serums he was using—it was all a mystery. El and Roberto hoped they could pull him away from the ballroom before he did anything drastic. As a backup, they had Amos hidden in the ballroom already. But that was plan B. Amos showing up would likely cause other problems considering most of the Court believed the Fae wanted to behead him.

El hated working off such shoddy intel.

"With the little information we have, Icarus' plan is good," El said.

"He says plans only survive until first contact."

El sniggered. "Ever the optimist."

Na'rina rose and ran her fingers over the velvet of El's dress. Her touch left a subtle white residue and she huffed, grabbing a towel off the dressing table. "We made it here," she said. "And Icarus already faced Mateo and Marie once. Between the two of us, we should be able to handle whichever one of them is here."

Icarus' contacts confirmed there was a ship, the *Observer*, shadowing the storm up the coast. He suspected either Marie or Mateo was aboard, controlling the storm, which left only one of them at the ball.

"I don't know if I can handle Dominguez," El admitted. Shock spiked through her. Besides Icarus, would she have admitted that to anyone?

But Na'rina didn't scold or scoff. She just picked up El's dress with the towel and unzipped the side. "Twiglet stairs problem," she muttered, pausing to finesse the zipper when it stuck.

El didn't know what she was talking about, but she grasped the sentiment.

Na'rina continued, "You'll have Roberto with you. He seems capable."

"He is, but we're both way out of our depth. And we're not the team you and Icarus are."

Na'rina swayed and the velvet dress swayed with her while she considered. "Even out of your depth, it's the right thing to do."

El's stomach flipped. *Separates the fish as follow the stream and the fish as fight the current. Always easier to follow the stream, but it's often flowing the wrong way.*

Almost as though she heard El's thoughts, Na'rina shrugged one shoulder with a tentative smile and said, "And you'll have Amos as backup if needed. And Felis, Dante, and Levi are standing by."

What a smorgasbord of people. El shared the smile and finally stood as Na'rina held out her dress.

"I just wish we had more intel," she said as the velvet slid over her head.

"We'll adjust as needed." Na'rina helped close the zipper and handed El a brush to fix her hair. "You look lovely."

El twirled to get a view of herself in the oval mirror in the corner.

She loved the dress with its smooth black texture. The back had two triangle mesh windows creating a broken hourglass separated by black velvet; the top window sat wide over her shoulder blades and narrowed to a point in the small of her back. The bottom started narrow at the middle of her thighs and then widened to hint at the curve of her calves. The beaded velvet separating them accentuated her hips and lower back with blue-black swirls. "Huh," El said, "for once, long black gloves won't look odd."

"You could pass for a nymph."

El paused in her perusal of the dress and met Na'rina's gemlike eyes in the mirror. The dryad winked at her.

"Rus is right, you are a mischievous sprite."

"Who me?" Na'rina grinned and picked up her own dress, a black and white satin number El had scrounged from the Strata room's wardrobe. There was a shrug to go with it to cover the aspens growing up Na'rina's arms. If El weren't so distracted, she'd be tempted to ask about them.

But tonight, there were more important things to worry about. El sobered and twirled the ruby engagement ring on her finger. On her other hand she wore a second ring, a thick silver band with an inner ring that rotated around the center. The larger base had been cast hollow so that poison could be held inside. The inner ring contained a pivoting needle that could be thumbed open. It could then be used to inject a person with whatever it contained in the reservoir. Currently the ring held the contents of the green vial Icarus had given her. It was another plan B of sorts. *Or plan C?* She was loath to use it considering how the contents were made. "Na'rina?" El asked.

"*Sa?*" Na'rina pulled the shrug on over her shoulders and slipped her comms piece into the hidden pocket in the lining. Icarus had explained that Na'rina found the comms' electrical hum seriously distracting. It astounded El that the Drydanda could hear the actual hum of such a delicate device. But, with some practice, Icarus had gotten Na'rina to the point where she could use it for a short time. *They work so well together.*

El tried to picture herself and Roberto before the symposium, smiling as they announced their courtship like it was the happiest day of their lives. The picture distorted, elongating and changing their smiles into funhouse mirror images. Too thin in some places and too fat in others. Roberto's offer tugged at her but a part of her believed it was mist. Beautiful to see but insubstantial to grasp. Thankfully, they weren't supposed to announce anything until her parents arrived tomorrow.

"Elodie? You alright?"

For once, El didn't mind the use of her full name. In Na'rina's raspberry accent, it sounded almost…beautiful.

"What you and Rus have—" for once words failed her. She tried again. "I've never seen him—" El liked Roberto. *But I don't see us together anymore.* There it was. She couldn't picture Roberto beside her anymore, especially after seeing Na'rina and Icarus together. She couldn't see being so completely herself with Roberto that, if she were a twiglet, she could curl up in his palm and fall blissfully asleep like she'd seen Na'rina do with Icarus on Riviera. And she *wanted* that.

Na'rina set aside the shoes she'd been about to slip on. She glided over on bare feet and took El by the shoulders, urged her to sit at the dressing table and took the brush from her fingers.

"Recent events have changed us all," Na'rina said as she began braiding El's hair into a dark crown. "But perhaps that's not a bad thing. Summer chills into fall; fall draws the curtain in for winter. Eventually winter bows to spring and spring lays the flowers for summer again."

451

Her fingers flew through the braid. El tried to make out the roots twining through her fingers in the mirror but the dryad quickly reached the end and carefully tucked it under to hide the tail. Then she stepped back. "Winter might feel bereft. But it does not last forever and when spring comes, it's all the sweeter for the remembered cold."

El couldn't have responded if she'd tried. She just watched Na'rina disappear into the bathroom and heard the faucet turn on.

Rus, you picked well.

With a shaking hand, El nabbed her clutch off the dressing table and peeked inside. It held a tiny dart and a blow gun. Such a small thing to have El in knots. Ambassador Marquin had given it to her along with a contract to capture and bring him Thomas Dominguez—she struggled to think of the man by his actual name, Thomas Inverro. Marquin didn't care about the danger to the people at the ball, the hurricane barreling toward them, or even the number of people who would *see* El take down Dominguez. All he cared about was Fae justice and he was bringing a contingent of guards from the Fae stronghold in Charleston to get it. He expected El to fulfil his contract before the night was done, regardless of the symposium.

She'd tried to refuse, and Marquin's response still left her cold.

"You can either bring me Thomas Dominguez alive or you and the rest of the Court can be lumped into his fate. It's your choice."

It was what Sophia had feared: destruction of the entire Sedanza Court for the actions of one Sedessan. El hated the manipulation but wasn't sure how to sidestep it.

Na'rina emerged from the bathroom with a washcloth, trying to clean some of the white residue off her face.

El snapped her clutch closed. She couldn't care less about the blowgun. It was a dumb idea. It was a weapon more suited to small rooms or forests than a ballroom filled with hundreds.

Marquin was desperate, trying to save his position at the embassy before Queen Lárissa found out his wife hoodwinked him and the Inverros had been caging mythics directly under his nose. He had to show he'd corrected the problem or he'd face his own Fae justice. Knowing the reasons for his manipulation didn't help El, however.

Na'rina huffed and almost tossed a shoe.

El tucked her clutch under her arm to help her.

"Do I have to wear these?" Na'rina asked.

"Can't go barefoot."

"Why didn't you bring flats?"

El just smirked. She hadn't thought it'd be a problem. *Maybe I can stick Dominguez with the dart by hand.* El slipped the shoe's straps around Na'rina's heel. *Except Dominguez is unlikely to allow me to get close.* And if Icarus or someone else encountered Dominguez, they'd be more apt to kill him than take him captive. Everyone except Na'rina, that was.

I should tell Roberto about the contract. For one night, they would be partners in crime again.

She helped Na'rina stand as someone knocked at the door. The dryad swayed, unsteady. El chuckled. "Hang onto Rus. He'll keep you upright."

Icarus flared his nostrils and wished he could stop his sense of smell for the evening. The perfumes, colognes, and buffet foods made his sinuses burn. He caught the achingly familiar breeze of Na'rina's aspen and mountain air fragrance and tilted his head a little more toward her as they approached the doors to the ballroom where a middle-aged man with too-big ears was checking invitations. Icarus held the Varela invitation in his hand. The houses could pick proxies, although it was rare, and Sophia had signed over the invitation to Icarus Teras and Na'rina Dafni. The last name Sophia had picked supposedly at random.

Icarus didn't believe that. Dafni in Greek meant laurel, or the prize the Greeks historically gave for winning their Olympic games. Sophia was hinting at Na'rina being a prize. If the laurel reference wasn't enough, the story of Apollo pursuing the naiad Daphne tipped the name over the edge of random and into the realm of insinuation. He ground his teeth and Na'rina squeezed his arm in question.

He gave her a smile, forcing himself to relax. She was picking up on his tension and she didn't need that.

Her silk empire-waisted gown accentuated her already thin figure, following the gentle curve of her hips and swaying against the tops of her feet as she took in the masses. Although she could shift her skin to white from its natural celadon—and had done so for the evening—she couldn't quite move like a human. There was a flowing quality to her that made the black and white flowers on her gown appear to flutter with her. She was mesmerizing. No matter what she wore, that flowing quality made the outfit part of her and her element.

Her fingers twitched on his arm again, but it was only a reaction to a man who bumped into her. She checked her arm, making sure she didn't leave residue on the man's jacket. The white to her skin made it powdery like her aspen's bark, but her thin gloves kept her from leaving marks on the elbow of Icarus' tux where her hand rested.

She'd never purposefully put herself in such a large group of humans before and her fingers trembled. Her tension was a knot in his chest from the vow. Icarus wouldn't have asked this of her if he'd been able to think of a better way to neutralize Dominguez' hurricane. His and Na'rina's part tonight was to neutralize whoever had been dosed with the oceanid serum. It probably wouldn't be Dominguez himself but one of his family. Until they figured out who it was, he and Na'rina had to play along among the people.

Dominguez was El and Roberto's responsibility.

Icarus scanned the crowd. There were no Sedessans, or other mythics, yet.

Na'rina squeezed his arm again, both in question and probably to reassure herself.

He leaned closer to speak, breathing in her aspen and wind scent again as he did. "Sophia picked your last name as a hint at you being a prize."

A line formed between her brows. "But a laurel is a plant. It seems logical."

"That's part of the fun for her," he said, keeping his tone light despite his irritation.

Na'rina considered that, swaying unconsciously until they had to step forward with the line. Finally, she shrugged. "She can think however she likes. Her view doesn't change who or what I actually am."

Icarus snorted a chuckle and kissed her temple.

She startled. "What was that for?"

"For being you."

She didn't get a chance to respond as they stepped up to the middle-aged man and Icarus handed over the invitation.

"Proxies?" he said, checking his master list. "Oh, I see. Thank the Varelas for their support the next time you see them, if you will, Mr.—" He finally looked up and his words died.

"We'll pass along your thanks," Icarus said and drew Na'rina into the ballroom.

Na'rina stopped inside the double doors. The ballroom had been strewn with rope lights that glittered against the dark stained-glass ceiling above. Her gaze traveled to the giant oak in the far corner, then up the trunk to the branches and glass above.

"With the rain outside, it looks like the leaves are moving," she said.

The skylight was slanted from the taller wall behind them to the outside wall with the oak tree. Rain coursed down the glass and Icarus tried to see it through her eyes. *It's like a ghost.* Before he could say it aloud, El and Roberto approached them.

"Notice the tapestries?" El asked. "I could scrape one with a knife and have dust butter."

Icarus snorted. The massive tapestries around the room depicted oak trees drooping in Spanish moss. It made the ballroom feel like a glade in a giant forest, but Icarus could see there was no lifeblood in the artwork and knew Na'rina could feel the difference. "Good luck tonight," he told his sister.

El winked as he pulled Na'rina away toward the buffet table.

Icarus handed Na'rina a plate as he asked, "See any mythics yet?"

Na'rina shuffled along, her hand straying out to touch the banner behind the table. "There's a goblin across the way."

Icarus spotted the shorter creature by the kitchen door. The goblin—a server—wore his human illusion with the unfortunate luck of having a bulbous nose and overlarge ears. Icarus wasn't surprised that the Sedessan houses had brought a few of their trusted servants. He tried to discern which house this one belonged to but didn't succeed before the goblin ducked into the kitchen.

Na'rina added grapes to her plate. "There," she said, "coming through the main door are two Sedessans I don't know."

One was an older man wearing a black suit with a pink ruffled shirt. A woman about El's age waltzed in on his arm. Her dress matched the older man's shirt in wispy layers similar to the pixies' style. If she twirled, it'd fan out around her legs like the petals of a flower.

"The De Leóns," Icarus placed them. El had told him about Arlo's poking at the Inverros. She suspected Arlo would do whatever he could to undermine the Inverros if he could do it without implicating himself. Icarus eyed him. El's suspicions were spot on. As Arlo pulled a chair out for Lucia, Icarus matched him to Rebecca Simms' memory of the Sedessan who had brought the flash drive from Rosharu. He hadn't placed Arlo before because the man had not aged gracefully. He'd grown out a heavy black beard to hide his wrinkles and splotchy skin, but none of it hid the effects of stress.

Leading Na'rina to a table, he whispered, "I'll be right back."

She grabbed his arm, confused.

He covered her fingers with his own. "He's the one who delivered the flash drive. I'll set up a time to speak with him later."

"Wait. I want you to hang onto this." She unclasped her necklace and held it out. For some reason, she hadn't restored it to its place beneath her skin.

"Why?" The store of zoi aima in the leaf had saved Na'rina more than once. He did *not* want to leave her without it.

"I want you to be able to shift even if I'm elsewhere."

He hadn't thought of that. Shifting into a lynx had also saved her more than once. Reluctantly he accepted the leaf and clasped it around his neck before he stepped away.

Arlo glanced up as Icarus pulled out the chair across from him.

"Think you're at the wrong table, old chap," Arlo said.

Arlo may have aged, but he sounded the same and his words triggered memories of holiday parties, teasing toasts, and spilled spiked cider. Icarus chuckled, fangs and all, at his reminiscing and Arlo went from cordially polite to confused and alarmed. Beside him, Lucia grasped his arm.

"Think I'm at the right place, old chap," Icarus said, picking up the British accent Arlo had used as he seated himself and leaned back. His hair covered his scared ear but, just to be safe, he tilted his head away slightly.

Directing their attention even more, he pulled the flash drive from his pocket and began spinning it end to end between his fingers. The drive alone probably wasn't enough for Arlo to make the connection between him delivering a flash drive for Rosharu and the device in Icarus' hand. It looked like any other plastic data stick, after all. So, he added a hint for the older Sedessan. "I almost got buried under a mountain of data this last spring and I hear you're the one to talk to about it," he said.

"Contracts go through our lawyer," Lucia hissed.

"No dear," Arlo said, patting her hand and dropping the British accent. "This is an old contract."

Lucia jerked back from her father. "How old? I know all our contracts."

Considering Rosharu's age, Icarus guessed this contract was old in the way family money was old. She may have had the De Leóns on retainer before Arlo was even born, much less Lucia. Yet he'd never shared the contract with his daughter. *Interesting.*

Instead of answering her, Arlo addressed Icarus, "No matter how old it is, however, tonight is not the time to discuss it." He slid a thick silver business card across the table. "Follow up with me later."

Lucia's face was turning red as her fingers wrapped like talons around her clutch.

Icarus made the card disappear into a pocket. "Enjoy your evening." He tilted his glass to them. The wine's odor, like heavy vinegar layered with too much sugar, hit his nose. He grimaced. *Marie must have picked something cheap.* Waving over a waiter, he handed the glass off as he stood to leave. When he turned toward his table, his stomach dropped.

Na'rina wasn't there. Her plate sat abandoned, and a grape rolled across the tabletop and dropped off the edge. *It's been less than five minutes. What happened?* Na'rina wouldn't have left on her own unless she'd seen Marie or Mateo and couldn't get his attention in time to follow. *She forgot her earpiece.* He'd wondered if the technology would do her any good. He tapped his thumb and forefinger.

"Na'rina? Na'rina, can you hear me?"

No answer. Then, "East side door, Rus," from El who'd probably seen the whole thing from the dance floor.

49

"You don't look happy."

Roberto's observation pulled El from her reverie. She tried to paint on a smile as he led her into a turn in their waltz. When she stepped back into Roberto's arms, he grimaced. "Now you look like you're in pain."

"Nerves," El said.

They promenaded and when they came back together, Roberto's expression had shifted from teasing to serious. "You know," he said, "I wouldn't pick another partner in crime. I—"

Not this! El cared for Roberto, but only time would restore any trust in him. "Marquin hired me to sedate your grandfather," she blurted. "He's headed here with a Fae contingent to take him into custody."

Roberto stopped dead on the floor, forcing El to stop too. A couple of dancers shot them startled glances, but he ignored them.

"Welcome everyone," a man greeted from the stage at the back of the ballroom. "If you would kindly find your seats, we'll begin the festivities."

Roberto's dance frame stiffened. For a moment, El thought he'd walk away like she had at dinner, but then he dropped his arms and touched her elbow to lead her to their table. As she took her seat, he unbuttoned his suit jacket and sat beside her, his motions precise.

Frog's breath, he's tense now. That might have been a mistake.

Servers brought out a pumpkin soup appetizer and the woman beside El leaned over, saying, "Can you believe this room? It's gorgeous."

El politely agreed but didn't strike up a conversation. The woman would be a great contact but El scanned the room instead, placing each Sedessan family. Besides them, there were human business leaders, government officials, and leading minds in mathematics, science, and electronics. It was a good turnout. *Who does Dominguez want to Compel?* El sipped her soup. She had no clue what Dominguez' ultimate goal was, and without that she had no way of guessing his next move.

"…Let me introduce our keynote speaker this weekend. He's a man many of you have heard about but have never had the pleasure to meet…"

They're announcing the keynote during dinner? Is Dominguez going to walk on stage in front of the Court? Will he appear human?

El glanced at Roberto. He sipped from his bowl but the tension around his lips spoke volumes.

"…and without further ado, let me welcome Mr. Dom Endo, the CEO of Intela Corp International, to the stage."

Thomas Dominguez climbed the steps, approaching the podium with gentle use of his cane. His facial lines were not showing, but his lifeblood was definitely a Sedessan's garnet.

"From everything I've heard, he's a brilliant man," El's table companion whispered, "and I hear his family's here tonight, too!"

El smiled, clapping politely, but she was gauging the ripple of apprehension running through the Court. Manuel Torres almost vacated his seat, but his wife grabbed his arm. *They realize they've been duped.*

Thomas had used Mateo to keep everyone distracted while he'd worked in the background, a shadow, to build the Inverros' strength and network.

As the clapping subsided, Dominguez greeted everyone. "Thank you for the warm welcome." Despite his age, his voice was steady and strong. Something flickered around the garnet edges of his zoi aima like an oily sheen.

What did he take? El took a sip of wine and tried to catch that weird sheen again.

"It is an honor to be here," Dominguez continued.

A server replaced El's bowl with a plate of roasted chicken, steamed broccoli, and wild rice. Above, rain streaked across the skylight in thick, twisting rivulets and the ballroom's lights shimmered against the movement, drawing her eye briefly. *Pay attention, El.* She sipped her wine again and had to steady her hand before setting the glass back down.

"…You might find it strange that the keynote speaker is already speaking and you've barely finished your soup." Dominguez gazed around with a friendly smile. In the psychic, a rope of scarlet color shot out from his lifeblood, there and then gone, like a solar flare. "You'd be right," he continued like nothing strange was happening. "However, we've been notified that the hurricane has unexpectedly turned toward us and has been upgraded."

The woman beside El groaned in dismay.

El slid a glove off to grasp Roberto's bare wrist under the table. *What's going on with your grandfather's lifeblood?*

Robert broke her contact to cut his chicken and shrugged.

A headache spiked through El's temple. She wanted to shout at him that he had to *talk* with his partner in crime.

"To make sure everyone has accommodations," Dominguez continued, "I've been asked to speak now so that after dinner, the King's Cathedral can find rooms for those of you who booked lodging elsewhere. Apparently, the streets are already flooding." He smiled again, this time reassuringly. "Don't be alarmed. This beautiful hotel has weathered many such storms. My sons," he gestured to the table where Ethan and Samuel were sitting, "will be at the tables in the back after dinner to help everyone."

The brothers' natural garnet was laced with a dull brown and green moss that El had seen before. She again touched Roberto's wrist under the table. *Why do your brothers have gnome zoi aima?*

Maybe to mitigate the backlash from grandfather's Compelling...especially from the other families.

El released his hand and took another sip of wine. The gnomes' ability to calm, if strong enough, could make the room pass out...or just leave everyone blissfully loopy. *And open to Compulsion.*

"Now onto my planned presentation," Dominguez said and the general muttering in the room settled. "Over the years, many people have led Intela Corp—"

"None quite so long as you," Arlo De León called drunkenly. The crowd tittered.

Dominguez chuckled softly and continued, "—fostering it into the magnificent company it is today. The reason it has stayed the course has been one simple concept. Legacy." He held up his gnarled hands. Zoi aima sparks flickered around his fingers. In the back of the room, a woman stood and quickly left. El recognized Renata Nevarez from her salt-and-pepper braid. "Would someone please check on her," Dominguez paused to say. Ethan rose to follow Renata. While everyone was distracted, Dominguez' eyes flicked up toward the skylight.

He's waiting for something.

"What we build with these hands," Dominguez continued his speech, raising his hands again, "passes to our children…" El tuned him out as he continued speaking about legacy and foundations for discoveries. Unease coiled in her stomach. *Renata's spooked and Dominguez is stalling.* She touched Roberto's wrist again. *What is going on?*

You have a sedative from Marquin? he asked.

Of course, but what does that have to do with anything? What is going on?

Roberto flipped his hand over and thumbed at his ring. He opened and closed a needle just like the one El wore on her right hand.

El's headache pounded. *You already brought a sedative?*

I came prepared, he answered. *Be ready to use Marquin's sedative when you get the chance.*

El tried to process beyond her aching head exactly why his answer bothered her. *When you get the chance,* she repeated to herself. If Roberto had a plan to use the ring, that meant he had a plan to get close to his grandfather. They'd assumed Dominguez would avoid them, but if Roberto knew that wouldn't be the case, he hadn't warned her. *What else hasn't he told me?*

On the stage, Dominguez smiled winsomely and gestured at the wall behind him. It lit up to reveal a floor-to-ceiling screen. "Our kind hosts granted me free reign in exchange for Intela Corp upgrading their systems," Dominguez' speech droned on. Again, he glanced at the skylight as he snapped his fingers and the wall's screen lit up with a spinning DNA strand. "We've come a long way in understanding our genetic code. We all dream of curing diseases…"

El leaned toward Roberto like she was whispering to him and pressed her thumb and pinky together to mutter, "Dominguez is stalling. Have you found Marie or Mateo yet?"

"Not yet," Icarus answered, "but we haven't caught up with Na'rina yet. She's headed for the roof." El caught the "we." Icarus must have called his wer-im to him.

El glanced upward. *The roof? That's not a coincidence.*

Dominguez snapped again, pulling El's attention back to the stage, and a second DNA strand appeared on the wall, this one a quadruple instead of double helix. "And such things are possible but far off…if we start with the human DNA on the right. However, if we start with the DNA on the left, we jump forward decades in our research."

A low murmuring had overtaken the ballroom. At the back of the room, Ethan returned with Renata in tow. She walked drunkenly, but El suspected it had more to do with the gnomes' calming ability than alcohol.

"I'm sure you're wondering where this DNA came from," Dominguez continued. "Since this is just a teaser, that's my secret for now," he winked and snapped a third time, "but I promise this is the legacy Intela Corp will leave for my children, their children, and their children's children."

A paused video appeared, showing a frail, unconscious woman on a hospital bed. Severe burns covered her entire left side. El's table companion gasped. El's stomach rolled, but she wasn't sure it was from the picture. Her vision swam as she tried to focus on it. *What's wrong with me?*

"I apologize for the gruesome image. Let me make it better." Dominguez snapped one last time and the video started. El barely registered the scene of a doctor healing the woman in seconds with what looked like a spray-paint can. She'd shifted focus to Dominguez and woozily watched the diaphanous zoi aima now flowing around his body. It reminded her of Sala's flames.

Am I hallucinating? The book said they weren't able to stabilize that ability. Dominguez wouldn't be immune to the fire. That makes no sense.

"I promise this is not sped up." Dominguez spoke into the silence when the video finished. "And I promise it's real. A lasting legacy to hand off to the next generation indeed." Dominguez gripped the podium. "And speaking of legacy, I'd like to shift now to something more personal. Would my son, Roberto, and Miss Elodie Varela please join me on the stage?"

El's brain stuttered and her vision swam again. She stood and clutched the table, fighting a swoon like she'd spent too long on a ship. "Roberto," she hissed. "I think I've been drugged." She wasn't even sure she *could* walk, much less climb the stairs to the stage.

Roberto shot her a glance, sighed with what looked like resigned frustration, and offered her his arm.

He knew. El leaned on him, fighting her wobbly legs. People would think she was drunk but she didn't care. What bothered her more was that Roberto wasn't surprised. *He knew this might happen.* El clung to Roberto's arm, trying to think.

Roberto had brought a sedative of his own. He still planned to stop his grandfather. Had he used her to get on stage and close to Dominguez? *Sa.* If he played it right, his grandfather would suddenly collapse in front of everyone and no one would be the wiser. They'd have dozens of witnesses to her and Roberto's innocence.

El forced her feet up the steps onto the stage. Dominguez glanced upward again at the skylight while he waited for them. *What's he waiting for?* Clutching even tighter to Roberto's arm, El realized she'd left her clutch with Marquin's dart on the table. *Dumb El,* she berated herself. *I seriously hope I'm guessing Roberto's intent correctly.* Although at this point, with her head swimming, she wasn't sure she'd gauged anything correctly.

Na'rina raced up the stairs, following the person she'd seen in the ballroom who had Alaya's familiar swirl of zoi aima but clearly wasn't Alaya. She shuddered. There'd been a strange reddish tinge to the lifeblood too. *What am I doing? I'm not prepared for this!* She gritted her teeth. *Plans rarely survive first contact. I'll adjust.* The sooner she stopped the person, the gentler the hurricane would be. Na'rina tripped on her heels and landed on her hands. Kicking the dumb things off, she left them behind.

Above her, shoes thumped softly on the carpeted stairs and someone gasped with over exertion. Then a door shrieked and the thumping and gasping were gone. In the sudden silence, there came a low hum. She froze, trying to place it. *Oh stars, I could have gotten Icarus' attention.*

She pulled the earpiece from the shrug's hidden pocket and inserted it into her ear. Then she tapped her thumb and forefinger together and sheepishly said, "I'm about to follow someone onto the roof." No answer immediately came. Na'rina peeked up over the railing and wrinkled her nose at the reek of onions that hit her, but she saw nothing.

She kept going and pulled the roof door open. It squeaked but the howling wind covered the sound as she peeked through. Stepping onto the roof, the heavy rain instantly drenched her and plastered her hair to her face.

Icarus' voice crackled in her ear. "Stay put. We're headed your way."

Na'rina tried the door handle behind her, hoping to slip back into the stairwell. It wouldn't turn. "Too late," she said. "I've found Mateo."

"Don't engage."

Don't have a choice. "Again, too late," she said.

Across the way, Mateo stood at the edge of the roof watching her. He smirked. "Marie insisted you'd survived," he shouted over the wind.

Na'rina gawked at the zoi aima thrashing beneath his skin. "What are you doing?" The tempest inside Mateo mimicked the storm above. His chest heaved for air. *His heavy breathing wasn't from climbing the stairs.*

"Picking something up from Marie," Mateo said like that should be obvious.

Marie's on the ship. A part of her was relieved she wasn't at the hotel. Another part, however, registered that the oceanid/sylph serum Mateo must have taken would make him very formidable in the use of the wind and rain.

"I won't let you do this," she said. She wasn't even sure what *this* was beyond him hauling in a massive storm, but that was enough. He was endangering lives. *Please, Icarus, hurry.* She didn't say it over the comms.

Mateo grimaced. "I'm not loco enough to want to go toe-to-toe with you, Señorita, but he is." His eyes flicked to the side. From behind the stairwell stepped the brute from the ship. He grinned and cracked his knuckles. "He wanted a rematch," Mateo said. "Who am I to refuse him? Now if you'll excuse me, I'll leave you to settle what you started on the ship." He turned to face the storm, pulling tendrils of energy like a magnet.

The captain appeared even bigger here than he had on the ship.

"Found the troll brute too," Na'rina warned Icarus as she chanced a glance at Mateo. He was reaching for the clouds and roiling zoi aima began streaming to his outstretched fingers. The control he was exerting tingled along Na'rina's skin, oddly similar to when Alaya drew water from the air. Answering, the storm surged closer. It wouldn't be long now before landfall.

The captain raced for her. Na'rina squeaked and darted across the roof to get away.

Icarus ran into the stairwell with Felis, Dante, and Levi close behind. Na'rina's initial comms had covered him calling for the other wer-im and it'd taken him a second to answer her. Even if Na'rina hadn't told him where she'd gone, however, her scent would have told him. Suddenly, the aspen and mountain wind disappeared under the stench of sweat and onions. *Troll.* He was glad Obek had warned him. As it was, he barely avoided the troll's swing when he came around the turn in the stairwell.

"Watch out!" He dove over the center railing, narrowly escaping the giant club that embedded itself in the wall. Falling past Felis and

Dante, he caught the next railing. His claws grated against the metal as he hauled himself back onto the stairs beside Levi.

"Time to play," a voice boomed above. There came a raspy laugh and then a spit. A loogie dropped between the floors.

Icarus' hackles rose as Felis and Dante backed down the steps to rejoin him and Levi.

Levi threw back his head and sniffed. "Trolls."

"Never fought a troll before," Dante admitted, the whites of his eyes showing huge.

Icarus didn't blame him. One troll was bad enough. More than one was a nightmare.

"Na'rina's facing Mateo above," Icarus said. "We need to make quick work of them. Levi, you're with me. Felis and Dante, come in behind us."

"Understood," Dante and Felis said together.

Icarus braced himself. Like Dante, he'd never faced a troll before.

"Now," he said and he and Levi rushed up the stairs, skipping steps as their legs stretched out. They reached the landing below the trolls and Icarus launched off the wall while Levi went low.

There were three of them. The lead creature looked like an overgrown goblin with tusks and cracking lips. The two behind him were bigger, their eyes peering over his shoulders in beady excitement. It was so rare for such beasts to wander into human society that Icarus had a moment of disbelief just before he clotheslined the first troll in the neck. It was like hitting an elephant.

Icarus howled, but then Levi hamstrung the creature, and the resistance disappeared as it fell backward with a bellow. Icarus landed on the thing's barrel chest and sprang off.

Leaving it for Levi to finish, Icarus ducked as the second beast swung, punching a head-sized hole in the wall. *At least it's his fist and not his club.* The club hanging from the creature's belt could probably take out the stairs.

The creature swung again and Icarus threw up his arms to block. The close confines of the stairwell kept him from ducking away. Both his forearms cracked. Pain erupted through his elbows and up into his shoulders as Icarus fell onto his back, stunned. He slid down the stairs, Levi jumping over him, until he fetched up against the first troll's body.

His arms popped, resetting themselves and renewing circulation. Icarus hissed his relief. *I'll never take the vow's healing for granted again.*

Felis vaulted over him to join Levi above. Icarus stood just as Dante passed. He started to follow when Dante spun back.

"Move!" Dante pushed him back down the stairs just as the floor seemed to jump under their feet. Icarus skipped backward over the dead troll and Dante followed a moment before another dead troll tumbled onto the landing. The odor of onion and feet made Icarus gag. *Two down. One to go.*

Icarus glimpsed movement on the landing below them, but he registered it as a familiar leafy green and ignored it. Another thump warned them before a heavy club landed on top of the two dead trolls.

Dante wiped sweat off his face. "Don't like fighting trolls," he said and waded back in. Icarus grinned. *Note to self, never take a direct hit from a troll again.*

As he joined Dante, his grin faded. Above, the third beast had

Levi's head pinned against the wall with one hand and was fending off Felis with a club in the other. Its span covered a good six stairs to begin with. With the club, it was easily keeping Felis at bay.

"What do we do?" Dante asked.

Above, Levi swung his bare feet up to rake his hind claws across the troll's stomach. Greenish blood gushed out over his feet, the troll's legs, and the stairs.

One more swipe.

But Levi didn't get it. The beast arched away from Levi's next kick, pressing even harder on the wer-im's head. He howled a gritty scream that sounded so much like Silas that Icarus' gut clenched.

"Grab the club," Icarus told Dante, gesturing at the dead trolls below.

"Hurry!" Felis again tried to get under the beast's reach and almost took a hit to the head.

Dante grabbed the club and hauled it back up the stairs. "Mighty heavy," he warned as he passed it off.

"Noted. Felis, be ready!"

Icarus hefted the thing two-handed. It was almost too big for him to wrap his hands around. Bounding up the stairs, he jumped off the stair directly behind Felis, pivoted on the wall above Levi's head, and came down on the troll's arm with the full weight of the club and his body.

There was resistance, a suspended moment where nothing moved, and then the arm snapped. The troll bellowed, deadening Icarus' hearing.

Levi collapsed as the pressure left his head.

Icarus landed on the troll. It twisted beneath him. He jumped to the step above, narrowly missing the beast's crushing bear hug. When it tried to follow, Dante and Felis pounced. They hit its back, pinning it to the stairs, and sank their claws into its neck from either side, slicing through both jugular veins.

In the sudden quiet, Levi retched onto the stairs and Felis gagged at the stench of stomach acid and troll blood. Levi's vow to Ver'rina already had his wounds healed, but Icarus was sure it did nothing for the taste in his mouth.

Icarus ducked past, heading for the rooftop. He found the door mutilated in its frame. He smashed a shoulder against it and grunted. It didn't budge.

"We need Amos," Dante said.

Icarus snorted, trying to kick the door this time. "He's not available."

"Try this." Felis held out a small, round lip balm container.

"Is that Rebecca's?" Dante asked, confused.

I could hug that girl. Icarus grabbed El's lip balm from Felis. "Everyone stand back. Especially you," he pointed at the twiglet who peeked at them from the landing below.

The creature ducked away.

A stream of zoi aima shot from Mateo's back. It held momentarily about three feet out, wavered, and spooled back into his body.

What was that?! Na'rina dodged around a large metal machine,

475

then vaulted over it to avoid the captain. All nymphs could push zoi aima out from their bodies a little. The Dandas like Alaya and Na'rina could extend it much farther, influencing things with their lifeblood, but she'd never seen it done by someone else. Na'rina jumped a metal pipe as she tried to figure out why Mateo would want to extend the zoi aima he was absorbing from the hurricane. Her feet skidded on the wet gravel, but she caught her balance before hitting the ground.

The captain followed, inexorably bearing down on her. "Can't electrocute me this time, nymph!"

Na'rina frowned, confused until she noticed a shimmer of energy over his shoulders. The Inverros must have given him something to protect him. She didn't want to get close enough to shock him anyway, but that meant she also had to figure out how to beat him when he was naturally stronger than her. She tested an antenna as she passed to see if she could break it off as a weapon. It bowed but didn't give and Na'rina gave up. He was too close for her to pause for too long.

"Can't run forever!" the captain taunted but she caught the frustration in his voice.

Sure, I can. Na'rina ran close to the roof's edge and stumbled at the sight below. The ocean pounded at the breakers on the far side of the bay, surging over top the rocks. Closer to the hotel, people were rushing to get away as the storm surge flooded the streets. The hurricane hadn't even made landfall yet.

A thicker zoi aima tendril shot out from Mateo, almost hitting Na'rina as it streaked toward the ballroom's stained-glass roof. She didn't want to see what would happen if Mateo managed to push the zoi aima into the ballroom below, but she also couldn't stop him while

476

dodging the captain. The streak wavered and retreated again.

Na'rina pushed off the wall to keep moving but she'd paused for too long. The captain swung her around by her arm just as lightning streaked across the sky and lit his face.

"And they warned me you'd be tricky to capture," he mocked.

Behind him, another thicker tendril shot from Mateo, reaching the skylight this time and vanishing into the ballroom below. The hair on Na'rina's arms stood straight up.

Desperate, she grabbed the captain's shirt and sucked in some of the storm's energy. His eyes went wide as a thin bubble of calm encased them. The energy rioted inside of Na'rina, making her skin feel like ants were crawling over her, but she held it. "I don't have to electrocute you," she said, "I just need you out of my way." And she released the energy with a shove.

El's skin crawled as Dominguez welcomed them to the stage.

"For those of you who don't know, this is my eldest grandson, Roberto, and his good friend, Elodie Varela," Dominguez told the crowd.

El's vision narrowed. So many people stared at them, including the entire Court. Arlo looked resigned. Renata, slightly sick. The Reyes might be planning their demise.

Dominguez is about to tie the Varelas to the Inverros. She slid her bare fingers onto Roberto's wrist. *You knew he'd drug me. You knew he'd call us to the stage,* she said.

I wasn't sure if he'd drug you, but I did plan on him calling us to the stage.

El wanted to shout at him for not warning her, but now wasn't the time. *Stop him,* she said instead.

About to.

"It is with great pleasure that I get to announce their engagement," Dominguez continued like he didn't see the undercurrents in the room. He grinned and El shuddered. The humans erupted with applause as Dominguez raised his hands for quiet and actual fire flickered between his fingers.

Now, Roberto! El released his arm, swaying on her feet as she gave him a small push.

Roberto thumbed his ring open. He smiled and patted his grandfather on the back, appearing to celebrate with him. Dominguez flinched.

Thank good—

Dominguez' lifeblood exploded in a starburst of light. El winced. Instead of passing out, the man pivoted and socked Roberto square in the chin. Roberto went down like someone cut his strings.

El found herself face-to-face with Dominguez, wincing as his zoi aima stabbed at her eyes. Behind him, the room erupted in shock and protest. El swayed, struggling to stay on her feet.

"Finally," Dominguez dismissed her as a threat, turning back toward the crowd. "Everyone. Sit. Down," he ordered.

The Compulsion rolled out from him like a shockwave. El collapsed. Right on the Compulsion's heels ran a wave of calm from Roberto's brothers like a chaser to a rough shot, but instead of smoothing out taste, it dulled El's sudden terror.

He's Compelling everyone without touch! El had to do something or, having just tied the Varelas and Inverros together, his actions would speak for both houses. *No, El, this is worse than that.* If the Fae arrived and caught Dominguez Compelling the room, they'd destroy the entire Court, and be justified in doing so.

El struggled to care, fighting her addled brain and the gnome-calm bathing the room.

Na'rina's microburst threw her backward and the captain halfway across the roof. The back of her knees clipped the parapet and

479

gave out. She flipped over the edge, seeing storm surge and flooding streets, then the rooftop again with a bewildered captain and, behind him, the stairwell door exploding outward and Icarus rushing through. Then she fell below the roofline.

Instinctively, Na'rina inhaled the storm's energy again and caught herself inside a calm bubble. Simultaneously, she exerted pressure with her zoi aima downward against the sidewalk below to stall herself midair. It was like she hacked a chunk of roots out of Mateo's tree. He stumbled above and caught himself on the rooftop's low wall.

Focus, El. Come on! Her head swam as she tapped her thumb and middle finger together repeatedly. Thankfully, the signal didn't require much willpower because she didn't have much to give. *This has gone pear-shaped. Time for plan B.*

Dominguez' painfully bright zoi aima flickered. Manuel Torres shot to his feet as the Compulsion faltered, and then stumbled when Dominguez' lifeblood steadied and the Compulsion hit full force again.

At that moment, Gladen responded to El's signal and dropped the illusion he'd been holding that hid himself and Amos against the tapestry by the kitchen.

"Stay put!" Dominguez shouted at Manuel.

Manuel stumbled but caught himself on a chair. "This won't stand!"

"It will," Dominguez said, "because it has to." Dominguez pointed at Manuel and fire shot from his hand. It hit the Sedessan in the chest. He screamed and would have spread the flames to his wife except a goblin servant tackled him and bore him to the ground, smothering him.

"Stop right there," Dominguez pointed at Amos.

Amos didn't react, still coming toward the stage.

El thrilled. Compulsion didn't work on a shielded mind and fire was only partially useful against a rock giant. Her relief melted as Dominguez pointed upward, shooting fire at the top of the tapestry behind Amos instead. It severed the ties and the huge banner slumped downward over the giant. Ethan and Samuel jumped on top, pinning him under it and flooding the area with the gnomes' calming. Amos might have a shielded mind, but emotional manipulation worked differently. The struggles under the tapestry began to weaken.

"Any other objections?" Dominguez asked. "Good. Someone go bar the doors."

A man rose, his eyes glazed, and ripped several tablecloths off the nearby tables to tie the doorhandles together. It was a mark of Dominguez' control over the room that no one reacted.

Na'rina's bubble fluctuated, threatening to pop. Before she lost control, she breathed in more of the storm and pressed upward, forcing her bubble to rise. The storm's energy tore at her inside, but she held it until she could roll back onto the roof.

Her bubble burst and rain pelted her. Na'rina sank to her knees. It would be harder for Mateo to throw her with the wind if she weren't standing. Going even farther, she laid down, gasping as she recovered.

She spotted Felis and Dante cornering the captain against an AC unit while Levi contended with more men coming out of the stairwell. Across the roof, she met Icarus' gaze. He'd been headed her way but now he paused as she pointed at Mateo. She tapped her fingers together.

"He's powering someone inside," Na'rina said. "We have to cut his control over the storm."

Icarus hesitated only briefly before veering toward the Sedessan. Instantly, the wind that had assaulted Na'rina shifted, trying to flatten Icarus against the roof.

In the time she'd been distracted, the tendril of zoi aima flowing from Mateo's back had become a river pouring into the ballroom. It made Mateo a starburst, funneling so much through him. She didn't want to know what the person inside looked like.

El's dealing with the other end of that. Na'rina swallowed hard. *How do I stop him?* The energy had shifted, disrupting Mateo, when she'd created her bubble, but she couldn't draw more without killing herself.

We can gift to our elements as well. It just fades faster. Alaya's words played in her memory. *Can I gift enough, fast enough, to kill the storm?* Na'rina had no idea, but it was the only idea she had. *I'll need help reaching far enough.* She closed her eyes, searching for a familiar, calm presence beyond the vortex around Mateo. Just like Icarus, the storm battered at her, eddies trying to fling her zoi aima about similar to how they did his physical body. Just as she started to doubt her plan, a still, quiet voice greeted her, *Hello, my Na'rina.*

Dominguez' lifeblood flickered again but he had solid control of the room now. El stared blearily. Between the gnomes' calming and whatever he'd drugged her with, her brain was mush. Deep down, she was revolted by Dominguez' actions.

El sat on the stage, unable to stand. Fire flickered over the back of Dominguez' hand while he talked to an immunologist who he was Compelling to believe he worked for Intela Corp and was finishing a particular study.

He must have burned through Roberto's sedative just like Icarus or Sala would have. The fire danced blue over his knuckles. *Fire…I can use fire…* El struggled to figure out how. *Sala…Sala's fire burned away my painkillers. Frog's breath, that's a terrible idea.* But she couldn't think of a better one. Roberto was out cold. Amos still struggled weakly under the tapestry. And no one else in the room was in any position to counter Dominguez. El hunched her shoulders, trying to get her body to respond. She fought her woozy brain and gnome-induced lack of care to inch closer to Dominguez.

Icarus fought his way toward Mateo. He didn't *want* to tangle with the man again, especially not in the mindscape. Na'rina had tried to encourage him that he'd made Marie bleed in their last confrontation, but he was under no illusion that he could do the same thing twice.

Maybe I can slit his throat before he reacts. Icarus doubted it. The mind tended to be faster than physical actions.

Icarus hit his knees to avoid an air duct that flew over his head. The storm was tearing things apart and the stronger it got, the more Mateo glowed like a light bulb. Icarus sank his claws into the gravel and kept trudging forward.

Hurry, Kadis, a familiar, multi-hued voice gasped in his mind, *Na'rina's working to counter him but we—we're weak.* Startled, he touched his chest, finding the golden leaf had sunk below his skin.

The psychic world engulfed Na'rina.

You're sure about this, my Na'rina? her grove asked. *I am no—not at my strongest.* She'd only ever drawn Na'rina across a great distance while calling their council. Unlike then, this wasn't below ground in other root systems, and they weren't growing for spring. Even as their zoi aima stretched off the hotel roof in search of an older, well-established tree, Na'rina could feel the grove's leaves fluttering to the ground in Colorado.

The Rina's doubts echoed her own, but Na'rina fought it. *We have to try.*

They followed the seething, muddy water through the streets, searching for something more than lawn shrubs. They needed something far stronger.

There! Her Rina suddenly turned down a side street and sank them into a thick-limbed magnolia that graced the front of a house.

Hmmm, he hummed, *hold tight, Dearie, this one's taking some branches.*

Na'rina curled into the magnolia's powerful zoi aima. He was perfect for her purpose. *I need your help,* she said. Na'rina pictured Mateo hauling in the hurricane.

He took a moment to process what she shared, then asked, clearly confused, *What do you propose, Drydanda?*

Na'rina hesitated. What she was about to ask might harm him even more because he'd feel the hurricane internally just like she did.

I'm not a fragile sprig, he encouraged.

I can gift a part of my abilities to you so you can pull energy from the storm, Na'rina finally answered. *It'll rob Mateo of a portion of the energy he's drawing in.*

The magnolia shuddered. *I'm not against helping, but even a Nolia as established as me isn't going to make a dent.*

One tree can't make a dent, but many can. I'll gift to every tree I can reach. What I need from you, beyond accepting my gift, is for you to pass my message ahead so I don't have to pause to explain. Na'rina didn't mention how huge a gamble this was. Even as she spoke, her Rina trembled with strain. They might not be strong enough to gift to enough trees.

The Nolia's thinking trickled through him in a slow, steady pace just like his sap. Na'rina held still, fighting her urgency to let him consider.

I will try, he finally agreed.

Na'rina's relief came through in the zoi aima she gave him. It flushed warmer than his usual lifeblood. The tree shuddered, losing leaves that the wind whipped away.

Do this. Na'rina inhaled and felt the responding reaction in the magnolia. A thin, calm layer of air appeared around his bark. He breathed again and the layer expanded, becoming a bubble like her own back on the roof. The magnolia chuckled. *It feels like I swallowed the wind. Continue on, Drydanda,* he said. *I will pass along your purpose.*

El's fingers finally closed around Dominguez' ankle. He flinched and looked down.

I never figured you for dumb, Dominguez spoke through the connection, and then flushed it with mental fire. It wasn't a fire meant to harm her physical body, but it assaulted her mindscape.

El whimpered but held on, digging into his skin and not responding. Just as she'd hoped, the flames cleared her head like a torched crucible burning out the impurities from silver. But it also burned her mental study to ashes, leaving El bare and defenseless. She whimpered again. *He's going to kill me.*

She gasped, her vision narrowing to nothing but where her fingers held Dominguez' ankle. Even if she'd wanted to, she couldn't let go. The fire lessened just before she passed out. She could feel Dominguez eyeing her lying limply, but finally he dismissed her again to turn back to Compelling a geneticist. The powerful Compulsion pressed out from him. Beneath it, El caught the deep satisfaction he got from scorching her bare.

The Varelas had been a thorn in Dominguez' side for decades and it was a triumph to reduce her to a mindless lump. His zoi aima flickered and the satisfaction shifted to frustration. He didn't know why

Mateo kept fluctuating the energy from the storm but it complicated things.

An idea hit El. It was just as terrible as her first idea, but it might give her an opening. With Dominguez focused on his current Compulsion, she kept her mind soft and crept toward his psyche. She was an infinitesimal flame, an ember left over from decimating her mental study. Just like the twiglet had become indistinguishable to Na'rina by becoming a part of her mindscape, El now slipped past Dominguez' wards as a tiny cinder and settled into the massive hearth he'd mentally constructed to contain the salamander's ability.

Boiling frogs, it's hot.

Sweat beaded on El's physical brow. If she wasn't careful, she would incinerate herself. The mental hearth around her cinder was solid. A huge brick fireplace roaring with flame.

It was the only thing in Dominguez' mindscape that wasn't cracking. El didn't need to search for a weakness as it was shuddering all around her. Beyond the hearth was a grand hall of an ancient castle. And the bricks in the walls were crumbling. Shimmers of zoi aima light threaded through those cracks, trying to hold it all together. *He's pushing too far. That's what makes Na'rina a Theos; she has a huge capacity for growth.* Dominguez did not, and it was starting to crack his mindscape.

A third terrible idea hit El. She thumbed her ring open, the one with the goblin ability, and waited. The energy from the storm was bolstering Dominguez enough to buffer himself. If she hit him while he was fully charged, he might be able to shrug off the effects of an extra ability. But if she hit him when he fluctuated again, it might just shatter him. El stayed quiet, waiting, as sweat started to drip off her face.

"I'm almost to Mateo," Icarus said over Na'rina's channel. The wind howled against him, threatening to send him sailing like a kite.

Across the roof, more of the captain's men had joined the fight against the wer-im. He'd get no help from them. The captain himself had acquired a new shield and Icarus winced when it connected with Dante's head. Levi skirted the group to approach the captain from behind. Icarus caught the captain's frustrated eyes briefly, then returned his focus to Mateo before he gave Levi away. His wer-im would handle the captain and his men.

Icarus' voice encouraged Na'rina on.

Just a little longer, she told her Rina.

Charleston was awash with old-growth trees. Hardy pines, supple palms, stands of cypress, huge oaks, and long-limbed magnolias. Na'rina lost count of how many she gifted to, but their becalmed bubbles stretched out behind her like an extension of her body, stealing energy from Mateo with each successive tree.

It's working. We just need a little more.

Her Rina gasped, *I'm—I can't feel—*

The Rina's presence flickered like a firefly. Na'rina grasped ahold as hard as she knew how. *This is killing you!*

I'm jus—just tired.

It was more than that, though. The grove's touch had become

insubstantial. *We've come far enough.*

Na, her Rina protested. *Mateo's—still holding. He's using the wind against Icarus. We need a little more.* Even as she spoke, her touch weakened and then returned. Before Na'rina could object, her Rina tried to move them farther and instead she disappeared altogether. Na'rina's consciousness whiplashed back to her body on the roof and nausea slammed into her. She gasped for air, her heart beating like a dwarf's drum.

The Rina's touch reappeared, humiliation tinging her presence. *We're not enough,* the Rina wept.

Na'rina burned against those words. They were too much like the twiglet's. *The trees are holding,* she said. *I can pull enough from the storm now personally to tip the balance.*

That will kill you! her Rina protested.

I'd rather that than both of us die. Before the Rina could protest more, Na'rina braced herself, and breathed deep of the hurricane. The storm whirled into her full force. It pressed against her skull and around her brain. She'd been sucked into a vortex and it was all she could do to hang on. She knew, vaguely, that her Rina was helping, but the chaos drowned out the grove's touch.

Na'rina gripped handfuls of the roof's gravel, digging the rocks into her skin, and breathed in more. Her bubble of calm grew by inches.

Across the roof, Mateo hit his knees and clawed to pull the energy she'd stolen back. He beat at her bubble with fists of wind and shoved her across the roof, bubble and all.

The river flowing from him to the skylight narrowed as Na'rina breathed in again. The edges of her vision darkened, and her temples pounded from pressure. She wasn't going to get very many more breaths.

I need more. Fighting to her feet, Na'rina stood and breathed in again, pulling so deeply her lungs protested. White and gray energy streaked toward her, hit her bubble, and shot right through to gather in her hands. She used it to push the bubble clear off the roof.

The wind died.

The calm swept over Icarus and Mateo.

The world held its breath.

Icarus lunged, catching Mateo's wrists. The man screamed. His draw on the storm vanished and the battle within Na'rina went eerily serene.

Icarus could feel Na'rina like a sharp lodestone in his chest. He'd acted in her momentary calm, but it wouldn't last long. And now his vision swam as Mateo elbowed into his mindscape.

A sunlit room with a menagerie of birds formed around them. A familiar golden cage sprang up around Icarus. He didn't fight it.

"So docile," Mateo commented. "So out of character for a wer-im."

If you only knew. He'd made a mistake on the ship. As Na'rina had pointed out, he'd fought the man entirely as a Sedessan in the mindscape where Mateo was stronger, but Icarus wasn't just a Sedessan.

Icarus grasped the bars, loudly clicking his claws against the metal, and grinned with his fangs showing. "In a zoo made for cats," he said, "you'd have to make the bars thicker than those needed for a bird."

Apprehension flashed across Mateo's face. The bars began to thicken beneath Icarus' hands.

He grinned even bigger. "You'll have to do better than that." He let the rage in—that part of him that Silas had always tried to coax to the forefront. "No one cages a wer-im—" if a dryad could use the rage, so could he, "—without regretting it!" Heat rushed through his body and his heart raced against his ribs. The shift washed over him so fast that Mateo was still looking at where his face had been when Icarus' paws hit the metal floor. He twisted, flattening his shoulders, and slid between the bars.

He smelled Mateo's fear in the acid tang in the air. Mateo was just taking a step back when Icarus pounced and caught him in the chest, sinking his claws inches into the skin. He bit at the man's throat.

They snapped back to the physical rooftop before he connected. Icarus' equilibrium wobbled at the sudden shift from mental lynx to physical wer-im body. "Don't want to die in your own mindscape?" he taunted, hiding his disorientation.

Mateo coughed and blood flecked his lips.

Punctured his lung. Icarus spun Mateo around to grab his neck, intending to finish him.

Kadis, our Na'rina needs you!

The world went white and thunder rattled the roof with a resounding *boom* as Na'rina's calm bubble vanished.

Dominguez' lifeblood had darkened to almost normal levels, but as soon as it dimmed, the fire dimmed with it and he spotted El.

What are you doing?! he asked. In his mindscape, he approached the hearth and beckoned with his fingers. El was forcibly pulled from the fire. She morphed from a small flame into her normal self.

Watching, she admitted. *Trying to understand.* She had to stall him.

None of you understand! Dominguez' shout bounced against El's brain.

Her patience slipped. *You're about to destroy the Court!*

I'm keeping us free! His disgust felt oily, but even more disturbing was the shuddering of the castle walls. *You think this risk is terrible? Wait until they decide we're second-rate citizens!*

She had no idea what he was talking about.

BOOM!

Both El and Dominguez snapped back to the physical ballroom. It shuddered and the glass above rattled. Dominguez recoiled like he'd been socked in the chest and his lifeblood flared brilliantly red. El recoiled and used the distraction to grab his ankle with her other hand and stab him with her ring. The hearth exploded and the castle started to melt.

She let go, scrambling to get away before the mindscape affected the physical world. She didn't make it far before Dominguez ignited with a roar so hot the stage popped and caught fire with him.

Na'rina sailed across the roof, thrown by her own collapsing bubble. *When will I ever learn!?*

She caught an AC unit and glimpsed the twiglet peeking out of the destroyed stairwell. The unit screeched and a chunk of metal came off in Na'rina's hand. She sailed backward again, tossed by the wind.

Catching the low wall between the roof and the ballroom's skylight, Na'rina stalled again, gasping at the water flooding down the slanted window below. Through the cascade, the majestic stained-glass Dry looked like it was waving its oak leaves at her. Something brilliantly red flickered beneath it.

Is that fire?

El rolled off the stage, dragging Roberto's heavy, unconscious body with her. She grabbed a tablecloth and smothered the flames covering him. Only then did she realize her dress had melted onto her legs. El screamed. *Terrible, terrible idea!* She flopped onto her back, writhing against the pain until her gasping became more painful than her skin. It felt like all the oxygen in the room evaporated, sucking her lungs closed.

The fire had caught the two tapestries on either side of the screen Dominguez had installed and was racing for the far sides of the ballroom. Its hellish light flickered over the massive oak in the corner, taunting the tree that it was coming. El gasped for air. Sprinklers hidden along the oak branches above groaned and started spurting water. The room hissed, but the fire continued to grow.

People were screaming. *We're going to burn.* There was no way everyone would get out. The doors were still barred, so unless someone somehow untied the doors against the press of fleeing people, they were all trapped.

El flipped over onto her hands and knees. A fit of coughing overtook her. She couldn't drag Roberto. Probably couldn't even get herself out.

A familiar, long-eared creature darted past her.

"Horaz!" she broke into coughing again.

The goblin froze with his hands in Roberto's jacket.

"Ice cream. Loads of it, if you get people out of here."

The creature's eyes brightened, then panicked as he took in the room. "Can't get all." He hauled Roberto over his shoulder. "No deal."

"Ice crea—," El fought another coughing fit, "—for any goblin who helps."

Horaz froze again. "Whole pack?"

"Whole pack," El agreed.

Holding Roberto over one shoulder, Horaz placed his fingers against his lips and let out a piercing whistle. The stream of Spanish he shouted after had goblins dropping their disguises right and left to grab humans. Some pushed their way through the crowd toward the doors. Others started hauling people up the walls to escape through vents. El's relief was short-lived. Horaz took off with Roberto. None of the goblins came for her.

El groaned. *Dumb El. Dumb goblin. Can't hold up my end of the deal if I'm dead!* El crawled for the nearest door. Even if she reached it, there was no way she'd get through. People jammed the opening, and she couldn't climb walls like the goblins. The heat on her back grew until El was scared to check her dress. It might be melted onto her back now. Something landed on top of her. She screamed and it took a moment to process that she wasn't burning. The familiar cracking of granite came just as Amos pulled her against his chest. His rock dome cast her into darkness.

"You'll burn."

"*Naaaa*," Amos slurred, loopy from being overdosed on gnome-

495

happy. "It'd have to be a mite bit hotter for that. I'm more worried 'bout us suffocatin'."

El's hands shook. She fisted them in her dress and pressed her face against Amos' bicep, trying not to cry. The ballroom was burning with hundreds of people in it. They'd failed.

Icarus blinked hard until the white from Na'rina's explosion vanished and he could see again.

Bodies littered the gravel where the wer-im and captain's men had fought.

Dante draped over the edge of the roof, hauling Felis back up over the side. *Felis got thrown.* Whether by Na'rina's explosion or someone else, Icarus had no idea.

Then he spotted the captain heading for Na'rina where she clung to the parapet. A streak of motion came at the man from the side. Levi slammed into the captain and they rolled. They fetched up against the wall to Icarus' left with Levi on the bottom, his hands and feet against the captain's torso like he was in feline form. With a triumphant, gritty yowl, he heaved, and the captain sailed up and over the low wall. There was a faint shriek as he disappeared.

"Felis! Dante!" Icarus shouted for the two. Their heads swung his way. "Take him! Don't let him touch you!" He pushed Mateo at them. The Sedessan hit his knees and keeled over.

Icarus raced toward Na'rina, sliding across the roof with the wind behind him.

Na'rina's resolve hardened. She could hang on long enough for Icarus to reach her. Suddenly, behind him, Mateo bolted to his feet and gave chase. Felis and Dante yelped and curved to intercept but she couldn't tell if they'd be fast enough.

"Kadis!" Felis shouted a warning. Icarus paid him no heed. Na'rina could see the singular focus on his face.

"Be Mitto…Be Mitto," echoed on the wind a second before Mateo ran past the ruined stairwell.

"Be. A. MITTO!" the twiglet yelled and launched himself into the wind. It shot him toward the skylight and directly onto Mateo's head. His tiny hands grabbed fistfuls of hair and Mateo screamed, flailing. He yanked the twiglet off and the creature came away with chunks of hair in his fingers. Mateo stared at him in momentary shock and then pitched the twiglet back into the wind.

The twiglet flipped end over end, shrieking.

I can catch him. Na'rina clamped her left hand tighter on the wall, glancing below at the red flickering oak skylight. Steam now hissed off it. *They're burning.* The oak looked like it was waving. *I can help them, but I need the twiglet's help.* The shrieking grew louder and Na'rina snatched the twiglet from the wind with her right hand. Her left screamed as it took her full weight.

You want to be a Mitto? she asked, refusing to look at Icarus rushing to save her.

Oceanfuls of willingness! the twiglet responded.

Na'rina could have kissed him. She let go of the wall and sailed out over the massive oak skylight, twiglet in hand.

One giant step, she whispered, fighting exhaustion.

One giant step, he agreed.

And she initiated the meld.

Icarus' world bottomed out. Na'rina sailed out over the skylight just as he reached the low parapet between the rooflines. He started calculating the distance when she blossomed into an explosion of blue and green zoi aima like a solar flare and disappeared.

"Kadis' claws!" Felis cursed. "Where'd she go?"

Icarus twitched. Felis and Dante held a slack-jawed Mateo right behind him. They all watched the skylight in shock.

Na'rina washed her and the twiglet's lifeblood over the dead oak's branches and then sank them through the chemicals coating the wood. It burned through their nerves. The twiglet whined but held tight, his trust both disturbing and complete, as she pressed inward, traveling through the branches toward the trunk and the oak's core. The closer they got, the hotter it became, and then they reached it. Fire blistered the outside of the wood but inside it was solid and pure.

Na'rina began frantically weaving their combined zoi aima tight to the grain before the fire ate too far into the oak.

I actually get to be a Mitto? the twiglet asked.

Na'rina just kept weaving. The fire was eating into the oak like

Theos Rising

fire ants biting her skin. *Please work. Please work.* She had no idea how anyone could survive inside the ballroom but if there was a chance, she had to try.

Is it working? the twiglet asked.

Na'rina paused. Although she didn't breathe, per se, as pure zoi aima, she wanted to gasp for air. *Nothing's happening.* The oak's core was now covered in flowing green and blue zoi aima but beneath remained dead. In desperation, she reached out to the Collective Wisdom. The memories surged upward like she'd broken a dam. Suddenly, she was that ancient Drydanda, Ara'marxia, the one who'd guided the transformation that sparked the myth the twiglet loved.

She hadn't known the Wisdom reached back so far.

The Drydanda wove her and the twiglet's zoi aima through a stick not much bigger than her arm until it looked like a tiny maypole. Then she dipped it into the flooding river and breathed, gifting to the dried branch a portion of life that wasn't just zoi aima or physical body, but both. The branch shuddered in her hand.

It was so much like gifting to the trees earlier that Na'rina almost laughed. She shook the Wisdom away, her tears choking her. *We need moisture,* she told the twiglet.

How? he asked. *We don't have roots or leaves and the fire's destroying anything already inside the oak.*

Na'rina could feel the rain pouring over the oak's branches above, but with the chemicals sealing the wood, she had no way to access it. *I don't know,* she admitted.

499

In Icarus' periphery, Levi vaulted up onto the parapet between the roof they stood on and the ballroom.

What is he doing?

The older wer-im then knelt, shirtless, with his hands stretched out like he was warming them over the heat from the skylight. Something writhed on his skin. The rough, white aspens traveled up his chest, flowed down his arms, and shot out his hands and down the low wall to splash through the cascading water below. The ballroom's roof shuddered from the aspens driving their way into the oak branches that wove through the skylight.

What in the world?

Icarus wasn't the only one captivated by the sight. The others stared gap-mouthed until Mateo shook and tore away from Dante to slap Felis' face. "Jump over!" he shouted.

Felis' eyes glazed and he jumped before Icarus could move. Belatedly, he tried to catch the larger wer-im but by the time his fingers closed on Felis' heel, his weight was too far forward and Icarus was carried onto the skylight with him. The rainwater swept them down the window. As Icarus tried to hang onto Felis, he spotted Dante's orange hair in the downpour too. Mateo wasn't with him.

The oak shuddered as white branches thrust into the dead wood. With them came a familiar, earthy zoi aima mixed with what could only be a wer-im's heated lifeblood.

Grandmother? Na'rina asked, shocked.

Na, answered Levi. *She is a part of me as I am of her. Now drink deep, my sprout, and move quickly.* And the aspen branches retreated, leaving gaping holes in the oak's varnish.

Na'rina did as Levi instructed, desperately drawing the water through the holes and deep into the branches. She flushed it downward into the trunk. When it reached the side burning within the ballroom, it hissed against the fire. Na'rina drew in more, pulling hard to saturate the oak's core before the fire reached too far. Something stirred along her nerves. *Now,* some part of her said, *breathe now.* She was weak, but as the prickling swiftly expanded, Na'rina pulled in a breath that wasn't air and *breathed.*

The oak exploded with a blinding, prismatic zoi aima. It writhed through the skylight's branches, twisting and twining into the wood, pulling the branches together into a cohesive whole and then racing for the trunk in rivers of light that left green, supple wood in its wake.

Ahhh, the twiglet sighed and then vanished, becoming part of the river. Instinctively, Na'rina wanted to hang onto him, but she knew she had to let him go. Instead, she tentatively reached out to touch the Dry's lifeblood as the transformation fully took hold. She found the unique mix of an oak's deep thoughts tinged with an overpowering, head-tilting, ecstatic curiosity.

Icarus sank his claws into Felis' shoe as they were swept down the slanted skylight. Rainwater poured over them, making the glass slick and the world a chaotic wash of lightning and stained glass. Dante collided with Felis. His weight tore Icarus' claws out of Felis' shoe. Just like Felis, Dante's eyes were glazed and he didn't react to the collision.

Icarus flailed, trying to catch them before they all sailed off the roof. Fully aware, he could break his fall. Felis and Dante, on the other hand, were in shock from Mateo's mental attack. Neither one would react. Icarus' fingers brushed Dante's arm just as the roof disappeared beneath them.

Icarus' stomach flipped.

Dante's body pinwheeled oddly under the torrent of water and he went tumbling before Icarus could get a firm hold.

Beyond Dante, Felis screamed, the fall breaking him from his shock. There was nothing Icarus could do for him. He'd either react and pivot to break his fall properly or he'd break on the sidewalk below. It'd only been a second since they sailed off the roof, but it felt like an eternity. Icarus had led them here. And now both wer-im might die, not in brawling as they all suspected they would someday go, but under torrential rain and from a Sedessan's mental spear.

Icarus twisted in the air, preparing himself for the landing. His sight blurred, becoming a mass of howling wind and driving rain until he oriented himself using the massive oak trunk in the hotel's wall. He tried to relax. Even being ready for the landing, it was going to hurt something fierce.

A warm, hard pulse, like a second heartbeat, flushed out from his chest. Then the world went white. Brilliant zoi aima shot out from the roof above in arching flares. They twisted and curled, transforming the raindrops into prisms before converging back onto the skylight

502

where they wove their way down the trunk beside Icarus in sparkling rivers of light.

Shattering glass joined the rush of pouring rain and wailing wind. Icarus covered his head just as the oak freed itself from the skylight above. Branches thrashed, splaying water sideways, and then one whipped out and snatched Icarus around the waist, stalling his headlong fall. He huffed from the force of it. Shaking water from his eyes, he found a chunk of dark green glass jutting out of the bark not more than a foot to his left. All around him, like the tentacles of an octopus, the massive oak had lifted its limbs, pulling the skylight's pieces apart to allow water to flood into the burning ballroom.

He didn't see Na'rina but Icarus' chest pulsed again, warm and steady.

Steam from the ballroom hissed upward in a thick cloud. Through the white mist, Icarus spotted Felis' legs in the curl of a nearby branch. He searched for Dante but didn't find him. But then, visibility was terrible.

Something crunched below, drawing Icarus' attention downward where thick roots had sprouted out of the oak. They thrashed and then dove into the earth, shattering the concrete sidewalk before disappearing into the soggy soil. It reminded Icarus so strongly of a kudzu vine tearing apart an Intela Corp research center that he chuckled. He didn't know how she'd done it, but Na'rina had transformed a dead oak into a living miracle.

El felt like a scalded rat that washed up on a riverbank after almost drowning in fire and water. For once, she was headache-free. She lay on top of a table that had been righted after the chaos with Icarus sitting beside her. Amos and the wer-im sat around a nearby table, playing cards like they weren't surrounded by debris.

"What's the tattoo thing?" Felis was asking.

"Not yours to know," Levi answered. "You dropped a card down your sleeve."

El tuned them out.

The morning's first rays glistened through the branches of the largest oak she'd ever seen. Fresh growth fluttered in the breeze. It'd grown within seconds, twining down two of the walls and, according to Icarus, expanding its trunk until it spanned more than twenty-eight feet, eating up the sidewalk and the roadway beyond. Bits of colored glass in the debris was all that remained of the actual stained-glass window.

El had expected to burn. She couldn't shake the memory of her lungs heaving for oxygen and Amos beginning to pass out. He'd started to break his protective shell, telling her to crawl for it, and then they were drenched in a deluge. They'd looked up to find a hollowed-out branch channeling water over their heads.

It'd soon moved to other areas but El couldn't shake the feeling

she'd been singled out for that early shower. She hoped she had. Icarus'
eyes held a wild edge. He insisted Na'rina was alive, that he could *feel*
her, but his eyes kept drifting toward the massive oak.

"You don't have to wait with me," El again tried to encourage
him to go find his Vow Protected.

"I wouldn't find her even if I searched," he insisted.

El huffed. She didn't want him in the crossfire between her and
the Fae when they arrived, but if she outright said that, he'd stick to her
even more. And the others wouldn't leave without him leading them.

"Why didn't you tell me about the Fae?" he asked.

El shrugged. "Habit. Fear. Some mix of the two." She traced a
branch with her eyes. It bisected the back wall, destroying Dominguez'
screen. The oak's actions had obviously been precipitated by the
Drydanda. No other mythic could have accomplished such a thing, but
in the chaos, Mateo had disappeared.

"Maybe work on that," Icarus said.

El shrugged again. It was hard to break lifelong habits that kept
her alive. Last night was the first time she'd seen the entire Court work
together. El had explained that the Fae were coming and, in a rare
moment of solidarity, they'd drawn together to fix the humans' memory,
wiping any trace of the Compulsions from their minds.

All human guests who hadn't been injured were now safely in
their rooms. The ones who'd been burned were in a nearby hospital.
Amazingly, only six had died. If the oak hadn't intervened, that number
would be much higher. Even still, El owed the goblins truckloads of ice
cream for doing what they could.

And now, due to the Court's actions, the humans remembered

an evening that went horribly wrong at the science symposium. They remembered Dominguez showing them a new experiment involving plant growth that had miraculously made the skylight's oak tree come alive. That led to the window springing a leak along the back wall, which then interfered with the new electrical system, sparking a massive fire. Trauma was difficult to override and so the Court hadn't even tried. They figured, by leaving the memory of the fire, the rest of their story would feel more real.

El swallowed the bitter taste in her mouth. She hated messing so deeply with people's memories, but at least now there wouldn't be headlines about new DNA strands or strange creatures climbing the walls.

A commotion at the main doors drew El's attention. She groaned, sitting up and trying to arrange her ratty dress over her legs. She wasn't sure why she even tried. Her leg bore large red blisters from her dress melting but they'd heal. The fabric, on the other hand, was toast. El tugged at her dress again anyway as Ambassador Marquin marched in, his shoes squishing in the sodden carpet. Two dozen Fae followed him.

Icarus hissed beside her, but she ignored him. He'd promised to let her handle this. The Fae arrayed themselves along the walls as the ambassador bore down on them.

"Señorita Varela," he greeted even while his eyes were drawn upward toward the oak. He paused and blinked, startled. With a visible shake, he looked back to El. "Where is Thomas Dominguez?"

No formalities. El's stomach rolled, registering the danger, but externally she just rested a chin in her palm. Fatigue pulled at her. "He's dead. Now ash." She indicated the muddy carpet. El had considered scooping up some of the goop and putting it into a small box to hand to Marquin, but she doubted he'd appreciate the cheeky gesture.

A dangerous gleam entered the Fae's slanted eyes. "Then you have a problem, Señorita." He waved in a circling gesture and his guards moved for the door. El guessed it was an order to round up the Court, but they wouldn't find anyone besides her.

All but a few of the Court had already checked out. Of those who remained, Roberto lay comatose, suffering massive burns, in a linen closet with his two youngest brothers guarding him. The boys weren't aware of Gladen holding an illusion over the closet door. Unless Marquin's guards were exceptionally good, they wouldn't even realize the small room existed.

Ethan and Samuel hadn't been found after Amos threw them across the room, so El had no way of knowing how they fared…and nothing to give Marquin now except herself. Renata had suggested offering Roberto to appease the Fae. El had refused, not because she was protecting him but because it was horribly wrong to hand over an unconscious, possibly dying man.

"Elodie Varela, I hereby proclaim the Fae and the Sedanza Court to—"

A hollow boom reverberated against the walls as the room's massive double doors swung shut. Above, the oak's leaves shuddered.

El jumped only to find Marquin had hardened the air around her. In her periphery the card game had become oddly statuesque. Icarus had also flinched. *He can't move either.* Instead of being angry, however, her brother was grinning, his teeth glistening.

"What are your intentions, Sedessan?" Marquin had whirled at the interruption but now he spun back and pointed at El. "You have already failed in your obligations! Any aggression now will only make this worse."

El shrugged. The hardened air allowed that much. "This is not my doing."

"I'll have you flayed," Marquin didn't hear. His finger almost hit El's nose as he leaned closer. "This affront against the Fae will not go unanswered. Do you think we aren't capable of wiping out the Court?!"

El gasped as the air around her tightened. A whimper escaped and all she could think was at least the consequences would be over quick. It was unfortunate Icarus had stayed or he could have been spared this. Beside her, he continued to grin. *Has he gone crazy?*

"IS THIS THE FAMED JUSTICE OF THE FAE?"

Marquin froze, eyes widening.

Something brushed El's toes, then climbed her legs, and surrounded her body like being submersed in a warm bath. As it enveloped her, the pressure on her chest lessened and she drew in a deep breath. She blinked her lens down to find a thin layer of zoi aima around her, pressing back against Marquin's hardened air.

"Who are you?" Marquin asked.

"Who are *you* to condemn an entire people for the actions of a few?"

El searched for the Drydanda.

Across the room, a thick branch creaked, stretching to the floor and splitting open with a resounding crack. A thin, disheveled man stumbled out of the hollow center and the limb snapped closed again.

"If you truly want justice, then take Mateo Inverro to your queen. It was Mateo who wrote your wife and invited her to Riviera's shores. It was he who worked alongside Thomas Dominguez to Compel you. And it was he who kept you away from the hotel last night by flooding the Fae's Charleston quarters. You will find evidence of this on the ship that the Varelas commandeered last night."

"And I'm to trust your faceless word? I don't think so. This one will answer to me!" Marquin pointed at El and crushed his fingers into a fist.

The zoi aima around El contracted, shuddered, contracted again, and shattered outward in a shards of glittering lifeblood.

Marquin recoiled like he'd been socked in the chest.

"You will trust this, Marquin Crostee, because I, Na'rina Drydanda, have vouched for it."

El gawked as Na'rina materialized in front of Marquin.

Icarus actually chuckled. He'd described the phenomenon of Na'rina emerging from a tree, but he'd never mentioned her eyes glowing a vibrant green as she did so or the aspen branches gently swaying on her arms as though in a breeze.

"Do you question *my* witness?"

El shivered.

Marquin took a slow, careful step backward. Belatedly, he bowed, fingers to forehead and eyes downcast in the deepest bow El'd ever seen beyond that given to Queen Lárissa.

"I appreciate your intervention before war was declared between the Fae and Sedanza Court, Na'rina Drydanda," Marquin's voice dripped honey but there was an underlying tremor. "Your kind, as always, does a remarkable job maintaining the peace. Now, I have a prisoner to transport and evidence to gather to present to my Queen. May I be excused?"

Na'rina's chin dipped and Marquin began issuing orders to his guards. The large double doors swung open with a wave of Na'rina's hand. Within moments, the Fae and Mateo were gone, leaving an eerie quiet in their wake.

"Stars above," Felis said, breaking the moment.

Na'rina swayed. El hopped off her table and rushed to hug her but Icarus got there first. She hugged them both instead. "That was magnificent!"

Na'rina froze, then returned their embrace. A creaking echoed in the ballroom and an oak branch coiled down to encircle all three of them.

"Thank you, Mitto." Na'rina caressed the bark on the branch.

"I am now Mitto?" a deep voice asked.

"*Sa*," Na'rina answered, "you are now Mitto."

Dante whooped softly but it was lost under the satisfied hum that vibrated the room. Finally, the branch retreated and other than the leaves fluttering in the breeze, all was still.

El twirled a pen and leaned against the study's desk while she eyed Ambassador Esmond—the new Fae ambassador—Sala, and Lady Ignatious sitting across from her. Despite Marquin's efforts, Queen Lárissa had not let him stay at the Riviera embassy.

This was to El and Sala's benefit if she played her cards right. As the new lead family of the Sedanza Court, the Varelas were required to help if asked with negotiations involving the Fae. Since El's parents were dealing with the ship details, including searching the Amazon for a particular mahogany tree for a surly Drydanda, El was left to handle matters at home.

She wore her negotiation mask.

Flame flickered at Sala's fingertips. Since waking from the stasis tank they'd found her in, she'd had a small, constant flame alive at all times. Lady Ignatious watched that flame with envy. She'd only spent one more day in a tank than Sala, but it'd left her unable to manifest the flame that lived just below her skin.

"I'm sure you understand," El said to Esmond, "why the fire elementals are hesitant to trust their current agreement with you."

Esmond was a sleek man in a tailored blue suit and brown leather shoes. The Queen expected him to smooth things over while also asserting her displeasure at the treatment of her previous ambassador. The responsibility must weigh on him but if he had a tell, El had yet to see it.

"That has been addressed," he said, "as the culprit is no longer living and his accomplice, Mateo Inverro, is in our custody."

"If that were enough to appease everyone, you would not have brought such a large Fae contingent to Riviera. All the elementals are asking is to be allowed to do likewise. Allow Sala Savatian, and any proceeding representatives, to bring five companions to the Fae Court and things can continue as the previous agreement." El was shocked they hadn't negotiated for companions in the first agreement as elementals could bolster each other's flame when needed.

"And shorten the representative's term to two years," Sala added.

"Do you not enjoy the company of the Fae, dear fire whisp?" Esmond turned a predatory grin toward Sala.

Sala flourished her fingers at him, fire dancing between them like a frog's webbing flickering with blue and red flames. "I rather think the Fae will not enjoy my company."

"We are willing to accommodate," Esmond said, holding Sala's gaze. "I would think two companions and a four-year term would please Queen Lárissa as long as we add a new elemental contingent here in Riviera."

El waved dismissively and said, "You're asking an elemental to live away from home for too long. Surely the Fae notice how the elemental's fire starts to dim after a while. It's to everyone's advantage to renew the representative more often. Three years and three companions make sense.

"As for a representative at Riviera, that's just excess,

Ambassador. The elemental's primary home isn't that far from here. If you need, all you have to do is contact them."

Esmond's predatory grin shifted to El. "Can't blame me for trying, Señorita Varela. Three years and three companions is perfectly agreeable."

Lady Ignatious shot from her seat, heading for the door. Sala slowly followed but paused to extend her hand to the ambassador, sans flames that had traveled to the tops of her ears.

"I will inform the Queen of your impending arrival," Esmond said, kissing the back of her hand.

Lady Ignatious grabbed Sala's elbow to escort her out, but she resisted, turning to El. Indecision played across her face. They'd been courteous since Sala's arrival that morning but now regret shone in the elemental's dark eyes. Sala suddenly extended her hand. Lady Ignatious gasped in protest.

El hadn't worn gloves to this meeting as a message to the ambassador that, if he chose to play foul, she wouldn't wear kid gloves either. El accepted Sala's grip, pleased with her unspoken apology.

"Thank you, Elodie Varela," Sala said, and then she departed.

After they left, Esmond rose. Like most people, he towered over El. "And what, Señorita Varela, do you gain from this?"

El refrained from shifting away as he stepped closer. He smelled of jasmine. *Part of an ability or does he just like the smell?* Either way, he was now close enough for El to feel the heat coming from his body.

"Naught y' need to know about," Amos said from behind him.

Warmth tried to blossom across El's face. She kept it in check, barely. She'd suggested hiring Amos as her bodyguard, emphasizing the advantages of having a guard with a shielded mind and, to her surprise, her father had overruled Sophia's reluctance. In reality, though, El wanted someone near who wouldn't betray her.

Amos had agreed on a trial basis.

Esmond stiffened at Amos' appearance but then flashed a half-sneer, half-grin. "The Queen's displeasure did not end with the death of the eldest Inverro," he said. "You'd be well advised to be a little more…accommodating in your dealings with the Fae."

Over his shoulder, Amos bared his teeth but El flicked her fingers in a staying gesture. "We are well aware of the Queen's disposition. We are, of course, willing to be accommodating. But neither," El stepped forward half a step, almost touching Esmond, "would she respect us if we gave way to all of her requests."

After a moment, Esmond took a step back and bowed shallowly, conceding. "Walking a fine line, Señorita," he said. Then he left, never glancing at Amos between the bookshelves. El's shoulders slumped as his steps faded.

What a snake. She hopped up to sit on the desk.

Amos hummed. "Y' were prepared for that."

"Roberto's advice," she admitted.

Amos approached and leaned, gently, against the desk beside her, folding his arms as he did. "Still talking to 'im?" he asked.

El nodded. Despite everyone's expectations, Roberto had survived the fire. Upon waking, he'd dove into rebuilding his family's standing with the help of Dylan and David. His entire household had crumbled. Grandfather dead, father imprisoned, mother and brothers running but still apparently steering Intela Corp. Roberto himself looked like he'd stood in a furnace, but his determination hadn't diminished. And that went for their engagement as well.

He let me walk blindly into a ballroom his grandfather was going to drug and Compel! He told me nothing of his actual plans. El couldn't get over that. Roberto said he'd thought they would take out Dominguez before things went so wrong, but El couldn't figure how he'd truly believed that when he'd told her nothing. She'd tossed the ring at him. He'd caught it, telling her he'd ask again later. El's fingers curled around the edge of the desk in irritation.

Amos nudged her and pulled out a list from his shirt pocket. "Come on, little Sedessan. That Horatio let me know a shipment arrived last night. Said somethin' about vanilla, chocolate slide, and ruby cherry needin' to be sent over to 'is cousin."

Ah, ice cream. That was something she could handle. El hopped off the desk and Amos handed her the list.

"Do you like hazelnut?" she asked.

A blindfolded dwarf led the wer-im. Obek had warned about that. He'd promised to send a guide to lead them into the dwarf's Appalachian capital, but he'd be blindfolded so that if he were asked about it later, he could honestly say he'd never seen the wer-im.

Icarus wasn't concerned about a blindfolded guide in the dwarven home. Although, as they walked, he did begin to appreciate how huge Mammoth cave was. The Appalachian dwarves didn't worry about humans exploring the cave system for that very reason. They'd barely scratched the surface and never come close to the city beneath.

"You're a half-wit kit."

Icarus' ear twitched but he stayed silent on Dante and Felis' conversation. He'd had no part in the fight with the captain on the roof and, as their current bickering dealt with when the captain threw Felis over the edge, he figured he didn't need to comment.

His fingers brushed the flash drive in his pocket. He hadn't been able to use it yet but El had confirmed the virus it contained would destroy whatever he plugged it into. With everything going on, he'd end up using it someday.

"Maybe," Dante admitted, "but you're still alive for it."

"I'm twice your weight," Felis grumbled. "I could've dragged you over the edge."

Their guide led them up a set of axe-hewn stairs cut into the wall of a large cavern. He carried a shuttered lantern that gleamed a tiny stream of light for the wer-im to follow.

"Buuuuttt, you didn't. So, all's good as ends good."

Felis huffed. "Half-wit."

"Maybe. Want a fireball?"

The spicy cinnamon tickled Icarus' nose.

Felis huffed again but accepted the candy, muttering, "Maybe it's you making me fat."

Their guide stopped at the top of the stairs and knocked on the iron-banded door that fit snugly into the stone. He set the lantern down and left, descending the stairs without a word.

Finally, the door swung silently open. Obek snatched the lantern, gestured them in, and latched the door behind them. Only then did he fully open the lantern to reveal a sitting room filled with haphazardly stocked bookshelves and several recliners facing a dead hearth.

Icarus frowned. The wood smoke and heat in the room didn't fit with the dead fire. As if to answer his unspoken question, Obek shoved a lever beside the hearth. With a soft grating, it swung around to be replaced by a burning wood fire.

Obek flopped into the nearest recliner. "Make yourselves at home." He gestured at the other seats. "I apologize that the welcoming party wasn't overwhelming but I'm not exactly in favor with my father and there's a standing order to arrest any wer-im near the city on sight."

Icarus sat and accepted the whiskey Obek offered.

"Now," Obek continued, "why'd you insist on meeting?"

Icarus set his whiskey on the round side table and rolled up his sleeve. Obek leaned forward, eyeing Icarus' forearm as he stood and activated the shield strapped to his wrist. It snapped open with a sharp snick.

"Baldim's beard," Obek cursed. He took the shield reverently when Icarus unbuckled it and handed it over. Running his rough fingers around the edge and along the seams, he drew the lantern closer and inspected the workmanship from about an inch away from the metal.

"You going to kiss it?" Felis teased.

"Maybe," Obek said, still focused on the shield.

Icarus knew when the dwarf's inspection found the coat of arms.

"Pyrgos," he breathed, recognizing the Rockies' dwarves etching. "This is recent work. Where'd you get this?"

"Off an Inverro guard."

"A Sedessan family?"

"The Sedessan family in charge of Intela Corp. That etching was also on the bottom of the tanks they were using to hold prisoners. I'm thinking your kin are sneaking those onto their work in hopes someone notices. They're alive, Obek."

The dwarf, usually so stoic, blinked misty eyes and sipped from his glass. They'd questioned if, after all these months, any of Obek's extended kin lived.

"We also found this." Icarus held out the folder he'd been carrying.

Obek hesitated to take it but finally accepted. Icarus didn't blame him. The Varelas had found a number of interesting things on the *Sansabria*. As a peace offering, they'd given Icarus some of the intel they gathered. Mixed in was this gem for Obek. Perhaps gem wasn't the right word. Double-edged sword might be better.

Inside were notes detailing the threats Mateo Inverro had used against King Olbin to keep him out of Intela Corp's way. Icarus hadn't known the king's sister was married to the Rockies king. It was straight up blackmail, but it gave them a strong lead on who'd captured Obek's kin and explained why his father had adamantly fought Na'rina during the summit.

Obek's breath hissed between his teeth, and he threw back the rest of his whiskey. He immediately poured himself more, scowled at it, cursed, and tossed the contents into the fire in disgust. The fire roared and then calmed, filling the room with the odor of burned alcohol.

"This is ugly, Wer-Kadis. For a dwarven king to have so little honor—" Obek shook his head. "I'll have to think on this. I can't let it ride but neither can I accuse him outright without being absolutely sure."

Icarus had expected that. Obek wasn't stupid. He would only act when he was ready. Tossing back his own glass, Icarus stood. "Keep the shield." It didn't suit Icarus' fighting style anyway, but it'd work well for the dwarf. "And let me know when you need me and the wer-im."

They both knew Obek would need the support.

The relief on Obek's face gave Icarus pause. On instinct, Icarus extended his hand and Obek shook it firmly.

Na'rina's bare feet rustled through the moldering leaves on the forest floor. She tilted her face toward the brilliant sunlight streaming through the needles above. A bone-deep exhaustion weighed on her. It was a good exhaustion, like a morning spent watering the reeds along the riverbank. She'd been layering healing zoi aima into her mother's seed tree. Fall was the wrong time of year for such healing, but she wasn't going to use the season as an excuse to avoid her mother anymore. Just that morning, her mother's consciousness had finally stirred, reaching out with lifeblood tendrils to touch Na'rina's cheek.

Tears brimmed in her eyes. The touch had been warm, full of encouragement. She'd feared anger or judgment but instead she'd received praise. It washed over her heart as rain over parched earth.

My Na'rina, her grove's sleepy voice interrupted her contemplations, *our wer-im has returned.* Her grove was recovering from overextending herself, and most of the time all Na'rina got from her was a vague awareness, but now there was excitement.

Na'rina grinned and took off for her seed tree while swiping her tears away with the back of her hand. She arrived before Icarus, like she hoped, and knelt in the dirt at the base of the massive tree. The earth shifted, opening up a small hole beneath the Rina's roots. Inside lay a thick, oiled canvas bag.

Na'rina pulled two things from inside it and replaced the bag. Thomas' book she set aside for now.

He's almost here, her Rina warned, excitement livening her sleepy, multi-hued tone.

Na'rina spun, holding the second item behind her back, just as Icarus emerged from the forest. He paused, raising a brow.

Na'rina flushed. *I must look guilty as a sprite.* She held out the item, a covered glass bowl, and smiled tentatively, "Welcome home."

"What is this?" he asked, accepting the bowl.

Na'rina loved the curiosity on his face but that wasn't her goal. Since Silas' death, Icarus' smile had become rare. But she'd seen it, unhindered and full of exuberance, when Marissa dumped a tray full of burritos in his lap. Na'rina didn't know if it was the food or Icarus' Niñera greeting him so enthusiastically, but she'd called El and arranged for Marissa to send something special for her hijo.

Icarus lifted the glass lid. The smell of cumin, sausage, and paprika wafted out of the breakfast burrito as the bowl, specially designed for this, started heating the contents.

Na'rina held out a spoon.

Icarus' startlement dissolved into a toothy grin, and Na'rina's heart melted into her stomach.

"Marissa's cooking?"

"El shipped it from Sedanza. Apparently, she brings food into the islands all the time, so shipping it out wasn't a problem." Na'rina shrugged and offered the spoon again.

Taking it, Icarus carefully set everything on the ground and took Na'rina into his arms. "How did you receive it? A P.O. box?"

Na'rina wasn't even sure what a P.O. box was. "Rebecca helped me."

He kissed her temple. "I've created a monster with a cell phone."

After a moment soaking in the warm joy swirling through his lifeblood, Na'rina pushed away and said, "Eat...I have some information to share."

A different light sparked in his eyes. Besides food, information was the other thing that drew Icarus like a moth to flame. Na'rina thrilled at finally being able to participate in his analytical side...although she didn't love what she had to tell him.

They settled with their backs against her seed tree and Na'rina opened Thomas' book to the back pages. "Did you know my grandmother's adept at reading Greek?"

"Have you considered how old she is?" Icarus asked around a bite of burrito.

Na'rina stilled, then shrugged. "She lives in a tree."

"So do you, yet you changed a twiglet into an oak last week. What kind of stories do you think *she* could tell?"

Na'rina shuddered. She *had* heard some of her grandmother's stories. Changing the subject, she tapped the page she'd turned to. "El mentioned Thomas' raving right before he ignited. I think I figured out what it was about."

Intrigued, Icarus set the empty glass bowl aside to read the journal entry. When Na'rina and her grandmother had gotten through the book, they'd been surprised to find that, after the text finished, Thomas' handwritten thoughts began.

"His wife?" Icarus' finger stalled mid-page.

Eager to explain, Na'rina said, "Thomas' wife was recruited by the very group your mother feared. She and Thomas used her position to keep tabs on the group, but then suddenly she just disappeared. Thomas couldn't prove it, but he was positive they killed her. He infiltrated the group searching for her and has watched them since."

"When he infiltrated the group was when he told the Court he'd made an alliance with them," Icarus guessed.

"I believe so. They believe things should go back to how it was under Zeus and his brothers. They believe Theos mythics should rule everyone, human and mythic alike. This confused Thomas because, as far as he could tell, none of the mythics involved are Theos mythics, but they're as close as anyone's seen in a long time, and he feared this.

"At the very end of his entries, he talks about them readying to announce themselves to the world and forcibly taking power. He didn't write an exact date, but he knew it was soon, which forced him to speed up his timetable. That's why he Compelled the symposium. He was trying to finish some of his serums to have mythics strong enough to combat this group. He didn't want to be ruled by them."

"This is the group that terrified Sophia?"

Na'rina nodded. "Those they can't control, they kill. Thomas saw it again and again. Ver'rina confirmed, in her way, that even she and Levi were trying to keep Mona'rina and Silas from their attention."

"This is Levi's avalanche."

Na'rina's stomach tightened. Discussion about Intela Corp or Thomas Dominguez tended to make her queasy. She leaned her head on Icarus' shoulder and waited as he thought it through. Finally, he closed the book and tucked her into his side. Na'rina leaned in, resting her ear against his chest.

"At least we know now," he said. "And we can face it together."

Now's the time. Na'rina opened her mouth to speak.

"And," he continued before she could, "we don't have to face them alone."

Na'rina went still. Was Icarus purring?

"I have my own surprise for you," Icarus said against her hair. He pulled a rolled parchment from his cargo pocket.

Na'rina pushed away to look at him, confused. "What is this?" she asked, accepting the document.

"Afre believes he failed you at the summit. This is his way of making up for it. He wanted to be here to present it to you but couldn't, so this comes with his apology." Icarus gestured for her to open it.

Na'rina unrolled the parchment to find it titled "Mythic Mutual Aid Alliance of North America." Under her fingers at the bottom was a block of signatures.

Onishla Oceadanda of the Pacific Coast

Oba Afre of the Fauns

Alaya Oceadanda of the Atlantic Coast

Na'rina's fingers stopped. "Alaya? Alaya's okay?!"

"She's recovering," Icarus answered.

Na'rina squeaked and slapped a hand over her mouth. The parchment rolled up on its own. Icarus chuckled. All that appeared to remain from her meld with the twiglet was a tendency to squeak when excited. If that was it, she'd take it, although it could be embarrassing at times.

Icarus tapped the parchment and she unrolled it again.

Tuckasegee River Naiad Coalition of the Smoky Mountains

Adrian and Sophia Varela of the Sedanza Sedessan Court

"Your parents signed? They're not North American."

Icarus snorted. "My minx of a sister bet me she could get their signatures and then convinced them to sign because their information network covers North America. Now I owe her a carton of ice cream."

"She's something else," Na'rina laughed. She could just picture the glint in El's eye when she bet Icarus. Going back to reading, Na'rina found her own name and Icarus' next. There were blank lines beside them for signatures.

Icarus Teras, North American Wer-Kadis

Na'rina Drydanda of the North American Dryads

A dozen more names followed theirs. King Olbin's was notably absent but that did not surprise her. The reality of what she held hit Na'rina. *We are not alone in this fight.* Her relief was followed by the bone-deep weariness she'd experienced earlier. She handed the parchment back to Icarus and stood up to ward it off a little longer.

Icarus set the parchment aside and stood up too, coming up behind Na'rina to slide his arms around her. "Are you still falling asleep in random places?" he asked. He must have seen her exhaustion.

Na'rina had pushed herself harder than ever before, especially as winter drew close. She slept more in winter anyway, but falling asleep with her forehead pressed against Mona'rina's seed tree hadn't been expected.

"Keep waking up with bark marks on my face," Na'rina admitted. "But Ver'rina burst out laughing when I asked about it, so I'm not too worried." A huge yawn overtook her.

Icarus laughed. "It's time to rest."

Now's the time. Na'rina turned in his arms. "Not quite yet," she said. "I have a question for you." Nerves made her voice squeak.

Na'rina pushed back from Icarus to hold his hands. Concern darkened his eyes and she just held his stare for a moment. He was her bulwark, the ground that shored up her roots. "You know in the dryad culture that handfasting is chosen by the female."

His eyes dilated and he went absolutely motionless. Behind him, two zoi aima forms coalesced into her grandmother and her mother. Na'rina almost stuttered. She had not expected her mother to witness. Behind them, the golden eyes of a mountain lion watched.

Na'rina took a breath and kept going. "For a Drydanda, handfasting is more. I hereby ask you, Icarus Teras, to be my handfasted mate, an extension of my soul and an anchor point to my roots. If you accept, know there is no breaking the handfasting. You will become a part of my Rina, my lifeblood, and my body. Do you accept?"

Her hands trembled in his while she waited.

"What you're describing is not just symbolic?"

"It is not."

"I accept."

We are satisfied, the watching Drydandas whispered and a low purring rumbled from the mountain lion.

Na'rina swayed. She hadn't really doubted Icarus' answer, but the words solidified her sense of connection to him. "So be it," she whispered. "Please hold still until this is complete."

She reached deep into her Rina's roots. They broke the ground to twist around his toes and up his legs. In counterpart, the branches on her hands grew, twining their fingers together and then advancing up his arms, across his shoulders, and down his chest.

Icarus' hands clasped her fingers tight as he watched in fascination.

Her zoi aima followed, flowing through the roots upward to fill in the aspen across his torso and connect the branches to their roots. Catkins curled and then hung from the branches, then fell to be replaced by unfurling green leaves. Those fluttered briefly in an unseen breeze. The wind grew stronger and the leaves shifted to golden before drifting to the ground to leave bare branches on his arms.

As the zoi aima paused, setting the transfer, Icarus' breath whispered in and out of his lungs. It was sweet to Na'rina's soul. It felt like her own breath. Her zoi aima retreated, the roots withdrew, sucking back into the ground with a soft thump, and the branches on his arms sank into his skin, becoming black and white tattoos.

Hello, Kadis, the Rina whispered, *and welcome to our life.* Then she retreated to her slumber again. Na'rina could tell he heard the grove's soft breath now.

He trembled and dropped Na'rina's hands to pull up his shirt and stare at the aspen trunk spanning his chest. Na'rina swallowed. *Was that too much?* Even if she'd described it, she wasn't sure she could have prepared him.

Icarus chuckled. "You," he spun and pointed at Levi, "speak in riddles too much."

The mountain lion huffed and turned away, heading toward Ver'rina's seed tree. Na'rina's mother and grandmother were already gone. Icarus chuckled again and turned back to Na'rina. He held out a hand covered by the tips of aspen branches. "Why did the leaves fall?"

"It reflects the current state of the grove."

He nodded and cupped her cheek. "I had hoped for this, but as you said, it was not my place to ask."

Na'rina leaned into him. "I wouldn't have minded if you did."

He folded her into his arms and kissed her temple.

"The avalanche will come," she whispered.

"We'll deal with it when it does."

Na'rina hummed and yawned, feeling that annoying exhaustion sweep over her again, now of all times. "Wake me in the spring then," she muttered.

"You should be asleep in your seed tree," Icarus replied as she drifted off.

Epilogue

"Got our work order for the day?" Frank asked Will as the man slid into the passenger seat beside him in the truck. The younger man had a terrible habit of forgetting the paperwork.

"Yeah, yeah." Will waved the clipboard and tossed it on the floorboard to buckle his seatbelt. "It's for an oak that damaged the King's Cathedral. There's another crew meeting us there 'cause it's a big job."

"All the jobs lately are big jobs," Frank grumbled. When a hurricane came through, dropping more than twelve inches of rain and hauling in feet of storm surge, it left a lot of wreckage behind. It was a great time to be in the tree service industry, but Frank was tired. "Let's grab coffee on our way." It'd be his third for the day, but he needed it.

They were sipping their coffees as they turned onto the street with the King's Cathedral. A lot of work had already been done to clear the roads.

Will set his cup in the holder and nabbed the clipboard off the floor. He perused it and tossed it on the seat. "Guess this thing's almost thirty feet wide. They built part of the wall around it. Seriously? Why didn't they have it taken care of long ago? They're right on the waterfront. Of course, an oak's going to damage things in a hurricane, especially if it's attached to the building."

"Beats me." Frank parked the truck. This wasn't an area of town he visited often. Bit rich for his blood. "Let's go take a look."

Will jumped out. Frank finished his coffee and grabbed the clipboard Will had left behind. As he joined the younger man on the sidewalk, looking over the orders, he almost bumped into him.

"What's up?" he grumbled, irritated.

Will pointed.

Frank followed his gaze to the hotel. His mouth fell open.

There wasn't an oak tree, but there was the clear outline in the bricks where one had been and a gaping hole in the ground from its roots.

Dumbfounded, Will asked, "Where did it go?"

Glossary of Mythical Creatures

Daughters of Medusa: Women believed to have sprung from the snakes on Medusa's head. They have similar abilities to Medusa, but technology has allowed them to wear contacts that prevent them from turning people to stone. Most work as mercenaries but not a lot is known about them.

Dwarves: A mythical race of short, stocky humanlike creatures who are generally skilled in mining and metalworking and who interact with both the mythic and human worlds. There are three races in the North Western Hemisphere: The Omichlodis or Appalachian line, the Pyrgos or Rockies line, and the now extinct Vathies Rizes or Cascade line.

> **Ak-Lea:** The leading family of the Omichlodis or Appalachian dwarves.

Fae: A very powerful type of mythic. These human-like creatures serve their queen and have an affinity for either summer or winter. They're a mixed bag, however, when it comes to abilities, which can include: teleportation, telekinesis, transparency, plant and animal affinities, emotional manipulation, and sometimes what they call identity finders.

> **Queen Lárissa:** Holds her court in the northern climes of Russia but the Fae also have an embassy on the seventh island, Riviera, of the Sedanza Island group.

Fauns: These creatures look like a man with a goat's horns, ears, legs, and tail. Here, fauns are lovers of truth and are friendly to those they feel deserve their loyalty.

> **Oba:** Title for the king of the fauns.

Giants: Only one is known to be living in the Western Hemisphere. Over time, they have shrunk in size but would be noticeable walking down a human's street.

Gnomes: Small creatures who love to live in and work the earth. Sometimes physically misshapen but friendly. They live in families and can send out a wave of calm to protect themselves.

Goblins: Highly intelligent humanoid creatures who usually judge their hierarchy by how ugly someone is. They love gold and ice cream and work hard as servants if paid well. They run in packs and rarely work alone.

Imps: Small gray or green creatures. Cousins to goblins but less intelligent and more mischievous. If in a group, they feed off the group hysteria.

Ior: Cousins to giants but not very intelligent. Likely to break things. Usually evil-tempered.

Nymphs: A mythological spirit of nature imagined as a beautiful maiden inhabiting rivers, woods, or other natural locations. Here, not all nymphs are female.

> **Auloniads**: Nymphs who inhabit wheat.

> **Dryads**: Nymphs who inhabit trees or forests.

>> **Drydanda**: Title for a queen of the dryads. This dryad typically has more mystical capabilities than the rest of her kind. For example, a Drydanda can travel any distance from her tree whereas most dryads are constrained to about a fifty-mile radius.

>> **Alam**: Formal name for a palm tree. If the tree has a nymph, the nymph's name carries this as a suffix, for

example: Alf'alam.

Ored: Formal name for a pine or spruce tree. If the tree has a nymph, the nymph's name carries this as a suffix, for example: Ser'ored.

Marxia: Formal name for a mahogany tree. If the tree has a dryad, the nymph's name carries this as a suffix, for example: Vell'marxia.

Meliai: Formal name for an ash tree. If the tree has a dryad, the nymph's name carries this as a suffix, for example: La'meliai.

Nolia: Formal name for a magnolia tree. If the tree has a dryad, the nymph's name carries this as a suffix, for example: Tella'nolia.

Rina: The name for an aspen grove. Aspens are usually more than one tree connected by their roots belowground. An entire grove bears the name Rina as a single entity. Any dryad attached to the grove bears Rina as a suffix, for example: Na'rina.

Dry: Formal name for an oak tree. If the tree has a nymph, the nymph's name carries this as a suffix, for example: Ana'dry.

Ptelea: Formal name for an elm tree. If the tree has a nymph, the nymph's name carries this as a suffix, for example: El'ptelea.

Naiads: Nymphs who inhabit rivers, springs, or waterfalls.

Oceanids: Nymphs who inhabit the sea or ocean.

Oceadanda: Title for a queen of the oceanids. This

oceanid typically has more mystical capabilities than the rest of her kind. For example, an Oceadanda can travel out of the ocean whereas other oceanids cannot.

Oreads: Nymphs who inhabit mountains.

> **Oreadanda**: Title for a queen of the oreads. This oread typically has more mystical capabilities than the rest of her kind. For example, an Oreadanda can travel any distance from her mountain whereas most oreads cannot travel beyond a specific range.

Sylphs: Nymphs who inhabit the air.

Salamanders or Fire Elementals: Creatures who are more fire than flesh. They can manifest as humanlike creatures or shift into flames.

Sedessan: A humanoid species that can pass messages psychically and alter memories through touch. Sedessans interact with humans on a regular basis, although humans are not aware they are "other." They are often hired as messengers if the mythic parties involved don't trust each other. Sedessans carry the stigma of being devious.

> **Sedanza Court:** Sedessan Court made up of six families living in a small island nation just off the coast of Venezuela and south of Trinidad and Tobago. The Court islands are protected by a technological dome, a Fae emotional deterrent, and one of the court families whose job for a decade is to mitigate human awareness of the islands. They usually reside in Venezuela for their time serving.

> **Sedanza Families:**

> **Inverro**: Living on Madridia Island, they are the leading family in the Court because of the size of their information

network. The family is made up of Mateo, his wife, Marie, and their five sons: Roberto, Ethan, Samuel, Dylan, and David.

Varela: Second Court family by information network standards. Adrian, Sophia and daughter Elodie live on the San Martez Island. They lost their eldest child, their son Icarus, in a hurricane.

Torres: Manuel and Gisele have three children: Gustavo, Estella, and Diego. They live on San Salida Island.

Reyes: Living on Eglesias Island at the southern edge of Sedanza, Carlos, Lila and their son, Alex, and daughter, Emilia, are rumored to be the Court's assassins.

Navarez: Family currently handling the human world's awareness from Venezuela. Enrique and Sara have two daughters, Renata and Teresa. Renata is known as a zoi aima savant when it comes to knowing exactly what someone is by their lifeblood. The family resides on the Las Mesas Island.

De León: Arlo and his daughter Lucia. Arlo also lost Lucia's older sister to a storm. They live on Santa Matia Island.

Asimi Court: Sedessan Court in Egypt

Sprites or Pixies: Mischievous, fairie-like creatures. Small cousins to the Fae who share many of the abilities of the Fae in smaller ways. Expert brewers of toxins, poisons, and antidotes.

Twiglets: Tiny, humanoid-like trees who live in stands of four to eight brothers. They are rarely seen.

Wer-im: A humanoid species, with claws that retract into their hands and feet, that bears resemblances to specific cats. Humans have sometimes called them were-cats but they are not always shape-changers.

They can often pass as human but must disguise tufted ears, stripes, and other catlike features.

Wer-Kadis or Kadis—Title for the leader of the wer-im. This wer-im holds his position by combat.

Glossary of Terms

The Circle: A group of ancient dryads, now totally part of their trees, who have succeeded in staying alive for the last phase of a dryad's life. During times when the Drydanda and her council cannot make decisions, the Circle steps in to vote for the "forest" or dryad nation.

Collective Wisdom: A genetic history of the dryads that is accessed as actual memories and is used most often by the Drydandas to help them in ruling.

Council: A group of five who help the Drydanda rule.

Hammer: One of the dwarven king's sons and captains

Handfasting: The mythics' term for getting married.

Kadivas: The official name for the leadership challenge, or fight, of the wer-im, used to determine the Wer-Kadis.

Mythic: Any creature humans view as mythical (nymphs, dwarves, elves, wer-im, Sedessans, fauns, etc.).

Omichlodis Mountains: Traditional mythic name for the Appalachian Mountains. This name is often used by the dwarves to indicate their race.

Pyrgos Mountains: Traditional mythic name for the Rocky Mountains. This name is often used by the dwarves to indicate their race.

Stray: A wer-im with enough diluted blood that he or she lacks some of the more prominent features of a full-blooded wer-im. They typically cannot vow and are not accepted into the wer-im culture unless named by a recognized wer-im or by a powerful mythic.

True Born: Usually a dryad is born from the mating of a dryad with another dryad or mythic, and a tree takes seed with the dryad's conception. Rarely, however, the tree seeds first in response to some kind of trauma. When this happens, the resulting dryad looks almost identical to his or her parent and has the same abilities, except stronger.

Vathies Rizes: Traditional mythic name for the Cascade Mountains. This name is often used by the dwarves to indicate their race; however, this race of the dwarves is also believed to be extinct.

Vow: The purer blooded wer-im can vow to a person, people group, or cause. This creates a link between the wer-im and his or her Vow Protected that helps in the protection of that person, group, or idea. Once given, it cannot be broken.

Vow Protected: The person, group, or cause that a wer-im has Vowed to help protect.

Zoi aima: The energy, also referred to as lifeblood, within any living thing.

Acknowledgments

So far in my writing journey, this book was the most challenging. I'm always trying new things, growing as a writer simply by exploring new ways to do something. The big challenge in *Theos Rising* was the multiple viewpoints. This naturally led to a more complicated plot and a messy rough draft. All that said, *Theos Rising* would not be what it is today without the massive support of a lot of people who continue to help me hone my craft.

Let's start with my Alpha readers, Curry Mitchell and Nate Zeiger. I cannot thank these two enough as they read the only marginally cleaned up and massive 172,000-word rough draft. Their feedback was instrumental in seeing what themes mattered, what could be cut, and more. Twenty percent is a ton to cut but they both were right: The story needed it. My heart may have bled some, but it was healthy.

My Beta readers were a huge help from there. Thank you to Mollie Bond, David Zeiger, Leslie Rohman, Haylee Rohman, Mom and Dad, Curry Mitchell, and Nate Zeiger. There are so many types of readers out there, and getting feedback from such varying views helped me see this story through many different eyes! Your feedback was invaluable.

Thank you also to Alan Feldman. Most of my life I've been around a smattering of Spanish but that doesn't mean I can speak it. Alan was kind enough to check the goblin's Spanish for me last-minute before I sent the manuscript to my editor.

Which leads me to Darren Thornberry, said editor. Darren notified me in 2022 that he might not be editing novels anymore. Then

I tentatively asked him if he'd still be willing to edit the novel I was working on. I didn't know when it'd be ready. I suspected it'd be really long. Obviously, Darren agreed anyway. I work with remarkable people. Even once I contacted him, a year later, to start the editing process, I had to push the date another month before giving it to him. Seriously, this book has defied all attempts to rein it into a timeframe. Despite that, Darren was wonderful and took *Theos Rising* from clean-ish to a polished manuscript. I can't thank you enough, Darren, for your patience and skill.

On to the artwork! At this point, I should probably just call Justin Allen my cover designer. He does amazing artwork and is so wonderful to work with. In 2023, he updated the *Quaking Soul* cover for me and then rolled almost immediately into the cover for *Theos Rising* despite the dozens, maybe hundreds, of emails back and forth to get *Quaking Soul* just right. Thank you, Justin, for your patience, professionalism, and outstanding artwork.

And thank you, Readers, for continuing the *Hidden Mythics* series with me and for your patience as I continue to figure out this thing called writing. I'd hoped this book would take one and a half, maybe two years to write and produce. As you probably know, it took way longer than that. Your enthusiasm and support mean the world to me and make writing all the sweeter.

And lastly, thank you to my husband, Nate. You read the manuscript almost as many times as I did and never lost faith that we'd reach publication. I wouldn't be writing without your unwavering belief in me.

Other Books by Jennifer M Zeiger

Hidden Mythics Novels

Quaking Soul
(Hidden Mythics Book I)

As the next in line to be Queen of the Dryads, or tree nymphs, Na'rina knows two things for sure. Her world of fauns, nymphs, dwarves and other mythical creatures must remain myths to the more populated human world to remain safe. And the wer-im, or werecats, who burned the dryad's trees long ago, are never to be trusted again.

But now a wer-im is warning them that humans are not only capturing mythics, but experimenting on them for scientific advancement. He wants to forge alliances to survive.

At first Na'rina refuses, but when her mother is captured, she finds the violent wer-im might be her only allies. But can Na'rina trust them? Or will her decisions doom the mythic world as she knows it?

Adventure Books
Discarded Dragons
Explore all 12 possible endings while getting to be a steam punk metal dragon.

Mystery of the Golden Shells

Explore all 10 possible endings in this mystery who-done-it on an island with wild magic.

The Adventure

Explore all 26 possible endings in this sampler with 3 distinct stories. Investigate the myth on Moonrise Mountain, explore a dangerous cave system for treasure, and compete in a medieval-style tournament.

Zap Dragon

Explore all 14 possible endings in this adventure where you get to be a metal dragon exploring the city. Just be careful: You might zap people by accident.

Jennifer M Zeiger grew up in the Rocky Mountains of Colorado and now lives in Texas with her husband, Nate.

She blogs multi-ending adventure stories and has now turned six of those into books—Three in *The Adventure* and now three stand-alones: *Discarded Dragons, Mystery of the Golden Shells,* and *Zap Dragon.* She also writes fantasy novels. Check out *Quaking Soul* for the first installment in the Hidden Mythics series.

jenniferzeiger.com

Jennifer M. Zeiger

Hello Dear Reader,

Thank you so much for reading *Theos Rising*! I hope you enjoyed it. It is only because of people like you that I'm able to do what I truly love.

If you enjoyed this book and would like to help, then please consider leaving a review on Amazon, Goodreads, or anywhere else readers visit. Word of mouth is a huge part of how well a book sells, so if you leave one, you are directly helping me continue this journey as a full-time writer. Thank you in advance to anyone who does. It means the world to me!

Many Blessings,

Jennifer M Zeiger

Amazon Author Page

Milton Keynes UK
Ingram Content Group UK Ltd.
UKHW011822140624
444031UK00010B/155/J

9 781735 122663